GILLIAN BENNETT

Traditions of Belief

WOMEN AND THE SUPERNATURAL

PENGUIN BOOKS

Penguin Books Ltd, 27 Wrights Lane, London W8 5TZ (Publishing and Editorial)
and Harmondsworth, Middlesex, England (Distribution and Warehouse)
Viking Penguin Inc., 40 West 23rd Street, New York, New York 10010, USA
Penguin Books Australia Ltd, Ringwood, Victoria, Australia
Penguin Books Canada Ltd, 2801 John Street, Markham, Ontario, Canada L3R 1B4
Penguin Books (NZ) Ltd, 182–190 Wairau Road, Auckland 10, New Zealand

First published 1987

Made and printed in Great Britain by
Richard Clay Ltd, Bungay, Suffolk
Filmset in Monophoto Garamond

For two Andrews – one living, one dead

Contents

Preface

There are not many subjects which have to be defined before they can be discussed, but unfortunately 'folklore' is one of them. Modern folklorists are victims of the subject's history and the baggage which the term brings with it. Everyone 'knows' that folklore is a body of old wives' tales, superstitions, fallacies, legends and quaint customs that linger on in backward country areas and provide evidence of outmoded belief-systems and pagan religion. It follows then that a book on the folklore of ghosts and E S P will be a collection of legends about 'cauld lads', boggarts, hauntings and exorcisms that are both undisturbing and unbelievable – an amusement for Hallowe'en. Fifty years ago, it may well have been just that. Readers will find this one very different, for both the study of folklore and the very definition of the term have radically changed since that time.

The first, introductory, chapter therefore aims to familiarize readers with modern trends in folklore study which will set this book in context. It has three sections, each of which by itself provides an entry into the descriptions and discussions of chapters 2 to 5. The first section considers the changing definitions of the term 'folklore' since the nineteenth century; the second section deals with the question of the truth or falsity of traditional ideas; and the third section assesses the value of listening to personal experience stories when studying folklore. Readers may begin at any of these three points, or read the introduction as a whole, but I do ask that they should look at at least one of these sections. I owe it to the women who spoke to me so entirely without disguise or reserve that those who read their personal stories should understand my own attitudes to their traditions.

There is one other respect in which the book may seem strange. Essentially, it is written back-to-front, so that present-day traditions are described at the outset, and not put into historical perspective until the final chapter. The logic of this arrangement is that it allows the presentation of today's folklore to follow immediately after the discussion of the modern definitions of the term 'folklore' itself. It also means that it can redress the historical bias of most books on supernatural traditions by placing the emphasis on the reality of present-day beliefs. If, however, readers feel that they prefer to follow the history of the traditions from the Middle Ages to the 1980s in a continuous chronological progression, they may start at chapter 6. The choice is, of course, theirs.

Gillian Bennett, December 1986

Acknowledgements

Very many thanks are due to my (necessarily anonymous) informants and to the dear friends who introduced me to them. To all of these, my gratitude and love.

Thanks are also owed to J. D. A. Widdowson for encouragement and advice with the research, to Andrew Bennett and Steve Roud for reading early drafts, to Paul Smith for friendship, to Derek Froome for proof-reading and to Matthew Bennett for typing. In addition, a great debt of gratitude is owed to the Centre for English Cultural Tradition and Language at the University of Sheffield and to the many scholars who have attended its conferences on legend, narrative and belief. My thinking has been so substantially influenced by them that I probably now claim their best ideas as my own.

Thanks, too, to David Hufford and the editor of *New York Folklore* for permission to reprint parts of 'Traditions of Disbelief'; to Linda May Ballard and the editor of Mistletoe Books for permission to quote the account of 'Holly Eve' from 'Before Death and Beyond'; to *Western Folklore* for allowing quotation from *California Folklore Quarterly* I (1942); and to Charles Skilton for permitting quotation from Fr Noel Taillepied's *A Treatise of Ghosts*.

Every effort has been made to contact owners of copyright material. Where this has not been successful, omissions will be rectified in future editions if the owners would be kind enough to contact me.

1 *The Study of Folklore*

The argument about folklore continues, even among folklorists.[1]
WILLIAM BASCOM

FOLKLORE: THE CHANGING DEFINITION

The term 'folklore' was coined originally by W. J. Thoms in a letter to the influential journal *The Athenaeum* (under the pseudonym 'Ambrose Merton') in August 1846. The name may have been new, but the study was already well-established, the Grimm brothers, most notably, having published their *Nursery and Household Tales* in 1812, and Jakob Grimm his *Deutsche Mythologie* in 1835. Since the seventeenth century, antiquarians had been writing about national 'curiosities' – ruins, ancient monuments, strange beliefs, outlandish customs – and it was this interest in 'popular antiquities' that laid the foundations for the study of folklore, as Thoms's letter makes clear. Suggesting that *The Athenaeum* should sponsor a nationwide search for bygones, he writes: 'How many facts would one word from you evoke, from the north and from the south – from John O'Groats to the Land's End! How many readers would be glad to show their gratitude for the novelties which you, from week to week communicate to them, by forwarding to you some record of old Time – some recollection of a now-neglected custom – some fading legend, local tradition, or fragmentary ballad!'[2]

Thoms's letter pinpoints elements which had been dominant in antiquarian pursuits and were to influence the evolving study of folklore for some years to come. The subject-matter was the 'novelties' of 'old Time', things neglected, fading and fragmentary. This interest was born in part out of romanticism and nationalism, as Thoms's letter later makes plain: the task is to be the nostalgic one of 'garnering the few ears remaining' of a dying peasant culture, and the practical one of using it as an archive of information which can be preserved until a British Grimm 'shall arise who shall do for the Mythology of the British Islands the good service which that profound antiquary and philologist has accomplished for the Mythology of Germany'. These elements – romantic nostalgia, nationalism, the search for myth, and the delight in curious titbits of information – in turn have dominated folklore theory for succeeding generations of scholars and collectors.

What the emerging study initially lacked was any theoretical structure or practical application. These were provided in the remaining decades of the nineteenth century first by comparative mythologists and then by the anthropological folklorists. The debates between the champions of these rival schools of thought brought to the study of folklore a vast and enthusiastic readership and kept it in the forefront of intellectual fashion until the outbreak of the First World War. In 1856 Max Müller, the leading Sanskrit scholar of the day, published his essay 'Comparative Mythology', which overturned all previous theories of myth and folktale. Over the next forty years, Müller refined, expanded and vigorously championed his argument that European religion, language and mythology had a common origin in ancient India, and that, in Greek legends and English fairytales alike, remnants of a pantheon of Vedic gods could be discerned.

He argued that tales and myths had originated in a 'mythopoeic age', when the development of religious thought outstripped the development of language, and abstract thought therefore had to be expressed through personification and concrete images. Eventually all that remained of the ancient beliefs were the names and the images, and thus myths were born out of 'the forgetfulness of language'. Careful study of etymology and comparative philology could reveal the stories in their true light as distant reflections of an ancient religion, solar myths, metaphors of the continual birth and rebirth of the sun and the battle between darkness and day.

Müller's followers, less careful and less scholarly, went further and indulged in ever wilder speculations, seeing the most humble fireside tale as an allegory of the operation of natural forces – lightning, storms or stars, as well as of the sun – according to their fancy. The familiar story of the boy with a goat that spits gold, a hen that lays golden eggs, a table that lays itself with food and a stick that beats thieves of its own accord is interpreted thus by Walter K. Kelly in *Curiosities of Indo-European Tradition and Folklore:*

The table in this story is the all-nourishing cloud. The buck-goat is another emblem of the clouds, and the gold it spits is the golden light of the sun that streams through the fleecy covering of the sky. The hen's golden egg is the sun itself. The demon of darkness has stolen these things; the cloud gives no rain, but hangs dusky in the sky, veiling the light of the sun. Then the lightning spear of the ancient storm-god Odin leaps out from the bag that concealed it (the cloud again), the robber falls, the rain patters down, the sun shines once more.[3]

Though extremes like this now seem plainly ridiculous, for nearly twenty years after the publication of Müller's epic essay, solar mythology held the field unchallenged, creating a new and long-overdue respect for folk narrative and putting folklore studies firmly on the map as central to human culture and experience.

After 1872, however, a group of vociferous adversaries, of whom the chief was the witty, prolific and erudite Andrew Lang, were ranged against the solar mythologists. Lang's onslaught on the mythological interpretation of folktales was initiated with his essay 'Mythology and Fairy Tales' and was waged without let-up in countless articles and books for nearly thirty years until the death of Müller. Lang's objections were born of his interest in anthropology and evolution. The supposition which these interests suggested was that, just as the animal kingdom had evolved over time, so might culture and thought evolve in a natural progression from simple to sophisticated, each society passing through identical stages of development. The advanced nations would once therefore have gone through the stage of culture now seen in 'primitive' societies. Just as fossils remained in the earth to show earlier life-forms, so cultural fossils might remain hidden in the thought of sophisticated societies, which would show traces of earlier beliefs and customs. The folklore of the people was just such a survival. These ideas were backed up by tracing a continuity between, on the one hand, the beliefs of primitive tribes and, on the other hand, elements in the folktales of European peasants. In the magic animals, talking trees and lucky gifts familiar to fairy stories, for example, could be seen the relics of the totemism, animism and fetishism described by missionaries and explorers returning from Africa and other wild places.

Lang's colleagues, whom the late Richard Dorson described as the 'Great Team' of British folklorists, were no less committed to the cultural evolution hypothesis. George Lawrence Gomme referred to 'the archaeology hid in our popular superstitions and customs', and, listing a variety of beliefs and practices comparable to those of 'savage life', commented that: 'both belong to the primitive history of mankind; in collecting and printing these relics of one epoch, from two such widely different sources, the Folklore Society will produce the necessary comparison and illustration which is of so much service to the anthropologist'.[4] Similarly, Alfred Nutt compared the science of folklore to that of geology and took it for granted that peasant customs and beliefs were 'the fossil remains by which the sequence of strata in the mental and social evolution of mankind can be determined'.[5] Again, Edward Clodd stated that: 'comparative anatomy has settled our place in the long succession of life; anthropology, in its branches of ethnology and prehistoric archaeology, has defined the differences between the races of mankind . . . What remains of abiding practical importance lies chiefly within the province of folklore to deal with.'[6]

Although in their later years the 'Great Team' were not without their critics – chiefly the 'diffusionists', who believed that the similarity of tales throughout the world could be more simply explained by borrowing and by the migration of people from place to place – the doctrine that the folklore of the people was a survival from cultural prehistory continued to be a major influence well into the present century.

The idea that the customs, beliefs and stories of the people are ancient myths or survivals from the nation's cultural past is still, of course, a part of popular ideas about the nature of folklore today, and pays tribute to the forcefulness and learning of eminent nineteenth-century folklorists. Another element in popular preconceptions about folklore, however, may be drawn from a scholar who, strictly speaking, was not a folklorist at all – Sir James George Frazer. His famous book of 1890, *The Golden Bough*, which is subtitled *A Study in Magic and Religion*, is a vast survey of pagan religions, agricultural deities and harvest rites. Central to its theme is the myth of Osiris – the Egyptian vegetation god who is constantly killed and constantly reborn. Other vegetation deities, like Adonis and Attis, the earth goddess Demeter, and Dionysus – the god who (in Plutarch's words) is 'destroyed, who disappears, who relinquishes life and then is born again'[7] – were all drawn into the net to aid the argument that at the root of custom and belief lay the rite of slaying a divine king to ensure the rebirth of the earth and the fertility of crops. It is, perhaps, more than anything else the popularity and fascination of *The Golden Bough* that is responsible for the vague feeling that folk festivals are, at heart, remnants of ancient fertility cults.

These, then, are the four theories from the history of scholarship that most influence the popular stereotype of the nature of folklore: firstly the notion, drawn from the antiquarians, that folklore is 'quaint', 'bygone' and 'curious'; secondly the idea, drawn from Müller and the comparative mythologists, that the customs, beliefs and stories of the people are relics of ancient myths; thirdly the idea, drawn from Andrew

Lang and the cultural evolutionists, that they are survivals from the nation's primitive past; and lastly the belief, drawn from Frazer, that they have their origin in pagan fertility cults. These are ideas which come from quite separate stages of the development of the study of folklore and from quite different scholars; each have, in their turn, been rejected as simplistic and unworkable. They are also the ideas which professional folklorists today are most anxious to get away from.

In the study of British folklore, it is as if all the clocks stopped soon after the Great War of 1914–18. Until then, brilliant theorists in gaudy colours had contended on a battlefield at the front-line of intellectual inquiry. But Müller died in 1900, Lang and Nutt in 1912, Gomme in 1916; and no new champions came forward to fill their place. Whereas anthropology gained acceptance as an academic subject, folklore did not, and gradually it slipped back into a genteel and amateurish anti-quarianism. On the Continent, however, life went on, and we have to follow the theoretical trail to Scandinavia and the USA in order to put the modern British folklore movement (and this book) in its context.

From at least 1890 the cultural evolutionists had been under increasingly successful attack from the diffusionists, and by the 1920s the stage was set for another of those massive shifts in definition and emphasis which mark the history of folklore studies. The researches of Kaarle Krohn, Professor of Folklore at the University of Helsinki from 1908 to 1928, into the Finnish national epic, *The Kalevala*, led him to believe that the 'runes' (oral epic poems) from which it was composed had originated in Estonia and Western Finland, far away from the north-eastern area where they had been collected. The travels of merchants and emigrants could not entirely explain this phenomenon, and he concluded that the runes themselves had spontaneously spread outwards in successive wave-like movements. From his attempts to document and explain this migration grew the 'historical–geographical' method – an entirely empirical approach to folklore, which relied on the collection and comparison of vast numbers of variant texts in order to study the history and diffusion of a particular poem or tale. The Finnish school has been immensely influential in modern folklore studies. It marked the beginning of a movement away from the grand search for esoteric meanings and mythological significance, towards intensive and scrupulous field-collecting, the amassing of archives, the indexing of texts, and sober, detailed work on individual narratives. The theorists of the great period of British folklore studies never collected the material on which their imposing structures were built themselves; since the publication of Krohn's *Die folkloristische Arbeitsmethode* (translated as

Folklore Methodology) in 1926, the personal collection of original material (in notebook, or on tape, film or video) has been a prerequisite of serious folklore study.

Though it is still taught at the University of Helsinki, the Finnish method has proved too dry and unexciting for many succeeding folklorists, who have felt, too, that it neglects the most fascinating questions about folklore. With a characteristic swing of the pendulum, therefore, scholars moved away from the study of history, texts and variants, and on to considerations of function and psychology. Rather than examining and comparing hundreds of versions of a single tale or proverb or ballad, folklorists began to ask what role that proverb or ballad played in the life of the individual who quoted or sang it, or what the underlying psychology of a story or belief could be that made it appear time and time again in popular traditions. In brief, what was the use of folklore – what *was* it, and what was the *good* of it? In a sense (though in a much more modest way) this was a return to the preoccupations with meaning that motivated the nineteenth-century theoreticians. But, whereas psychological perspectives on folklore turned back, at least some way, towards abstract speculation, functional approaches remained strongly empirical.

Two of the greatest figures of psychology, Freud and Jung, were both much interested in folklore. Freud leaned heavily on mythology, fairytales, jokes, superstitions and popular taboos in his *The Interpretation of Dreams* (1900); and Jung not only contributed serious studies of UFO sightings, synchronicity, belief in spirits and trickster tales, but also based his central ideas of the 'collective unconscious' and 'archetypes' on his extensive knowledge of folklore and mythology. Freud's friend and biographer, Ernest Jones, wrote a classic study of night-time assault traditions, *On the Nightmare* (1931); and the Freudian approach to traditional beliefs can also be seen in Erich Fromm's *The Forgotten Language* and Gershon Legman's studies of erotic literature and jokes (1964 and 1968). Among the present-day folklore establishment, Alan Dundes has produced several Freudian analyses of jokes and legends.

The functional approach has, however, had a more enduring effect on folklore scholarship. Like earlier theories it has its roots firmly planted in anthropology (the subject which, like literature and linguistics, constantly intertwines with the study of folklore). Its academic ancestry goes straight back to two early pioneers – Franz Boas, the champion of diffusionist theories, and Bronislaw Malinowski. Charting the relationships between the two disciplines in an essay of 1953, William Bascom, Professor of Anthropology at the University of California at

Berkeley (and former student of Melville Herskovits, himself a student of Boas), observed that anthropologists collected a great deal of folkloric material which remained unused because, on the one hand it was peripheral to anthropology, and, on the other hand, it was ignored by folklorists who were still overly concerned with the textual analysis of oral literature. Throwing down the gauntlet he says:

The anthropologist, to speak frankly, often feels that his colleagues in folklore are so often preoccupied with the problems of origins and historical reconstruction that they overlook problems of equal or even greater significance, for which one can hope to find satisfactory solutions. He looks to them for guidance in the literary analysis of folklore, and for cooperation on the problems of style and of the creative role of the narrator. He would welcome their cooperation in recording local attitudes toward folklore and its social contexts, in analyzing the relation of folklore to culture and to conduct, and finally in seeking to define its function.[8]

He took up the final challenge himself in his presidential address to the 1953 meeting of the American Folklore Society, where he delineated 'Four Functions of Folklore', following and expanding the ideas put forward by Malinowski in his 'Myth in Primitive Psychology' (1926). The functions he suggests are: entertainment; the validation of ritual and the institutions of society; education; and 'maintaining conformity to accepted patterns of behaviour'. How right Bascom was can be seen simply by looking at representative types of folklore – festivals, legends and jokes. The major Western festival, Christmas, provides entertainment and validates the rituals of the Church and the central social institution, the family; legends entertain and educate; jokes also entertain, and maintain conformity by mocking outsiders, failures and deviants. Children's folklore fulfils all four functions, as even a cursory glance into Peter and Iona Opie's contemporary classic, *The Lore and Language of Schoolchildren*, amply illustrates.

Clearly, in calling for an exploration of folklore function, Bascom caught the mood of the time. In other respects, too, he was remarkably in tune with the age, for, since the 1960s (when folklore became established as an academic discipline at several universities in America), literary analysis, problems of style and creativity, and the study of the context of folklore have become overriding concerns among American scholars.

The literary analysis of style in verbal folklore (proverbs, ballads, tales, legends, anecdotes and so on) has also been much influenced by structuralism. A great deal of excitement was aroused by the publication in English in 1958 of Vladimir Propp's classic of Russian formalism, *The Morphology of the Folktale*, in which he studied the folktale collection of Afanás'ev to try to discover underlying patterns. He began by distinguishing between the actions of the tales and the characters who performed those actions. For example, a certain action might be ascribed to a man in one tale, but to an animal or even an object in another. Clearly, the enduring and unchangeable (therefore definable) aspects of the tales were not the characters but the actions or situations (which he called 'functions'). Through detailed analysis of a hundred tales, he concluded that every one of them was stitched together out of thirty-one 'functions' arranged in a set order into two basic patterns – either a quest or a conflict. There were obvious precursors of this type of analysis (notably the Danish scholar Axel Olrik's study of 'the 'Epic Laws of Folk Narrative' and Lord Raglan's study of The Hero of Tradition'), but, after Propp, the search for pattern was definitely on, producing studies of the 'morphology' of traditional American Indian narrative, French folktales, Turkish epic and Afro-Caribbean trickster tales.

A still more potent force in the folklore scholarship of the last twenty years has been contextual study – the most empirical of all folklore methods or theories to date. Its intellectual parentage is functionalism and ethnography (especially that late offshoot of sociolinguistics, the ethnography of communication). Its method is detailed and sympathetic description; its premise that we cannot understand folklore or its function unless we also understand in the greatest possible detail the contexts in which it is used. Alan Dundes, in one of the earliest essays on the subject (in 1964), puts the argument thus, giving as his example the case of riddles:

Whereas folklorists have long been unwisely content to publish just riddle texts, anthropologists have prided themselves upon their inclusion of some mention of the function of riddles. Accordingly, in the latters' preface to their riddle collections, they may list some of the various functions of the riddles, eg., their use in courtship ritual. However, they rarely, if ever, give any indication of just which riddles . . . are used for which functions . . . One reason for collecting context is that only if such data is provided can any serious attempt be made to explain WHY a particular text is used in a particular situation.[9]

Contextual study is therefore a necessary tool, as well as a refinement, of functional approaches to folklore. That this sort of approach was what Bascom had in mind in his 1953 address can be seen by the fact that it was he who edited (in 1977 under the telling title *Frontiers of Folklore*) a set of papers written by pioneers of the contextualist approach – Alan

Dundes, Dan Ben Amos, Roger Abrahams, Richard Bauman, Dell Hymes and others.

With the development of stylistic and contextual studies (and their joint offspring, the analysis of performance) the move to a non-doctrinaire, descriptive theory of folklore was complete. Gone were attempts to construct grand schemes of meaning or origin, or to define for ever and always what sort of things counted as folklore. The detailed ethnographic work undertaken simply showed that the contents of folk-lore fluctuate, its meanings vary, and its origins can never be finally known. The feeling of most folklorists today is that the subject has to be defined, not in terms of *items* ('fragmentary ballads', or 'fading legends', or whatever) but in terms of *processes*.

Folklore is usually seen as a body of beliefs, activities, ways of doing things, saying things and making things that are acquired 'through the skin', as it were, by talking to, watching, socializing and communicating with other people. Folklore is a form of culture – an informal, almost spontaneous, culture that can be distinguished from popular culture because nobody makes money out of it, and from 'high' culture because it is never taught in schools.

Having thus (at least for the time being) answered the question 'What is the "lore" in "folklore"?' an even larger question inevitably raises itself: 'Who, then, are the "folk"?' In the past, as we have seen, the answer was invariably 'peasants', or 'old codgers and granny-women'. Indeed, there are folklorists in Britain today who will still give the same answer – though there aren't many peasants left and the grannies are probably busy watching *Dynasty* on their videos – but, outside the folk museums and the schools of Celtic studies, most folklorists today are looking at very different answers. Dan Ben Amos, in his startling essay of 1971, 'Towards a Definition of Folklore in Context', argued, for example, that folklore was simply what was passed on in 'face-to-face' situations when 'both performers and audience' (he is speaking speci-fically of storytelling here) are 'in the same social situation and . . . part of the same reference group'.[10] Earlier, in 1965, Alan Dundes had put this more bluntly: 'The term "folk" can refer to *any group of people whatsoever* who share at least one common factor. It does not matter what the linking factor is – it could be a common occupation, language or religion – but what is important is that a group formed for whatever reason will have some traditions which it calls its own'[11] [his emphasis]. In each of these definitions the important points are that folklore is informal and interpersonal, and that it is not confined to races, nations, geographical regions or other large-scale groupings but may be small-scale and self-contained. Once, then, you have thus defined the 'lore' of folklore in terms of communicative processes, and the 'folk' in terms of communicating groups, you have moved a very long way from W. J. Thoms, the solar mythologists and the seekers after 'survivals'. You have, for instance, to think of the following types of people as having their own folklore: educated people, urban people, young people, people like you. The commonest answer, therefore, that folklorists today would give to the question 'Who are the "folk"?' is 'We are.'

These are the ideas that motivate what one might call the 'New Folklorists' in Britain. One cannot illustrate these ideas better than by quoting some of the definitional statements put forward for discussion at a recent seminar on the future of folklore studies in this country. Firstly, Steve Roud:

Folklore is not for me essentially rural, or the province of an illiterate peasantry, or racially-determined, or dying out ... Our responsibility (or one of our responsibilities) is to document and report as accurately, sensitively and humanely as possible ... in such a way as to bring real insight on human life and society. We betray that responsibility by wittering on about ritual origins ... or perpetuating a rosy view of a romanticised past.[12]

Secondly, Marion Bowman:

It is not now necessary to locate some decrepit, rural, materially-deprived, preferably illiterate (or, in Scotland, Gaelic-speaking) peasant who has never been tainted by the media or travelled outside his/her community to find the stuff of folklore. City bankers circulate legends about computer fraud; a graduate wears a St Anne medal to discos to help her find a prospective husband; scientific research staff worry about a haunted lab.; nurses know not to put red and white flowers together in a hospital ward. Folklore is all around us, whoever and wherever we are, and we are all folk.[13]

This book has been researched and written very much within this framework of ideas and attitudes. First and foremost, it is based on fieldwork – face-to-face conversations with more than a hundred people living within a few streets of each other in a city suburb. Though I did not myself know the people beforehand, I was introduced to them by a third person who had lived among them for twenty years and was himself present throughout the interviews. Most of the people I talked to were elderly – not because I think that old people have a monopoly of interest in the supernatural (in fact, they proved to be distinctly more sceptical than younger people), but because my go-between was himself not a young man. The vast majority were women. Again, this came about more by accident than design. Among retired people there simply are more women than men. In addition, women are more willing to talk and are more likely to be at home during the day. The book therefore concentrates on 107 interviews with women between the ages of forty-six and ninety-six (the vast majority were over sixty) and aims to present a full picture of the belief-system of this homogeneous (and, I think, typical) group.

Secondly, folklore study is unlike social sciences such as sociology in that it prefers small-scale studies to large-scale surveys. What it loses in universal significance by this approach, it gains in understanding. A folklorist, sitting by the fire talking to a friend-of-a-friend is likely to be given frank answers and the sort of details about the informant's life and times that put beliefs, opinions and personal experiences into context. In this, the difference between sociology and folklore study (or 'folklor-istics' as it is often termed today) mirrors that between documentary and oral history. Whereas the former can claim to be more 'factual' (whatever that is), the latter can put living flesh on the bare skeleton of historical account. As informants speak, their choice of significant events or key concepts or favourite quotations, their language and their intonation – all these can reveal the values and attitudes that inform the past they describe or the beliefs they express. And this is immensely valuable information.

Thirdly, this book in no way seeks out the bizarre legend or untypical, though perhaps exciting, experience (of this, more in the following section). As we have seen, folklorists today define their subject in terms of informal cultures which we share by virtue of belonging to human groups. The full-blooded ghost stories with howling storms and dogs, hollow voices echoing in cobwebby attics, white-clad figures flitting through the gloom of old houses by the light of a single guttering candle are the stuff of literary fiction, not folklore. Fact is more prosaic. The strange experiences we have and talk about to others, and which go to make up the belief-traditions which our group share are, as the women I spoke to said, 'just little things' – less baroque but more believable; less flamboyant but more fascinating.

TRUTH AND FALSITY IN FOLKLORE

In the previous section I have tried to show how, by successive stages, folklorists moved away from the idea that folklore is a body of quaint, old-fashioned left-overs from some shadowy pagan past. It goes without saying, then, that we also can no longer accept another old idea – that folklore is fallacious, nonsensical and wrong-headed (though many people today still do equate folklore with falsity). This just isn't the case. Whatever its reputation, folklore has a remarkable capacity for turning out to be correct after all. Traditional remedies are one obvious example. It used to be the practice to cut apples into rings and to hang them up until mouldy for use as a poultice on infected wounds or, alternatively, a poultice of mouldy bread would be recommended. Now, of course, we have penicillin instead, which, as the *OED* says, is 'a therapeutic drug first discovered in mould'. Similarly, the friendly practice of 'kissing a child better' is neither sentimental nor useless, saliva having been found to have healing properties. Again, South American Indians traditionally chewed coca leaves as a pain-reliever and stimulant: for all its abuses, cocaine, the derivative of those leaves, is surely one of the most effective analgesic drugs available to the medical profession. The list is extensive.

Even some semi-magical agricultural practices and ghost stories have been found to be not altogether baseless. Hillbillies of the Ozark Mountains traditionally planted crops according to the quarter of the moon. Leafy crops were sown in the 'light' (i.e. the waxing) of the moon, and root crops in the 'dark' (i.e. waning) of the moon. The idea was that as the moon waxed it would pull plants upwards, and as it waned it would pull them downwards. Daft as this sounds, it might have worked reasonably well, for it seems that the moon not only controls the tides, but also affects the water-table. Legends, too, often contain grains of useful information. A case in point is the legend of Bryn yr Ellyllon, a burial mound near Mold in Clwyd, haunted by a 'golden knight' according to Robert Chambers in *The Book of Days*. When the barrow was excavated in 1832, it was found to contain a skeleton of a man wearing a corselet of bronze overlaid with gold. Tradition had obviously retained knowledge of the burial but, by the 'Chinese whispers' effect of continuous oral transmission, had transmuted an armoured soldier into a ghostly golden knight.

Other bits of folklore have never been doubted and there is no reason at all to think they are false. Traditional weather lore is at least as reliable as the predictions of the Meteorological Office. 'Red sky at night, the shepherd's delight' works very well as a guide to tomorrow's weather; 'Rain before seven, clear before eleven' will not apply to Ireland, Wales, the Lake District or any place to which you go on holiday, but it's reasonably accurate elsewhere. Proverbs contain incontrovertibly useful advice. 'A stitch in time saves nine', 'You can take a horse to the water, but you can't make it drink', 'More haste, less speed', are all sensible guides to action.

Folklore, then, is not necessarily wrong. Like every other body of knowledge, from physics to philosophy, it may be true or it may be false. Only time, experience or experimentation will tell.

This is as applicable to supernatural folklore as much as to anything else – though it takes some courage to say so, for, of all types of folklore, this is the one that seems least respectable and least believable in a so-called scientific age. The main trouble for folklorists is that we have got ourselves into not one, but no less than three, classic vicious circles. Firstly, no one will tackle the subject because it is disreputable, and it remains disreputable because no one will tackle it. Secondly, because no one does any research into present-day supernatural beliefs, occult traditions are generally represented by old legends about fairies, bogeys and grey ladies. Furthermore, because published collections of supernatural folklore are thus stuck for ever in a time-warp, folklorists are rightly wary of printing the modern beliefs they do come across for fear of offending their informants by appearing to put deeply felt beliefs on a par with tales of chain-rattling skeletons and other such absurdities. Thirdly, because no one will talk about their experiences of the supernatural there is no evidence for it, and because there is no evidence for it no one talks about their experiences of it.

Two brave folklorists and one brave psychologist have tried to break out of this double-bind. In writing of 'The Psychological Foundation of Belief in Spirits', Carl Gustav Jung says: 'There are universal reports of these post-mortem phenomena . . . They are based in the main on psychic facts which cannot be dismissed out of hand. Very often the fear of superstition, which, strangely enough, is the concomitant of universal enlightenment, is responsible for the hasty suppression of extremely interesting reports which are then lost to science.'[14] This point will be dealt with in more detail in chapter 4, for, since Jung's day, psychologists interested in bereavement and grieving have given attention to the 'post-mortem' phenomena to which he refers.

Here, however, it is specifically folkloristic approaches I want to consider. Very similar attitudes to Jung's inform the work of Andrew Lang (1844–1912) who writes with so much force and conviction and presents such innovative ideas that he must be listened to. Lang wrote extensively on the supernatural for magazines and journals and also produced two full-length books, *Cock Lane and Common-Sense* (1894) and *Dreams and Ghosts* (1897), of which the former is probably the best book on the subject written in the English language. It is in part a historical review of the history of ghost traditions, and in part an energetic argument that the evidence for ghosts is as good as the evidence for anything else. Its central theme is that 'Common-Sense' cannot adequately account for phenomena such as those which occurred at Cock Lane in the mid 1700s. According to Lang, 'On every side we find in all ages, climates, races and stages of civilization, consentient testimony to a set of extraordinary phenomena', but we are bullied by common-sense into accepting feeble rationalizations: 'of all the wanderers in Cock Lane, none is more beguiled than sturdy Common-Sense if an explanation is to be provided. When we ask for more than "all stuff and nonsense", we speedily receive a very mixed theory in which rats, indigestion, dreams, and, of late, hypnotism, are mingled much at random.'[15] The chapter which bears the same title as the book illustrates the ridiculousness of 'common-sense' explanations in five famous cases of haunting. The silliest explanation of them all, it seems, was given to one Alexander Dingwall, who was plagued by persistent mysterious noises. His daughter suggested that the sounds were made by a fox which was trying to attract the hunt, so it would have an excuse to run about and get warm. Lang's tersest and most trenchant defence of tradition, however, comes in the preface to the book. This is worth quoting at some length:

In many cases, as we show, the explanations offered by common-sense are inconsistent, inadequate, and can only be accepted by aid of a strong bias which influences the reasoner. No doubt the writer himself has a bias. He is conscious of a bias in favour of fair play and ordinary logic . . . Fair play and right reason have rarely been applied to these subjects [. . .] Common-sense bullied several generations, till they were positively afraid to attest to their own unusual experiences. Then it was triumphantly proclaimed that no unusual experiences were ever attested. Even now many people dare not say what they believe about occurrences witnessed by their own senses.[16]

However, in succeeding generations of folklorists there have unfortunately been few to follow Lang's robust line. In Britain I can think of none; in America the record is rather better. The last forty years have produced scholars like Louis Jones, Wayland Hand, Lynwood Montell and William Wilson who have recognized the interest and value of studies of folk belief and have written about the supernatural without sneers and heavy whimsicality (a rare feat).

Most in tune with the spirit that infused the thinking of Jung and Lang, however, is David Hufford (Associate Professor of Behavioural Science at the Pennsylvania State College of Medicine), who in 1971 began work on a group of night assault traditions usually collectively termed 'The Nightmare, or The Old Hag'. The story-line, if one may call it that, of the Old Hag is that you wake up in the night filled with an overwhelming sense of dread and terror. Into the bedroom comes something unutterably evil, which approaches the bed. While you lie on your back powerless to move or cry out, the Hag rides you until you can no longer breathe. You come to, drenched with sweat, cold and exhausted, but mercifully the Hag has gone. The common explanation is that it is a dream or hallucination born out of familiarity with Old Hag stories. Simply, you are experiencing things you already 'know' sometimes happen; you are, in a sense, pre-programmed to have these sorts of experiences through the strong suggestions born of superstition and fear.

It is, indeed, extremely hard to believe that such exotically bizarre occurrences could have any basis at all in actual experience, but Hufford has been able to demonstrate that, if we shed the traditional explanations (i.e. that the Old Hag is summoned by witchcraft) and concentrate on the phenomenology of the experience (i.e. the sense of an evil presence, immobility, a feeling of pressure on the chest, suffocation, exhaustion and terror), we find that we are dealing with something that is, after all, a not uncommon, real occurrence. His researches have led him to formulate two theoretical propositions which are extremely challenging to students of supernatural folklore. The first is formally presented in his book *The Terror that Comes in the Night* (1982). Putting it simply, perhaps over-simply, the argument is that, rather than traditional beliefs determining the nature of any strange experiences we may have, the traditions have grown up to explain the strange experiences we *already do have*. It is not tradition that pre-dates experience, but experience that pre-dates tradition. The 'experience-centred' approach to supernatural folklore, as he calls it, demands that folklorists do what they have never done before – *believe* their informants, or at least *not disbelieve them on the basis of their own beliefs*.

Hufford's second theoretical proposition is set out in an article the reasoning of which closely resembles that put forward by Lang in *Cock Lane and Common-Sense* over ninety years ago. As far as matters of the supernatural are concerned, Hufford suggests that two opposed groups face each other in mutual incomprehension – believers and sceptics. It is customary to see only the believing group as having a 'folklore' and adhering to established traditional patterns of thought. But, he argues, the sceptics rely just as much on received attitudes and standard responses that are culturally determined – the sceptics, too, have their folklore. The cornerstone of their arguments is that there is very little genuine experimental evidence. Traditions of the supernatural, they say, develop from repressed psychological desires, the need to control children by threatening them with bogeymen, over-imaginative (or just plain lying) storytellers, or folk etymology. Their second, overlapping, line of reasoning is that where people do actually 'see something', they must be mistaken. They are, perhaps, under the influence of LSD, or alcohol, or delirium, or stress, or maybe they are psychotic. Alternatively, they have simply misinterpreted something quite ordinary and everyday, or have mistaken coincidence for causality. At the last ditch, the materialist will fall back on the argument that, even if none of his/her arguments will fit the case in point, given time and the advance of scientific knowledge, a 'rational' cause *will eventually be found*. These arguments are remarkably consistent and come from people of all ages, social classes and degrees of education – they are 'traditions of disbelief'.

It has been my aim in writing this book to stand outside both traditions, and to describe the beliefs of the women I spoke to in both their positive and negative aspects. Though it is obviously more interesting to present the opinions of the believers among my informants, I shall also try to show not only what the traditional counter-arguments are, but also the point at which believers themselves draw the line and place taboos on the subject.

It follows that no judgements have been made about the credibility or otherwise of the beliefs and the belief-systems, the stories and the arguments described in Chapters 3 to 5. I have no more reason than right to doubt my informants' observation, reliability, intelligence or honesty, so I must treat their beliefs and experiences with respect and sympathy. But, and it's a big 'but', I can only accept their *explanations* for the occurrences they report by stepping inside the supernaturalist tradition, and I do not see that that is necessary. I think I can believe them without believing their explanations. Having said that, I have to admit that, unless I step inside the opposing camp and accept the rationalist tradition, I am left with no explanations at all. All I can hope to do is to use the history of ghostlore in the English-speaking world and the insights of psychology to set the beliefs I speak of in context and, by viewing them from these different perspectives, reveal the fascinating interplay of tradition and experience which underpins belief in supra-normal occurrences.

Lastly, it must be said that the supernatural traditions I found were not the ones I expected: the research showed up areas of belief that I was not previously aware existed. Having been brought up on literary ghost stories, naturally I expected to be told several standard ghost legends. I did not come across any. The beliefs discussed and the stories told to me were often very far from what I expected. But then they were stories told from personal experience, not learned from books.

LEGEND AND MEMORATE

As we have seen, modern approaches to folklore demand that the researcher works from original, recorded material based on face-to-face interviews; that this material should be collected from people 'inside' the tradition being investigated; and that folklore should be regarded as the possession of all of us, not just of a few selected peasants and old-timers. In all these senses folklore comes (to use the title of a recent book) 'from mouths of men'. It follows, then, that a lot of our raw data is reminiscence and personal narrative. This sort of material immediately raises two very large questions for the researcher. How far can we be sure that reminiscences are not purely idiosyncratic, and how do we present the informants' words to the reader?

The reliability of oral testimony in general has, of course, been very thoroughly discussed in Jan Vansina's modern classic, *Oral Tradition*, and less academic consideration may also be found in the works of folklorist and oral historian, George Ewart Evans (especially in *Where Beards Wag All*). Here, however, it is specifically the question of whether personal experience stories of the supernatural ('memorates') may be regarded as reliable guides to tradition that I want briefly to consider.

In the past, it has been the practice for folklorists to eschew personal testimony and to look for the more enduring patterns that are thought to be observable in legends. This position is admirably summed up by two past presidents of the Folklore Society. In his Presidential Address to the Society in 1927, A. R. Wright said: 'I set aside a considerable collection of ghost stories made by *The Daily News* in November last, because they are mostly alleged individual experiences . . . and not the traditional or other stories of the countryside that interest us.'[17]

Nearly sixty years later, very similar opinions were expressed by Dr Carmen Blacker in a paper given at the Society's conference on the folklore of ghosts in 1980: 'We shall not be concerned with first-hand testimonies of apparitions such as might interest the student of psychical research, but rather with . . . the "tradition" of ghosts, what is made of the shocking, often horrifying experience of perceiving an apparition of the dead, the stereotypes into which, as though by some magnetic force, the mind tends to elaborate these bare perceptions.'[18]

There is much to say in favour of such positions. They rely on tested and tried distinctions: between the communal and the personal, the cultural and the idiosyncratic, the enduring and the ephemeral. Folklore as a discipline concerns itself with the communal, the cultural and the enduring; the personal is only of interest where it is moulded by these wider forces. The rub, of course, is that in practice we can often only make clear distinctions between the communal and the personal, the cultural and the idiosyncratic, the enduring and the ephemeral by laying down a priori 'rules' about what *is* communal and so forth; in effect defining tradition in terms of what folklorists *say* it is.

The distinction between 'tradition' and 'modernity' is particularly artificial in the case of supernatural folklore because, if we outlaw newly collected memorates and insist on studying only old legends, we will be in a perpetual time-warp, never admitting up-to-date evidence about what 'the stereotypes into which . . . the mind elaborates . . . bare perceptions' presently are.

We tend to think of tradition as fixed and unchanging, but it isn't really quite like that. The fact that traditions are passed on by word of mouth or by other forms of interpersonal interaction means that, though there are elements that remain constant over time, there are others which change. As a song or story or belief is passed on, each person preserves the outline but forgets a little, invents a little, alters a little, adapts it to his or her own uses, so, though there is always continuity, there is also variation and selection – the agents of change. Legends are no less ephemeral than memorates if they are orally told. We tend to think that they are enduring only because we keep on reading them in print. Where fieldworkers have tried to rediscover legends which they have read in their predecessors' collections, they have often failed. Robert Hunt, famous for his *Popular Romances of the West of England* (1865), plaintively remarked that he had made an earlier legend collection as a boy in 1829, but: 'I have within the last year, endeavoured to recover these stories, but in vain. The living people seem to have forgotten them.'[19] Perhaps that is to be expected over the course of thirty-six years, but only a few years after Hunt had worked on his boyish project, the West Country novelist, Mrs Anna Bray, published her *Legends, Superstitions and Sketches of Devonshire*. Hunt found little trace of his old stories in her collection either, and concludes: 'This work proves to me that even at that time the old world stories were perishing . . . Many wild tales I heard in 1829 appear to have been lost.'[20] One cannot think that the West of England is peculiar in its predisposition to change. In folklore, loss and gain is exactly what one would expect. Legends, in their written form, merely catch and suspend one moment in the eternal flux of tradition: they endure because they are written down, not because they are in some way more real, more rounded, or more 'traditional' than memorates.

Indeed, memorates are just as 'traditional', though in a rather different way. Each one may be ephemeral (because it has not found its way into print) and each one is personal and individual (because it is the teller's story and no one else's), but together they are, nevertheless, communal, cultural and enduring. They are so because they are the embodiments of received attitudes and beliefs – tradition in action. They are told because the narrator believes them to be true, because they 'really happened', because they are 'the *one thing* that made me really believe'. They are for folklorists, therefore, the best possible evidence for the existence of an on-going tradition. By listening to, collecting and studying memorates, one studies tradition at work – giving meaning to meaningless perceptions, shaping private experience into cultural forms, showing how ancient concepts are adapted to the modern world and individual needs. Memorates may be personal, but they are seldom entirely idiosyncratic. They are remarkably reliable guides to the current state of a particular belief or tradition.

However, collections of memorates made from field-recordings are more difficult to handle than collections of legends from printed sources. Spoken English is full of false starts, digressions, hesitations, repetitions, *non sequiturs*; people don't talk in sentences but tend to string ideas loosely together and leave the hearer to sort out the relationships between them. Again, speakers assume that they and their listeners share a common background and so logical links are often omitted; yet, on the other hand, they seem never to assume that they will be believed, so their speech is packed with seemingly irrelevant details of the 'It was Wednesday. No, I tell a lie. It must have been Monday because I was doing the washing, and our Brenda had just popped in to say she was expecting twins' variety. None of this matters in conversation (unless it is carried to excess), but, as soon as real speech is copied down word-for-word and set on the printed page, it looks uncouth and comical and it is sometimes hard to follow what is going on. We simply are not aware that we really do speak like that, for we are a literate society and are used to the neatness and finish of written English. A story, transcribed exactly as it was told, is therefore likely to seem very strange and to make wearisome reading.

In the past, therefore, it was the practice to re-write oral narratives, preserving the story, but tidying up the wording, tightening the narrative line, and generally 'improving' it so that the rough edges were knocked off and it acquired a literary shape and polish. This was the practice of the Grimm brothers in their *Nursery and Household Tales*, for example, and of the seventeenth-century collector of folktales, Charles Perrault, and of many others since. The result is a neat, readable narrative like the following account of 'The Guardian Black Dog', a legend well-known at the end of the nineteenth century. This version is taken from Augustus Hare's *The Story of My Life*.

> *Brancepeth Castle, 3 January, 1885*
>
> Mr Wharton dined. He said, 'When I was at the little inn at Ayscliffe, I met a Mr Bond, who told me a story about my friend Johnnie Greenwood, of Swancliffe. Johnnie had to ride one night through a wood a mile long to the place he was going to. At the entrance of the wood a large black dog joined him, and pattered along by his side. He could not make out where it came from, but it never left him, and when the wood grew so dark that he could not see it, he still heard it pattering beside him. When he emerged from the wood, the dog had disappeared, and he could not tell where it had gone to. Well, Johnnie paid his visit, and set out to return the same way. At the entrance of the wood, the dog joined him, and pattered along beside him as before; but it never touched him, and he never spoke to it, and again, as he emerged from the wood, it ceased to be there.
>
> 'Years after, two condemned prisoners in York Gaol told the chaplain that they had intended to rob and murder Johnnie that night in the wood, but that he had a large dog with him, and when they saw that, they felt that Johnnie and the dog together would be too much for them.
>
> 'Now that is what I call a useful ghostly apparition,' said Mr Wharton. [21]

This is very nice, very entertaining, very well told, but many students of oral literature would feel that it is 'homogenized' – that everything individual, idiosyncratic and intrinsically *oral* has been taken out, to leave a bland uniformity that makes it indistinguishable from literary narrative.

Since the 1960s, therefore, scholars of oral narrative have increasingly moved towards presenting verbatim texts. First came texts which were left *almost* as originally spoken: only the 'um's' and 'er's', the false starts and the hesitations were taken out, so that the story could be followed and due credit given to the skill of the storyteller. This seems, for example, to have been Richard Dorson's practice in his great collection of American folklore, *Buying the Wind* (1964). Recently, scholars such as

Elizabeth Fine and Bill Ellis in the USA, and Herbert Halpert and J. D. A. Widdowson in their work on Newfoundland folk narrative, have argued that texts should be transcribed not only absolutely verbatim, but also with as many paralinguistic and kinesic features as possible (voice, pitch, tempo, intonation, as well as gesture, body movements, changes of posture, and so on).

Not many narrative scholars today would defend the practice of re-writing oral material into literary forms, but each one has to decide how 'verbatim' their 'verbatim' text is going to be in any situation. Here, I am going to revert to Richard Dorson's practice of tidying up texts (but making absolutely no other alterations), so that they are easy to read but still retain their individuality and their eccentrically oral characteristics. At the same time, I shall try to show some of the vividness of the speech by using italicizing to show stress, capitals to show marked change of pitch or loudness, dashes to show pauses, and quotation marks to show when the narrator assumes a 'quoting voice'. A typical story will therefore look like this:

'I think yes! Because of *my mother-in-law's* experience.

'About three days before she died, she *told* me she was dying, and that her *husband*, my father-in-law, and his *sister*, had been to *see* her and they told her that everything was PERFECTLY all right, and – Oh, I was just flabbergasted, because she was the sort of person with *no* imagination WHATSOEVER. She *couldn't* have dreamt it up! She wasn't the type.

'*He* died about ten months before *her* and the *sister* died about fourteen, fifteen months before. Oh, she was quite happy. She'd talked to them, you know. She was quite relieved.

'That was my own experience, because I'd be about twenty-eight. I hadn't *come* across anyone so SURE, and, had she been a very imaginative, chatty sort of person, probably I wouldn't have taken any notice, but she was ABSOLUTELY convinced. I mean, who am I to say that she didn't hear them, see them or speak to them?

'She was going to join them. It was eerie at the *time*, but as I've got older I've thought more about it, "Oh, yes! There must be something *in* it!"'

In its own way, this is a great story. Though the events are not assembled in chronological order, though the story-line is interrupted by digressions and comments and though the clauses are joined together into somewhat haphazard sentences, it has what a re-written story never has – immediacy, vividness, energy, conviction, directness. These are the hallmarks of good oral storytelling. It is different, no doubt, from literary narrative, but it is no less effective.

All illustrative material will, therefore, be memorate – the personal experiences of the women I spoke to – transcribed from tape-recordings 'almost verbatim' (that is, with only the 'um's', 'er's', fillers and false starts omitted). Stories such as these are the most effective way of showing what people actually believe – they save many paragraphs of explanation and discussion because they are more direct and vivid than any commentary can ever be. They are believed to be true by those who tell them, and are used to illustrate points of view and explain the finer points of an argument. As Sir Philip Sidney said of the poet, so might the women say of the storyteller:

he doth not only show the way, but giveth so sweet a prospect into the way, as will entice any man to enter into it [. . .] He beginneth not with obscure definitions, which must blur the margent with interpretations and must load the memory with doubtfulness; but he cometh to you with words set in delightful proportion [. . .] and with a tale, forsooth, he cometh to you, with a tale which holdeth children from play, and old men from the chimney-corner.[22]

NOTES

 1 Bascom in 'Folklore and Anthropology' (Dundes, ed. (1956), p. 23).
 2 Cf. Dundes, ed. (1965), p. 5.
 3 Quoted in Dorson, (1968), pp. 173–4.
 4 Quoted in Dorson, (1968), p. 223.
 5 Quoted in Dorson, (1968), p. 237.
 6 Quoted in Dorson, (1968), pp. 250–1.
 7 Quoted by Graves in *The New Larousse Encyclopedia of Mythology* (1959), p. 160.
 8 Cf. Dundes, ed. (1965), p. 33.
 9 Dundes (1964b), p. 256.
10 Ben Amos (1971), p. 13.
11 Dundes, ed. (1965), Introduction, p. 2.
12 Personal communication with the author.
13 Personal communication with the author.
14 Jung in 'The Psychological Foundation of Belief in Spirits', *Collected Works*, Volume 8, p. 316.
15 Lang (1894a), p. 173.
16 Lang (1894a), p. 5.
17 Wright (1927), p. 28; and see Giraud (1927) for the collected ghost stories.
18 Cf. Davidson and Russell eds (1981), p. 95.
19 Hunt (1865), p. viii.
20 Hunt (1865), p. xi.
21 Hare (1896), vol. 5, p. 425.
22 Sidney in 'Apology' (1959 ed.), p. 25.

2 Patterns of Belief

Man prefers to believe what he prefers to be true.[1]

FRANCIS BACON

Belief in occult forces is both endemic and ancient, one of the most enduring matters of interest. As Le Loyer wrote in the sixteenth century, it: 'is the topic that people most readily discuss and on which they linger the longest because of the abundance of the examples, the subject being fine and pleasing and the discussion the least tedious that can be found.'[2] For this reason, it has been one of the most commonly studied of all types of folklore. Writing on the subject abounds, from the sermon stories of the Middle Ages to the popular ghost gazetteers, investigative writing and legend collections of the present day.

That in dealing with supernatural beliefs we are dealing with immensely widespread traditions can, of course, be taken for granted. We may read, for example, of ghosts in both Old and New Testaments, find ghost stories in the classics and the Icelandic sagas, as well as among communities in modern London. Poltergeist reports come from ancient Egypt and from sixteenth-century Italy, as well as from eighteenth-century London and twentieth-century New York. Anthropologists have pointed out the intimate connection between tribal religion and belief in spirits, and folklorists and sociologists have documented similar connections in Western thought. Similarly, precognition, horoscopes, omens and premonitions and other forms of divination have been a staple of popular belief in many ages and cultures, part of 'ane old imprescriptible tradition'[3] as Robert Kirk called it. Just as the antiquary John Aubrey reflected in 1696 that: 'How it comes to pass, I know not, but by Ancient and Modern Example it is evident, that no great Accident befalls a City or Province, but it is presaged by Divination, or Prodigy, or Astrologie, or some way or other',[4] so I read in my horoscope today that the moon being at the full, and my airy sign inimical to water, I 'would be unwise to take a sea-voyage' this week.

It is common, however, nowadays to think of supernatural belief as declining in modern Britain. 'Common-sense' people argue that in a scientific age there is no place for fanciful anachronisms such as ghosts and ESP, or feel that such beliefs are 'childish' or 'irrational', or point out that most religions nowadays are opposed to such 'superstition', or ask what possible purpose a belief in the supernatural could serve and why we should continue to tolerate night-fears born out of tales of headless monks and other palpable absurdities. Ghosts and such, they all agree, are surely too great a strain on our credulity and too great a restriction on our freedom.

Historians and psychologists have also hastened to assure us that 'the social function of belief in ghosts is obviously much diminished and so is their extent',[5] and that 'ever since that age of enlightenment [the eighteenth century], percipients in England, and presumably much of Western Europe, have attributed to the dead an ever-diminishing social role',[6] or that 'we no longer need a vivid community of the dead'.[7] Folklorists have compounded the error by printing collections of readable – but unbelievable – legends and calling them the 'folklore' of the supernatural.

In order to redress the balance two points must be made. Firstly, all these writers are plainly operating from within the rationalist 'tradition of disbelief'; they fail, perhaps, to recognize the strength of the supernaturalist tradition because it is so far from their own ways of thinking that they simply do not see it. Secondly, they have all relied on written accounts for their data. For historians that has principally meant the records of the Society for Psychical Research (SPR) and popular ghost books; for folklorists it has meant local histories and nineteenth-century legend collections. If, on the basis of these accounts, researchers conclude that modern ghosts are pale and purposeless shadows of their former selves and that nobody believes in them anyway, it is hardly surprising. On the one hand, the motiveless apparitions of the SPR are motiveless because all traditional embellishments, such as the attribution of purpose and significance, have been carefully excised from published accounts, not because the informants *themselves* thought them motiveless. On the other hand, the white ladies and cauld lads of nineteenth-century country legend, though they may once have been believed, almost certainly wouldn't gain credence in towns and cities nowadays. To find out what people really believe about the supernatural, there is no alternative but to go out and *ask* them.

Of late, sociologists have done just that. Geoffrey Gorer, for example, conducted a survey through a national newspaper for his *Exploring English Character*, which included questions about palm-reading, horoscopes and ghosts. More recently, the sociology department at Leeds University have conducted a study into what they call 'common' religion (folklorists would call it 'folk' religion), asking questions, among other things, about life after death, ghosts, telepathy, clairvoyance, fortune-telling and horoscopes. Gorer found that 30 per cent of his respondents believed in palm-reading, 20 per cent in astrology, and 17 per cent in ghosts. The Leeds team found that 14 per cent believed in astrology, 35 per cent in fortunetelling, 36 per cent in ghosts, 54 per cent in clairvoyance, and 61 per cent in telepathy. Gorer's figures suggest quite high levels of belief; the Leeds figures are higher still, and do not at all give the impression that belief in the supernatural is declining. It would seem from their results that a quite substantial proportion of the population, of all ages and social classes, share these ancient traditions. Clearly the psychologist Gustav Jahoda rather under-estimated the extent of belief when he wrote:

There is clearly a substantial minority of the general population in England . . . (and probably in other European countries as well) who hold decidedly superstitious beliefs. Moreover, detailed breakdowns according to social background of the informants indicate that such beliefs are by no means confined to the poor and ignorant [. . .] If one takes into account the fact that people are apt to be somewhat shamefaced about superstition and liable to deny holding any such beliefs when faced with a strange interviewer, the evidence becomes even more impressive. Superstition is still very much with us, and it is possible that some forms of it may be on the increase. Therefore it is well worth trying to understand the nature of this complex phenomenon, which is a general human one not confined to distant peoples.[8]

Give or take a 'superstition' or two (a sure sign that he was writing from within the rationalist tradition), Jahoda is very much on the mark here.

His remarks also hold a substantial clue to the reason for the different figures obtained by Gorer in 1955 and by the Leeds team in the 1980s. Gorer sent out written questionnaires for respondents to fill in, whereas the Leeds team employed trained fieldworkers to interview people face-to-face. Obviously, the more impersonal the approach, the more 'shame-faced' the respondents and the more likely to 'deny holding any such beliefs'. Yet among friends and on informal occasions, as Le Loyer rightly observed, the topic is 'fine and pleasing', the one 'people most readily discuss and on which they linger the longest'. All depends on the context in which questions are asked or discussion engaged in.

*

When I set out on this project, then, it seemed likely that a small-scale study, which could be conducted not only face-to-face, but informally through discussion and conversation as well as through question-and-answer, and in the presence of a familiar and trusted intermediary, would show even higher levels of supernatural belief in the community. And so it turned out. What seemed to be particularly helpful was not only that the interview was kept friendly and relaxed (informants themselves often turning questioner and asking for *my* opinions and beliefs), but also that, as the study progressed, I could adapt the wording of my questions and prompts to fit in with the phraseology the women themselves used. For example, I found very early on that I had to drop terms like 'the supernatural' altogether: for my informants it was not a neutral, nor even a factual, term – its connotations were wholly evil and taboo. As long as I said I was doing research on 'the supernatural', I had only negative reactions, ranging from denial to hostility and even real fear. As soon as I took to speaking in vague fashion about 'the mysterious side of life', the women relented, showed decided interest and were eager to talk. Similarly, when I started out, I had simply followed the practice of people like Gorer and had blankly asked, 'Do you believe in ghosts?' and everybody had promptly said 'No'. Luckily, I was soon put on the right track by a woman who said that she didn't believe in ghosts, but she knew that a house could be 'spirited' and in fact she had once lived in a house that 'wasn't right'. On the same day, an old lady said that she didn't believe in ghosts, but 'funnily enough, whenever someone's going to be ill in my family, my mother comes to me'. These linguistic clues obviously led to two distinct categories of what I dare not now call 'ghosts': on the one hand, evil entities inhabiting houses and, on the other hand, the friendly, warning spirits of the family dead, which I grew to call 'witnesses' (see chapter 3). I was able to follow these clues and from then on talked about '*things* in houses' and experiences where dead parents and husbands 'come to' the living, without alarming or offending anybody.

Likewise, initially I had kept to the conventional practice of distinguishing between 'omens' as material signs of death or danger and 'premonitions' as non-material signals that something is amiss somewhere. I had to learn by trial and error that the women themselves distinguish between omens and premonitions principally according to the *outcome*, the word 'omen' being used where death or severe danger ensues, and the word 'premonition' where less awful fates await – marriage, perhaps, or a minor accident. In addition, the term 'telepathy' might be used in either case (as in the phrase 'a telepathy with the future'), as well as in its dictionary sense of 'the action of one mind on another at a distance through emotional influence without communication through the senses'.

A final, very important, advantage of informal, face-to-face interviews is that informants do not have to be pressed to give clear yes/no answers as they would have to do in a written questionnaire or formal survey. Very often they like to phrase their answers with a little face-saving ambiguity. In these circumstances, if they are pushed to say whether 'I think there may be something in it' means 'definitely yes' or 'definitely no', they will probably say 'no', even though that is far from their real opinion. Also, the approach allows informants to express partial belief as well as unashamed conviction, and that gives a fairer and more accurate picture overall. There are problems here, of course. If the informant will not herself plainly answer 'yes' or 'no', the researcher is left to make the judgements (with the danger of getting it all wrong). With practice, however, one can learn to pick up linguistic clues which are good and reliable guides to belief or disbelief.[9]

These adaptations to the language of the questions and prompts all undoubtedly help people to relax and to be more frank and open. The figures for belief in various types of supernatural tradition are therefore higher here than in previous studies – and, I think, a little nearer to the truth. Of all the women I interviewed, well over half have some measure of belief in extrasensory perception (ESP), telepathy and the continued presence of the family dead, and almost half of them also accept the possibility of poltergeists and hauntings.

If we concentrate on the retired women, who formed the vast majority of the informants (87 out of 107), some very interesting patterns of belief emerge. In the first place, the women fall into two distinct camps – believers versus sceptics (adherents of the supernaturalist and rationalist traditions discussed in chapter 1). The crucial sticking-point is their attitude towards the status of the dead. Rationalists of the 'once you're dead, you're dead' school discount not only belief in spirits but also most forms of divination and precognition; supernaturalists of the 'there are more things in heaven and earth, Horatio' school would not only believe that the ghost of Hamlet's father was real enough but also firmly trust in ESP. The former group answered 'no' to most or all of my questions, the latter group 'yes', or 'there must be something in it'. Only 17 out of the 87 older women reserved their position, or gave mixed answers in which they confessed to a belief in ESP but dismissed belief in the continued presence and influence of the dead. It suggests that the supernatural is a topic that is discussed frequently and seriously among them, so that individuals are pressurized into taking sides and seeking refuge in the stock arguments and attitudes provided by their team in the philosophical tug-of-war.

That believers are on the winning side (at least numerically) may be seen in the high percentage of belief given overall to a group of very old traditions – warnings in the form of the ubiquitous premonition, 'ghosts' and 'revenants' (though these, as we have seen, are terms the women themselves would certainly not use) and omens of death and disaster. Among the 87 older women, the highest faith is placed in what they call 'premonitions' – ineffable warnings that 'something's going to happen'. A massive 77 per cent of them hold it to be possible to be so forewarned and 43 per cent of them are *certain* that it can happen as they are themselves 'a little bit psychic'. The next most popular idea is telepathy: only 10 per cent think it does not and cannot occur, whereas 53 per cent are convinced it is a real phenomenon which they have experienced themselves and a further 14 per cent think that it is at least likely. Sixty per cent of the older women believe that 'the dead never leave' them, 44 per cent with conviction, 16 per cent with only slightly less certainty. They are less likely, however, to believe that *evil* spirits are around in the form of poltergeists or haunting ghosts, though even here the figure is larger than might have been expected (14 per cent expressing convinced belief and 27 per cent thinking the phenomenon possibly really occurs). Another 11 per cent speak in this context about 'happy' or 'unhappy' houses, reflecting, perhaps, the last remnants of the ancient belief in household spirits. The final group of traditions accorded considerable approval are omens of death in the form of mysterious noises, the scent of flowers, broken mirrors, dreams, visions and phantoms. A surprising 55 per cent of those asked still put some trust in these old tokens ('signs and wonders' as one lady rather biblically described them), half of whom are quite convinced about it and can cite personal examples.

It must be stressed that these women are not ignorant or ill-educated; nor are they socially or geographically isolated. They are dignified, sensible, experienced women, living in a middle-class suburb of a large city. Neither are they in any way eccentric; on the contrary, they are pillars of the Church and local community, essentially 'respectable' in even the narrowest sense of that unpleasant term. It is a tribute to the staying power of tradition that women so conventional should still hold to these ancient beliefs in an age which is almost *officially* considered to be rational and scientific, and it surely indicates that the extent of belief in the supernatural has, for a long time, gone unrecognized and under-estimated. Probably the levels of belief in the community are really higher still. In the privacy of their own hearts many people would no doubt, under the cover of dark, slip over the lines from the official rationalist camp into the unofficial supernaturalist enclave.

When fortunetelling and astrology are discussed, however, the picture changes, and a second type of polarization in belief-patterns emerges. Whereas the women give substantial approval to ESP and belief in good spirits, they are decidedly less enthusiastic about fortunetelling and astrology. Here, it is the rationalists who are numerically stronger, and even entrenched supernaturalists are often sceptical. Sixty-four per cent of all the older women, for example, are dismissive of astrology, whereas only 2 per cent believe in it completely and only 25 per cent admit partial belief. The percentage of disbelievers rises to 75 per cent in the case of fortunetelling; only 15 per cent of informants are sure it works and only 9 per cent think it might do. These are fascinating patterns, so, before going on in chapters 3, 4 and 5 to present a detailed picture of the women's beliefs through their own words and stories, I want briefly to look at the attitudes which seem to predispose some women (but not others) to belief, and to some beliefs (but not others).

By listening to all the conversation recorded on the interview-tapes, it is possible to pick up a very good general picture of the mental furniture the women carry round with them, and this is most instructive when trying to understand the why's and wherefore's of belief. Judging from this background information, it seems that it is social and philosophical considerations that determine *whether* women accept traditions of the supernatural, and moral factors that decide *which* traditions they accept. The women I interviewed are elderly, conventional, churchgoing, and very much geared to traditional roles and pursuits. Their beliefs and attitudes are bound to be influenced by considerations of morality, and their morality by received ideals of the relationships of women to men, individuals to society and mankind to God. Like it or not, these women have been taught by the society they have grown up in that the ideal member of their sex is an intuitive, gentle, unassertive person, geared to a caring and supportive role rather than to direct action, independent thought or concern with self. Whether a particular traditional super-natural belief is acceptable seems to be directly governed by these basic assumptions. Popular beliefs reflect permitted behaviour. Premonitions and telepathy score so highly on their belief-scale because, par excellence, they are intuitions; because they come unsought, not as the result of the active pursuit of knowledge; and because they turn outwards from the self to the immediate circle of family and friends. They are feelings about and for other people – love of others made manifest, defeated by neither time nor distance, and felt in the deep recesses of the heart where none may challenge their authority. In contrast, fortunetelling and astrology are intellectual pursuits – a learned ability to interpret purely material signs; deliberately sought experiences which effectively devalue intuition. In addition, they are self-centred not other-person-oriented. It is a woman's own fortune that is told, and her own fate that is read in the stars; other people are thrust into the role of supporting cast and she steps centre-stage. Such behaviour is not permitted, so such traditions are not believed.

Similarly, the women are much more likely to say that they believe in good spirits than bad ones. As they describe it, they are made aware of the souls of the good dead more often through sensing their presence than by seeing them in physical form; on the other hand, haunting ghosts and poltergeists manifest themselves through material means. Again, when a dead mother 'comes to' her distressed daughter, she comes unbidden, and her presence is evidence of mutual caring, proof that other-person-centredness works even from beyond the grave. In contrast, a person who hears mysterious footsteps in the attic, or witnesses doors opening of their own accord, or sees apparitions of unknown people passing up the stairs is surrounded by a world of *strangers*, where intruders creep even into the heart of the family and invade the circle round the hearth.

Moreover, hauntings and poltergeists are dangerous and unpredictable and, time and time again, the women show a strong reluctance to believe in anything which makes the world seem unsafe. Premonitions, telepathy and the presence of the good dead are reassuring proof of the efficacy of human caring, the existence of another, better plane of life, the love of God for mankind and the harmony of his creation; fortunetelling, astrology and evil spirits on the other hand make the world seem less safe and predictable, unsettling the known order of things and introducing uncertainty into tidy lives. So one is believed and the other is not.

These are the patterns which appear over and over again as the women describe their beliefs and experiences. A traditional belief is accepted most readily if it depends upon the utilization of intuition, imagination, insight; if it is an involuntary experience rather than a chosen activity; if it enhances or extends interpersonal relationships;

and if it gives reassurance of the goodness of God and man. If a concept challenges these values, it is far less likely to be accepted. It is not oversimplifying matters to say that the degree of belief accorded any traditional idea can be predicted by its position on four continua – from intuitive to objective, from unsought to sought, from interpersonal to selfish, and from safe to dangerous. So, whereas 60 per cent of the women believe in the presence of the good dead, and still more believe in premonitions and telepathy (all intuitive, unsought, interpersonal happenings that encourage a feeling that the world is safe and good), scarcely more than a quarter have much belief in astrology and fortune-telling (acquired skills or deliberately sought, self-centred experiences that introduce an element of the unknown into ordinary living). Between these two extremes lie traditional concepts like hauntings and omens, which approximately half the women believe in. About 41 per cent, as we saw earlier, are prepared to believe in poltergeists and hauntings – at the 'wrong' end of three continua, but at least *unsought* encounters with the supernatural. Rather more (55 per cent) were prepared to accept omens – dangerous in consequence, but (as we shall see in chapter 5) other-person-centred and unsought.

It does seem, then, that the acceptability or otherwise of a supernatural tradition depends to a large extent on its morality in the women's eyes, and, in turn, that that morality is dependent on their perception of a woman's 'proper' role and persona and their need to see the world as an orderly, harmonious sphere for God's goodness and human affection.

Some of the same themes are important in understanding why it is that some women cling so strongly to supernatural beliefs, while others are embedded within the dominant rationalist tradition of British society. In a broad sense it is these same moral attitudes, mediated by social situation and intellectual orientation, that are determining factors here, too.

As far as social situation is concerned, one would imagine that factors such as ageing, widowhood, solitude and the loss of family ties would be of paramount significance in disposing middle-aged and elderly women to a belief in the supernatural. One might think that fear of death would lead the elderly to a search for immortality; widows might seek to hold on to lost husbands; lonely people, lacking the love and companionship of the living, might turn to the dead for comfort. Strangely enough, though all these suppositions seem so obvious, none of them are borne out by the present study. I found that readiness to believe does not increase with increasing age in any fixed progression and is not more observable in widows and those who live alone than among married people. However, there is one very significant aspect of social situation which does seem very strongly to predispose women towards belief, and that is a reliance on, and love for, family.

One simple way of showing this is by selecting a representative group of women to whom kinship and family are obviously important and comparing the incidence of supernatural belief among them with that in a contrasting group of women with apparently much less family feeling. When listening to the tapes, it is quite easy to distinguish the 'family woman', because all her talk, whatever its ostensible subject, is liberally sprinkled with references to dead and living members of her clan – aunts and uncles, nieces and nephews, parents and grandparents. On the other hand, in complete contrast, there is the woman whose conversation, though maybe thoughtful, entertaining and fluent, contains few or no references to other people, neither to friends nor to family. Though these relationships may exist, they do not colour her thinking, memory and discourse as they do for the 'family woman'.

Sixty-two out of 107 of the women I interviewed fall into the first category – they are 'family women' – and it is amongst these that supernatural belief is strongest. Fifty-two out of the 62, for example, believe that the souls of dead friends and family still surround them and sometimes may be communicated with. In contrast, only 8 out of the 29 non-family women cherish any such idea and 17 are quite sure that such things cannot happen.[10]

Belief in the supernatural allows the continuation of relationships of mutual love – parent and child, husband and wife – even when one of the partners is separated by distance or death. It enhances the traditional female role and secures for the believer a continued place in society as she has known it. A younger woman might well regret the limitations imposed on these older ones, the way their lives have been restricted and the subordinate roles that have been forced upon them, but the women themselves salvage a great deal from their lifestyle, and, through their concept of the spiritual/supernatural world, endow their role with something of the holy.

Moral issues play their part, too, in the philosophical orientations that dispose some women to belief and others to scepticism. One of their primary values, as we have seen, is the concept of order. It is, to a very large extent, the different ways in which the women seek to find order in the chaos of fate and chance that determine whether they adhere to the supernaturalist or to the rationalist tradition.

Supernaturalists respond to the unpredictability of human life and the oddities of human experience by adopting a mystical view of life which sees the world as a semi-magical place governed by unrevealed laws. They say, for example:

'The world's a great study and a great puzzle'

'There are more things in heaven and earth than we dream of'

'The world's so wonderful, isn't it? And we just don't *know* what there is'

'There is far more to know than we are ready for yet'

'It's such a beautiful, wonderful universe, anything is possible'.

Though the world as they see it is incapable of being thoroughly understood and is perpetually surprising, it is, nevertheless, integrated and purposeful, and guidance, help and divine providence mitigate the worst effects of ignorance and chance.

Though most of the women profess adherence to the tenets of Methodism or other major Christian denominations, elements from other religions and sects form a stable part of their faith. The belief in re-incarnation is particularly dominant, notably in its Buddhistic form of infinite progression towards perfection. Again, the doctrine of personal revelation and divine intervention, borrowed from charismatic, fundamentalist sects, is a frequent aspect of their thinking. For these women, it would seem, academic distinctions between the natural and supernatural, the normal and the paranormal, are virtually meaningless. All believe in an afterlife in which 'we will meet again', and this view informs a world-view in which 'the dead never leave' them, and the boundary between the mundane and spiritual worlds is a flexible one.

Alternatively, they may have a great sense of the world's mystery but not formulate their philosophy in specifically theistic terms. Rather than seeing a world in which 'God moves in a mysterious way', they see a world of psychic wonders. Many of this group claim to be 'a little bit psychic' and several said that they had been offered the chance to train as mediums (a chance all had turned down). Invariably these are women of great intellectual curiosity, open-minded and discursive. The dominant impression is that the psychic powers they claim are correlations of, extensions to, or substitutes for, conventional religion and also constitute a claim to special social status – membership of a sort of intuitive élite. Mysticism gains for its adherents a relaxed acceptance of life's oddities and the chaos of the material world. It allows them to control disorder and take away its sting by accepting it.

The sceptual tradition is also a response to anxiety about chance and fate, but here the strategy is to ignore or deny the disorder, by means of either determinism or materialism.

The effect of the deterministic approach is to make the world mechanical by presupposing an immutable divine plan. Life is a machine which God has set in motion and which, once running, cannot be stopped or altered. There is no result to be gained nor purpose to be served by such things as astrology or fortunetelling. Though the future is ordained, it *is* the future and therefore cannot be apprehended in the present. Hence there can be no possibility of omens or premonitions either. No jot of one's fate can be altered; warnings, prophecies or helpful revenants are therefore irrelevant and therefore do not exist. This gloomy Knoxian doctrine is widely held, not only by the sole Scottish Presbyterian I interviewed, but also by members of other denominations and by those very few who professed no religious affiliation at all – another example of an imported doctrine that has enough explanatory or pragmatic power to be incorporated in popular religious belief. This attitude is summed up neatly in the words of the informant I shall call 'Evelyn' (all place and personal names are, of course, fictitious): 'My father used to say that from the moment you're born to the moment you die, your life is mapped out for you. He says *nothing* will alter it.' Deterministic women are thus resolute, stoical and unflinchingly negative in their attitude to the supernatural.

The materialistic approach, which other adherents of the rationalist tradition adopt, is a sort of 'ignorance is strength' philosophy: they simply refuse to think about fate, disorder or the supernatural at all, they do not *let* them exist. They say they 'do not go in for it', they do not 'bother with it', they 'do not believe in delving'. Their approach to life, they say, is to 'take one day at a time' and to 'meet troubles when they come'; they describe themselves as 'a day-to-day person' or say 'I'm not fanciful, I'm more practical'. This group of women is the least religious of all, the least speculative and the least talkative. Although brief descriptions and statements are all they want to offer, the outlines of their philosophy are nevertheless still apparent. They are practitioners of what one might call 'simple realism': they deal with discrepant experiences by denying them, riding them out, or by correcting them by the application of simple rules of 'common-sense', so that the world can be made a reliable 'machine for living in'.[11]

These, then, are the patterns of morality, social situation and personal philosophy that seem to have most significance in deciding whether an individual woman will subscribe to the supernaturalist or rationalist school of thought, and whether individual traditions will be accepted by the majority of the community or not. Briefly summarized, optimum conditions for supernatural belief seem to be reliance on, and love for, family; the placing of a high value on interpersonal relationships; a metaphysical philosophy in which chance and fate are seen as part of an unrevealed benevolent plan; and a traditional 'female' morality, which places great value on intuition, caring, unassertiveness, unselfishness and order.

These attitudes run like a thread through the women's thinking and, in both general and detail, influence their beliefs about the dead and ESP – the subjects of the following chapters.

NOTES

1 Francis Bacon, *Aphorisms*.
2 Quoted by John Dover Wilson in his introduction to Lavater (1929 edn), p. x.
3 Kirk (1976 edn), p. 111.
4 Aubrey (1696), pp. 33–4.
5 Thomas (1971), p. 605.
6 Finucane (1982), p. 222.
7 Blauner (1966), p. 382.
8 Jahoda (1969), pp. 25–6.
9 See Appendix (page 213).
10 In order to see whether it might just be a general sociability that conditioned women to accept supernatural beliefs, I ran two checks. First of all, five women who talked a good deal about friends, though not about family, were added to the group of 'family women' to make a larger group of 'social women', and, secondly, twelve women who, while not talking much about either friends or family, were yet voluble and discursive, were added to make a group of 'talkers', and the figures were then calculated for both new groupings. Both returned lower percentages of believers than the original group of 'family women' (i.e. 83 per cent belief among 'family women'; 78 per cent among 'social women'; 66 per cent among 'talkers'). It appears, therefore, that the single most significant correlative of a belief in the supernatural is devotion to family and family-life. Simply, there is strong evidence that people who put a high value on personal relationships are reluctant to give them up even when death intervenes.
11 The phrase is, of course, Le Corbusier's architectural maxim.

3 *The Dead*

It is not to be denied, and we are all very well aware that many persons of quality and distinction, learned men, too, and sober, level-headed folk, who fear God and reverence the truth, have solemnly declared and avouched that they have on occasion both seen and heard Spirits.[1]

FR NOEL TAILLEPIED

So wrote Noel Taillepied in 1588, and things have not changed much since. People today are just as likely to have experiences which they interpret as supernatural and to tell stories about them. These narratives (memorates) are very good guides to present-day traditions, and through them we may not only see how culture shapes individual experience, but also how individuals (and the society they live in) shape culture.

On the subject of the dead there is, of course, a very long cultural tradition; the stories quoted here and in the following chapters provide a commentary on that tradition as well as an up-date of it. They feature two distinct kinds of spirit. At one extreme there are the spirits of the good dead who surround their descendants and continue to provide protection, love and reassurance. The women I spoke to may very well believe in other types of supranormal encounter as well but, if they do, they never mentioned it. No-one spoke, for example, of animal ghosts, or of haunted gardens, churchyards or crossroads. It may be that these have dropped from the traditional stereotype altogether – or maybe they were not mentioned simply because the subject never came up in conversation: it is hard to tell. Perhaps we do therefore lack a comprehensive picture of supernatural traditions in the community. However, what we *have* got is a clear and full description of two opposed poles of belief – the wholly evil and the wholly good.

THE EVIL DEAD:
HAUNTINGS AND POLTERGEISTS

At the evil pole there are the meaningless, malevolent, disruptive phenomena that the women refer to as '*things* in houses', 'spirits', 'ghosts',
'poltergeists', or 'haunted'/'wrong'/'nasty'/'unhappy' houses. This
grouping conflates two separate categories recognized by modern
psychical researchers – that is, 'poltergeists' and 'hauntings' – both of
which have long ancestry in popular belief.

Poltergeists are some of the oldest types of manifestation recognized
in Western culture. Andrew Lang refers, for example, to the existence of
an ancient Egyptian papyrus addressed to the destructive spirit of a dead
wife. In medieval times such accounts were the stock-in-trade of a
priesthood anxious to impress the reality of purgatory on their con-
gregations. Again, in the late sixteenth century Taillepied was writing
about: 'Demons and Sprites [that] will upset furniture; bastinado, nip,
thump and batoon persons, throwing stones and tiles at them; holding
doors and jamming them so fast that it is impossible to open them;
marauding high and low throughout the whole house, endamaging
property and perilously molesting men and women, even sometimes (if
God so permits) endangering life and limb.'[2] Such evils continued to
hold the public imagination well into the modern age. Joseph Glanvil's
seventeenth-century account of 'The Daemon of Tedworth' continues
to make appearances in books on poltergeists even today and the
Mompesson house in Wiltshire, where the manifestations were supposed
to have occurred, is open to the public. An even more famous account is
John Wesley's story of the disturbances at his father's home in December
1716. More recently there have been outbreaks at Borley Rectory (of
dubious authenticity according to psychical researchers Dingwall,
Goldney and Hall) and at Runcorn.

Tales of the restless dead are equally ancient and widespread. One of
the most popular stories of all time is Pliny's account of the philosopher
Athenodorus who was plagued by a very noisy spectre until, in
phlegmatic fashion, he followed it into the garden, discovered its bones
and gave them decent burial (see pages 155–6). In 1572 the arch-
rationalist, Ludowig Lavater (of whom more later) was admitting that
'Daily experience techeth us that spirits do appear to men' and citing the
following examples which contain very similar motifs to Pliny's story:

Many times in the nyght season, there have beene certaine spirits hearde softely
going, or spitting, or groning, who being asked what they were, have made

answere that they were the soules of this or that man, & they nowe endure extreame tormentes. Yf by chaunce any man did aske of them, by what meanes they might be delivered out of those tortures, they have answered, that in case a certaine numbre of Masses were soong for them, or Pilgrimages vowed to some Saintes, or some other such like deedes doone for their sake, that then surely they shoulde be delivered.[3]

In the eighteenth century, the antiquarian Francis Grose gave an amusing description of popular ghost beliefs which forms a bridge between these traditions and more recent beliefs. Give or take a sneer and exaggeration or two, this is a fair checklist of the stereotype of haunting in modern popular literature and ghost legends:

if any discontented maiden, or love-crossed bachelor, happened to dispatch themselves in their garters, the room where the deed was perpetrated became for ever after uninhabitable, and not infrequently nailed up. If a drunken farmer, returning from market, fell from Old Dobbin, and broke his neck . . . that spot was ever after haunted and impassable. In short, there was scarcely a bye-lane or cross-way but had its ghost, who appeared in the shape of a headless cow or horse, or clothed all in white glared with its saucer eyes over some gate or stile. Ghosts of superior rank, as befitted their station, rode in coaches drawn by six headless horses, and driven by headless coachmen and postillions. Almost every ancient manor house was haunted by one or other of its former masters or mistresses . . . and, as for the churchyards, the number of ghosts that walked there, according to the village computation, almost equalled the living parishioners.[4]

In the 1950s, an American folklorist, L. C. Jones, conducted a survey among his students which, though differing in emphasis, still presents much the same picture of a haunted house (though there is no mention of crossroads and bye-lanes, etc.). He lists the manifestations they thought typical of such places as: mysterious footsteps in attics or cellars or on the stairs, noises, moving furniture, lights which switch themselves on and off, bedclothes uncannily twitched off in the night by unseen hands, sudden breezes from nowhere, ineradicable bloodstains, and strange feelings of unease and cold.

Though the women I spoke to were more reluctant to talk about evil spirits than any other topic – less inclined to tell stories or expand their answers beyond a brief 'yes' or 'no' – they obviously do still think there may be something in these ancient beliefs, and, where one can piece together a picture of their concept of the evil supernatural, it fits re-markably well into this familiar pattern. Throughout the women's mem-orates and stories, familiar themes and motifs keep recurring: mysterious footsteps, self-flushing toilets, cold winds from nowhere, lights and rappings, displaced objects. A group of typical stories give the flavour of these experiences:

Molly's story

'We lived in a house that was spirited. It was a lady committed suicide in the house, and then no one would live in it. *We* lived in it. We were desperate for another house. We went to live in it.

'We had *all* kinds of things happened. Otherwise I wouldn't have believed in it, because I *do* believe in spirits. I don't say *ghosts*. I don't know whether they're the same – I imagine they are really.'

[G. B. : 'What happened there?']

'Oh, well, the toilet used to flush when nobody was in, and we'd hear somebody walking in the passage and we'd go to the door and there'd be nobody there, and my mother was hanging washing up one day in the attic. You know, we'd two big attics, and she was hanging washing up one day and somebody came up behind her and gripped her by the shoulders. And she thought it was one of *us*, but it wasn't.

'We didn't live long in that house. It got a bit unnerving.'

Agnes's story

'Again, I remember Wolfgang, a German boy who used to stay with us, telling us the story about his uncle, the pastor . . . He had an uncle who was a Lutheran pastor, and the uncle told *him* or it was strong family knowledge.

'They moved into this equivalent to the Manse, whatever they call it, and it was quite empty and not a very nice sort of place altogether. It was a bit *grim*, and his uncle wasn't a *bit* happy about it. But, anyway, they settled down, the family did.

'And he was in his study writing his sermons, and suddenly all his books came off the shelf and flew all over the place, and his papers – his sermons – were all fluttering about like leaves. And the uncle wasn't really very concerned, he thought there was a sudden wind though there wasn't a window open or anything. And he went out into the other room, passage, or what-have-you, and asked his *wife* and she said, "No. Nothing. *Why?* What do you *mean?*"

'And it happened again. Every time he went to sit down to do any study, all his papers flew up all over the place.

'Now, I know to make the story *real*, I should say what it was that had *caused* this, and Wolfgang did connect it up to something, but *that* I've *forgotten*.'

Georgina's story

'And I was brought up waiting for the Second Coming. My mother used to say to me often, "You'd better ask God to forgive you before you wake up, because you may *never* wake up and you'll find yourself in HELL." And I used to go to sleep often terrified that I hadn't been really forgiven for whatever it was I'd done. And therefore I know in my own mind that the Last Day was a feature that I waited for with *horror* sometimes, and sometimes, if I felt that I'd been saved, I could almost *look forward* to it. And my grandmother would expound it all in great detail and I would feel the mixture of thrill and terror, depending on how I thought I was placed in the Elected. But having been brought up with that kind of thing, I'm quite sure I developed a kind of poltergeist – not *entity* . . . but I'm quite sure that my mind was concentrated on the terrified occult. It was *forced* in that direction because I daren't think of the things I was being led to believe. Some of them were *too terrible* to accept . . .

'And I remember distinctly, for several weeks, lying awake and listening to tappings above the doorway in the bedroom, and they were definite and positive tappings. I didn't imagine them, because they aroused me and terrified me and I knew they were not of *my world*. These tappings used to continue for quite a long time and strange lights would come through the window. These lights appeared through the window and they were *static*, and they used to occupy a space in the middle of the room where an *illumination* . . . Now, I never *saw* anything in the way of a *Being* or anything of that kind, it was merely a *light*. And that happened several times and was also associated with the rappings. They were hard, harsh rappings that couldn't have been made on a wall or a door. That's the *point*: I've only just thought of that *now*! They were *above* the door and yet they were rappings on a *hard substance*. Now, a wall hasn't got a hard substance like that. FUNNY! I hadn't thought of that till just then.

'There was a space in the corner behind my parents' bed – I slept in the same bedroom. It was a common thing among working-class people in those days when space was crowded. And, in my parents' bedroom in which I was sleeping, there was one corner where "Hob" lived. Now, I *knew* he was "Hob". I *knew* him. I met him frequently. I used to meet him in dreams and half-dreams. My recollection of Hob is of him sitting on a gate. Now, I may have seen something like that in books but . . . And I was always terrified to go past him.

'Now, I woke up several nights terrified of Hob and also terrified of the tappings I heard, and my mother used to come up, but I daren't tell her. I just daren't *tell* her that kind of thing. I didn't tell her about Hob and where Hob lived. I used to tell her I'd had a dream about pirates.'

Stephanie's story

'Oh, well. The *first* one was when Martin and I went to see *Hello Dolly* at Drury Lane, and this was a few years ago now. And we all stood up, you know, to give them an encore or something – I forget now – and SUDDENLY . . . there wasn't a door opened or anything . . . We just turned *round* and there was this very, very cold, CHILLY feeling. Everybody turned round at once. There was *nothing*, no doors opened or anything, nobody . . . For *some reason* we all turned round at once. There was this *cold chill* at the back of us. It was a very UN-CANNY feeling, a very STRANGE feeling. And it wasn't until *afterwards* that we *knew* there was any ghost floating round in Drury Lane.

'So that was *one*. That was it. That was *very* strange, that. That was a *really chilly* thing. That was the ghostly one.'

Sandra's story

'I've heard of *one or two* people who had experiences like that. I mean, I go for music lessons on a Saturday morning, and this little room where I go, years and years back a lady was supposed to have hung herself there and there's supposed to be a *spirit* THERE. And doors are mysteriously banged and music's flown about and this sort of thing.

'But I think one would have to *see* it. I would be *frightened to*

DEATH, you know, but I'd only have to *see* it and it would
convince me.'

A linguistic analysis of these and the handful of other memorates which
were told on this subject shows that the words which crop up most
frequently are: *house, go, attic, stairs, door, somebody, cellar, nightmare, family,
disappear*. The women speak, for example, of a father who 'all of a
sudden, heard footsteps coming up the cellar steps'; a daughter who
wakes to find a 'nightmare' apparition bending over her in the 'very old,
tall house' where she is staying; of a child who hears two ghosts talking in
the attic; of a 'funny thing' happening in a house which is 'kind of
haunted'; of another house where 'a little old lady' in old-fashioned
clothes 'keeps going up and down the stairs'; of waking up to find
'somebody' disappearing through the bedroom door; of a family who
have to 'leave everything and *go*'; and so on. All these motifs, words and
turns of phrase may be found time and time again in accounts of hauntings
from medieval sermon stories to popular ghost gazetteers. The original
experiences are real enough, but, as they are mentally rehearsed or turned
into public narrative, they are being moulded by cultural expectations.
So, they are not only put into the 'proper' context of darkness and
solitude, and located in no-go areas such as cellars and attics and deserted
old houses, or betwixt-and-between regions such as stairs, gates and
doorways, but they are also explained to others (to the potential or actual
hearer) in terms of traditional causality. Molly says that 'a lady committed
suicide in the house', Sandra's lady 'was supposed to have hung herself
there', Agnes is worried that her story will not be 'real' unless she can 'say
what it was that had *caused* this' and Georgina's experiences are accounted
for by psychological disturbance severe enough to attract the other-
worldly and allow it to manifest itself. Elsewhere, the evil supernatural
has been permitted to enter into the orderly mundane world because
someone 'very sensitive' has been on hand to respond to and interpret it,
or because its territory has been invaded by rash people trespassing in
cemeteries or playing with Ouija boards.

These transformations are being performed on real experience neither
consciously nor cynically, but in order to understand and classify it.
Telling other people about strange happenings in stories and memorates
is another way of dealing with them; and, the more the women narrate
to each other, the more their stories become traditionalized. They neither
make them up nor tart them up; rather they use the traditional embellishments to help classify the experience for themselves and others.

Here, as elsewhere, traditionalizing events in this way is a strenuous attempt to make sense out of them, to bring discrepant experiences within the compass of the known and understood.

One can see these processes at work very clearly in a sad, strange little story which Inez tells. She is presented with a very peculiar domestic situation for which no rules of interpretation exist. She can only explain the situation to herself in terms of conventional ghostlore, and yet she knows all along that it is neither quite appropriate nor relevant to her situation:

Inez's story

'Now, this is a funny thing. I married a man who had been married before, and when we came to set up our own house he had *everything* from the old house brought in and it had to be exactly in the same *way*. *Nothing* had to be altered. And if any china was broken, it had to be bought just the same. I didn't *realize* this, mind you, when I married him, but still . . .

'There was a big photograph of his wife . . . a big *lithograph*, really, of his wife, right over the mantelpiece, sitting in a chair. And I used to have *nightmares* she wasn't really dead. She was alive in the attic. *We hadn't* GOT *an attic!* Or she was in the basement room, which we hadn't got *either* – neither attic or basement!

'But I had to do everything in the house as she *said* so. And when I went cleaning round the house, sometimes I'd *knock* myself against the sideboard or whatever, and I'd feel *she'd* knocked me against the sideboard. This was just because I had to have everything the same, you know, that's the only thing.

'But to *think* she was alive and telling me, and that if I got knocked or trapped in the furniture, I thought *she* was doing it. It *did* affect me, as I say, always having this photograph in *front* of me, and having to have everything the same way.

'For about a fortnight before the anniversary of her death he wouldn't speak to you. He was always rushing off, you know to the cemetery. Of all the days in the year, Christmas Day it was too! You kind of felt *she* was the boss, you know.'

Personal experience narratives like these are substantiated by a number of local legends and rumours about hauntings and haunted locations.

Carmen's legend

'And there was a house in Torkington Street and that was haunted by the father, and every time they used to take anybody back to the house he'd *start*. Things like throwing things, making things *go*. The father used to make *doors* slam and it was awful! I actually *knew* that girl.'

Cynthia's legend

'There've been so many *cases*. There was one family locally a few years ago – council house down near Ramsbottom Gardens there – and *that* family just had to give up and go *out*! The local priest, vicar or whatever – *clergyman* – had gone in and tried to exorcize it. Literally things had just been thrown round the room, and they'd just *had* to get out. And there was a case in New York, wasn't there? I *think* it was New York – anyway, *America* – they made a *film* about it.'

Marilyn's legend

'There was a house in Farwood, and there was a woman and she'd never been out of her room in *ages*, because they couldn't *get in* the room, because the bed was constantly going up and down, and things kept flying *round*, and they tried to *exorcize* it, but it was no success, and all the rest of it.

'But that was when *The Exorcist* was going round. *That* could've had a lot to do with it.'

Marilyn's final comment, like Cynthia's remark about the New York poltergeist being made into a film, points up one characteristic of these rumours and some of the memorates too – that is, the direct influence of literature and the mass media in transmitting belief in the evil supernatural and shaping public conceptions about it. One can see this in the consistency of the motifs and language from older to more recent accounts and from written to oral stories, and also in the way media-and-book-acquired knowledge of the supernatural creeps into personal accounts. There is also more direct evidence of this influence in the form of the non-narrative comments the women make on the subject – references to the written word ('I've *read* about it' and 'You *do* read about that in the paper, don't you?') occurring almost as frequently as references to the spoken word ('I've heard of *so* many people who . . .', 'people *do* say . . .', 'so many people have reported these things'). There is obviously a high degree of interaction here between literary and oral tradition and between public and private belief.

Alongside these accounts, however, there runs another stream of folklore that probably comes from a much more purely oral source. In the middle of Georgina's account of a standard poltergeist manifestation, for example, there suddenly appears the figure of 'Hob'. Though she says she may have seen a picture in a book, and though she appears to think she has made this name up herself, 'Hob' is in fact a familiar figure in folklore. According to Katharine Briggs's *Dictionary of Fairies*, Hob or 'Hobthrust' is a creature which, though considered beneficent in many traditions, is yet mischievous and unpredictable enough to be associated in others with the Boggart (bogey, bogle, barghest), a rather more unpleasant character altogether. Georgina's 'Hob' is a sort of amalgam of both Hob and Boggart types. She associates him with the gate, and some would argue that the etymology of the term 'barghest' is 'bar' + 'geist', that is 'gateghost'; yet he is obviously connected with the house, and Hobs are often resident household spirits. In tradition, these spirits may be either good and helpful, or bad and tricksy. Regional legend collections are full of stories of Hobs and Boggarts associated with local stately homes and humble farmhouses alike, and the idea that a house could have other residents than people is certainly a well-established British oral tradition.

Faint echoes of these beliefs may be heard, perhaps, in the references to 'happy' and 'unhappy' houses, which was the response of many women to questions about hauntings and poltergeists:

'If you go into a house you know what it feels like. You feel the atmosphere when you walk in.'

'A happy house . . . Sometimes when you go into a house you think, "Oh! I feel *happy* here!" and other houses, "No. I'm not very *keen* on that house!"'

'But the people have all been *good* who've been in that house. My sister said she felt happy whenever she came into it. She's been so happy since she went in there.'

'There's one or two places that I hate and always have, and I don't know *why*. I think there *are* places that emanate sort of malignant, sort of nasty feelings.'

'We had a *technician* at *work*. *She* had this feeling. They moved

into this *house*. She said, "Oh," she said, "the first night, I *was*
unhappy! Like *you*," she said, "I don't know what it *was* and,"
she says, "as far as I know, there'd been a divorce – the previous
couple had been divorced," and she said it was an *unhappy* house,
very unhappy *atmosphere*.'

A longer account of such feelings and their consequence is provided in
an amusing story which Berenice tells:

Berenice's story

'Well, I'm in two schools of thought about that [i.e. poltergeists
etc.] Because . . . we've never moved *ourselves* but O H, B O Y I've
bought a lot of houses for *other* people. And we've gone round
looking for houses and bungalows for older people – flats and
things – and sometimes I've gone into this really G R O T T Y property and thought, "O H! This is *lovely*!" and I've gone into a
beautiful new house or bungalow and said, "Oh no! I couldn't
live *here*!" The house . . . there's always an *atmosphere*, something
wrong with it. I can't put my finger on it.

'But a friend of ours – a funny little story, I don't know
whether it will interest you – he moved from Corbridge after he
got married, *remarried*, and wanted to move out of the area. So
he went to live at Doonesbury, and he was in this house for
quite a while *very happily*.

'Then he decided that another house they liked across the
town was a bit bigger and they rather liked it, and they moved
into this house.

'They actually moved *into* this house, and they got everything
straight, and Ron sat down with a cup of coffee and a cigarette,
and he says, "I CAN'T STAY HERE! WE'RE MOVING OUT."
And his wife played P O P with him! And he hadn't even *slept* in
the house! And he just *wouldn't* . . .

'Now, he is *very* sensitive – for a *man*. Particularly sensitive.
And he *re-negotiated*, and they bought their old house *back*!

'But I *mean*, everybody *laughed* at him, but there *must* have
been something *in* it!'

These accounts, while perhaps reflecting a tradition less influenced by
literature and the media than full-blown hauntings, yet help unravel the
rationale behind both concepts and show them as aspects of a single idea.

Words like 'atmosphere' and 'feelings' keep recurring; as do references to unhappiness, 'wrongness' and divorce, or, alternatively, happiness, goodness and loveliness. When the women discuss the matter in more detail, a clear and consistent picture emerges. As they see it, the events and emotions of former residents' lives remain locked in the house where they lived in the form of 'energy' or 'waves' or an 'aura' – something which, if it is pleasant, the present resident can absorb and benefit from, but which, if it is unpleasant, they will have to contend with or submit to. Malignantly directed, this energy may transform itself into a force which can throw or displace objects or echo the events of real life by sighing, walking about, switching lights on or off, closing doors, flushing toilets and so on. Alternatively, it may simply create an atmosphere so unpleasant that it cannot be endured. This is, both literally and metaphorically, the 'spirit' of the house. Equally well, the spirit and the memories of the house may be wholly good and may make those who live in it happy, healthy and wise. The older the house, the more likely it is to have a history which may thus manifest itself. Agnes puts this well when she says:

'If it is possible you can get the voices of people who are living, you can get their voices in the air, that people can speak to you on the telephone from Australia, New Zealand, as if they were in the same room; and I've read or heard that every single word that's ever been spoken, every sound that's ever been made since the world came into being, is still here – well, I think that your vibrations are all around you. And if there's evil – Hitler, or any of the dreadful atrocities, burnings at the stake – there's been heaps and heaps through history – you couldn't have terror and horror and violent physical pain and hatred and evil and it just disappears, just because the people have died. It's still there! And the same with very good people.'

This logical, and apparently scientific, reasoning makes the foundation of the believers' case. In addition they are able to point to the existence of the ceremony of exorcism, to the many reports of 'reliable people', and to the unlikeliness of people wanting to deceive others on such an important point or of several people spontaneously 'imagining' identical phenomena in a single location.

Claudia, Dora, Meg and Lettie all give replies which combine some or all of these typical arguments in the apt language and sincere puzzlement which characterizes all the women's thoughts on this difficult and delicate matter:

Claudia

'I've sort of *wondered* about that. It seems a bit fantastic in a way
. . . and yet it must happen, because, I mean, I think there's
something in the Prayer Book, isn't there? I think there's something *in* it.

'That's what makes you wonder. There *must* be something
besides *us*, mustn't there? Probably, you know, going back in
history, perhaps where a lot of evils happened in a certain place.
The place may have *absorbed* that atmosphere. It's sort of *carried
on*.

'But why you should get people of today living in a *modern*
house, which happens sometimes . . . Unless it's the people *themselves*. You know, they've got some sort of aura.'

Dora

'Yes! I think that's quite *possible*. I think it's quite possible that
there are sort of *waves* going from people that influence the
situation. The sort of people who've *reported* these things are
people that you can rely on their *word* about it. I mean, you get
people, you get *ministers of the Church of England*, who SWEAR
that they've *heard* this sort of thing.

'Are you finding that young people scoff at this sort of thing
more than the old people?'

[G. B.: 'No. Quite the contrary.']

Meg

'You *do* read that in the paper, don't you? Well, I think it *must*
happen to *them*. Well, they couldn't imagine it, *surely*? I mean,
when they say things move and all THAT. They do, don't
they?'

[G. B.: 'Well, I don't know, it's never happened to *me*.']

'No, nor to *me* either. If they get a *minister* to come and
exorcize it . . .? When I read about it, I've *believed* it. I don't
think you can *imagine things like that*. I know people are *queer*,
but . . .'

Lettie

'Well! I don't know *what* to think! There must be *something* in it. *Something* must have happened. They can't possibly have *imagined* it – all the tremors and things, can they? I shouldn't *think* so, anyway.'

So popular science, oral tradition, peer-group discussion and literary ghost stories from books, films or TV combine to provide a coherent tradition with an appealing rationale – a tradition sufficiently lively to find acceptance among 41 per cent of the women. Even among the 55 per cent of the group who are sceptical, one can detect an underlying recognition of the strength of the opponents' case. Though there are, of course, those for whom the matter is so frightening and so taboo that they will not 'bother with it', they are in the minority. It is more common for disbelievers to feel that there is a definite case to answer and to argue quite forcibly that events have been misinterpreted, or that there are so many fakes that one cannot trust what one hears; that the people who tell the stories invent them for ulterior motives (principally so that they can get a new house); that the reports are unsubstantiated personal opinion, or that the percipients must have 'bad nerves' or be 'nervous, sensitive types'. On occasion, this latter argument even fades into the grudging admission that some people may possibly be 'sensitive' enough to 'sort of receive the message' and be generally 'sort of psychic'.

More significantly, the majority of the sceptics are inclined to feel that, though they disbelieve (and need to disbelieve), they could be persuadable, given the right conditions. They say:

'I think I'm sceptical really. Until probably if anything happened to *me*. Then it might be a different *thing*.'

'No, I don't *think* so, *not* having experienced it. I'd be scared to death probably, and I certainly wouldn't go near it if I knew of anything.'

'I don't know, but if there *was* a ghost in a house, I wouldn't go and *live* in it!'

Quite obviously, traditions of the evil supernatural still have quite a foothold in the minds of ordinary people in twentieth-century British society, and the old-fashioned poltergeist has not entirely lost its power to haunt and thrill.

THE GOOD DEAD:
WRAITHS, FETCHES AND WARNING GHOSTS

At the other pole of the supernatural spectrum there are the very different happenings and occurrences caused by benevolent spirits, and these are accorded much more general belief by the community. Unlike manifestations of the evil supernatural, these are never referred to as 'ghosts' nor dressed up in the familiar paraphernalia of legendary hauntings. Whereas stories of poltergeists, spirits and '*wrong* houses' are, as we have seen, couched in terms of conventional 'spookiness' – attics, cellars, stairs, doors, nightmares, a mysterious 'somebody' who 'disappears' or haunts the house so that the rightful occupant has to 'leave everything and *go*' – the good supernatural is described in subjective terms and reflects the relationships of the family life (*feel, see, think, say, come,* [*a*]*live, there, mother, father* are the most frequently recurring words used), and is seen as an extension of ordinary life. They are *natural*, never 'supernatural', occurrences. Whereas the ghosts or poltergeists which haunt unhappy houses are always unknown and unwelcome intruders, the good dead whose presence is felt or who are heard or glimpsed around the family home are loved, familiar, trusted, needed and welcomed. They are figures of power and authority (dead husbands and lost mothers), or representatives of the caring outer circle of the family nexus (aunts and uncles, nieces and nephews, grandparents), desperately missed siblings or deeply lamented children. This community of the loving dead is thought to surround living people and may occasionally interact with them, effortlessly bridging the gap between the spiritual and the mundane worlds.

Dead loved ones are thought to exist alongside the living rather than to have returned from a distinctly separate place, as the relational prepositions the women use in their stories show (*to, with, by, beside, around,* and *in,* which all imply nearness, are used five times more frequently than words like *back* and *from*). That 60 per cent of the women believe in this type of supernatural operation is perhaps hardly surprising, for glimpses of dead loved ones, echoes of their familiar voices and feelings of their presence give the strongest possible proof of the unity of the cosmos and the benevolence and harmony of God's creation, demonstrating to the believer the knowability of the world and the security of human life.

Three typical stories encapsulate the major ideas that structure this complex belief-system:

Alma's story

'But I know . . . A cousin of mine she was very, very old when she died. She was very *sensitive*. We knew her mother wouldn't last – she was downstairs. My cousin had gone to bed. They'd been sitting up with the mother, and she had gone to bed.

'And she said her father came and woke her and he said, "Your mother *wants* you," and she got up, went downstairs. And her brother was there and he said, "What have *you* come for?" and she said, "Well, my father came and said she *needed* me." *He* said, "*Father?* Father's DEAD!"

'And she said, it was *only* after . . . She said, "Oh," she said, "He came *in*. I heard him *cough*, and he came in," and he shook her and said, "Your mother *wants* you," and she got up.

'And she said it was only when her brother said, "FATHER? Father's *dead*!" AND HE'D BEEN DEAD YEARS.'

[G. B.: 'What happened next?']

'Oh, she *died*. She died very soon after that.'

Vera's story

'My mother was *highland*. Once or twice I *see* her come *back*. She comes if there's anything *ill* going to happen in the family or anything like that – any *trouble* or anything.

'When my brother-in-law died, that was the last incident that happened in the family. She *came*. I could SEE her, you know, quite distinctly. And I said, "Well, something's *happened*, something's going to *happen*." And I heard but a day or two after that Henry had died suddenly.

'And any trouble in the family, she's *there*. She's always come. But I FEEL her. SHE'S THERE – and not very far away. I don't know. Isn't it strange?'

[G. B.: 'Mmm! Do you actually *see* your mother or are you just *conscious* of her?']

'I just feel her *presence*, yes, and there's like a *grey shadow*.'

Rachel's story

[G. B.: 'Did *you* ever have anything like this happen?']

Only when I was doing that *house*, and yet I wasn't a *bit* afraid of it!'

[RACHEL'S DAUGHTER (aside): 'Bill, that was her brother

who'd died, told her how to paint the house for his wife to sell.']

[G. B.: 'What about that? What Bill told you?']

'Well, like, when I was doing the *cupboard*, he'd say, "Now tosh inside that corner, Rachel!"'

[G. B.: 'Tosh?']

'*Paint*. That's a right old-fashioned word for "paint". "Now tosh inside that corner, Rachel. Do it *proper*." AND YET! ... I didn't turn round to look for him, but it was his *voice*. And he HELPED me to paint that house! It's really funny. He said, "Paint it *lightly* and very *quickly*. Paint it light and very quick, the *gloss paint*, not like the other, the undercoat ..."

'And HONESTLY, he *helped* me paint that house! Well, I think he wanted to THWART my brother-in-law, because he was right nasty about it. He said, "You won't get a B ... hundred pounds for that house!" And we got £390 for our Ellie, Bill's *widow* like. That's a *long while* since, love.

'And I went up every night, four doors away, and I PAINTED the *lot*! Kitchen and all! I *did*! Upstairs! *Everywhere*! And it looked something LIKE when I'd finished you know, and I was really proud of it! But prouder when the money came and our Ellie had her share.

'And I never told my husband. He used to say, "There's a terrible smell of paint, Rachel," and I said, "Get away! You've got paint on the *nerves*, Arthur!" But he must have been right, because it was *me*, you know! I'd a pair of our Bill's old overalls and I used to put them on when I went up, and I FELT HE WAS HELPING ME. *It's true*! And I could have stopped there all night.

'And Arthur says, "Where the HELL have you *been*?" and I said, "I've been *right over the back* with the dog." Poor Judy! Poor Judy had never been *anywhere*! If only that dog could have *talked*, she'd have had a story to tell!'

As represented in these very typical accounts, the essential difference between the evil and the good supernatural is the absence or presence of *purpose*. Evil occurrences are meaningless and intrusive disturbances of the natural order; they have causes but no functions. Benevolent manifestations, on the other hand, are not only caused by events in the mundane world, but are also purposefully *directed* towards them. Whereas ghosts have 'no business to be here' in both senses of the phrase, the

good dead have *every* reason to be around. Alma's father is there to
convey to his daughter a message his dying wife is too ill to send herself;
Vera's mother warns of her son-in-law's death; and Rachel's brother
uses her as the vehicle of justice for his widow. Each of these revenants
has been recalled to the realm of the living by events occurring there,
and has not only a reason for appearing, but also a role to play. They are
agents of order, not disorder.

This contrast is very neatly demonstrated in a little memorate which
Audrey tells:

Audrey's story

'And then *one* night ... NOW, this is the thing that *made* me
believe it!

'I'm very fond of playing patience. It's a form of *therapy* –
when I'm depressed, I play *patience*. And JOHNNY, that was my
late husband, ALWAYS used to steal up *behind* me and pinch a
CARD! And I was playing patience one day, and I got the first
lot out: they were *all* there the first game. The SECOND game, I
found out the two of spades was *missing*. Now I ONLY play
patience in the *lounge*. I never play it in the *dining-room*. SO, I
searched HIGH AND LOW for this two of spades, and I *could*
NOT find it anywhere. I looked under the CUSHIONS, you
know how you look *anywhere* for things?

'And then, about three days *after*, the rent man came.
And I always take him into the dining-room to pay the rent.
And I hadn't been in the dining-room because I only use the
dining-room in the *summer* – there's no heating in it except the
electric fire. And DO YOU KNOW, that in the centre of the *table*
was that two of spades? DEAD CENTRE.

'So, of course, I went to Miss Luke, the medium – it *did* quite
frighten me, it STARTLED ME – "Oh," she said, "that was
Johnny playing one of his TRICKS on you!"

'Wasn't *that* strange?'

Audrey is alarmed when she finds that an object (the playing card) has
been displaced, for it is just this kind of apparently purposeful but
basically meaningless phenomenon that is associated with poltergeist
activity. The occurrence quite literally does not make *sense*: 'It *did* quite
frighten me, it STARTLED ME,' says Audrey. The medium, however,
allays her fears by re-interpreting the experience for her, and she does

this by introducing the idea that the removal of the card was deliberate – one of the late Johnny's practical jokes. From being a meaningless and disorderly, therefore frightening, happening, it becomes proof of the continued presence and influence of the loving if mischievous, Johnny: the 'thing that *made*' Audrey 'believe it'. This radical re-interpretation has been achieved simply by introducing the idea of purposefulness.

Notions of cause and consequence, purpose and order run through all the stories the women tell about the good dead. They are so basic to belief, so entrenched in traditional habits of thought, that they even structure the narratives themselves. By following structural clues in the stories, therefore, we are able to distinguish distinct aspects of the women's system of belief about the influence of the spiritual world on and in the earthly sphere.

Commonly, memorates about the family dead have five standard components. The narrator almost always starts by marking the onset of a story with a remark such as Audrey's 'And then *one* night ... NOW, this is the thing that *made* me believe it!' or Alma's 'But I know ... A cousin of mine,' and then either gives a little general background information, or very briefly summarizes the information which is to come. Only Rachel, who is getting forgetful, launches straight into the middle of her story without observing these preliminaries. Just as invariably, they plainly signal the close of the story, usually with some form of evaluative gloss which pulls the ends together and allows the audience to comment. Alma, for example, adds quite a lengthy discussion to her story, which was omitted in the first transcription for the sake of brevity. She says: 'But I *do* know for a *fact* that she's had one or two different *experiences* like that. It wasn't that she'd been drinking – she was very SOBER!!! I've always been interested in anything like that. It's fascinating.' Similarly, Audrey and Vera invite audience-comment in identical phrases 'Isn't/ Wasn't that strange?' These devices are, of course, common to most or all forms of oral storytelling, as ubiquitous as the 'Once upon a time' and 'And they lived happily ever after' of folktales, and identical in purpose, serving as signposts or boundary-fences to mark the borderline between narrative and ordinary conversation.

There are also three central elements which narrators may choose to use in memorates, though they do not necessarily utilize all of them or arrange them in the order they are presented in here. The first of these narrative building-blocks is a more-or-less precise and leisurely scene-setting which concentrates in particular on analysing the state of mind or health of the protagonist, so that the hearer is given a picture of the context of the occurrence and the condition of the percipient. The second narrative element is, of course, some mention of the experience itself, though, strangely enough, this may be extremely brief and imprecise (one would not gain much useful information, for example, about what it is *like* when a dead mother 'comes to' a living daughter from Vera's account). The third component is some description of the consequence of the visitation, the 'what happened next?' story-element.

Some stories use all five structural elements (as well as many other details beside); others use only two.

A good deal of useful information about the nature of the women's belief in the good supernatural may be obtained by looking at the ways in which they combine these elements in their stories. Though a narrative may, perhaps, be surrounded by circumstantial information, snippets of detail and lengthy boundary-markers which obscure the outline, the story-core is always one of three permutations of the central components. The storyteller may speak of her condition at the time of occurrence and the nature of the happenings themselves; of the happenings and their consequence; or of all three: in each of these story-patterns, distinct beliefs about the operation of the spiritual world may be discerned.

The simplest and briefest narratives are those which describe the condition of the percipient and the subsequent appearance of a revenant. Invariably they concern the impending death of one or other of a loving pair – a husband and wife, a parent and child, a woman and her fiancé. In one type, though the condition of the percipient is described in some detail, that condition is in no way abnormal or alarming: on the contrary, everything is as ordinary as can be. Into this ordinary environment, steps the extraordinary – in the shape of some loved person known to be a long way away. He or she is, of course, dead or dying in that far place. I collected only two stories on this theme, one a family legend and one a memorate, but fortunately both are neat examples of the type:

Ella's story

'But I know ... Some years ago, it was at the end of the First World War. My husband was quite young and he was *away* with his older *sister* – on holiday or something. And the young man his sister was engaged to APPEARED BEFORE THEM in the bedroom, *as plainly as anything* in his UNIFORM. He said it was just as if he was almost *there!* And he'd been KILLED just at that *time* in the *War!*'

Gloria's story

'Only one time that I vividly remember, and this was many years ago, and we were in Spain. And my husband's mother . . . we *wanted* to take her with us, actually, but she wouldn't come. It must be about eight years ago, and it was about two o'clock in the morning. Now, it wasn't *dark* or anything. We'd just come back from a nightclub, and my husband was in the bathroom cleaning his teeth. And I just said to him . . . and we hadn't had a lot to *drink* or anything . . . I said, "That's *funny*! I've just seen your MAM! Isn't that SILLY?" Now, all the lights were on.

'And I forgot all about it until the next morning. We were going out to this BOWLING they have in the open air, and we had a *telegram* saying that his mother had *died*. That was unexpected because, although she had sugar diabetes, when we left her about eight days previously she was *well*.

'And she'd died, as the coroner thinks, about quarter to *two* on the Tuesday night. But it was the Wednesday morning before they found *out*, because the bedroom door was *locked* and they couldn't get *in*.

'Now THAT . . . And I've never forgotten that. It's VERY funny.'

In the other sort of 'condition' story it is the percipient who is dying, as in the memorate example quoted in chapter 1, where Berenice explains that 'About three days before she [the mother-in-law] died . . . her *husband* . . . and his *sister* had been to *see* her and they told her that everything was PERFECTLY all right.' Here the appearance of the already dead to the nearly dead person is a sign that they are soon to be together again.

Elsewhere, as in the stories below, the dead person comes back specifically to accompany a beloved relative to the otherworld. In each case, the narrator takes some trouble to describe the precise conditions which caused the revenant to appear, stressing dates and times and places, or giving a history of the fatal, or near-fatal, illness, or otherwise establishing beyond doubt that there was good reason for the happening and that it arose out of the proper circumstances and in the expected context. The following accounts are typical:

Lettie's story

'But I saw my *father*. My *father* was the first to die, and he died at *three* o'clock in the morning. Then TWELVE MONTHS AFTER *mother* died at three o'clock in the *afternoon*. Well, she died from cancer of the jaw, so I mean, it was nothing to SMILE about.

'But just before she *died*, I *felt* that whatever there *was* – EVER there was! – *father* had come to *meet* her. YES!

'Because she just sat up and she gave that SMILE (of course, I think they *do* sit up before they die, but . . .) And she sort of held her arms out, and it was just that SPECIAL SMILE she always kept *for* him . . .'

[G.B.: 'You think she actually saw him?']

'I DO! I DO! OH, YES!'

Kathleen's story

'But I do think you can *see* people that's *died*. I do think there's summat at the other *side*, and I've EXPERIENCED it, as I say.

'And my daughter, she lives in Corbridge now, her youngest daughter's nearly sixteen now, and when she was only about three it was the *kidneys* that were wrong with her, and they sent a district nurse to her. My daughter had a very bad time with that last child – she's *four of them*, two married now, one [*sic*] still at home – and she was very close to her father, my daughter was, she was the *eldest*.

'And I didn't know for quite a long while after, and I knew it must have been the crisis – my granddaughter must have been passing through the crisis – because she seemed to *turn* after that, on the mend. And I didn't know for quite a long while after.

'And my daughter said, "Mum," she said, "I've SEEN MY DAD as *plain* as I can see *you*! And he STOOD at the bottom of the bed as though she was going to die." She says, "He was ready to take her! But she turned for the BETTER, you see." But she said, "He STOOD at the bottom of that bed with his arms up!"

'Some people think you imagine these things, but *no*! I'VE HEARD MY HUSBAND'S VOICE, and there's not been a *soul* in that flat!'

These themes are frequently echoed in non-narrative remarks like: 'I've heard people say that just before you die, you seem to *see* them,' or 'I only believe they might come back at your death.'

Again, these are the ideas which also structure an account which Clara gives of a recent illness:

Clara's Story

'But I'll tell you *something*. I haven't even told my *sister* this.

'I've been quite ill just recently, and it's been one of those horrible things that didn't get diagnosed until it was almost too late. I hadn't been feeling well for well over a year, and I'd put on an *awful* lot of weight and was *so* tired that it was like an illness. I just couldn't drag myself around – I don't know *how* I dragged myself around. And fortunately for me, I got two *lumps* in my neck, and, of course, this started the ball rolling then. They were *thyroids*, I had an inactive *thyroid*.

'But I just couldn't go to the office or anything like that at all. It was just impossible. And I was so TIRED and so WEARY, when I dozed off in a chair it wasn't like an ordinary little catnap, it was almost like a coma.

'And there was *so* many times during that short period WHEN I USED TO IMAGINE my mother was coming into the room. And she'd been dead for about fifteen or sixteen years. 1964, *seventeen* years at the end of the year.'

[G.B.: 'You never actually *saw* her?']

'No, it was just a *feeling*. I haven't even told my sister. And I felt at times almost as if she was *talking* to me. And I just *passed it up* because I don't really *believe* it.'

When I remarked that 'That's where you differ from a lot of people, because a lot of people would say she was *really* there . . .', Clara replied, 'Well, if I *had* thought *that*, I'd have been really *sure* I was dying, because I would have thought, "Oh, my GOD! This seeing my mother's DYING!" But I don't think that way at all She thereby expressed belief even as she denied it, and illustrated its nature even as she dismissed it.

Four more stories of this 'condition' type, though contributed during discussions about the return of the dead, do not actually feature revenants. They do, however, provide additional evidence that it is commonly thought that the dying are afforded some kind of supernatural experience and that the occurrences of these visions, being glimpses of the next world, are signs of impending death. Kathleen, for example, tells two short stories after her account of her granddaughter's illness. In one a dying acquaintance sees 'The Master' and in the other a fatally sick man keeps saying 'What a beautiful picture!' In a third story, the narrator tells how her husband died exclaiming, 'It's *wonderful*! It's *wonderful*', and in a fourth a dying grandfather sees the gates of heaven.

What is in common between all these accounts is the emphasis the storytellers place on the *context* of the occurrence. Ella and Gloria stress the ordinariness of the situation: a boarding-house bedroom or hotel room, the absence of darkness or mystery, and the presence of the everyday event (Gloria's husband is prosaically brushing his teeth; the brother and sister in Ella's story are presumably getting ready for bed). In contrast, Lettie's and Kathleen's stories, and Clara's too, feature the extraordinary conditions of fatal or near-fatal illness. In every case, careful attention is given to dates and times and persons. Ella says the events happened 'at the end of the First World War'; Gloria is even more precise – it was eight years ago, at two in the morning, when they had just got back from a nightclub; Lettie is exact about both father's and the mother's deaths, matching them up neatly; Kathleen gives a mini-history of her daughter's life; and Clara is specific about the onset of her illness, its duration and the period that has elapsed since her mother's death. Even the narrators of the four short stories about dying are careful to set the events in appropriate times and places. The ordinary conditions of Ella's and Gloria's stories contrast with the extraordinary events and thus *authenticate* them; in the other stories, the extraordinary conditions *explain* the even more extraordinary events that follow. Throughout, therefore, there runs a theme of order and purpose which, in the words of Bronislaw Malinowski, 'brings down a vague but great apprehension to the compass of . . . domestic reality,'[5] and makes the world safe and predictable because governed by understood rules of cause-and-effect.

On other occasions, however, there are no precipitating conditions which can account for the appearance of a revenant – no sickness, no danger, no dying. The speaker merely says 'I see her come back', 'she actually saw her', 'my mother came to me in the night', 'I could see my brother disappearing in the distance', and so on. When this happens it is assumed that, lacking a cause in the present, there must be a cause in the future. The story then is shaped in terms of expected *consequences* and takes the form of a description of the visitation plus an account of the

outcome. As revenants are never purposeless, and the percipients themselves can see no reason for the visitation, it is reasoned that the
dead person must know something the survivors don't and has come to
alert them to the danger. Usually, of course, the warning is of an impending death. Vera's story (page 51) is most typical of these, because it
features a family revenant and a family death. Elsewhere, however,
revenants may warn of burglaries or accidents:

Dora's story

'They had burglars in the house about two years ago. And, just
before this happened, one of my aunts APPEARED to her – my
aunt died four years ago. And she actually *saw* her but she didn't
say anything.

'She said to me afterwards, "I'm *sure* she was trying to WARN
me."'

Carrie's story

'Well, it's FUNNY. DO YOU KNOW, if anyone's going to be ill in
my family, my mother comes TO me. I always know. My mother
comes TO me.

'You know, when our Wilfred used to be ill, I used to get on
the phone and I'd say, "Hello, Florrie. How *are* you?" And
she'd say, "*I'm* all right. But WILFRED'S in bed."

'And before I had my back done, like before I fell in the
cemetery, in the night my mother come to me and she says,
"You can't SLEEP," or something like that, "You can't SLEEP,
can you?" She's STOOD at the side of the bed, and I've not been
well *since*.

'Isn't it STRANGE how she comes TO me every time?'
[G.B.: 'You can actually *see* her?']
'YES. She's stood at the side of the bed, and then it's gone.'

'Condition' and 'consequence' stories show the dead in some of their
most enduring roles – as 'wraiths', 'fetches' and warning ghosts. A
'wraith' is the apparition of someone who has just died or is about to
die, or, alternatively, of someone in acute distress far away and needing
the support of loved ones. Strictly speaking, in tradition a 'fetch'
is one's *own* wraith – one sees one's soul as already separate, a sure sign

of imminent death; but in practice the term is often stretched to en-
compass traditional family omens of death or the family ghost who comes
to 'fetch' one to the next world. Warning ghosts are self-explanatory, as
commonplace as they are ubiquitous. These three categories of apparition have been very well-established in British tradition for many
centuries.

The wraiths described in Ella's and Gloria's stories are at heart
updated versions of a common type of medieval precognitive vision or
apparition. Several of these may, for example, be found in the *Dialogues*
of Pope Gregory the Great, written at the end of the sixth century,
popular for the best part of a thousand years, and probably originally
based on oral stories in contemporary folklore ('Old wives' tales',
according to the Reformer Ludowig Lavater). Others may be found in
the *Liber Exemplorum*, a thirteenth-century preaching manual, and in
Caesarius of Heisterbach's *Dialogue on Miracles*: stories written by and for
the clergy for use in sermons, and reasonably accurate guides to what
was generally considered believable at the time. As befits the times,
these 'exempla' feature the visions of holy hermits and ascetics, who see
the good being received into heaven and the bad facing horrible punishments at the moment of their death.

The wide political and moral significance of accounts such as these,
however, was extensively eroded by the theological debates of the
Reformation (see chapter 6), and by the late sixteenth century such
apocalyptic visions had been watered down to a feeling that, 'oftentimes
a little before they yeld up the ghost, and some time a little after their
death, or a good while after, either their owne shapes, or some other
shadowes of men, are apparantly seene'. [6] The feeling that wraiths and
visions are common accompaniments of death, however, remained
strong. Six of the twenty most famous British ghost stories from the
period 1690 to 1890 concern wraiths, of which the most often quoted
are Aubrey's account (from 1696) of the wraith of John Donne's wife
who, while he was abroad, appeared to him in great distress carrying a
child in her arms (his wife had at that time given birth to a stillborn
baby), and the account in Richard Baxter's *The Certainty of the World of
Spirits Fully Evinced* (1691) of the wraith of Mary Goffe, who, while she
was in a coma, went to visit her far-distant children (see chapter 6).

Wraiths are indeed a commonplace of oral tradition. Stith Thompson's
The Motif Index of Folk Literature (1955), a six-volume catalogue of
story-elements which regularly occur in Western European folktales and
legends, has twenty-four entries for wraiths, including familiar motifs
such as:

- person sees her own wraith
- seeing one's own wraith a sign that person is to die shortly
- wraith of dying woman goes to see children for last time before death
- wraith gives information of death in the family
- wraith investigates welfare of absent person
- appearance of wraith as an announcement of person's death
- appearance of wraith as calamity omen.

Warning ghosts have an even longer history. The principal role of revenants in medieval times was to reinforce the Church's teaching about purgatory, and ghosts almost invariably returned to warn of the punishments, pains or pleasures of the next world; returned from purgatory because of some unrequited crime; could not rest until it had been confessed and absolved by the priest; and, according to the thinking of early Protestants, it was 'on those apparitions of spirits, as on a sure foundation their [i.e. the Catholic] purgatory is chiefly builded'.[7] After the Reformation, when the doctrine of purgatory was rejected by Reformist theologians, the British warning ghost took on a more secular role, a role which became increasingly emasculated in succeeding centuries until it became geared to purely domestic concerns, like the burglaries and accidents Dora and Carrie tell of.

Joseph Glanvil's famous story of Major Sydenham is one of the last in the old mould of warning ghosts; while the legend of the Phantom Hitchhiker is typical of modern legends. Between the two lie three centuries of evolving tradition, in which continuity may be detected as well as change, and which link the homely stories my informants tell with the baroque, loquacious revenants of the past.

The Ghost of Major Sydenham

Concerning the Apparition of the Ghost of Major George Sydenham ... to Captain William Dykes ... be pleased to take the Relation of it as I have it from the Worthy and Learned Dr Tho. Dyke, a near Kinsman of the Captains, thus:

Shortly after the Major's death, the Doctor was desired to come to the House to take care of a Child that was there sick, and in his way thither he called on the Captain, who was very willing to wait on him to the place, because he must, as he said, have gone thither that Night, though he had not met with so encouraging an opportunity. After their arrival there at the House ... they were reasonably conducted to their lodging, which they desired might be together in the same Bed; Where, after they had lain a while, the Captain knockt and bids the Servant bring him two of the largest and biggest Candles lighted that he could get. Whereupon the Doctor inquires what he meant by this? The Captain answers you know Cousin what disputes my Major and I have had touching the Being of a God, and the Immortality of the soul. In which points we could never be resolved, though we so much sought for and desired it. And therefore it was at length fully agreed between us, That he of us that dyed first should the third night after his Funeral, between the hours of Twelve and One come to the little house that is here in the Garden, and there give a full account to the survivor touching these matters, who should be sure to be present there at the set time, and so receive a full satisfaction. And this says the Captain is the very night, and I am come on purpose to fulfil my promise. The Doctor dissuaded him, minding him of the danger of following those strange Counsels, for which we have no warrant, and that the Devil might by some cunning device make such an advantage of this rash attempt, as might work his utter ruine. The Captain replies, that he had solemnly engaged, and that nothing should discourage him: and adds, That if the Doctor would wake a while with him, he would thank him, if not, he might compose himself to his rest; but for his own part he was resolved to watch, that he might be sure to be present at the hour appointed. To that purpose he sets his Watch by him, and as soon as he perceived by it that it was half an hour past Eleven, he rises, and taking a Candle in each hand, goes out by a back door, of which he had before gotten the Key, and walks to the Garden-house, where he continued two hours and a half, and at his return declared that he had neither saw nor heard anything more than what was usual. But I know, said he, that my Major would surely have come, had he been able.

About six weeks after the Captain rides to Eton to place his Son a Scholar there, when the Doctor went thither with him. They lodged there at an Inn, the sign was the *Christopher*, and tarried two or three nights, not lying together as before at Dulverton, but in two several Chambers. The morning before they went thence, the Captain stayed in his Chamber longer than he was wont to do before he called upon the Doctor. At length he comes into the Doctor's Chamber, but in a visage and form much differing from himself, with his Hair and Eyes staring, and his whole body shaking and trembling. Whereat the Doctor wondering, presently demanded. What is the matter, Cousin Captain? The Captain replies, I have seen my Major. At which the Doctor seeming to smile, the Captain immediately confirms it, saying, If ever I saw him in my life I saw him but now. And then related to the Doctor what had passed, thus: This Morning after it was light, some one comes to my Bed side, and suddenly drawing back the Curtains, calls *Cap. Cap.* (which was the term of familiarity that the Major used to call the Captain by). To whom I replied, What my Major? To which he returns, I could not come at the time appointed, but I am now come to tell you, *That there is a God, and a very just and terrible one, and if you do not turn over a new leaf* (the very expression as is used by the Doctor punctually remembered) *you will find it so.* (the Captain proceeded) On the table by, there lay a Sword which the Major had formerly given me. Now after the Apparition had walked a turn or two about the Chamber, he took up the Sword, drew it out, and finding it not so clean and bright as it ought, *Cap. Cap.* says he, *this Sword did not use to be kept after this manner when it was mine.* After which words he suddenly disappeared.

The Captain was not only thoroughly persuaded of what he had thus seen and heard, but was from that time observed to be very much affected with it. And the humour that before in him was brisk and jovial, was then strangely altered . . . Yea, it was observed that what the Captain had thus seen and heard had a more lasting influence on him, and it is judged by those who were well-acquainted with his Conversation, that the remembrance of this passage stuck close to him, and that those words of his dead Friend were frequently sounding fresh in his Ears, during the remainder of his Life, which was about two years.[8]

The Phantom Hitchhiker

A newly married couple were on their honeymoon and were returning in late July from a visit to the World's Fair in Chicago. The last day they were on the road was very stormy, and driving slowly they saw an old woman at the side of the road hailing a ride. They picked her up, and during a brief introduction learned she was from Ringsted, Iowa. She told them not to go to the Fair after September first, for the Enchanted Island was going to sink into the Lake. Silence followed, and when the young wife looked around to talk with the old woman, the woman was gone. The couple were puzzled and decided to go to Ringsted to investigate their passenger. They stopped at the place where the old woman said she had lived, but the persons living there at the time informed them that the woman had lived there but that she had passed away a year before. The couple described the old woman, and the residents of the Ringsted home said that those clothes were the identical ones in which the old woman had been buried – and that it was exactly a year to the day that the old woman had died.[9]

The process by which the warning ghost changes its sphere of influence from the religious to the domestic will be discussed in chapter 6, which will outline the history of the ghost traditions from the Middle Ages to the present day. Meanwhile in the following section, I want to go on to describe other beliefs about the souls of the dead, especially the women's entrenched conviction that members of the family still surround them as constant witnesses of earthly affairs and occasional intermediaries between the spiritual and mundane worlds.

THE GOOD DEAD: WITNESSES

The supernatural type I want to discuss here may seem something of a novelty because it has not made a strong appearance in previous work on the folklore of ghosts. It is however, I believe, an essential part of modern supernatural traditions – a belief vigorously transmitted and tenaciously clung to.

The types of the supernatural belief discussed so far, for all their drama, appeal, and irrefutable longevity, are a relatively small part of my informants' belief-system. Just less than half the women were prepared to accept the notion of evil spirits haunting houses, and few had personal stories to tell on the subject. Though very many more believed in the good supernatural, tales of wraiths, fetches and warning ghosts were relatively scarce (seventeen in all), and there were no casual references to such phenomena in chat and conversation. What the women did speak of extensively was a type of experience encountered much less frequently in legend and literature – the feeling of the 'presence' of the dead around them, and their strong belief that these presences could witness and, if

necessary intervene in, the lives of descendants and survivors. Though
there is entrenched belief in these sorts of experiences, though it is
obviously a traditional belief in the sense of being continuously and
vigorously transmitted among the peer group, and though if one
searches one can find substantial clues to such beliefs being a part of an
older folklore too, this is essentially a 'hidden' tradition. Indeed, there is
not even a *name* for such spirits, though I myself think of them as
'witnesses', for this term embodies their main characteristics.

Experiences of witnesses are the single most important aspect of the
women's supernatural beliefs. Few are prepared to discount them totally,
for they embody all the qualities that figure most prominently in their
moral and philosophical value-scale. They are intensely intuitive experiences; they graphically symbolize the power of love and its triumph over
death; they are based on interpersonal communication, often of an inter-
nal telepathic kind; and they render the world a safe and protected environment. Of all supernatural types, witnesses are also the most purposeful.

This concept of purposefulness is most clearly revealed by the fact
that speakers give their narratives a neatly symmetrical before-and-after
structure (for memorates are the public expression of private belief and
therefore are always carefully shaped according to cultural expectations).
In witness narratives we find all five basic components typical of revenant accounts. As we saw earlier, memorates about wraiths and fetches
combine descriptions of the content of the visitation with an account of
the experience itself, using scene-setting material and boundary-markers
to shape them into proper narrative form; and memorates of warning
ghosts are composed using another grouping of elements in which an
account of the visitation plus its consequences are central. In witness
narratives, narrators are careful to give not only proper preliminary
detail and boundary-markers, but also a full account of both context and
consequence of the witness's intervention.

Narratives on the subject have a neat symmetrical structure: an account of the context of the occurrence or the condition of the percipient,
a description of the encounter, and a résumé of its outcome – with the
first and last elements neatly matched together. The context of the
visitation is invariably given as some sort of 'lack' [10] in the narrator's life
and the consequence is invariably seen to be the liquidation of that lack
– as purposeful and safe a supernatural encounter as could be.

In some cases the lack is a lack of health: then the dead lend a hand
and the sick are returned to health. Or it might be a lack of peace of
mind that troubles the protagonist: in which case, the dead give reassurance and support, as in Ruth's account:

Ruth's story

'One of our guild members was saying she always remembers when her daughter was *very* very young. I think it was *measles* she had, but she had it *very* very badly, and she was *delirious* with it, you see. And she *had* to go out of the room, and she was *very* very worried. And she *suddenly got the feeling* that her MOTHER who had DIED had sort of *reassured* her that the child would be all right while she was out of the room.

'And she said, when she came back, this child was as CALM and QUIET as ever! She thought . . . she just *felt* her mother had been present, helping her.'

In other stories the lack is of some necessary object, in which case the dead communicate its whereabouts to the living.

Elisabeth's story

'And I remember once particularly, not terribly long after my husband died, there was some little . . . I had a note to say something about *income tax*, you see, and I couldn't *find* any details. And I suddenly thought, "Of *course*! He took it *in*! I *remember*!" Because I remember he said, "Oh, I better put this income tax return *in*. Let's get in the car and *go*."

'We JUMPED in the car and went over. And I remember it so well, because we went to this new building. I sat in the car while he ran up the steps, and the man was just locking the door, and he gave it *to* him, you see. And I remember ABSOLUTELY. And I remember when it *was*.

'And I had been PUZZLING and WONDERING and I *did* say to him, "Oh, DO *tell* me where it *is*!" Quite soon after that, you know, he . . . I was REMINDED that we *took* it. AND IT WAS SO!

'And I rang up the accountant, whoever it was, and I said I could even give the approximate date, and it *was* so, you see. They had mislaid it or something.

'It's extraordinary, though, isn't it? It's quite *strange*.'

In yet other cases, the lack is a lack of knowledge or information so acute as to constitute a danger. Here the dead step in to provide necessary instructions and so avert the peril:

Agnes's story

'Dad had been dead now for about three years probably. Ned
was working at the time of the story for a local farmer, Sam
Black at the Manor Farm at Dell. And he used to have to go to
market with these cart horses, bigger horses than ours but still
cart horses. And he was going to Bradbury market one terrible
frosty day. It was a dark morning, *early* morning, and the leading
horse slipped and fell.

'Ned would be at this time only fifteen or sixteen at the *most*
and NO experience. He was STUCK in a country lane with a
horse – and the *load* all UP like *this* – the one horse had dragged
the other horse down. And he didn't know WHAT to do A
LITTLE BIT! And he said – this is the story – you know how
you do? "Oh, HELP ME! HELP ME! What shall I *do*? What shall I
do?" and saying it out loud.

'And he said Dad's voice CAME TO HIM QUITE CLEARLY,
said, "Cut the girth cord, Ned! Cut the girth cord!" And he cut
the girth cord and the leading horse got up and he was able to
go. And he got to Bradbury very shaken, very frightened, but
the load intact.'

In all these accounts, as in many others, the dead are shown as active for
good in the mundane world – providing information, carrying messages,
reminding, strengthening and supporting distressed survivors. They are
thus part of a chain that reaches from the supernatural to the natural
sphere – a *part* of the natural world, not an intrusion into it. They
therefore provide for the women the strongest possible evidence not
only of the survival of personal identity after death, but also of the
continuance of the important structuring relationships of family and
kinship. The beliefs are thus an extension, and to an extent a consequence, of the women's strong faith in some form of life after death.

As we saw, the majority of them are churchgoers (Methodists mainly,
with a few Roman Catholics, Anglicans and Jews), and of the 31 women
who were specifically asked whether they believed we 'might meet the
dead again' in the next world, 23 were fairly confident it would happen,
and 5 hoped that it might be possible; only 3 were sceptical. Elsewhere,
though they were not directly asked, in responses to questions about the
souls of the dead, the women *imply* belief in an afterlife through stock
formulae such as 'faith is a great thing', 'there must be *something* on the

other side', and 'it would be very disappointing to go through life and not have a feeling that there *is something there*'. A few women are sadly preoccupied with wrongs they have done to those now gone, or with failed relationships now beyond repair, but most are comforted by the thought of meeting dead loved ones, in some form or other, after death. Though they are careful to speak of '*souls* rising again' or of contact with the dead being 'only a *spiritual* thing', their faith in an afterlife is at heart a surprisingly material one. If the spirits of the dead survive with the personality remaining intact, as they seem to believe, it follows logically that memory and affection also remain, and it follows too that these spirits must *be* somewhere, and not necessarily far away. Joan and Mary express the prevailing ideas most aptly:

Joan

'Well, it's Saint Paul, wasn't it, said, "We're encompassed with a great cloud of witnesses." So I do *think* that they have some interest in the people left behind.'

Mary

'I think they're *here*. I don't believe that there's a deadline, and, above, that's heaven, and below, that's earth underneath it. I don't believe that.'
[G.B.: 'They have to be around us somewhere?']
'Yes! That's why you suddenly sense a presence, isn't it?'

It is in the context of this view that women say 'the dead never leave me' and expect to be understood at both the metaphorical and the literal level, or speak of their attachment to their homes or to photographs of dead friends thus:

'I've been there forty-five years. I wouldn't really like to *leave* there, because I always feel that my mother and father are there.'

'I don't take flowers to the cemetery at anniversaries. I put them in the *house*, near the picture, and I say, "This is where they *are*. They're with *me*."'

As has been observed by anthropologists, historians and philosophers of science, attachment to family and religious conviction are often pre-requisites of belief in the supernatural,[11] or maybe supernatural belief is an extension of the love and faith born of family and religion. Heaven is all around for such people, and love defies death.

If one had to find an image for this world-view, the best one would be the vanilla slice. Mundane life is the slab of custard in the middle, the spiritual world is the crust which surrounds it. The crust is not quite solid or separable – bits of it keep flaking off and finding their way into the custard. Similarly, the spiritual world encompasses the mundane one and filters into it; the boundary is flexible and shifting, and does not consistently keep the two worlds distinct from each other. In this world, God does literally 'see the little sparrow fall' and can stop it falling. If he should miss it, then the good dead, in the capacity of guardian angels, can intervene to prevent the tragedy.

So it is that the women say:

> 'I'm not really *religious*, but I have *beliefs*. Since my husband died and I've been alone, there's such a lot of things that happen that I've thought, "Well, there must be somebody *behind* that's helping me."'

> 'I'm sure you must sometimes have said to yourself, "Oh, I *wish* I hadn't done that!" because something was *telling you* not to? What *was* that something? Perhaps it *was* from the spiritual world, I don't know. But *something* has told you NOT TO DO IT!'

Alternatively they may refer to other people's experiences of such things and compare it to their own sad lack of such support:

> 'So many – I'm speaking of *widows* now – find comfort. They say, "My husband's walking beside me." "It must be a very good thing to have," I say. "What a *help* it must be! But," I've said, "I've *tried*. I've tried, not to *contact* him but to feel he's *around*, but . . . no. No."'

> 'You do hear different people *speak* of it – that they've been in *touch* and all this sort of thing. But it's never happened to me. *I* can't say, "Well, yes, I had the feeling that a soul was at the side of me telling me anything." You know, you'll hear somebody say, "Well, I just sort of *sensed* that he was at the side of me."'

*

Thus it is the common opinion that the spiritual world permeates the mundane one and that the dead may perpetuate their role of parent or spouse as guardian angels mediating between two worlds, continuing to interest themselves in the small concerns of daily life and if necessary coming to the rescue, armed not only with their former love but also with their present superior knowledge.

All accounts of these occurrences therefore are firmly rooted in the domestic sphere. Three women tell of the intervention of the dead in times of sickness (as Ruth does in her story on page 67); three happenings involve house purchases; three tell of lost documents or objects (as Elisabeth's story on page 67 does); three tell of receiving timely instructions (including Agnes's story, page 70 and Rachel's on pages 51–2); and in three, dead relatives give necessary strength and skill. In other stories they give peace of mind in a crisis, come to see how their children are getting on, tuck a grandchild up in bed as they always used to do in their lifetime, or (as in Alma's story on page 51) bring a daughter to a dying wife. These events always happen in familiar surroundings – the bedroom principally, but also elsewhere in the house or in the family car. Only in Agnes's story do events happen away from the home. Mothers are the most common type of 'witness', then fathers and husbands. Children and friends figure in four stories and a brother, a grandmother, and a 'lady in white' in three more. The 'lady in white' is the sole example of an unknown and unnamed 'witness'. In half the cases the stories involve some sort of communication between the dead and the living. Words like *ask*, *tell*, *say*, *hear*, *speak*, *listen*, *call*, *reassure* and *remind* recur very frequently.

On some of these occasions the witness's voice is plainly heard but just as frequently the communication is a telepathic one. In five stories the narrator actually sees her visitor and in another five she 'feels her presence'. Objective experiences are thus just as common as subjective ones: as many women insist that they heard or saw the dead person 'quite clearly' as say that 'it was only a spiritual thing' or it was 'as though' he/she was really there. Similarly, fairly equal numbers of women tell, on the one hand, of events which happened once or twice on specific, well-remembered occasions, and, on the other hand, of 'feelings' that are 'always with' them in whatever they are doing.

Two typical stories show the uniformity of the theme but the contrasts in the way it is presented:

Violet's story

'My mother's been dead a long time, but I *always feel* that if I'm in any trouble, I can feel the NEARNESS of my mother. I mean, my mother was a good woman – we were all brought up Chapel. And I FEEL as though she's near me and she helps me. It doesn't make it any *easier* for me. I mean, it doesn't go *away*. But I feel she's *there*.

'I went through a very bad time quite a few years ago. My husband had a very bad illness. I couldn't have gone through that on my own *strength*. Now, whether that help came from up *above*, which I really think it *did*, I got HELP. And my mother was at the side of me I'M SURE! Because I couldn't have gone *through* it on my OWN.

'I lost four of my family in three months. So, as I *say*, I DIDN'T BEAR that on my own. I did come *through* it. And I really do *think* ... I always feel that in any time of trouble my *mother* – not my *father*, my *mother* – is very close BY me.'

Kate's story

'Well, ACTUALLY, a long time ago, when I was a young girl my *mother* died. And we were living in this house where we were all very unhappy. And I REMEMBER my mother coming and saying "Go!" Now I REMEMBER that *distinctly*!'

[G. B.: 'And your mother was —?']

'She'd *died*, yes! It's quite true, that. I wakened up and I thought, "Yes! She's RIGHT! We've got to *go*!"'

[G. B.: 'And did you?']

'We did. We did, yes.'

Such beliefs in the power of the dead to see and intervene in the affairs of ordinary life have power to explain a wide range of strange occurrences; for example that commonplace, but yet perplexing, experience of the surfacing of unconscious into conscious thought – those familiar, involuntary perceptions, intuitions and recurrent thoughts that seemingly miraculously solve long-standing problems. Elisabeth's story is essentially of this nature and elsewhere another lady, Maura, has a long, complex account on the same theme. She is asked by a friend to help him sort out the possessions of his late wife. During the clearing-out, they find a letter from a building society about a substantial (secret) investment the wife had made. The widower cannot claim the money unless he can find the paying-in book, which, of course, he knows nothing about. Maura promptly says, without knowing why, 'I expect it's hidden under the paper in the bottom of the wardrobe.' And that is exactly where they find it. Maura interprets her sudden inspiration as a message from the dead woman. Similarly, in one of her many racy stories, Audrey tells how she loses her pension-book:

Audrey's story

'Well, it's a funny thing happened. I lost my pension-book one day and I couldn't find this pension-book *anywhere*. NOW, I always put it in one place, keep it in one place. I have it in a pochette, you see.

'I'd taken my money out, I put my pension-book back and I put it in the sideboard drawer which I've always *done*. SO one Thursday – it was pension day – went to get it and it wasn't THERE! And I thought, "That's darned funny! I NEVER left my pension-book out at ALL!" And I searched and SEARCHED for it and couldn't find it *anywhere*, so I said, "It's NO USE! I'll have to go to the Post Office and see what the post master will say about this," and *on my way to the Post Office* something kept on saying in my brain, "Look behind the electric *fire*! LOOK BEHIND THE ELECTRIC FIRE!"

'Anyway, I went to the Post Office. I *knew* I hadn't lost it outside, and he said nobody had brought it in, and he said, "You'd better to go to the main Post Office," you see. So, coming back, this, "LOOK BEHIND THE ELECTRIC FIRE," so I looked . . .

'When I got in, I looked behind the electric fire, AND it was absolutely *full* of soot! Now, the lady upstairs, because I live in a downstairs flat, had had the chimney sweep in, and she'd said, "There's hardly any soot down my chimney," but it was all down MINE!

'So I thought, "I'd better clean this OUT!" I DID get lots of soot out! So, I cleaned this soot out and I thought, 'Well, I'd better go down now and see about getting some money from the Social Security," and, as I was going out of the back door, I thought, "Those *tissues* look funny!" – I keep some tissues on the Welsh dresser in the kitchen, and they were *flat* on there, you see, lying *flat*, you know. I thought, "Well! What's WRONG with those tissues?" And I lifted the tissues up AND underneath was my pension-book!

'Now I have an idea myself – I know it sounds *silly* – that Johnny wanted me to find out that there was soot behind the electric fire, because it was *dangerous*, you see. And I thought *he* thought the only way of telling me was to hide my pension-book. It might just come into my head to say, "Look behind the electric fire." WASN'T THAT FUNNY?

'Because, a pension-book, I wouldn't *dream* of putting it underneath the tissues! I've always for years put it straight back as soon as I've taken the money out, so I know where *it is*.

'But I think it was Johnny telling me. Don't *you* think that?'

Witnesses, then, are active in a way that fetches, wraiths and warning ghosts are not. The latter only *appear* (and occasionally speak, though not always to the purpose); they are made meaningful by the interpretation put on them, not by virtue of anything they do, and their significance lies in their presence only. Witnesses, however, accomplish changes in the mundane world by some form of indirect intervention by means of communication with the living.

In one way this makes them a very traditional form of revenant – their activeness links them, for example, to the interfering and loquacious ghosts of the seventeenth century and earlier. But the homeliness of the encounters, the domesticity of the revenants' interests, the humdrum little affairs they concern themselves with – all these seem to cut them off from the ghosts of mainstream tradition. 'Witnesses' who hide pension-books or help paint houses seem far removed from the great ghosts of tradition with their religious missions, huge significance and potential for menace. It is fetches, wraiths and warning ghosts, with their interest in matters of life and death, that are recognizable as traditional revenants. It is easier to find their counterparts in ancient accounts than to find precursors for the witness type.

Before dismissing this lively belief as 'untraditional' or exclusively modern, however, there are several points which have to be considered. Just as it is not to be doubted that the concept of hauntings and poltergeists owes as much to popular ghost stories, the mass media and literary accounts as to ideas in oral circulation, so do notions of fetches, wraiths and warning ghosts. They can be encountered time and time again in literature, legend-collections, films and TV. It is typical of literate societies that there should be this continuous interaction between formal and informal learning, and between written and oral literature. We must remember, however, that in such a society it is those informal beliefs that fit most closely into formal stereotypes that are most easily seen and recognized. It does not follow that ideas which are not instantly familiar or immediately referable to a written source are not traditional. Tradition is a little more flexible than that. In the first place, we may have traditions which have become submerged and, in the second place, absurd though it seems on the face of it, we may have modern or even new traditions.

A tradition may be submerged, or more precisely 'hidden', because, though it continues to evolve in an endless chain of face-to-face encounters, nevertheless it may never break surface on the official, or public, level. Perhaps it is never newsworthy or commercial enough to be exploited by the popular media, nor quaint and striking enough to be taken up and re-worked by men of letters. This is specially true of supernatural folklore in a literate culture. Hauntings, warnings, wraiths and fetches are dramatic happenings, and their histrionic qualities can be continuously used and re-used – as ammunition in philosophical or religious arguments, as motifs in works or art, as entertainment, thrills and horrors, or as a means of making money. Stories of encounters with these sorts of revenants, therefore, turn up time and time again in both educated and popular literature, and are honed and polished with great skill to make unforgettably impressive accounts that can serve a variety of useful purposes. A story such as Glanvil's tale of the Ghost of Major Sydenham, for example, has plainly gone through all these processes. Though such stories continue to be folklore, they are also a part of popular and/or educated culture and are thus highly visible. There are other types of supernatural encounter, however, which do not have the same immediate power to thrill, and traditions about these may remain submerged below the level of popular awareness, so that when attention *is* drawn to them they appear to be entirely unfamiliar and strangely new. By reading and detective-work, however, their ancestry may be established just as clearly as that of the more visible beliefs.

In the second place, it must be remembered that traditions may be as easily passed from person to person as from generation to generation: what is important is that there should be continuous transmission and a feeling that it is important that the information *should be* thus transmitted. The *direction* of this transmission, however, is not ultimately significant

– traditions may just as easily be transmitted, so to speak, 'horizontally' among friends and acquaintances as 'vertically' down through the generations. Where in a close community, people daily exchange information, news and views – as in school playgrounds, church coffee-mornings, college staffrooms, or works canteens – a folklore quickly builds up and is passed on among peers. Such traditions are not only lively and meaningful but just as 'traditional' as any which have been kept going over several centuries.

That belief in 'witnesses' is part of a vigorously transmitted modern folklore among the community of women I interviewed (and almost certainly among other similar groups, too) is, I hope, obvious; that they have an ancestry in older traditions can be established by seeking for clues among historical texts and what little serious work there is on the folklore of ghosts today.

Some early impressionistic evidence that the witness type may not be an idiosyncratic modern invention but may well have a lineage in older folklore is provided by a comparison of the lexis of representative texts. A word-list compiled from witness stories shows that the twenty-five words most frequently used by narrators are (in order of frequency) *dead, feel, see, mother, father, think, say, come, alive, there, house, plainly, happen, bedroom, bed, husband, know, (a)wake(n), night, as though, tell, presence, always, help, lose*. This list is surprisingly close to one compiled from the work of the seventeenth-century antiquarian, John Aubrey, one of the earliest folklorists, who was intensely interested in supernatural lore. When stories from his *Miscellanies* of 1696 are analysed to find which words are most frequently used in connection with 'apparitions', 'spirits' and 'ghosts' (as he calls them), we find they are *dead, bed, say, saw, ask, tell, (a)wake(n), vanish, friend, wife, look, appear, go, come, fancy, advise, alive, dream, nothing, ill, noise*. One third of the words in the two lists therefore are identical, another six are related (*mother, father, husband* reflect female orientations to kinship; *friend* and *wife* are male orientations; the modern phrase '*as though* he was *there*' is roughly comparable to the older '*fancy* that he *appeared*'; and *help* is not dissimilar to *advise*). Where differences do occur, they are in the degree of subjectivity/objectivity of the report, not in the content. Basically, shorn of the elaborations typical of the period, the essence of the old stories is surprisingly similar to that of the modern ones, the emphasis in both cases being on the coming of the apparition in familiar shape, on its being there (often in visible form), on the communication with it, and on the result of the encounter. This indicates that many of the assumptions about such visitations have remained fairly constant in spite of changes in surface detail, in literary and oral styles and in cultural climate.

Four of Aubrey's stories do indeed directly feature apparitions that have strong affinities with the witnesses of modern tradition. He recounts, for example, two stories which were plainly in vigorous transmission at the time of writing. The first concerns the will of Sir Walter Long of Draycot (see p. 174 below). On three occasions when a clerk tries to draft a paper which will disinherit her son in favour of the children of Sir Walter's second marriage, the phantom hand of the first Lady Long is seen hovering reproachfully over the paper. The second story also concerns a dead first wife who is troubled about the fate of her children. Her ghost appears to show the place where the settlement on them is hidden, and thus they gain their inheritance. Here we plainly have the motif of the dead mother still active to protect those she loved in life – we are really not a far cry from Rachel's house-painting brother (also concerned about justice for survivors) or Elisabeth's dead husband (who reminds her of the whereabouts of lost documents).

Elsewhere in Aubrey's collection, we find ghosts who effect cures. In one story – the truth of which is vouched for by the Archbishop of Canterbury no less! – an old man is kind to a mysterious stranger dressed in outlandish clothes 'not seen or known in those parts' and, in gratitude, the stranger cures his lameness. In another, a ghost appears with an eccentric remedy for ague (to lie on one's back from ten to one daily). Though the surface detail of these stories – weird strangers, ghosts, recipes, ague – is unfamiliar, the underlying idea that the dead have power to help and cure remains in witness traditions. It is the rationale behind Ruth's story, for example, and behind another account in which a 'lady in white' comes to a sick child and tells her to get better ('Funnily enough,' says the narrator, Ella, 'from then on she was all right. She got better').

A text of some thirty or forty years later provides even stronger evidence of the existence of some sort of 'witness' tradition in times gone by. In 1729, that great journalist, publicist and exploiter of popular tastes, Daniel Defoe, under the alias 'Andrew Moreton' was compiling his most famous work on the supernatural, *The Secrets of the Invisible World Disclos'd*. At the outset, he puts forward the proposition that 'almost all real apparitions are of friendly and assisting angels and come of a kind and beneficent Errand',[12] carefully explaining, in what must surely be the expression of a common viewpoint, that the mistake in learned thinking is 'that we either will allow no apparition at all, or will have every apparition to be of the Devil; as if none of the Inhabitants of the World above, were able to show themselves, or had any Business among us'.[13] Defoe's bracketing together of 'assisting angels' and the souls of the dead, his talk of 'kind and beneficent Errands' and 'Inhabitants of the World above' directly reflect the women's phraseology about witnesses, and his argument that the dead do indeed 'show themselves' here and have 'Business among us' is precisely the rationale of modern opinion.

It is very difficult to follow the trail of the witness through the rest of the eighteenth century and the early decades of the nineteenth century. By the 1730s, educated opinion was firmly set against the concept of supernatural powers[14] and there is a gap in serious writing on the subject from then till the turn of the century.[15] When the topic was taken up again in the early decades of the nineteenth century, the clergy, medical men and philosopher–scientists who interested themselves in it came armed with an entrenched rationalistic stance which led them to see such beliefs only as evil nightmares of the mind that the populace needed freeing from. Though supernatural belief undoubtedly continued to flourish in this period, it was as an unofficial, submerged and discredited system. This makes it hard, at this distance of time, to reconstruct its precise nature.

It is not, in fact, until the publication of a popular collection of ghost experiences by Catherine Crowe in 1848 that we can pick up any substantial clues to the supernatural folk beliefs of the age. Rambling, discursive, credulous and romantic, Mrs Crowe brings together a massive collection of narratives and a body of theoretical speculation. She is usually considered the first British writer to use the term 'poltergeist', and her chapter on that phenomenon (unfortunately in the second volume which is now difficult to obtain) is a classic of its kind. The first volume deals with precognitive and telepathic dreaming, warnings, wraiths, *doppelgängers*, apparitions and the afterlife. Crowe's collection places traditional texts higgledy-piggledy alongside memorates, family stories, and contemporary rumours, so it gives a very clear idea of what were the continuing traditions of the time and what was considered to be believable. In her narratives, ghosts can be seen in some very traditional roles – paying debts, revealing murders and otherwise returning because they died with something on their mind. The commonest theme, however, is the return of parents to offer love and comfort. These are ideas which continue to appear in the best of popular literature (though not in folkloristic texts, geared, as they were, to the collection of old country legends), through the remaining years of the nineteenth and early decades of the twentieth centuries. There is thus plenty of evidence to suggest that revenants who return out of love for family or home, or in order to serve the interests of survivors, were a steadily growing feature of the supernatural stereotype during the nineteenth century.

It is significant that, in his 1959 study of American ghostlore, folklorist L. C. Jones lists one of the five principal types of ghost behaviour as warning, consoling, informing, guarding or rewarding the living, for these are very much the functions of 'witnesses'. He goes on to remark that some years prior to writing the book he conducted a survey of the 'mood displayed by American ghosts'. Though this count showed that 58 per cent of them were 'completely indifferent to human values good or bad', 29 per cent 'couldn't have been nicer'.[16] There is no way of knowing what Jones's data-base was, whether written legend or personal experience, but it is likely that legendary material predominated as it usually does in such work. Even so, a figure of nearly 30 per cent for benevolent apparitions in such a survey suggests the existence of a lively contemporary tradition of friendly revenants, and gives further evidence that the witness type of supernatural encounter is more deeply rooted than might, at first sight, be suspected. More up-to-date evidence from America can be found in folklorist Larry Danielson's recent study of the narrative style of sixty-nine paranormal memorates culled from archive transcriptions, folklore collections, popular paperbacks and *Fate* magazine.[17] He observes that in over 40 per cent of cases 'the apparitions described in the accounts are purposeful, most of them involved in helpful missions to the living', and 86 per cent 'appear to some person with whom the appearer has some strong emotional bond'.[18] Danielson notes that his findings closely correspond with those in analysed surveys from 1890 to 1962.

A final, contingent, piece of evidence for traditions of friendly, visiting ghosts comes from Ireland. Among many accounts of frightening apparitions and alarming hauntings in the archive of the Ulster Folk Museum, Linda-May Ballard reports the following pleasanter belief. The informant explains that:

on . . . Holly Eve [Halloween] you would . . . they used to sweep up the ashes and clean the floor all round, and in near the grate here they would leave a lock of ashes, and smooth it down, and when they came down in the morning they would see the tracks of the feet, where they would be sitting, warming themselves. That's on All Souls' Night too. They're supposed to get out on All Souls' Night, you see. The souls will get out of purgatory . . . and they would say they'd always get home . . . This would be the tracks of the people's toes where they would be sitting round the fire warming themselves on All Souls' Night, you know. That was a custom in them days. My mother always done it,

she always swept up the ashes and left a wee ... round the grate here, and
smoothed it down, the way she would see if they had come. If ... if you see, if
they seen the tracks of the toes in the fire ashes ...

Quoting this account, Ballard observes that it blends folk and religious
tradition together and appears to 'be more of an act of affection than
propitiation, the dead being welcomed into the house'.[19]

Each of these bits of information contributes a piece to the jigsaw
picture of the friendly witnessing ghost. The Irish account shows dead
people returning to their homes and welcomed there; the American
surveys indicate the helpfulness of the visitation and the bonds between
visitor and visited; Crowe's stories have all these features; Defoe's and
Aubrey's earlier writings specify the kinds of errand the dead may carry
out in their role as 'assisting angels' in the world of the living. Throughout all the accounts run threads that link the humble witness of modern
tradition to the great ghosts of the past – their active purposefulness,
their awareness of events transpiring in the earthly domain, and their
power for good in the lives of former loved ones. The idea of the
witness is thus the epitome of a philosophy that sees the creation as
whole, ordered, hierarchical, harmonious and more than a little magical.
Here, perhaps, in the folklore of the twentieth century we may see the
last remnants of the medieval world-view.

NOTES

1   Fr Noel Taillepied, *A Treatise of Ghosts*.
2   Taillepied (Summers edn), p. 106.
3   Lavater (1929 edn), pp. 71–2.
4   Grose (1790 edn), pp. 2–3.
5   Malinowski (1982 edn), p. 137.
6   Lavater (1929 edn), p. 77.
7   Lavater (1929 edn), p. 110.
8   Glanvil (1681), pp. 181–4.
9   Beardsley and Hankey (1942), p. 306. The legend is undated. Both these accounts bear
    the imprint of literary over-writing. They have greater shape and polish than
    verbatim oral texts would have, are more elaborate, give a larger number of causative
    and logical links, and employ the mannered phraseology of literature.
10 The term is Alan Dundes's. See Dundes (1964a).
11 See especially Butler (1983), where, in attempting to establish the date at which the
    occult element in slave religion in the southern states of America emerged, he
    argues that 'the collective practice of either African or Christian religious rites
    emerged only after family life and kinship systems developed among the surviving
    slaves' (p. 61), and that the occult practices followed, not preceded, Christianization.
    It has long been assumed that ghost belief flourishes best in settled communities –

by implication, these are often assumed to be rural communities, as in Rockwell (1981) where she writes, 'I would venture a speculation that belief in ghosts can only be a significant part of a culture where long-continued intensive agriculture makes a continuity both of habitation and of human family generations possible. It is to the established family hearth that the ancestors return to give advice and warning' (p. 43) – but the major relevance is not location, I believe, but the feeling of family and 'roots'. Arguments for the importance of settled family life in the establishment of ghost traditions may also be found in Thomas (1971) and Blauner (1966).

12   Defoe/Moreton (1729), p. 6.

13   Defoe/Moreton (1729), p. 16. See chapter 6, below, for an account of the assumed relationship between apparitions and the Devil.

14   It is significant, for example, that the last texts (in English) devoted to disproving witchcraft – Hutchinson's *An Historical Essay Concerning Witchcraft*, and de Daillon's *Daimonologia* – were published in 1718 and 1723 respectively, and that the last of the Witchcraft Acts was repealed in 1736. Discussions of the supernatural invariably mingled with discussions of witchcraft and the two were almost inseparable in learned and popular thought (see chapter, below), so the outlawing of one strongly indicates the decline of the other.

15   Andrew Lang puts the gap in outspoken public interest 'roughly speaking' at 1720 to 1840. Lang (1894a), p. 8.

16   Jones (1959), p. 55.

17   Danielson (1983).

18   Danielson (1983), p. 201. See also Taillepied (Summers edn), p. 95. A ghost, he says, 'will naturally, if it is possible, appear to the person whom he has most loved whilst on earth, since this person will be readiest to carry out any behest or fulfil any wish then communicated by the departed'.

19   Ballard (1981), pp. 29–30.

4 The Rhetoric of Tradition and Taboo

'Well, I *have* seen my mother sometimes – occasionally. But whether that's occasions that she's been on my mind or something . . .'

[G.B.: 'How did you come to see your mother? Did she . . .?']

'It was in the night. Whether I was dreaming about her I don't know. I saw her quite plainly. It only happened once to me. But whether she was on my mind or not I don't know, and I can't remember whether perhaps I was a bit low.'

[G.B.: 'How long ago was this, Vanessa?']

'Oh, I can't say how long.'

[G.B.: 'When you were younger?']

'No, the last few years. And it just came over me whether it was a warning that I *was* going to meet her or something. I never said anything to anybody about it.'

VANESSA

Though it is always fascinating to describe a present-day belief and delineate its ancestry in older tradition, there is an equal fascination in looking at *why* people hold the opinions they do. Often the arguments for and against belief are just as traditional as the beliefs themselves.

Vanessa is plainly thoroughly *au fait* with both rationalist and supernaturalist arguments about the return of the dead, for her reluctant account attempts both sets of explanations for her strange experience. She plainly cannot entirely decide whether what she saw was objective or subjective. On the one hand, she uses the familiar language of ghost belief ('I *have* seen my mother', 'I saw her quite plainly') and relies on traditional assumptions about the reasons why the dead may return ('and it just came over me whether it was a warning that I *was* going to meet her'); on the other hand, she wonders whether she was perhaps dreaming or whether it happened simply because 'she's been on my mind or something' or because she herself was feeling 'a bit low' – states which might lead to her making a perceptual mistake.

Vanessa's answer encapsulates themes we frequently meet in discussions of ghost belief. Supernaturalist arguments are based on 'crediting my senses and those of all the world' (Glanvil): rationalist arguments on the observation that 'many natural things are taken to be ghosts' (Lavater). Both arguments are traditional: we may not only hear them on the lips of women in a city suburb in twentieth-century Britain, but also read them in philosophical and religious writings of the past (as the quotations from Glanvil and Lavater illustrate). In this chapter I want first to look at traditions of belief and traditions of disbelief, then to examine attitudes towards spiritualism – taboo for both believers and unbelievers among the women I interviewed.

TRADITIONS OF BELIEF

One cannot do better by way of introduction to traditions of belief than to return to Glanvil's story of the Ghost of Major Sydenham. As was his usual practice, Glanvil appended an 'Advertisement' to this relation, which specified how he had obtained the information and what reliance could be put on it. He writes:

it will not be amiss to take notice what Mr Douch writes in his second letter to Mr Glanvil, touching the character of the Major and the Captain. They were both, said he, of my good acquaintance, Men well-bred, and of a brisk humour and jolly conversation, of very quick and keen parts, having also been both of them University and Inns of Court Gentlemen.

Here is the believer's first line of argument – their informants are well-known to them, lively, intelligent people, neither melancholy nor stupid. The reasoning continues along a second, equally well-worn path.

I cannot understand that the Doctor and the Captain had any discourse concerning the former engagement to meet, after the disappointment of that time and place, or whether the Captain had after that any expectation of the performance of that promise which the Major had made him. Thus far Mr Douch.

Glanvil then goes on to enlarge on what Mr Douch has written:

And truly one would naturally think, that he failing the solemn appointed time, the Captain would consequently let go all hopes and expectations of his appearing afterward. Or if he did, that it would be at such a time of night as was first determined of, and not at the morning light. Which season yet is less obnoxious to the Impostures of Fancy and Melancholy, and therefore adds some weight to the assurance of the truth of the Apparition.[1]

Here Glanvil is trying another approved tactic – to undermine the rationalists' case by insisting that there can be no deception or mistake. He insists that it would have been well-nigh impossible for the Captain and the Doctor to have concocted such a tall story or for the apparition to have been induced by the Captain's anxious expectation. Furthermore, the apparition comes in daylight not at the agreed time, a fact which makes it more believable, because, at this time, the Captain would not only have been able to see clearly but would have been in cheerful morning mood, not likely therefore to be subject 'to the Impostures of Fancy and Melancholy'.

Similar reasoning underlies his thoughts about his most famous 'Relation', the story of 'The Daemon of Tedworth' – a long, rambling narrative constructed partly from rumour and hearsay and partly from Glanvil's own experiences while a guest in the affected house. This was a poltergeist case – thought to be witchcraft at the time – which aroused immense contemporary interest. A certain Mr Mompesson, a magistrate, confiscated the drum of an itinerant drummer and thereafter was plagued by insistent drumming noises around the house. The drummer, though jailed in Gloucester for theft, seemed to know all that was happening at the Mompesson house in Wiltshire, and was said to have remarked, 'I have plagued him and he shall never be quiet till he hath made me satisfaction for taking away my drum.' On this evidence, he was tried for witchcraft, convicted and sentenced to be transported. The manifestations thereupon promptly ceased. By some means or other, however, the drummer escaped from the convict-ship and returned. The troubles at Mr Mompesson's house began again immediately. The story made considerable impact at the time and was the cornerstone of many arguments in favour of supernatural powers. Glanvil himself investigated the case somewhat in the manner of a present-day psychical researcher. His conclusions on the matter are interesting, for they reveal the underlying bias of his thinking and the entirely traditional nature of his arguments.

Mr Mompesson is a Gentleman, of whose truth in this account I have not the least suspicion, he being neither vain nor credulous, but a discreet, sagacious and manly person. Now the credit of matters of Fact depends much upon the relators who, if they cannot be deceived themselves, nor supposed anyways interested to impose upon others, ought to be credited. For upon these circumstances, all Human faith is grounded, and matter of Fact is not capable of any proof beside but immediate sensible [i.e. 'sensory'] evidence.[2]

Similarly, Glanvil's contemporary Richard Bovet, in introducing the fifth 'Relation' of his *Pandaemonium: or The Devil's Cloister* (a story about a phantom funeral), writes that it was 'A strange Apparition, which was seen by a Man, as he was going home two Miles in a Winter Night, near Kineel by the River Forth in Scotland', that the man the strange events happened to was 'in no wise in drink, nor was he at all of a Timorous Nature', and that 'This story I have heard related by several Persons of good Repute, that lived in the same Town with him, who had it from his own mouth. The man I have several times seen . . .'[3]

Again, Richard Baxter, in *The Certainty of the World of Spirits Fully Evinced*, says of his second narrative (the famous story of Mrs Bowen of Llanellin, whose dead and decomposing husband tries to get into bed with her) that Mrs Bowen is 'very much praised for her true piety and courage' and that Mr Samuel Jones, who vouches for her, 'is a man of known learning, piety and honesty'.[4] Similarly his fourth narrative happened to a 'pious, credible woman yet living in London',[5] the informant for the sixth narrative is an 'ancient, understanding, pious and credible man',[6] and those who told him about the wraith of Mary Goffe 'all agree in the same story, and everyone helps to strengthen the other's testimony' and, moreover, 'they appear to be sober, intelligent persons'.[7]

These are exactly the arguments used by my informants in their discussions. 'There've been so many *cases*'; 'the people who've *reported* these things are people that you can rely on their *word* about it. I mean . . . you get *ministers of the Church of England*, who SWEAR that they've *heard* this sort of thing'; 'it wasn't that she'd been drinking – she was very SOBER!!!'; 'it wasn't *dark* or anything . . . we hadn't had a lot to *drink* or anything'; 'they couldn't imagine it, *surely?*'; 'I *knew* that girl'; 'I've EXPERIENCED it, as I say'; 'I can see it to this day!'; 'I REMEMBER that *distinctly*'; and so on *ad infinitum*. All these arguments are ultimately based on trust in the reliability of human testimony and the accuracy of human observation, as they were in Glanvil's time and have been both before and since. Believers point out that both religion and tradition are firmly in favour of the continued existence of the souls of the dead and that there is sound empirical evidence that they do interact with living people. This evidence is drawn not only from folklore and literature, but from personal experience and the stories of friends and relatives.

There is one particular experience, which I believe helps to substantiate supernatural traditions by providing strong apparent evidence for the justice of its claims (or perhaps even being the ground in which such traditions grow), and that is bereavement. I want, therefore, to digress a little and for a brief space to discuss the psychology of grieving. It is particularly relevant in the case of my own informants, because it was almost universal among them to have lost an important member of the family. Most of them were between sixty and ninety-six years old and more than a half of these elderly women had lost the one person they had held dearest. By virtue of their age, in fact, all but a handful had also lost many of their closest kin – brothers, sisters, husbands, parents, even children. It would be strange if so recent and overwhelming, as well as common, an experience should not have had a profound effect on their thinking about the status of the dead.

The psychology and physiology of bereavement have attracted a good deal of attention in the last twenty years, especially among psychologists and psychiatrists interested in normal and pathological grief reactions. The first, and still most complete, analysis of the behaviour of recently bereaved people was Lindemann's 1944 study based on observed field data, and this still remains the starting-point of more recent work. Almost twenty years elapsed, however, before Lindemann's findings were rediscovered and taken up by others. From psychology, Bowlby, Parkes, Marris, Weiss, Glick, Schulz and Kastenbaum,[8] in particular, have contributed to our knowledge of the normal processes of mourning; the sociologist Geoffrey Gorer also devotes a chapter of his *Death, Grief and Mourning in Contemporary Britain* to the experience of loss. In all this work there is substantial agreement that the bereaved person attempts to deny the irrevocability of the loss and institutes within him/herself a process of searching for the dead person which, among its other symptoms, takes the form of illusions of the presence of the dead and hallucinatory perceptions.

Peter Marris, for example, quotes the following as typical of the early stages of mourning among the seventy-two London widows he studied, 'inability to comprehend the loss, brooding over memories, clinging to possessions, a feeling that the dead man is still present – talking to him and of him as if he were still alive'.[9] Of his seventy-two widows, thirty-six experienced a sense of the husband's presence, and fifteen continued to behave as if he were still alive, a process Marris calls a refusal to 'surrender the dead, reviving them in imagination'.[10] Similarly, of the eighty people interviewed by Geoffrey Gorer, thirty-one experienced what he calls 'lucid dreams' of the dead – five of them, bravely refusing his definition, maintained that what he called 'dreams' were reality.

In many cases the illusion of presence is strong and vivid enough to constitute an auditory or visual hallucination of the dead person. This phenomenon was first noticed by Lindemann, and his findings have since been borne out by Glick *et al.*, Marris and Parkes. The *British*

Medical Journal, too, carries a survey by a Welsh GP which records an incidence of almost 50 per cent post-bereavement hallucinations (auditory and visual) among his sample of 293 local people, and he notes that these are common during the first ten years of widowhood. The barest description of this state of mind is provided in an account which my imformant May gives of her feelings after the death of her mother:

May's story

'I don't know whether it was just my imagination . . . I was the only daughter and I had two brothers. And my mother and I were rather close – very close – and she lived with us for seventeen years after my father died. She was nearly ninety when she died and she was really only seriously ill the last twelve months. She had a stroke which left her memory impaired but not her faculties. She couldn't remember people and places [. . .]

'But after she died, I *never* felt she'd really gone. Her presence seemed to be particularly in her bedroom. And it was about twelve months after until her room felt empty to me. And it was very *strong* at times. I would go UP. And I used to wake up in the night and think I heard her, because she slept with her door open and so did we – to hear her – and I was CONFIDENT I'd many a time heard her *cough*. Well, that would be sheer imagination, of course.

'But it was the emptiness in the room. And it was quite twelve months – after we returned from the second holiday after she'd died – and then I realized the room was empty.

'I've never expressed it before, but it was WITH me all the time in whatever I was doing. She was THERE somehow, either sitting watching me or . . . But suddenly the house was empty.

'But I couldn't express it really. It was a FEELING. I came back, and before that I'd always felt she was about somewhere. And it had gone.'

Here, then, is a solid basis for the belief that the dead surround the living 'like a great cloud of witnesses'. If, as Glanvil wrote, 'matter of Fact is not capable of any proof beside but immediate sensible [i.e. 'sensory'] evidence', then such experiences provide all the proof necessary. One may see this plainly in an account which Margot gives of her post-bereavement sensations and in the interpretation which she puts on them:

Margot's story

'And again! I have PROOF of *that*! My *grandmother*, who, as I said, I lived with as a child, when she . . . after she died . . .

'I always had the habit, ALWAYS, that I always had a bedroom at my grandfather's house, and, from time to time, I would remove and go and live back there, because he LIKED me to do that, you see. And I *slept* in the bedroom I'd had as a *child*. And my grandmother always, ALWAYS, when I was in bed, the last thing she did was ALWAYS to *come* into the bedroom and sort of TUCK ME UP when I was lying there. And I FELT this *whenever* I went back to that house.

'I always *felt* that someone came into the bedroom when I was in bed. Not a FRIGHTENING thing, a GOOD thing, a COMFORTING sort of thing.'

[G.B.: 'Very nice. Very nice.']

'Oh, yes, it WAS! IT WAS! There's nothing frightening about anything like that, I don't think!'

[G.B.: 'And it definitely felt as though she was there?']

'Oh, yes! I sort of had the sensation of the door opening, because she always liked the bedroom doors closed you see, and I *always* had the feeling that the bedroom door was being opened and closed and . . . Nothing frightening about her, no.'

The weight of evidence such experiences provide can be seen by the fact that of thirty-eight women who spoke of such feelings and sensations, only six interpreted them as illusions or hallucinations. Even May is not a hundred per cent unambiguous. Though she insists for the most part that 'that would be sheer imagination, of course' and says it was just a 'feeling', she does, nevertheless, speak without these qualifications when she says 'I realized the room was empty' and 'She was THERE somehow'. The other narrators speak simply of husbands and parents actually returning or continuing to exist. Note, for example, how easily Margot shifts from speaking about there being 'nothing frightening about anything like that' to there being 'nothing frightening about her'. For the majority of my informants, tradition gets to work on the experience simultaneously with it. It is interpreted through religious traditions about the immortality of souls and folk traditions about the ability of those souls to perpetuate themselves at least for a while in their former environment: that is, through a tradition of ghosts. Well might people argue, then, that the evidence for ghosts is as good as the evidence for anything else. In fact, in times past, as we shall see in Chapter 6, it was the empirically verifiable ghost-figure that underpinned belief in the hierarchy of the supernatural world and (in the last resort) confirmed the existence of God Himself.

It is therefore the interaction of tradition with accounts of personal experience that forms the basis of the believers' case. It is very clear in the present research particularly, that, for the majority of people, 'good evidence' of the truth of traditional concepts is empirical and oral. For them, the best evidence of all is personal experience, and then, in descending order of merit: the eye-witness accounts of peers; the reports of 'sensible' people; media reports; and written accounts. Reasoned argument follows a poor sixth. In 69 per cent of cases where the informants express some measure of belief in the supernatural, their answers are glossed with an appeal to experience. In some cases these are brief statements such as 'I've read about that' or 'Well, I've experienced it'; elsewhere a full-blown memorate may be offered. Typical answers to questions are made up of a brief 'yes', followed by a short explanation and then an illustrative story. Alternatively, the speaker may launch straight into narrative. So, when asked about whether the dead can return to this world, for example, the first ten of my informants replied as follows:

1 'Yes! I do. I don't know whether you would call it superstition or . . . But I do believe it's close to you in time of trouble or anything. Particularly my mother. I feel her presence, and I will say this . . .' [See May's story, page 87].

2 'Oh yes, yes, yes. Oh, yes. I do, yes. And again! I have PROOF of *that*! My *grandmother* . . .' [See Margot's story, page 88].

3 'My little boy was drowned in the brook in Cardale village. Did you not know? Well, I can tell you about that. I can tell you what happened with that . . .'

4 'I do. I do believe, but my family don't. But I'll give you an idea . . .'

5 'I think I must be a little bit psychic. I had one rather strange experience . . .'

6 'Oh, definitely, definitely, because my mother's been dead a long time but . . .' [See Violet's story, page 72].

7 'Well, it's a funny thing happened . . .'

8   'Isn't it extraordinary that? And I remember once . . .' [See Elisabeth's story, page 67].

9   'Yes, well, ACTUALLY, a long time ago . . .' [See Kate's story, page 72].

10   'Yes! You see, my mother died when I was very small, and . . .'

Eventually, of course, these 'proofs' stand or fall by whether personal experience can, or cannot, be relied upon: it is the reliability of testimony that is the shibboleth that ultimately distinguishes believers from non-believers. Believers implicitly have faith in human perception and human truth, trusting that: (i) people see accurately and interpret correctly what happens in the world around them; and (ii) that they have no reason to lie or mislead others when they report these experiences. Sceptics, on the other hand, will not take these things for granted – indeed, their case is ultimately based on the assumption that not only are people frequently misled themselves, but also that they do indeed sometimes have cause to mislead others.

There can be no compromise or mediation between these two viewpoints, only a greater or lesser awareness of the strength of the opponents' case and a corresponding willingness to meet their objections. Here the balance of power, so to speak, has drastically shifted from the Middle Ages to the present day. Four hundred years ago, it was the sceptics who had to prove, rather than assert, their opinions; now the position is reversed. Believers show themselves defensively aware of what the sceptics' arguments are likely to be. They realize that the majority view is firmly set against the reliability of human testimony (especially oral testimony) and that there are few now who would boldly assert with Glanvil that 'the credit of matters of Fact depends much upon the relators who' (given minimum safeguards against lies and stupidity) 'ought to be credited', so they insist that their informants are of the *highest* probity, the perception seen or remembered with *the most distinct* clarity, and, moreover, that such cases are both numerous and well-documented and *do not depend on the evidence of a single person* however reliable. All these are, at heart, ploys designed to pre-empt the disbelievers' probable argument that oral testimony is anecdotal and 'unscientific'.

We can see this as a reflection of the move towards new standards of scientific verifiability – initiated by the Renaissance and accelerated by the New Philosophy and Galilean science, which redefined the nature of

the 'proof' required as 'immediate sensible evidence' in terms of empirically testable hypotheses – a move which by the eighteenth century
had officially enshrined scepticism as the *sine qua non* of 'science', and
'science' as the unofficial religion of educated people. Thus it is that
sceptics do not feel the need to recognize, and be ready to answer the
believers' case. Their arguments are baldly asserted and boldly phrased,
as we shall see.

TRADITIONS OF DISBELIEF

For a catalogue of the arguments mustered by adherents of the traditions
of disbelief which has grown up in the light of scientific scepticism,
there is no single source better than Ludowig Lavater's *Of Ghostes and
Spirites Walking by Nyghte*, translated into English in 1572. Though, as an
ardent Reformer, Lavater had a particular theological reason for wishing
to discredit ghost traditions, his arguments are nevertheless representative not only of the thinking of his sympathizers and contemporar-
ies, but also of modern opinion. The aim of his book is to prove that
apparitions are 'not the souls of dead men as some have thought.'[11] To
this end, part 1 is given over entirely to discussing a variety of misapprehensions which might lead people to think they have seen a ghost. So
chapter 2 argues that much ghost belief is derived from 'Melancholike
persons and madde men, imagining things which in very deed are not',
and chapter 3 that 'Fearfull menne, imagine that they see and heare
straunge things'. Chapter 4 asserts that 'Men which are dull of seeing
and hearing imagine many things which in very deede are not so',
chapter 5 deals with tricks used to scare children into obedience, jokes
and pranks played by young men and legends and tales, reasoning
that, 'Many men are so feared by other menne, that they suppose they
have heard or seene spirites', and chapters 6 to 10 enumerate what he
sees as deliberate deceptions perpetrated by disingenuous monks and
priests upon simple people. In chapter 11 he argues that 'Manye
naturall things are taken to bee ghosts'[12] and that 'Simple foolish men
hearing [night noises] imagine I know not howe, that there be
certayne elves and fairies of the earth, and tell many straunge and
marvellous tales of them which they have heard of their mothers and
grandmothers'.[13]

Chapters 12 and 13 give momentary credit to established folklore,
admitting that 'spirits do often appeare and many straunge and marvellous things do sundry times chaunce,'[14] but by chapter 14 he is back to

listing possible errors and deceits and arguing, 'That in the Bookes, set forth by the Monkes, are many ridiculous and vaine apparitions.'[15] The remaining chapters of the first part are given to a description of supernatural happenings that he cannot disprove by these arguments and which he will later redefine in terms of 'a good or evill Angel, or some other forewarning sent by God'.[16] Even here, however, he cannot resist taking a side-swipe at contemporary folklore, arguing that, though there are those 'who thinke it a gay thing, if many straunge sightes appeare unto them', a man of true piety will not be much troubled with such things because 'he knoweth well what he ought to deeme and judge of them'.[17] Elsewhere he insists (as has so often been asserted since) that the incidence of apparitions and visions is declining, and that, though there are undoubtedly accounts of spirits in the Bible, there are fewer than people assume. Later in the book he deals specifically with these biblical accounts, giving two whole chapters to Saul's raising of the prophet Samuel through the mediumship of the Witch of Endor. He is wonderfully scathing about this story, bluntly asserting that 'If the witch had called for Samuell whilest he lived, doubtless he would not have approched unto hir. And how then can we believe that he came to hir after his death?'[18] Likewise he demolishes with equal style and aplomb other important biblical accounts, including that dealing with the appearance of the ghosts of Moses and Elias to Jesus (*only* to Jesus, he argues, and obviously he would be an exception to the general rule); and the Resurrection account where the Apostles thought they saw Jesus' ghost (they were mistaken, he says flatly, or else what they saw was really an angel sent by God).

The arguments of parts 1 and 2 are finally summarized in resounding style: 'I pray you what are they? If it be not a vayne persuasion proceeding through weakness of the senses through feare, or such like cause, or if it be not a deceyte of man, or some naturall thing . . . it is either a good or evill Angell, or some other forewarning sent by God.'[19] Putting aside Lavater's sectarian insistence that monkish tricks and lies are responsible for many supposed supernatural experiences, and the argument (entirely of its time) that though *ghosts* do not exist, *good and evil angels do* and may be mistaken for apparitions, the reasoning in the first 160 pages of *Of Ghostes and Spirites Walking by Nyghte* is very similar to that heard on the lips of people today.

Most of these familiar arguments are used at one time or another by the disbelievers among my informants. In particular, the women stress the lack of independent evidence for the proposition that the dead return, or condemn it as inherently implausible, saying:

'No! Because nobody's come back, have they?'

'Well, *I've* never had any experience of anything.'

'Nothing has *ever* happened to *me*!'

'You only *ever* hear it at fourth hand or something.'

'No, because you must go back thousands of years, mustn't you? Well, I mean, if people are going to come back from all those years, well I can't see how it *can* be!'

'I have a theory that you're put on this earth for so long and that's your span of life. It's like a flower. A flower dies – another one doesn't grow in its place, you've got to plant something else, haven't you?'

'No, as far as I'm concerned, once you're dead you're dead. Look at the animals for that.'

'I do think our bodies die like the plants and flowers do.'

Elsewhere they baldly assert that people who report hauntings and other phenomena:

'have put the wrong interpretation on it'

'are probably very highly strung and imaginative'

'doing that just for the publicity'

'doing it just to get a new house',

or they say that:

'when people are very bad with their *nerves*, they think *all sorts of things*!'

'it's only what *they* believe. Anybody else coming to live in that house would probably not be affected.'

Where they have to face popular opinion at first hand and respond to acquaintances who report subjective experiences such as the 'feeling of presence', they are politer, but nevertheless just as negative. Usually such occurrences are attributed to the power of dreams and desire:

'My mother still thinks of him so much – of her son so much – that she sometimes does come down in the morning and say he was in the room with her, but, you know, whether that's half-dreaming or not, it's hard to say.'

or to the influence of past associations:

'I think that is rather involved in one's teaching from childhood and when there is distress or any other crisis we probably revert to what we've been taught and go over it again. That's how I think I'd explain that.'

'I think one might feel that one has been helped by thinking about them, but whether any actual spirit comes to help you I should rather doubt. I think it's more *inside* you. You get the comfort and strength from contact with whoever it is that you're thinking of rather than that they come specially to help you, in the spirit or any other way.'

'Well, I think you live through your parents a lot during your life. Personally I think an awful lot of the way you were brought up and the things they say as regards religion and everything does stay with you and you tend to talk about it at times.'

'Oh! I think you can feel the presence there sometimes. But that is only a spiritual thing.'

Sometimes sceptics maintain their disbelief by simply refusing to think about such matters at all:

'I don't *want* to know about it. If there's anything on radio or TV, I switch off.'

The arguments and attitudes are plainly traditional. Here, for example, is David Hufford enumerating the arguments he has isolated as important in traditions of disbelief as he has studied them:

Disbeliefs about supernatural agents begin with the argument that traditions about such agents generally develop with very few experiential referents. The forces operating ... are believed to consist of four overlapping kinds – 1. unconscious pressures from repressed needs and the operation of primary process impacting on traditions through projection; 2. social needs leading to the development of social controls from the 'opiate of the masses' to the 'bogeyman'; 3. the creative urge that leads to hoaxes, and the fabrication and modification of legends by prevaricating raconteurs; 4. folk etymology – from solar myths to devil's footprints.

These forces operating on narratives and beliefs through many repetitions are believed to give rise to many traditions and traditional accounts believed to support them, often without the involvement of any significant experience. These traditions in turn are believed to condition certain experiences of believers in a way that gives rise to accounts that have the misleading appearance of supporting evidence for the traditions.

When actual experiences are involved at all, they are generally thought to fall into one of four classes. First there are hallucinations, believed to be relatively uncommon, most often occurring in one of three kinds of situations: (a) under the influence of psychotropic substances ranging from alcohol to the opiates and alkaloids such as L S D; (b) under extreme physical or psychological stress – as in vision quests or during delirium; (c) among psychotics – especially highly creative psychotics, who manage to become shamans and mediums rather than being institutionalized. The conformity of such experiences to traditional expectations is said to he high and is believed to be a consequence of those expectations.[20]

Likewise, another eminent American folklorist with an interest in the supranormal, Donald Ward, traces the various attempts to explain psychic phenomena, observing that:

The Age of Enlightenment ... introduces a new attitude prompting learned men to make concerted efforts to eradicate superstition, and to dismiss the apparitions of supernatural creatures as the hallucinations of unenlightened minds.
  It was not, however, until the development of empirical research of the latter part of the nineteenth century, coupled with the emergence of folklore as an independent discipline that the explanations of such encounters begin to be based on empirical evidence and on systematic analysis.[21]

He goes on to compile a list of six explanatory theories presently on offer, as follows:

Supranormal experiences are thought to be conditioned by:
  1 atmospheric and other natural conditions
  2 physiological disturbances
  3 emotional associations
  4 dominating personal concerns
  5 the subject's Frame of Reference
  6 objective reality
  7 psycho-physiological states[22]

Only the sixth of these alternative explanatory theories allows for the possibility that the experiences may be objective ones, and this view he firmly attributes only to professional parapsychologists.
  Though 400 years divide them, between Lavater's list of common sixteenth-century misapprehensions and Ward's list of present-day explanations of supernatural experiences, four arguments remain constant – that is, that they may be caused by physiological disorders, psychological distress, stress, or failure to perceive the environment accurately. Between Lavater's list and Hufford's 'traditions of disbelief' there are a further four points in common – supernatural experiences are said to be conditioned by childhood fears of bogeymen and other threatening figures of social control, by the too-vivid imaginations of storytellers, by hoaxes, or by madness (divine or otherwise).

The women I interviewed also covered much the same ground (though naturally, they expressed their opinions in less specialist terms). Unusual occurrences were attributed variously to physiological or psychological disorder, failure to report or interpret experiences accurately or to see or hear sufficiently distinctly, to emotion and desire, to a too-vivid imagination, and to plain simple lies and deceptions for ulterior motives. All are part of 'ane old imprescriptible tradition'.

HISTORICAL INTERLUDE

In the annals of folklore history, probably the best-known debate between representatives of the traditions of belief and disbelief is that between Andrew Lang and Edward Clodd in the 1890s. As their dispute is an almost perfect illustration of the debating strategies of the two sides, it is worth describing in some detail.

Andrew Lang was not only an expert and prolific writer on ghost traditions, but also a member of the Society for Psychical Research; Edward Clodd, on the other hand, was a stout-hearted rationalist who scandalized Victorian society (and provoked the former Prime Minister, W. E. Gladstone, to withdraw his subscription to the Folklore Society) by arguing in his presidential address of 1896 that the rites of Christianity were but part and parcel of a long line of similar practices going back to the cult of Dionysus and beyond.[23] Both men were formidable debaters: the tradition of belief could have had no quicker a thinker to represent it than Lang; the tradition of disbelief no more emphatic and committed a follower than Clodd. It was the rapier versus the hammer.

Battle was first joined by Clodd in his 1895 presidential address which set out to demolish the reputation of the SPR: 'Superstitions which are the outcome of ignorance can only awaken pity . . . the art of life largely consists in that control of the emotions and that diversion of them into wholesome channels, which the intellect, braced with the latest knowledge, can alone effect.'[24] Superstition disguised as science, however, merits scorn rather than pity. The SPR, by encouraging belief in the possibility of communication between the living and the dead, promulgates superstitions of this second type. What they advocate is just 'barbaric . . . philosophy', 'the old animism' writ large, decked out with 'precious phrases'. Time, space and the laws of gravity are all ignored by its adherents, merely 'untrustworthy observers' who keep their minds in water-tight compartments, 'suspend or narcotize [their] judgement, and contribute to the rise and spread of another of the epidemic delusions of which history provides warning examples'. 'The Society will sell you not only the Proceedings . . . but glass balls of various diameters for crystal-gazing from three shillings upwards.' Entrenched and secure within the dominant tradition of disbelief, Clodd does not trouble to explain the grounds for this round condemnation. He plainly feels that it is not necessary to enter into serious discussion about 'the twaddle of witless ghosts' – it is simply enough to say that it *is* twaddle. It is not until he has to take on Lang, in fact, that he is forced to justify these opinions and discuss specific instances. Until then, he sits comfortably secure in the conventional tradition where few will challenge him.

Lang, however, when he is moved to defend the SPR, has not got the same security of consensus behind him. He feels he has to argue both longer and better to make his point. So, in his 'Protest of a Psycho-folklorist',[25] he immediately gets his teeth into Clodd's argument, taking the latter's assertions point by point, citing cases and examples, up-braiding his President for being himself unscientific, for being led by his prejudices to miss good opportunities for useful folkloristic research, and for ignoring both tradition and empirical evidence. All classic strategies in the believers' repertoire.

He begins his attack with a deft *argumentum ad hominem*: 'Mr Clodd asks us to contemn the "superstitions" of Dr Alfred Wallace, Mr Crooke, Professor Lodge, Mr A. J. Balfour and all of the eminent men of science, British and foreign' who support the SPR – a fine piece of name-dropping, if ever there was one! Then he moves on to a blistering attack against Clodd's remarks about the sale of crystal balls:

That many persons are so constituted as to see hallucinations in glass balls I cannot possibly doubt, without branding some of my most intimate and least superstitious friends as habitual liars. I see nothing odd in a glass ball, but if I give my friends the lie, then I act as the dreamless Irish king would have done, had he called all men liars who averred that they could dream. Granting, then, that such hallucinations exist, why on earth should they not be studied like any other phenomenon? Is it because you can buy a ball for three shillings? Is it because savages explained the facts as they explained almost all facts? Or why is it?

To have such hallucinations when looking into crystal balls, he argues, is just as much an individual peculiarity as, for example, having hyp-nagogic illusions, and: 'If Mr Clodd has these, he believes in their existence. Even if he has not, he probably believes because so very many people do have them.' Then Lang closes in for the kill with a *coup de grâce* typical of the tradition of belief – an appeal to superior evidence:

'To everyone who thinks of it, the existence or non-existence of such subjective pictures must be a matter of evidence. I have enough to satisfy myself, and perhaps, if Mr Clodd had as much, he would be satisfied also.'

The name-dropping and the appeals to human experience continue: 'I have Dr Carpenter on my side'. 'Mr Crookes, a distinguished man of science . . .' 'Australian blacks, Presbyterians, Celts, Platonists, Peruvians, Catholics, Puritan divines [were all] witnesses', 'Mr E. B. Tylor . . . attended seances', 'Mr Darwin's own mind was open on the matter', 'countless French, German and Italian savants . . .' 'the Irish say, the Welsh say, the Burmese say, the Shanars say, the Negroes say, that there are such and such phenomena', 'the evidence . . . of cameras and of the eyes of living and distinguished men . . .', 'the evidence of living and honourable men', and so on throughout the whole essay.

Lang's second line of attack/defence focuses on the rationalist's dismissive explanations of unusual occurrences. A lighthearted suggestion of Clodd's – that psychic phenomena are the result of a disordered liver – is disingenuously taken seriously and then stood on its head: 'If Mr Clodd explains all by "a disordered liver", then a disordered liver is the origin of a picturesque piece of folklore. That piece of knowledge is acquired for the race.' This idea is then pursued in a spirit partly serious, partly humorous, Lang suggesting that a 'real' scientist and a 'real' folklorist would surely be hot on the trail of such vital clues to the origins of folklore:

Take another even more extreme example, the folklore of levitation. Some man or woman is seen by witnesses, who often give evidence on oath, to rise in the air and stay therein. I have elsewhere shown that this story is as widely distributed as any *Märchen*.

Then comes D. D. Home, and professes to do the trick. What an opportunity for a folklorist! One can imagine a President of the Folklore Society rushing eagerly to examine Mr Home, and to explain at once and for ever the origin of this chapter in folklore.

Clodd, he implies, would have 'rushed' in the opposite direction!

Similarly, on the matter of ghostly lights, another familiar motif in folklore, the SPR has collected many contemporary accounts. Rather than sneering at them, folklorists should be grateful – *especially* if Clodd is right in thinking all such accounts mere delusions. Here is the chance to examine raw data scientifically: 'with what gratitude should we thank the SPR for providing us with nascent delusions *in situ*, as it were, so that we may compare these with similar delusions in history'. This is

true science, he argues, and men like Tylor who attended seances 'I call
. . . not "superstitious", but "scientific".'

After twelve pages of detailed and spirited argument, he returns to
the subject of crystal-gazing and rises to his grand finale, engaging in a
last bit of name-dropping and winding up his argument about what is
truly scientific:

When psychical students are accused, *en masse*, of approaching their subjects
with a dominant prejudice, the charge, to me, seems inaccurate (as a matter of
fact) and, moreover, very capable of being retorted. Not the man who listens to
the evidence, but the man who refuses to listen (as if he were, at least negatively,
omniscient) appears to me to suffer from a dominant prejudice [. . .] Of all
things, modern popular science has most cause to beware of attributing prejudice to students who refuse its Shibboleth.

After this onslaught, Clodd is compelled to marshal his arguments. In
his 'Reply to the Foregoing "Protest"',[26] he focuses his attack not this
time on the content of the S P R's research, but on its methods – 'which
under the guise of the scientific, is pseudo-scientific'. As an illustration,
he cites the case of the *Census of Hallucinations*. However, instead of
criticizing the reliability of its methods and findings (which were, indeed,
suspect) he sidetracks into a typical bit of special pleading. A quarter of
the accounts in the *Census*, he says, were given at second hand, and, what
is more: 'the table "dividing the answers according to the nationalities
of the persons answering" shows, as might be expected, that more
women than men answer the question in the affirmative, and that the
lower the intellectual standpoint the higher are the "percentages of
affirmative answers and hallucinations". England thus contrasts
favourably with Brazil and Russia.' If women and Brazilians believe
they have seen or been touched by persons or things which appeared not
to be 'due to any external physical cause', he implies, then, of course,
such hallucinations *must* be due to mere superstition and prove nothing!

Think, too, of the people who manned the inquiry, he urges: 'One-
tenth of the collectors were drawn from classes not highly educated, as
small shopkeepers and coastguardsmen. Nor does the *personnel* of the
committee itself inspire our confidence. I should prefer five thor-
oughgoing sceptics to Professor Sidgwick and his wife, Miss Alice
Johnson, and Messrs Myers and Podmore (the two ladies taking, it
appears, the more active share in the whole business).' Q E D : If women
take the more active role in a survey, no wonder the findings are 'biased'!
After this proof, could 'anyone in his senses' accept the conclusions of
the *Census*?

We are, of course, on very familiar ground here – back, for instance, with the arch-sceptic of the witchcraft debate, Reginald Scot, who asserted (in 1584) that: 'as among faint-hearted people; namely women, children and sick-folk [supernatural beliefs and traditions] usually swarmed: so among strong bodies and good stomachs they never used to appear'.[27] Believers' reports, the rationalists imply, are literally 'old wives' tales' and *therefore* can be treated disrespectfully and dismissed as serious evidence.

After this bit of typical reasoning, Clodd moves on to express the conventional opinion that strange experiences need not be attributed to the operation of supernatural forces, but are most probably caused by physical or mental disorders:

who doubts that they are the effect of a morbid condition of that intricate, delicately-poised structure, the nervous system [. . .] Voices, whether divine or of the dead, may be heard; actual figures seen; odours smelt; when the nervous system is out of gear. A mental image becomes a visual image, an imagined pain a real pain [. . .] This abnormal state . . . may be organic or functional. Organic, when disease is present; functional, through excessive fatigue, lack of food or sleep, or derangement of the digestive system [. . .] Only the mentally anaemic, the emotionally overwrought, the unbalanced, are the victims.

Having gone through this familiar list of naturalistic explanations for unusual occurrences and perceptions, Clodd then moves on to state in uncompromising terms the grounds on which his scepticism, and that of all adherents of the tradition of disbelief, is ultimately based: that is, the deceivability of human senses and the willingness of unscrupulous operators to exploit that deceivability. Of levitation, for example, he argues:

I should want the levitation repeated many times before many witnesses. I would not trust my own eyes in the matter. I cannot forget that man's senses have been his arch-deceivers, and his preconceptions their abettors, throughout human history: that advance has been possible only as he has escaped through the discipline of the intellect from the illusive impressions about phenomena which the senses convey.

Then, neatly turning the tables on Lang by quoting one of the latter's 'authorities', he adds:

And I fall back on the words of Dr Carpenter . . . 'with every disposition to accept facts when I could once clearly satisfy myself that they were facts, I have had to come to the conclusion that . . . there was either intentional deception on the part of interested persons, or else self-deception [. . .] There is nothing too strange to be believed by those who have once surrendered their judgement to the extent of accepting as credible things which common-sense tells us are entirely incredible.'

Finally, in resounding terms, Clodd arrives at the last argument in the catalogue of traditional arguments – that, even if no rational explanation of the strange occurrences is forthcoming as yet, *in time* one will be found. Before succumbing, for instance, to tales of mystic lights, he says, we need much more 'terrestrial light' on the subject, in order to find 'the naturalistic explanation to which the belief must ultimately yield'.

Returning to the fray, he takes on the question of fire-walking, which, he says, is in no way mystic or mysterious really – 'the whole thing is a trick'. The Fijians who are known to be able to do it have extraordinarily calloused feet – they bathe them in dilute sulphuric acid, singe and prick them, and use oil of vitriol or alum on them to make them tough and pain-resistant. Science can explain such 'mysteries' very easily: 'it is well-known that a man may hold his naked hand in a stream of molten iron so long as the hand is kept moist. The intense heat causes the moisture to retain its spherical form, so that there is a sort of film between the hand and the metal, rendering the heat perfectly bearable.'

As a science, he concludes, folklore will abide by proper scientific attitudes, principles and methods. And, as such, it will also repudiate the SPR and all its works, for its investigations are 'worthless, being vitiated by imperfectly guarded methods, and by the preconceptions of the researchers'. 'The psychical researcher represents a state of feeling, the folklorist represents an order of thought.' Folklore, therefore, 'marches not with any method which tends to confusion rather than to order, and which postulates unknown causes to explain effects which known causes are sufficient to produce'.

One can imagine how strong Clodd's joy must have been when a great scandal hit the psychic world. Eusapia Palladino ('an uneducated Neapolitan woman', according to Clodd) had achieved an international reputation as a medium and attracted considerable attention and support. Even the *Spectator* had given her a favourable write-up; as Clodd puts it, the journal had 'indulged in "high falutin'" talk on this triumph of psychical research ... admonishing scientific men that at their peril did they stand aloof, or still insist that the thing "was a trick, a fraud, and nothing else"'. However, put to the test in a private sitting, Eusapia was, in Lang's colloquial phrase, 'busted up' – found to be cheating. Clodd could not help but gloat over Lang, and reserved the first part of his 1896 presidential address for kicking his opponent while he was down: 'that an illiterate, but astute, Neapolitan conjuror should have thus befooled men of high intellectual capacity justifies my strictures on the incompetence of scientific specialists off their own beat to detect trickery.'[28] Warming to his point, he cites other instances of deception by mediums, rejoicing, for example, that 'that colossal old liar, Madame Blavatsky', was reported to have said:

'I have not met with more than two or three men who knew how to observe, and see, and remark what was going on around them. It is simply amazing! At least nine out of every ten people are entirely devoid of the capacity of observation and of the power of remembering accurately what took place even an hour before. How often it has happened that, under my direction and revision, minutes of various occurrences and phenomena have been drawn up; lo, the most innocent and conscientious people, even sceptics, even those who actually suspected me, have signed *en toutes lettres* as witnesses at the foot of the minutes! And all the time I knew that what had happened was not in the least what was stated in the minutes.'

Clodd goes on to quote other instances of mediums who had been 'busted up', concluding triumphantly by quoting Lang himself (from 'a half-bantering letter where one hears him whistling to keep up his courage'): '"it really looks as if 'psychical research' does somehow damage and pervert the logical faculty of scientific minds"'.

Though it looked as if luck had dealt the winning hand to Clodd, Lang did not stay down for long. Indeed, in the preface to the new edition of his *Cock Lane and Common-Sense*, he had his last attempt: 'to make the Folk-lore Society see that such things as modern reports of wraiths, ghosts, "fire-walking", "corpse-lights", "crystal-gazing", and so on, are within their province.'[29] There is an element of despair, however, detectable in his complaint that:

As he [i.e. the author] understands the situation, folklorists and anthropologists will hear gladly about wraiths, ghosts, corpse-candles, hauntings, crystal-gazing, and walking unharmed through fire, as long as these things are part of a vague rural tradition, or of savage belief. But, as soon as there is first-hand evidence of honourable men and women for the apparent existence of any of the phenomena enumerated, then Folklore officially refuses to have anything to do with the subject. Folklore will register and compare vague savage or popular beliefs; but when educated living persons vouch for phenomena which (if truly stated) account in part for the origin of these popular or savage beliefs, then Folklore turns a deaf ear. The logic of this attitude does not commend itself to the author of *Cock Lane and Common-Sense*.

Such an attitude, he regrets, stems from the fact that minds are already closed:

The truth is that anthropology and folklore have a ready-made theory as to the savage and illusory origin of all belief in the spiritual, from ghosts to God. The reported occurrence, therefore, of phenomena which suggest the possible existence of causes of belief *not* accepted by anthropology, is a distasteful thing and is avoided.

Somewhat wearily, he goes through the familiar arguments – testimony to the supernatural comes from 'undeniably honest and absolutely contemporary' sources; not one of the explanations offered by the rationalists holds water; and the evidence for ghosts is as good as the evidence for anything else:

We cannot expect human testimony suddenly to become impeccable and infallible in all details, just because a 'ghost' is concerned. Nor is it logical to demand here a degree of congruity in testimony, which daily experience of human evidence proves to be impossible, even in ordinary matters.

Indeed, in the last resort, he argues, rationalists are as 'unscientific' as they claim that believers are. Any of their explanations 'is a theory like another, and, like another, can be tested' if only they would deign to do it. But they will not, for their prejudices are too deeply ingrained:

Manifestly it is as fair for a psychical researcher to say to Mr Clodd, 'You won't examine my haunted house because you are afraid of being obliged to believe in spirits', as it is fair for Mr Clodd to say to a psychical researcher, 'You only examine a haunted house because you want to believe in spirits.'

And there he rests his case.

It is not possible to say who 'won' this dispute: there can be no victory where defeat is not conceded, just as there can be no discussion where there is no meeting of minds. Lang and Clodd simply stand either side of a great divide, entrenched in opposed traditional philosophies, using opposed traditional arguments.

We are fortunate, however, to have such a detailed record of their long-standing debate for not only is it a fascinating chapter in the history of folklore, it also shows how even the most astute and ardent debaters do not (and perhaps cannot) step outside the arguments allotted to their team in the philosophical tug-of-war. Though cogently stated and enthusiastically expressed, their arguments are almost entirely predictable; they would be very familiar to a long line of disputants. Lang says no more and no less than Joseph Glanvil and Richard Baxter in the seventeenth century or Margot, Violet and Kate in the twentieth century. Clodd's opinions and arguments are just those that Lavater and Scot used four hundred years ago and those that sceptics employ today.

The one great difference between the two sets of disputants, however, lies in their willingness to engage in argument in the first place. Adherents of the tradition of belief, being always on the defensive, have their reasons ready – rehearsed and polished up through constant use. They have been in the minority since the Reformation and must needs stand up for themselves or be put to shame. Adherents of the tradition of disbelief, on the other hand, are less ready and loquacious as a rule. In the first place, because they are a part of a dominant trend, they need seldom defend their opinions from hostile criticism; in the second place, the arguments for disbelief, being less rehearsed, are less well-known; and thirdly, a dominant trend will attract the person who is unwilling to think about the subject anyway. One who regards a subject as taboo will take refuge in majority opinion, for that is where silence lies.

The greatest taboo, and the greatest silence, is of course reserved for illicit 'delving' into the unknown – for the spiritualism over which Lang and Clodd debated so fiercely.

TABOO: SPIRITUALISM

Unwillingness to elaborate or explain a point of view comes to a head when the conversation turns to spiritualism. Here believers and sceptics alike are reticent: obviously this is an idea which threatens the world-view and principles of both groups and has the strongest taboo placed upon it.

The threat it poses for unbelievers is that it apparently provides dramatic evidence that the world is not as knowable and, so to speak, un-supernatural as they would like it to be. Where their scepticism is worn as a mannerly social garment or as a suit of armour, rather than as a deliberately chosen, reasoned point of view (a respectable way of avoiding thinking about things which might frighten them), then spiritualism presents a challenge they would rather avoid. For believers, spiritualism is threatening because it undermines the very foundation of their beliefs. If the dead can be summoned at will by strangers and have no purpose for their appearance but to answer foolish questions at the whim of a medium, then they cannot be the sort of intuitively apprehended community of carers that present-day believers envisage. Indeed, they must begin to take on some of the qualities of the feared 'ghosts', 'spirits', or 'things in houses'.

Thus we find that sceptics nowadays indulge in contorted sophistries such as, 'I'm R C, you see, and we believe that, yes, spirits do come back, but not in the way spiritualists think. It's not spirits, but *souls* –

"souls will rise again"', and believers back off rapidly and become suddenly conventional, 'I don't know whether one can go *deeper* into it, I think one might get bogged down in spiritualism and that kind of thing – which *I do not* believe in. I don't think one should try to *recall* dead people. I hope nobody tries to bring *me* back when I pop off! Now, seriously though, I don't agree with that *at all*.' For both groups, to 'delve' (as they call it) into the supernatural, deliberately seeking out strange experiences and experimenting with fears and faith, is to court disaster both personal and spiritual. Delving is strictly taboo.

It is almost impossible to persuade a non-believer even to talk about the subject: it obviously makes too fearsome a dent in the deterministic or materialistic armour. For many believers, too, it is a subject best avoided. No doubt there are many who would feel as the clergyman in the following newspaper account (taken from a provincial evening paper) does:

A BOOM FOR GHOSTBUSTERS

More people than ever are seeing ghosts – especially the young and the jobless who try to look into the future – claims church exorcist the Rev Tom Willis of Bridlington. He says one person in 10 will see a supernatural apparition. Mr Willis, who has exorcized hundreds of ghosts in 15 years as official exorcist for the diocese of York added: 'People are turning to spiritualists, tarot cards and Ouija boards – but all they do is stir up restless, often mischievous spirits.'[30]

Again, this strikes me as an entirely traditional point of view. One can see it echoed more elegantly and logically in the detailed exegesis which my informant, Louisa, supplies:

'One thing that used to worry me a little bit was when my son was interested in the tarot cards. He had a set of tarot cards and in periods of depression he would cast them, and I think he firmly believed in them. What I feel about that kind of thing is that there may be some kind of occult influence that is invoked because the reader of the cards and the subject, too, both firmly believe in the influences that are being cast by the cards, and I somehow feel that there may be an interference, a *participation*, of some occult influence.

'Well, after all, they're so *old* and they're *mystic*. The magicians of the last century and the first part of this used to *accept* the tarot card readings – Aleister Crowley and people like that –

and I feel there is an evil influence, not a good one, as I do about lots of spirit happenings.

'I feel they're not influenced at all or originated by human agencies, but by disembodied non-existencies. But I have a strong belief that (I'm choosing my words carefully but I'm not sure "belief" is the right word), but I have a strong *feeling* that we are surrounded by a world that has never been *corporeal*, had physical existence, and that they're *there* and can be invoked by minds that actually *leave gaps* in the defensive armoury for them to get through.'

If this genuinely horrifying thought underlies, or is one of the concepts that underlie, the general reluctance to 'delve', then it is hardly surprising that so many women refuse to think about occult practices, or defensively stress the limited nature of their experience, or turn to humour or introspection when giving accounts of the seances they have actually attended.

In spite of the anxiety the subject evokes and in spite of the fact that all but one of my informants rejected the tenets of spiritualism, a number did say that they had visited a medium at least once in their lives. There are fourteen accounts of such visits in all and, judging by these, the activity seems harmless enough. According to their stories the medium merely discusses the relationship between mother and daughter; makes prosaic predictions about future events or pronouncements about the sitter or the dead relative; diagnoses disease; or says that a dead relative has a (usually trivial) message for the sitter. Nevertheless, the accounts are very defensive ones. Half of them begin with explanations or disclaimers such as:

'Well, talking about the one and only seance I was ever persuaded to go to ... It was just after my mother died. I absolutely adored my mother and I was just in the mood to make any sort of contact.'

'When I lost Miriam I went – as we all do, well, like some of us do – to see a spiritualist.'

'I lost a brother in the War and I went to ... Gosh! I've forgotten what you call them now ... a seance. It was fashionable, I think, after the War, you know.'

Visits to mediums are excused as being a youthful group activity, or an experiment contemplated because of family beliefs or connections, or because seances were a fashion. Speakers stress that they have been only once, or were persuaded to go, or went to please their daughters or aunts. No one confesses to going because she believes in spiritualist doctrine or ceremony.

The stories themselves are often as humorous or cautionary as Hilda's:

Hilda's story

'This is about my aunt, my mother's sister. She went into everything very fully, not cautious and level-headed like my mother. She went and had her spirit guides drawn for her by an artist, a medium. And one of them was a sadistic-looking nun and one was a Red Indian. And she had one of these portraits in each of her bedrooms, and the one in my bedroom was the sadistic-looking nun. And I said, "You can take *that* down, before *I'll* sleep in there!"'

Alternatively, and more interestingly, they may be made into evaluative life-reviews, so that the focus of the account is turned away from the seance and on to the psychology of the sitter. A story told by Margot is a fine example of this type of transmutation. She focuses first on her subjective response to the experience and then uses it to explore the relationship between an invalid mother and the unmarried daughter who cares for her. She begins with a lengthy dissociative introduction: 'No. I once had a most remarkable experience. I went with a gang of girls I worked with in the office at the time, to a *spiritualist's* meeting, which I *don't* go in for at *all*, because I firmly believe that if there are any spirits around, they should be left in peace. I don't want anybody whom I knew or loved sort of *dragged* back to . . .', and then goes on to give a brief account of the seance, again stressing aspects of her attitude that separate her from 'spiritualists'. She says, for example, that, though she did not go intending to 'scoff' at the proceedings, she was in a mood to take precautions against being cheated (such as sitting apart from the friends she had gone with). Thus she establishes her credentials as a 'scientific' observer rather than an involved participant. Next, she stresses aspects of the seance that were unexpected – the 'spiritualist lady' comes in 'very bright and cheerful, not a bit glum or anything'.

These contrasts are the frame for an experience which 'shook me to my foundations first go off'. The medium detects the relatedness of Margot and her friends immediately and announces that there is no way she can reach such an unbeliever, but tells her that she is wholly dominated by her mother and memories of her mother. This account constitutes the first half of her story. The second half then goes into a discussion of her relationship with her mother, and the focus is turned away from the seance experience and on to interpersonal relationships and the ties of love and duty. Thus the nature of both experience and account have been changed, and the taboo has been removed by the application of proper morality. Here, as in the majority of the women's stories about mediums and seances, the illicit nature of the experience is transformed by being shown to be merely another reflection of their morality and philosophy. Like accounts of other supernatural experiences they become stories about relationships, love and caring, and exhibit aspects of larger views about ESP, the healing power of the dead, telepathy and the continued protection of the dead members of the extended family. But the taboo is still there and is never quite removed.

When we go on in the following chapter to look at the women's ideas about ESP and related topics, we shall see a similar taboo operating against deliberate attempts to see into the future. Essentially, in the women's view, encounters with the supernatural should be *unsought*. Any attempt to take the initiative in such matters is to repeat the sin of Adam – to abuse gifts freely given by demanding more; to attempt to usurp the power of God by claiming the right to equal knowledge.

NOTES

1   Glanvil (1681), p. 185.
2   Glanvil (1681), p. 83.
3   Bovet (1951 edn), pp. 138–40.
4   Baxter (1840 edn), p. 44, quoted in full in chapter 6.
5   Baxter (1840 edn), p. 55.
6   Baxter (1840 edn), p. 57.
7   Baxter (1840 edn), p. 99, quoted in full in chapter 6..
8   See the bibliography.
9   Marris, quoted by Gorer (1965), p. 127.
10 Marris (1974), p. 26.
11 Lavater (1929 edn), Author's Preface, unpaginated.
12 This and previous quotations are from Lavater's initial list of contents, unpaginated.
13 Lavater (1929 edn), p. 49.
14 Lavater (1929 edn), p. 53.
15 Lavater (1929 edn), initial contents list, unpaginated.
16 Lavater (1929 edn), Author's Introduction, unpaginated.

17 Lavater (1929 edn), pp. 88–9.
18 Lavater (1929 edn), p. 129.
19 Lavater (1929 edn), p. 160.
20 Hufford (1982b), p. 49. Quoted by permission of the New York Folklore Society and the editor of *New York Folklore*.
21 Ward (1977), pp. 212–13.
22 Ward (1977), pp. 213–17.
23 Clodd (1896).
24 Clodd (1895a).
25 Lang (1895b).
26 Clodd (1895b).
27 Scot (1651 edn), pp. 25–6.
28 Clodd (1896), pp. 37–40.
29 See Dorson, ed. (1968), vol. 2, pp. 458–63.
30 *Manchester Evening News*, 24 February, 1986.

5 ESP and Other Experiences

To say absolutely, that all dreams, without distinction,
are vain Visions and Sports of Nature . . . and to banish
all Divination from the Life of Man . . . is contrary to
Experience and the common Consent and Agreement of Mankind.[1]

JOHN BEAUMONT

HISTORICAL PERSPECTIVES

To control the future, or at least have sufficient foreknowledge of it to
be able to divert the worst effects of time and chance – these are almost
universal aspirations, reflected in a multiplicity of divinatory rituals,
systems and beliefs from medieval times to the present day.

Shakespeare's *Julius Caesar*, for instance, a play which deals with large
events, is also large in prophecies. Apart from the soothsayer's famous
'Beware the Ides of March', Caesar is warned not to go to the senate by
his wife, an augur and by a host of weather effects both natural and
unnatural. When the plot against him begins to thicken, Casca 'with
his sword drawn' enters with Cicero to stage directions specifying
'thunder and lightning', and when Cicero asks him why he is trembling,
he answers in no uncertain terms:

> Are you not moved, when all the sway of earth
> Shakes like a thing unfirm? O Cicero
> I have seen tempests, when the scolding winds
> Have riv'd the knotty oaks; and I have seen
> The ambitious ocean swell, and rage, and foam,
> To be exalted with the threat'ning clouds:
> But never till tonight, never till now,
> Did I go through a tempest dropping fire.
> Either there is civil strife in heaven;
> Or else the world, too saucy with the gods,
> Incenses them to send destruction.
> [. . .]

> A common slave – you know him well by sight –
> Held up his left hand, which did flame and burn
> Like twenty torches join'd; and yet his hand,
> Not sensible of fire, remain'd unscorched.
> Besides – I have not yet put up my sword –
> Against the Capitol I met a lion . . .
> . . . and there were drawn
> Upon a heap a hundred ghastly women,
> Transformed with their fear; who swore they saw
> Men, all in fire, walk up and down the streets,
> And yesterday the bird of night did sit,
> Even at noonday, upon the market-place,
> Hooting and Shrieking.

As if this wasn't warning enough, Caesar's wife Calpurnia reports that:

> A lioness has whelped in the streets;
> And graves have yawn'd and yielded up their dead;
> Fierce, fiery warriors fight upon the clouds,
> In ranks and squadrons and right forms of war,
> Which drizzled blood upon the Capitol;
> The noise of battle hurtled in the air,
> Horses did neigh, and dying men did groan;
> And ghosts did shriek and squeal about the streets.

When Caesar proposes, though not in so many words, that 'a man's got to do what a man's got to do' and that he is above such trifling warnings, Calpurnia objects that though:

> When beggars die there are no comets seen;
> The heavens themselves blaze forth the death of princes

and, very reasonably under the circumstances, persists in her warnings. Eventually, Caesar gives in, telling his advisers that it is to please his wife that he stays at home:

> Calpurnia here, my wife, stays me at home:
> She dreamt tonight she saw my statua
> Which, like a fountain with a hundred spouts,
> Did run pure blood; and many lusty Romans
> Came smiling and did bathe their hands in it:
> And these she does apply for warnings and portents,
> And evils imminent; and on her knee
> Hath begg'd that I will stay at home today.

The traitor, Decius, reassures him that Calpurnia has misinterpreted her dream, and Caesar foolishly prefers Decius' flattering view of the matter. Never was man more extensively advised by human and inhuman intervention to stay at home than Julius Caesar was, yet he persists in his plan and pays the penalty of death by multiple stab wounds.

Similarly, his enemies are warned dramatically against taking up arms. Before the last, fateful battle, Brutus sees the ghost of Caesar who, like a 'fetch', announces that they will meet again 'at Philippi'; and the arch-plotter Cassius receives plentiful omens about the outcome of battle:

> Coming from Sardis, on our former ensign
> Two mighty eagles fell: and there they perch'd
> Gorging and feeding from our soldiers' hands;
> Who to Philippi here escorted us:
> This morning they are fled away and gone;
> And in their steads do ravens, crows and kites
> Fly o'er our heads, and downward look on us,
> As we were sickly prey: their shadows seem
> A canopy most fatal, under which
> Our army lies, ready to give up the ghost.

Well might the dramatis personae of this play – no doubt like the audience who watched it – feel that:

> ... When these prodigies
> Do so conjointly meet, let not men say,
> 'These are their reasons, – they are natural';
> For I believe they are portentous things
> Unto the climate that they point upon.

Shakespeare, of course, is an excellent source for contemporary belief, so much was he in tune with the folklore of the age (as well as much indebted to it for both plots and dramatic effects).

According to Fr Taillepied writing in France about eleven years earlier, political traumas are always thus presaged by various signs and wonders (Cicero, he says, called them 'ostenta', 'portenta', 'monstra' and 'prodiga'), unfavourable omens in warfare are commonplace, and thieves may be detected by the fact that, if they spill wine on the table at dinner, it will seep through the wood rather than run off it. 'There is no one who reads this', he says, in phrases which echo the rhetoric of the 'tradition of belief' very closely, 'who cannot readily remember similar omens and forewarnings which have befallen either himself or his friends, or which he has been told of by trustworthy and intelligent persons.'[2]

Similarly, the sceptic and Reformer, Ludowig Lavater, prefaces chapter 17 of his *Of Ghostes and Spirites Walking by Nyghte* with the remark: 'That there happen straunge wonders and prognostications, and that sodeyn noises and cracks and suchlike, are hearde before some notable alterations and chaunges.'[3] He is able to quote extensively from the classics and contemporary folk traditions to prove it:

divers times it cometh to passe, that when some of our acquaintance or friends lye a dying, albeit they are many miles off, yet there are some great stirrings or noises hearde. Sometimes we thinke the house will fall on our heads, or that some massie and waightie thing falleth down throughout all the house, rendring and making a disordered noise: and shortlie within a few months after, we understande that those things happened, the very same houre that our friends departed in. There be some men, of whose stocke none doth dye, but that they observe and marke some signs and tokens going before: as that they heare the dores and windowes open and shut, that something runneth up the staires, or walketh up and downe the house, or doth some one or other suchlike thing [. . .] In Abbeys, the Monks servants or any other falling sicke, many have hearde in the night, preparations of chests for them, in such sorte as the coffinmakers did afterwardes prepare in deede.

In some country villages, when one is at deaths dore, many times there are heard in the Evening, or in the night, digging a grave in the Churcheyarde, and the same next day is so found digged, as these men did heare before.

There have bin seene some in the night when the moone shined, going solemnlie with the corps, according to the custome of the people, or standing before the dores, as if some bodie were to be carried to the Church to burying. Many suppose, they see their owne image, or as they saye, theyr owne soule, and of them divers are verily persuaded, that except they dye shortlie after they have seene them selves, they shall live a very great time after. But these things are superstitious. Let every man so prepare himselfe, as if he shoulde dye tomorrowe, lest by being too secure, he purchase himselfe harme.[4]

Lavater's chapter 17 is a superb list of ómens of death which, judging by his comments, are still an active part of the folklore of the time. He also reports details of how murder-victims bleed afresh when their murderer approaches them, the occurrence of 'sympathetic weather' before coups and treachery, phantom armies being seen and heard before the outbreak of war (facts which he attests to by extensive reference to Roman history), and the appearance of wraiths as announcing their own death – believing them all to be 'forewarnings sent by God'.

A hundred years later most of this elaborate structure was still intact, as we can see by reference to the list of 'portents' and 'omens', which the antiquary and folklorist, John Aubrey, amasses in chapters 3 and 4 of his *Miscellanies* of 1696. These are accounts of current rumours, contemporary legends and personal experiences. On 1 May, at Broadchalk in Wiltshire, he says, his mother observed a strange celestial phenomenon when 'going to see what a clock it was by a horizontal dial'[5] and 'the next remarkable thing that followed' was the imprisonment of King Charles on the Isle of Wight, which 'lieth directly from Broadchalk, at the x a clock point'. Indeed, Charles I's death seems to have been almost as extensively prefigured as Julius Caesar's, for Aubrey also notes that when he was:

a Freshman at Oxford, 1642, I was wont to go to Christ-Church to see King Charles I at supper: where I once heard him say, 'That as he was Hawking in Scotland, he rode into the Quarry and found the Covey of Partridges falling upon the Hawk': and I do remember this expression farther, viz, and I will swear upon the Book 'tis true. When I came to my Chamber, I told this story to my Tutor: said he, 'That Covey was London'.[6]

As if this was not enough, Aubrey reports that an ineradicable bloodstain dropped from a bird's breast on to a bust of the King, and that it is 'well-known' that at his trial the top of his staff fell off. James II led a similarly omen-full life, if we are to believe Aubrey, and there are many instances of thunder, lightning, storms and prodigies to presage the fate of other unpopular or insecure monarchs.

Perhaps the best accounts of omens and second-sightedness as construed by people of the middle and late years of the seventeenth century, however, are to be found in Robert Kirk's *The Secret Commonwealth*, probably written in 1691, and in Richard Baxter's *The Certainty of the World of Spirits Fully Evinced*, also of 1691 but containing material from earlier decades. We are indebted to Kirk for a very full account of the phenomenon of second sight. Kirk's belief was that such powers afforded to men (though not often to women!) the capacity to see ghosts, fairies and wraiths of various sorts, and that 'these forecasting invisible People among us'[7] forewarned them of death and disaster. *The Secret Commonwealth* is a great source of contemporary local legends and beliefs, including three particularly delightful stories. In the first of these a man enters an inn and is told by a seer that he will die in three days' time. In anger, he kills the seer, and two days later he is hung for his murder. In the second story, a minister and a seer are walking down a narrow lane when the seer tells the minister to stand aside for a moment or two. The minister refuses, for he can see no reason to do so.

Both men are knocked over by an invisible force and the minister is lamed. After they have carried him home, someone comes to toll the knell for a parishioner who has suddenly died. It was, of course, his phantom, rushing from his body, that they had encountered in the lane. In the third story, a seer is sitting down to a meal when he abruptly ducks his head to one side. He explains that a friend of his in Ireland has just at that minute threatened to throw a dish of butter in his face. Of course, they check this preposterous information, and, sure enough, they find that it is true. The Irish friend has indeed made such a threat in order to test whether the seer is capable of receiving his message.

Elsewhere in *The Secret Commonwealth*, Kirk copies out a letter from Lord Tarbett to Robert Boyle, which gives an excellent flavour of beliefs about second sight in Scotland. This letter makes it plain that it is thought to be very common especially in the Highlands and Islands. The examples he gives are surprisingly homely for the period. From his own personal experience, he recalls that his servant on one occasion warned him not to enter a certain inn because he had just 'seen' a coffin coming out of it. During their stay, the innkeeper has an apoplectic fit and dies. In another personal experience story, a second-sighted man sees armies coming through a field of barley which has not yet been sown. Elsewhere, seers predict a young lady's marriage and subsequent widowhood, that a man will have his legs broken, and the death of a man with an arrow in his thigh. In this last story, the supposed victim dies without suffering from an arrow wound, but there is a disturbance at his funeral, during which shots are fired and an arrow pierces his thigh. An account in Martin Martin's *Description of the Western Isles of Scotland* (quoted extensively in John Beaumont's *An Historical ... Treatise of Spirits*) substantiates this homely picture. Omens of death include death howls, wraiths and smells of fish or meat emanating from the fire (by this account, children, horses and cows are particularly prone to such visions).

To Richard Baxter we are indebted for some fascinating letters about contemporary death-tokens in Wales. These include corpse-candles, phantom-fires and sightings of the wraiths of those about to die. According to Baxter's correspondent, John Lewis, 'dead men's candles' are particularly common omens of death. These were flickers of marsh gas like will-o'-the-wisps, which were particularly common in church-yards at that time, owing to sloppy burial practices which left gaseous rotting corpses half-buried or half-exhumed. These lights, rising up round a funeral party going to bury a newly dead person, were thought to pre-figure an imminent death among the mourners (the Tan-wed, which another correspondent also refers to later, is a similar phenomenon).

John Lewis writes that: 'It is ordinary in most of our counties, that I never scarce heard of any sort, young or old, but this is seen before death, and often observed to part from the very bodies of the persons all along the way to the place of burial, and infallibly death will ensure [sic].'[8]

Likewise John Davies of Generglyn tells Baxter that corpse-candles:

are common in these three counties, Cardigan, Camarthen and Pembrook, and, as I hear, in some other parts of Wales [. . .] If it be a little candle, pale, or blueish, then follows the corpse either of an abortive, or some infant; if a big one, then the corpse of someone come to age; if there be seen two or three, or more, some big, some small, together, then so many, and such corpses together; if two candles come from diverse places, and be seen to meet, the corpses will be the like; if some of these candles be seen to turn a little out of the way, or path, that leadeth unto the church, the following corpse will be found to turn in that very place, for the avoiding of some dirty lane, or plash, etc. [. . .]

Another kind of apparition we have, which commonly we call Tan-we, or Tan-wed, because it seemeth fiery. These before their decease, do fall upon freeholders' lands, and you shall scarce bury any with us, be he but a lord of a house and garden, but you shall find someone at his burial . . . that had seen this fire to fall on some part of his lands. Two of these, at several times, I have seen myself [. . .]

Sir, so many of these evidences, as I saw not myself, I received from understanding and credible persons and such as would not lie, no, not for a benefice; and yourself may receive the same from me, as from one that was never too credulous, nothing superstitious, and as little ceremonious.[9]

The eighteenth century, for all its supposed enlightenment and rationalism, was hardly less influenced by the desire to predict death and foretell the future, though interest began (at least in public) to be confined to the poorer and less well-educated classes. Mary Beer's *Prophetical Warnings* and Robert Nixon's *Cheshire Prophecies* were particularly popular, the latter running to twenty-one editions before 1745 and remaining in print until 1878. Twelve books and chapbooks of 'Mother Shipton's' prophecies were published between 1715 and 1795, and Ebenezer Shipley's publications on occult science and fortunetelling were almost as popular. Shipley wrote seven titles between 1784 and 1795, of which *A Key to Physic and the Occult Sciences* and *A Complete Illustration of the Celestial Science of Astrology* seem to have been the most popular, the former (a combination of astrology and herbal remedies) running to six editions between 1794 and 1814, and the latter (with the later revised 'new' edition) also appearing six times within the space of only six years. Neither should we forget that the seventeenth-century astrologer, William Lilly, remained popular throughout the period, three reprints of his *Life and Times* being produced between 1715 and 1774, and that the famous *Old Moore's Almanack* (which first appeared as a broadsheet, 'Vox Stellarum', in 1697) steadily increased in size and circulation throughout the eighteenth century.

Further evidence of the widespread appeal of divination, dreams and prophecies may be found in the fact that John Abercrombie's very popular *An Enquiry Concerning the Intellectual Powers and the Investigation of Truth* (*par excellence* a rationalist overview of popular supernatural ideas) devotes a whole chapter to dismissing cases of precognitive dreaming. Abercrombie relates some of the best-known accounts of his day and explains them away with elegant, though elaborate, logic: 'A gentleman sitting by the fire on a stormy night, and anxious about some of his domestics who are at sea in a boat, drops asleep for a few seconds, dreams very naturally of drowning men, and starts up with an exclamation that his boat is lost. If the boat returns in safety the vision is no more thought of. If it is lost, as is very likely to happen, the story passes for second sight.'[10]

Elsewhere antiquarians such as Francis Grose list 'Corpse-candles – Second sight', 'Omens – Things lucky and Unlucky' and 'Superstitious methods of obtaining Knowledge of Future Events' among their collections of 'Popular Superstitions'. As omens of death, Grose is able to compile a three-page inventory, which includes items such as:

- hearing screech owls
- hearing three knocks at the bed's head
- having a bleeding nose
- rats gnawing the hangings
- the breaking of a looking-glass
- coffin-shaped coals leaping from the fire
- seeing a 'winding-sheet' on a candle
- corpse-candles
- tan-wed
- the tick of the death-watch beetle.

He also has three rather more macabre popular prophecies – if rigor mortis is late setting in on a corpse, then another death is to follow; a child who does not cry at the christening is not long for this world; those who marry early die young.

Over time, the content of these omens remains fairly constant. Visions such as apparitions and wraiths keep number one place as omens of death, for example, followed closely by noises of various sorts (especially bangs and creaks round the house), mysterious lights, fires in the sky, ordinary things perceived in extraordinary situations (night birds seen during the day, footsteps heard where no foot passes, unaccustomed breakages) and other upsets to the natural order of things. It is worthwhile noting, too, that what we nowadays call 'telepathy' and 'astrology' are neither of them modern ideas. Astrology is an extremely ancient form of divination; telepathy, often called 'sympathy', is one of Grose's 'Popular Superstitions' and receives attention in earlier writing, too, notably Balthasar Bekker's *The World Bewitched* (1691), where he advocates a strikingly modern theory that such occurrences are caused by bodily 'emanations' attracted to each other by love.

However, as time goes by, the accounts of 'sympathy', or 'fore-warnings', become a little less dramatic, the range of tokens a little more restricted, the omens themselves imbued with a rather more homely character. This is exactly the same development as we find in traditions about ghosts and revenants (see chapter 6). From the late sixteenth century onwards, belief in the supernatural is subject to attack from the political, religious and intellectual establishments, gradually becoming so unfashionable that it is, in a literal sense, almost un*think*able. Writing in 1676, Joseph Glanvil puts this well when he discusses the decline of belief in witches which was taking place (to his regret) in the England of his day: 'those that deny the being of witches, do it not out of ignorance of those Heads of Argument of which they have probably heard a thousand times; But from an Apprehension that such a belief is absurd, and the thing impossible'.[11] The 'Heads of Argument' remained (and remain) the same: 'there *must* be something on the other side'; there 'must be other intelligent Beings other than those who are clad in heavy Earth or Clay';[12] it is 'the common consent and agreement of Mankind' that these things exist and happen; to deny them is 'contrary to ex-perience'; reliable witnesses (intelligent, trustworthy, honest people all of them) vouch for their truth; to say 'These are their reasons – they are natural' is simply not a convincing enough explanation. As Glanvil says, everyone is familiar with these arguments and they might recognize the strength of this traditional reasoning *were they ever to consider it dispas-sionately*. But that, they do not (and perhaps cannot) do. Intellectual fashion since the Reformation has become so strongly set against supernatural beliefs that gut reactions are that such things are 'absurd' or 'impossible' – unthinkable.

It is a tribute to the staying power of tradition that belief in supernatural entities and effects ever survived the onslaught of changing philosophical fashion. But it has reacted to attempts to destroy it like elastic, stretching and thinning out rather than letting itself be severed completely; and it has responded to being banished from thought by lodging in feeling. Thus in the nineteenth and twentieth centuries, we see three interlinked processes at work: the survival of the more extravagant belief-traditions in legends and literature (which, nevertheless, continue to function as a reservoir of concepts and examples); the toning down of orally transmitted lore, so that there are fewer, less baroque omens confined to homelier contexts and less portentous outcomes; and the internalizing of the experiences, so that 'feelings' and 'dreams' dominate the phenomenology of forewarning, rather than the monsters and prodigies of the pre-scientific age.

By the mid-nineteenth century, therefore, there were two main strands in popular and folkloristic writing about foreknowledge. On the one hand, antiquarian William Hone was able to list fifty-three separate types of divinatory ritual in only two pages of *The Year Book* of 1832; on the other hand, George Lawrence Gomme, president of the Folklore Society from 1890 to 1894, in his selection *English Traditions and Foreign Customs* taken from the pages of the *Gentleman's Magazine*, included a fat section on 'prophecies and dreams' from the years 1751 to 1820. Similarly, collectors of out-of-the-way information like Robert Chambers could compile a familiar list of death-tokens (including a reference to the ominous quality of the late onset of rigor mortis, 'winding-sheets' on candles, 'coffins' in the coals and the ill-effects of burying a body on Sunday or failing to take the Christmas decorations down before Candlemas) and devote six columns to 'the folklore of playing-cards', but at the same time give five-and-a-half columns to the experience which he called 'mystic memory' and which we would call '*déjà vu*'. Likewise in 1866, William Henderson, one of the best-known collectors of regional folklore, compiled a list of death omens, which plainly contained up-to-date information (hallucinatory calls, the grip of a dead hand, deformed lambs, hens laying an all-female brood), as well as older items such as the tick of the death-watch beetle or the noise of the house falling down; and that indefatigable picker-up of unconsidered psychic trifles, Catherine Crowe, collected in 1848 seventeen narratives about 'prophetic dreams', both legends and personal experiences, and thirty-five pages of accounts of 'double dreaming and trances', i.e. telepathic dreams and ESP experiences. Elsewhere, however, other influential compilations of supernatural legends give an equal or greater amount of space to dreaming. Robert Dale Owen, for example, devoted sixty-nine pages of his *Footfalls on the Boundary of Another World* (1861) to the subject; Frederick George Lee, DD, in book one chapter 5 of *The Other World* (1875) assembled seventeen accounts of dream-warnings, three of 'presentiments' and six of second-sight, alongside his fifteen accounts of omens preceding the deaths of kings and other public figures. Lee's later *Glimpses in the Twilight* (1885) gave two whole chapters to the subject, chapter 2 dealing with 'warnings of danger or death, by dream or otherwise', and chapter 4 with 'remarkable dreams and supernatural occurrences'.

Naturally, not all of this information is 'folklore', as we should define it today, nor is it all contemporary material, but it does give good guidance about what was considered to be believable, interesting and topical at that time. Dale Owen and Lee, for example, had a particular axe to grind, using (as so often writers before them had used) accounts of supernatural intervention as weapons against what they saw as the increasing atheism and materialism of their age. In a propaganda war such as this, incredible, irrelevant material out of step with current attitudes and assumptions would serve no useful purpose. Indeed, these writers were popular and influential, continuing in print for many years – a sure sign that they were (even if unintentionally) attuned to contemporary popular beliefs.

Two avenues into the future seem, then, to have been thought worth exploring in the nineteenth century – on the one hand, omens of death and divinatory practices designed to discover one's personal fate; on the other hand, prophetic or telepathic experiences in dreams and visions. In compiling *The Handbook of Folklore* (1890), one of the fullest and most penetrating field-manuals of the day, Gomme spent a chapter on 'magic and divination', explaining that 'the methods employed in divination are very numerous, and the results perfectly fortuitous', but nevertheless instructing folklore fieldworkers to inquire 'What methods are employed for divining future events?' and 'What omens are believed in?' Gomme listed the types of possible answer thus:

The future is divined in dreams; by the entrails of animals; by the flight of birds; by the sight of various animals of a lucky or unlucky character; by single combat; by throwing chips, stones, wreaths, molten lead, etc. into water to see what sort of ripples they make, to observe whether they sink or swim, or what curious shapes the water assumes; by casting lots; by shooting arrows; by spinning a coconut, a teetotum or a knife; by a shoulderblade; by means of a magic drum, a sieve or a key and a Bible; by pulling petals off a flower and speaking certain words each time a petal is removed; by the growth or death of a tree specially planted for the purpose; by the stars, etc. etc.[13]

Obviously much of this curious list was drawn from the anthropological literature so popular with folklorists of the late nineteenth and early twentieth centuries: it is hard to think that single combat was common in English villages in 1890, or that town dwellers had much access to teetotums, magic drums or the entrails of animals. Undoubtedly, some of the less exotic divinations were commonplace, however. Lucky and unlucky animals are obvious examples. There are still people who think that whatever you are doing when you hear the first cuckoo of spring, you will continue to do for the rest of the year; there are others who ritually say 'rabbits, rabbits' on the first day of every month; and others who remember having to say 'Good morning, Mr Sheep' to the first lamb of the year. Children and young people still de-petal flowers reciting 'he loves me, he loves me not' and spin paper discs to find their future fate. Legends tell, too, of the comic outcomes of exploits with Bible and key.

Belief in omens was obviously very widespread in earlier days and took its impetus from a wide range of peculiar occurrences and situations, combined with the universal desire to impose order on the unruliness of the present and to discover the vagaries of the future. In writing *The Handbook of Folklore* (1914), Charlotte Burne, the first woman president of the Folklore Society, wrote thus on the subject of omens and divination:

No unexpected or unusual occurrence is too trivial to be the subject of an Omen. Mysterious sounds, knocks, bells; accidents to inanimate objects, as implements, tools, pictures ... personal accidents or sensations, shivering, tingling, stumbling, cries, or actions of birds and beasts, wild or domestic; dreams; unusual appearances in the fire or the heavens ... unaccountable events, such as flowers or fruit-trees blossoming out of season, or a space omitted in sowing a crop; or any thing, person or animal, seen or encountered at the New Year, or on beginning a journey or any other enterprise; all these are everywhere liable to be taken as Omens.[14]

In her earlier *Shropshire Folklore* of 1883, Burne had given a paragraph of examples, which might be called 'the folklore of bread':

Omens are drawn from the appearance of the bread after baking. If four loaves adhere together on being taken out of the oven, it is a sign of a wedding; if five of a funeral (Clee Hills). A loaf which turns over as it rises in baking is a sign of a wedding (North West Shropshire). A Staffordshire cook informs me that a cake she made shortly before Miss A—'s wedding rose in the oven till it nearly tumbled over! If a loaf parts in two when one is in the act of cutting it, it is a sign of a parting. In January, 1879, an inquest was held at Prior's Lee (in the colliery district) on the body of a woman named Ann Woolley, who had been found drowned. Her husband stated that on the day of her death she had been baking, and during her absence on an errand he went to take the bread out of the oven, when he found 'one of the loaves cracked right across', and immediately knew that something had happened to his wife. This 'caused him to go and look for her', and he found her drowned in a pool not far from the house, into which she seemed to have fallen accidentally.[15]

The second strand of tradition – dreams and visions – though never entirely distinct from belief in omens and portents, began to have its chief expression through the concept of second-sightedness. One of the fullest and clearest descriptions of this old idea as it was conceived of from the eighteenth century onwards is, by good chance, supplied in the elegant language of no less a person than Dr Johnson. He writes that it is:

an impression made either by the mind upon the eye, or by the eye upon the mind, by which things distant or future are perceived and seen as if they were present. A man on a journey, far from home, falls from his horse; another, who is perhaps at work about the house, sees him bleeding on the ground, commonly with a landscape of the place where the accident befalls him. Another seer, driving home his cattle, or wandering in idleness, or musing in the sunshine, is suddenly surprised by the appearance of a bridal ceremony, or a funeral procession, and counts the mourners or attendants, of whom, if he knows them, he relates the names, if he knows them not, he can describe the dresses. Things distant are seen at the instant when they happen ... This receptive faculty (for power it cannot be called) is neither voluntary nor constant. The appearances have no dependence upon choice: they cannot be summoned, detained, or recalled, the impression is sudden, and the effect often painful.[16]

These two dominant strands of tradition about encounters with the future may still be plainly seen in the folklore of the twentieth century.

FOREKNOWLEDGE TODAY

Today, belief in foreknowledge flourishes unabated, though transmuted by modern needs and conditions. Very large numbers of the women I interviewed have considerable interest in fortunes and divination: most confess to having visited a fortuneteller at some time in their life; nearly all of them read their horoscopes in the evening papers to see what might befall them the following day; and a few say they have seen signs or tokens of coming disasters. Likewise, the visionary type of encounter persists in their stereotype of E S P, though the term 'premonition' now replaces the older 'presentiment' in their vocabulary, and references to 'telepathy' and 'being psychic' outnumber references to dreams and second-sight.

Clearly, belief in the possibility of foreknowledge is a vivid part of their mental furniture. Their conversation is full of vague generalizations, references to their mothers' opinions and to what 'they' or 'people' think ('You *hear* people *say* these things', 'They do *say* that', 'There *are* people *like* that') and so on, which strongly suggest that the topic is often talked over within the family and social circle. Another indication that these matters are part of a vivid dialogue of contemporary belief is that there exist well-established counter-arguments – the equivalent to the rhetoric of disbelief we looked at earlier. As far as fortunetelling is concerned, these take the form of arguing that any correspondence between prediction and outcome is coincidence, or that recourse to a clairvoyant is merely superstitious or irrelevant because the future is 'in the Maker's hands' or, most commonly, a neat argument that the skill of the clairvoyant lies more in her ability to 'react to your reactions' than to any genuine psychic powers. As Ada says:

> 'Well, I mean, if you go and have your hand read like I used to do when I was young . . . I *mean*, if you *think* about it afterwards, they ask you questions in such a roundabout way, and by the time you come out, you think to yourself, "I've gone and told her all she wanted to *know*! She didn't read my hand: I was *telling* her what to read in my hand!"
>
> 'Well, *really*! When you're sat on the train coming home, you think to yourself, "WELL! *She* hasn't read my hand. I've read it to *her*!"'

When the women move on to discuss omens and premonitions, the ready-made counter-arguments are more numerous. Apart from obvious objections such as that such beliefs are superstitious, open to religious objections, and, being based on chance coincidences, deceptive, the women assert that such notions are 'fanciful', or 'sheer imagination', or use other such generalized rebuttals. In addition, they employ sophisticated arguments which counter belief in detail as well as substance. Such strange feelings and mood changes are 'really' due to a variety of natural causes – unconscious anxiety, low spirits, poor health, atmospheric conditions. Precognitive dreams are explained very much in the way that Abercrombie explained them in 1830, as chance re-shapings of the previous day's events (and thus in no *need* of explanation, supernatural or otherwise). Similarly, states of unease and the utterance of involuntary thoughts cannot be due to psychic powers, but are merely the natural working out of observations and impressions unconsciously acquired over the course of time. All the evidence thus points to there being an established folklore about forewarnings, which is subject to the sort of discussion, scrutiny and debate that keeps the traditions in the forefront of conversation, and thereby ensures that they are not only kept alive, but are also continuously updated.

The patterns of belief are, as always, most clearly seen in the stories which people tell about their own experiences. For example, the story below is an account of a typical visit to a fortuneteller:

Stella's story

'I once had my *fortune told* and it *has come true*. Yes, yes, it has – because, I was only young but she said I wouldn't have any children. And I was passionately fond of children. I said it was *ridiculous*. I said she was a liar. It was STUPID to say that, for it's TRUE you see.

'And all the time I kept saying to my mother after this, "She said I wouldn't have children. It's RIDICULOUS, isn't it?" And she said, "Oh, yes, it is!" But, you see, I never did. So you see, there was something *in* that.

'And she told me at the *time* that I was courting or had a boyfriend, and she said she could see a ring but she didn't think it was a wedding ring, and then there was no ring. WELL! I couldn't believe *this* EITHER!

'And when I did get engaged, the friend I'd been with said, "Oh, what did she mean? You'd get a ring but not get another ring?" And I said, "Oh, it's a lot of nonsense!"

'And when I was engaged, I broke it off and married this other fellow. So there it is: that's all I can tell you.'

Judging by the women's accounts, palmistry and tea-leaf reading seem to be the most common methods employed by professional fortunetellers, though many, like Stella, concentrate on the message they are given rather than on the details of how the predictions were arrived at. As in this account, marriage, engagements and domestic arrangements are the stock-in-trade of such prognostications, though money matters often figure large, too.

A story of this type involves the ubiquitous horoscope:

Norah's story

'I read my horoscope but it's just like water off a duck's back, isn't it? I don't *believe* in it, really. Because once my horoscope told me that I should buy some Premium Bonds, and I went out and *bought them*! and they've never won YET!

'Yes, I remember reading it and it said something about buying some Premium Bonds, and I went out and bought some LIKE A LUNATIC! And I just went OUT and bought this five pounds' worth of PREMIUM BONDS, but I never *won*!

'So I don't think I'll believe in it AGAIN!'

Elsewhere women tell of having their charts read to ascertain their character:

Dorothy's story

'I did once send up, I think it was to *Katrina*, and foolishly sent some money for a horoscope. It was about twenty pages long and it only told me what I knew myself.

'I'm very aware of my faults and shortcomings – it *was* rather rubbing it in!'

Other stories feature traditional omens of death. In one of these, the speaker hears a banging noise in the bedroom furniture; and in another, the narrator sees the 'Angel of Death'.

Norma's story

'I always remember before my husband died . . . I had a chest-of-drawers quite close to my bed, and there was such a BANG in it. You know, funny noise, not like a creaking like you get from . . . A BANGING as though something was HIT. And it was about a *fortnight* after that my *husband* died, and I've always ASSOCIATED it.'

Rose's story

'And I'll tell you another peculiar thing.

'Auntie Edie, when she died, she went to stay with her *son* for the last few months. And we went up on the Saturday, in January 71, and ... Poor thing! Bernard, her son, met us at the station at Ludford and took us to Chesney. And I said, "How's Aunty Edie?" and he said, "She's not too good, Rose," he said. "We think she's sort of gone into a coma." So I said, "Oh has she?" and he said, "Yes."

'ANYWAY, we got in and we went up to see her and she was lay on the bed this way ... And there's one window *there* so that was the only source of light apart from the door – and with her face turned to the light. I went up and looked at her, and she wasn't saying anything. She was laid there so peacefully, half-gazing at the light. So whether there was any sight in the eye, I don't know.

'ANYWAY, "I can't do with this!" I said (Oh, God! I'd been the week before and done all the cleaning up and taken the Christmas decorations down for them, because they'd no time to do anything. And I'd come *again* to sort of tidy up for Bernard and Joyce – that's the son and daughter-in-law) –

'So I said, "*I* know what I'll *do*! I'll take Patch" – that's the dog, or is it "Butch"? – "I'll take her out for a walk. We'll go for a *walk*. I'll go upstairs first and spend a penny."

'SO ... You go up the stairs like THIS, you see, and *there's* the bathroom and the toilet. NOW, THAT'S Aunty Edie's bedroom, *that's* Bernard's room, and *that's* the spare room ...

'SOME, NOT ME. I'M not having the *door* shut, am I? OH, NO. *I'm* having the door *open*! So, I'm sitting there like this, doing a *wee*, you see. And MY CLOAKED FIGURE went past. WELL, I just *literally* FROZE! I said, "It's AGES and AGES since I saw *that*!"'

[G.B.: 'A particular thing that you regularly saw?']

'YEAH! And I just LOOKED! MY GOD! The ANGEL OF DEATH! It *had to be*!

'So I went down, "Come on, dog. Let's go for a walk." I was right you know. That thing, it never came downstairs. It stayed there all afternoon, that did. My husband said to me at dinner-time, "What's the matter?" I said, "Don't worry, it'll keep. It'll keep." Well, sometimes these things are very frightening.'

*

Elsewhere, in narratives and conversation, the women tell of hearing the sound of a brick hitting against the house-wall, of a broken looking-glass, of the persistent smell of lilacs in the house, and the appearance of apparitions and other ominous figures as preceding death or serious accident in the family.

The second, visionary, strand of tradition is represented by stories about premonitions, telepathy and vague 'feelings' of unease, which are justified by the ensuing events. Sometimes these refer to happy events, as in Inez's story:

Inez's story

'Well the only personal experience I have had . . . One day, in the office, I was going past one of the girls – not a *young* girl – and I knew nothing about her personal life except that she lived with her parents and was very good to them, very devoted. And, as I passed by her, I turned round to her and I said, "RITA, SOMEONE'S GOING TO ASK YOU TO MARRY HIM!" I FELT the –

'And then, the next day, she came in and said the man next door, a widower, had asked her to marry him. And they got *engaged*.

'And that's the only thing I know of *personally*.'

On the majority of occasions, of course, the foreknowledge is of tragic events:

Iris's story

'Well, I think I believe that. One particular occasion was Mrs Robertson.'

[IRIS'S MOTHER: 'Yes, the doctor's wife.']

'Well, you know, she was in hospital, going in to have her *hip* done. And when the matron came down the ward, she came to her bed, and Mrs Robertson turned round and said to her, "You've no need to tell me. It's my husband. He's *died*."

'And he was *killed*, he had a coronary on the road.

'And she *did*, she *turned round* and said, "You've no need to tell me. I know it's my *husband* and he's *died*." And he'd just collapsed at the wheel, veered to the side.

'And THAT's the only one that I've *known*.'

So it is that many of the old concepts and ideas are still a part of present-day folklore, and that at least two strands of tradition have survived in modern thinking about knowledge of the future. On the one hand, various conventional ways of discovering what is to happen through reading signs in the material world; and on the other hand, subjective feelings, dreams and visions about the future. What is particularly interesting, however, when we look more closely at modern thinking, is that nowadays, it seems, people no longer make quite the same distinctions between the various types of forewarning as they did in the past. Whereas in the past, unless the folklorists and antiquarians who tell us of these traditions were mistaken or imposed their own, inappropriate, classification system on the material they collected (which is always possible), omens would have been classed with fortunetelling, divination and augury, and regarded as slightly different from second-sight. Nowadays it seems that seeing omens of doom and danger has crossed the divide and come to be regarded as another example of powers of ESP. Folklorists, however, have yet to catch up with this change of attitude.

The folklorist's conventional way of thinking of traditions of forewarning still groups omens with forms of divination on the grounds that all involve the interpretation of some material sign or other. An astrologer reads the stars, a seaside fortuneteller examines lines on the hands of her customer, 'sensitives' study the faces or intimate possessions of those they seek to understand or whose future they want to predict, women tell their fates in their teacups, young men cast the tarot cards, and so on. All these skills rely on the ability of the practitioner to read signs correctly. On the other hand, premonitions are 'signals' rather than 'signs' – subjective states of mind which 'mean' what they mean because they are directly caused by the events rather than related only indirectly to them by virtue of conventional symbolism. On this classification, 'omens' clearly fit into the first grouping, for they are objective happenings or appearances that predict events, as it were by proxy, because someone is there to say (as Shakespeare's Cicero does in *Julius Caesar*) 'I believe they are portentous things', and to interpret accurately what it *is* that they portend.

We can see, however, that the women interviewed for this study do not themselves make these sorts of distinctions. For example, accounts of perceiving signs were often given in response to questions about 'premonitions'; visionary perceptions, disembodied voices, mysterious noises round the house, all of which consistently appear in folklore collections as 'omens of death', were often cited as instances of 'premonitions'. Elsewhere, even more confusingly, they might crop up as signs which an amateur fortuneteller 'delving' into the future sees in someone's cup or hand. Conversely, the clearest account of what a folklorist would call a 'premonition' (i.e. a precognitive intuition or signal) was given as an 'omen' of a death. Clearly, the two terms are used to a large extent interchangeably.

To muddle the conventional classification further, the women might speak of fortunetellers having 'a telepathy with the future', or give two accounts of a single experience, the first time as an example of 'being on the same wavelength' as someone else, the second time calling it a 'premonition'; or they might describe what are clearly precognitive visions or *déjà vu* experiences as 'telepathy'. Stories of telepathy, too, tell of the same sorts of occurrences, feature the same range of dramatis personae (the narrator and her family and friends), focus on a similar range of accidents, injuries, deaths and (to a lesser extent) marriages, and rely alike on the twin concepts of intuition and communication.

Plainly omens, premonitions and telepathy are all seen as instances of ESP and are grouped together under the umbrella of that popular concept without troubling too much about their exact status or nature. Where they are differentiated, it is by virtue of the gravity of the outcome. Forewarnings about really bad things tend to be termed 'omens'; warnings about lesser events, 'premonitions'; and advanced information about happy or trivial or undisturbing things, 'telepathy'. Experiences such as these are very extensively believed to be both real and valuable. 77 per cent of those interviewed have some measure of belief in premonitions; 67 per cent believe that telepathy is possible; and 55 per cent think it is possible to receive an 'omen' of death and disaster. Many of the women claim to be 'a little bit psychic' and even more say they can sometimes 'get on the same wavelength' as some other person. These are also very popular subjects for discussion, eliciting the readiest, fullest responses and many stories (just under one-third of the total number of narratives were devoted to telling personal experiences of ESP).

The women are far less willing to believe that more formal means of viewing the future are efficacious, however. Only 27 per cent think that horoscopes are at all useful, and only 24 per cent believe in palmistry, tea-leaf reading or other means of divination; there is also far less conversation on these subjects, a much greater tendency to dismiss the idea with a laugh, and only sixteen stories, of which two are designed to show how wrong the predictions were and six of which show the practices in more sinister light. It seems strange that women should make the sharp distinction between some aspects of traditions of foreknowledge and others – on the one hand, apparently regarding the possession of psychic powers by lay people like themselves as genuine and valuable; on the other hand, seeming to regard professionals' claims to psychic abilities as either spurious or dangerous.

The solution to this riddle can be worked out when one looks at their conversation and narratives on the topics in more detail.

From the content of the stories, the way they are told, and the throwaway remarks the women offer about other people's experiences, we can piece together the clues which help explain these sharp divergences of attitude, and also see how individuals adapt traditional ideas to their own values and needs.

Stories about omens, premonitions and telepathy typically feature ordinary women who, while engaged in their ordinary routine about the home or the office, suddenly 'feel' or 'know' that 'something's going to happen', or perhaps see or hear something unusual and unaccountable. After a short time, three days or three weeks, someone dies or has an accident or is admitted to hospital or gets married – just as was foreseen. The storytellers invariably are precise about places and times and persons, giving the sort of detail and specificity that shows they are serious about being believed. Almost always the scene is set in 'the daily round, the common task', as the narrator walks down the road, does the shopping or the housework, lies in bed or (as in Rose's case) visits the toilet; and the precise date is clearly remembered (the events are said to have happened 'in January 1971', or 'three years ago last November', or 'only yesterday morning'). The 'feeling' or 'knowledge' relates to some member of the family, most commonly mothers, sisters, husbands, brothers and nephews, or to some close friend. Usually its precise meaning cannot be identified immediately; subsequent events will reveal its significance. Narrators call it 'being psychic' or having a 'sixth sense' or 'second-sight' or 'affinity'; alternatively, they refer to the experience as a 'premonition', a 'hunch', or a 'feeling', or say that they 'just *knew*', or that they '*think* things that come true'. Only a few of the stories feature signs or tokens of death, but, where they do, these signs are very traditional ones – the sound of a brick hitting the wall, bangs in furniture, broken mirrors, the scent of flowers, dreams and apparitions like Rose's 'Angel of Death'. More commonly, the forewarning comes to them in the form of a strange physical or emotional state. The women say things like:

'I do believe in premonitions, and the feeling *I* get if it's something not very pleasant is a coldness, a chill. Suddenly, for no reason at all – I can be so happy and everything seems all right – and then suddenly (and it's a horrible feeling) really physically go quite cold and shudder, and then whatever it is I *think* about it.'

'If there's anything going to happen, then my tummy gives a sort of roll and I say, "Hello! What's going . . . Something's going to happen today!"'

'I think one has a very *strange* feeling when something very important is going to happen, that you can't explain. Can't *explain* it. Almost as if one's on the edge of a *cliff* and you FEEL that something TERRIBLE is going to happen, but you can't put your finger on it.'

'Sylvia says, "Oh, you're *psychic*, mother!" I'll say, "No I'm not!" but I *do* know that different things have happened and I've seemed to . . . at the back of my mind, it's as though I've *seen* something *before*.'

These feelings are often not explained even this clearly, speakers merely saying 'I get such a *queer* feeling', or 'I *know* what's coming', or 'It has come true just as I *dreamt* it', or explaining that:

'You start *thinking* about somebody who's close, but a long way away, and there's a *need* to think of them. Afterwards you find that it's been at that precise time.'

'Usually if there's going to be any sickness or anything related to my family, I usually feel very much – I wouldn't say "depressed", but I get the FEELING that something in the future isn't going to be very good. I think I must inherit that from my mother, because SHE *very* often knew all *along* that these things were going to happen.'

The result of these omens and premonitions, hunches and feelings ranges from bereavement to the non-arrival of visitors, though death and ill-health are by far the most common outcomes. Throughout all the stories there is a vagueness about the nature of the experience, which assumes that the hearer already knows what it is and can fill in the details from his or her own experience or 'common knowledge'. More than anything else, if proof were needed that traditions about forewarnings are still an active part of today's folklore, it is this assumption that the outlines of the concept are too familiar to need spelling out which affords such proof. The gaps in the stories indicate the narrator's reliance on knowledge supposed to be shared and common: that is, on a common folklore. Other indications of just how active and well-established these traditions are can be seen in the respondents' total lack of surprise at the questions: in the fact that they have a received vocabulary for talking about the experiences, which includes ancient terms such as 'second-sight' and 'a sixth sense', as well as neologisms such as 'a psychic sense'; and in that they frequently quote their mother's or grandmother's opinions or refer to 'those little ideas that people *used* to have'. Throughout, there is also substantial agreement about what sorts of encounters with the future might be afforded to those 'sensitive' enough to receive them.

All these typical patterns in experiences of forewarning and the way they are presented may be seen in Rose's and Norma's stories quoted above and in the short selection which follows. We begin with another of Rose's many offerings on the subject:

Rose's story (2)

'Oh, I have my little visions! Was it three years last November? We were in the kitchen washing up, my husband and I, you see. And we have a window *there*, where the sink is, and a window *there*, so you sort of go round and the back door's *here*.

'And I said, "Ooh!" And it's DARK, you know, it's *November* and it's *dark*. He said, "What's the matter?" I said, "I've just seen a MAN standing in that corner!" And he *looked* at me and he said, "Oh, GOD! There you go *again*!" So I said, "OK, then!"

'Sixth of November it was. Comes the Tuesday, the following Tuesday, and I've been out shopping. I come back, turn into the top of the road. What greets me? THREE FLIPPING POLICE CARS, with their lights going round, you know, and a CAR all smashed up on the side and MY SON'S TRUCK, which was parked outside, BUMPED FORWARD into the *lamp*, the lamp *down on top of it*!

'And I said to my husband, "What's *happened*?" "Oh," he said, "You'll find out in a moment."

'A knock went on the door and I opened the door. GUESS TO WHAT? A POLICEMAN! THE SAME GEEZER that I'd seen in the corner. I'D SEEN HIM! I'd *seen* the MAN IN THE BLUE GARB!

'Ooh, no! I'm a great believer in the supernatural, yes I am! And there are more things in heaven and earth than we dream about.'

Phyllis's story

'I've never had *experiences*, but I *do* remember . . . My brother was killed in the War . . .

'We were very close and we grew up together, and he was killed when he was nineteen, you see. And I was always very upset about this. And he was wounded in the *leg* and he *died*, after having a blood transfusion.

'And, do you *know*, I had a DREAM that night. I could SEE my *brother*, with his *leg* all SHRIVELLED. That was *before we knew*, you see.

'That's the *only* funny experience *I've* had.'

Edna's story

'NOW, we were only *talking* about this . . .

'I have a *cousin*, and when he was a baby, when he'd be about eighteen months old, whenever he was passing *trees*, "Ooh! Those bushes are going to prick my *eyes*!" And, I mean, he was too young to be aware of what could happen.

'WELL, he went in the War. He was just eighteen when he went in the War. They went over a *mine*, and he was BLINDED.

'Well, NOW THEN, his mother was living with us at the time. He'd no father and she was living with us. Before she opened the *letter*, before *my aunty* opened the letter, my mother said, "It's his EYES! MY GOD! It's his EYES!" I can't remember what it was she'd dreamt, but she'd DREAMT SOMETHING about it!

'Now, we were only *talking* about that this *weekend*!'

Sylvia's story

'My *sister* died some years ago and she was desperately ill. And we'd been to see her in hospital on the Sunday.

'And on the Sunday *evening*, the specialist phoned and said that the crisis was over and she would be on the mend.

'And I could HEAR her TALKING to me ALL evening. And *suddenly*, at five to six she just said, "I'm sorry, Sylvia, I can't hold on any longer." And the phone went, and it was the hospital. She'd *died* at five to six.

'But it was as if she was actually in the *room* with me! And said, "I'm sorry, Sylvia, I can't hold on any more."'

Inez's story

'I've got up some mornings and thought, "I must do so-and-so, because somebody might *come*." And they HAVE come, you know. You know, tidy the kitchen or whatever. And I've thought, "Isn't it a GOOD JOB I DID it? They DID come!" Or I've made a batch of scones for unexpected visitors, and they HAVE COME! But I can't say who it *was* going to come. Just that *somebody* might come knocking on the door.'

Cynthia's story

'I've never experienced it myself, but I have a friend, a colleague, and SHE does, and I KNOW she does!

'She has DREAMS, and she'll come in and say very *vividly*, and she knows what's *happened* and it DOES COME TO HAPPEN! It may not be SOON.

'And it's happened a lot of times with her. I've known it happen with *her*. She might dream of, say, a FIRE or a national DISASTER – something like that – and it DOES come to happen.

'She comes in some mornings quite BOTHERED when she's had one of these dreams very vividly, it's always a *dream*. It's always in the *night* when she's sleeping. Something DOES happen afterwards.

'As I say, there have been national disasters, there have been *personal* disasters to *her*, there have been personal things to *friends* and *colleagues* that don't directly affect her. And she's come in and she's told us that it IS going to happen. And they're not the kinds of things you can STOP. I know for a *fact* that she's dreamt things that have come about. And she's not Scots or any of these people that have, are supposed to have, second-sight, as far as I know. So that can happen.'

When we come to look at the women's stories and remarks about fortunetelling and astrology, we find that they not only have a quite different atmosphere from stories like these, but also a quite different type of detail.

In contrast to the specificity about places, times and persons in the stories we have looked at so far, tales about fortunetelling and astrology are considerably vaguer and more general. Narrators are content to say that the events happened 'ages ago', 'when I was younger', 'once', or 'one time I remember'. Though the events took place away from the ordinary environment, the location is seldom described in any sort of detail. The dramatis personae, too, are only vaguely spelled out – often as not, they are simply described as 'we', 'this woman,' or 'she'. It is seldom, too, for a teller of this sort of story to reveal how the fortuneteller arrived at her diagnosis: we are not told whether she used a crystal ball, or cast the cards, or read the palm. Almost invariably, the account is very objective, so we do not get to understand the narrator's frame of mind, motivation or reactions, either. We are simply told about the message which 'this woman' delivers. So the total effect – in contrast to that of stories of E S P – is impersonal and distanced. Rather than trying hard to convince their hearers, tellers of fortunetelling stories have a 'take-it-or-leave-it' attitude to their narratives.

Another interesting observation is that the predictions which are featured in these stories are quite different in several ways from the forewarnings afforded by E S P. In the first place the message about the future is quite clear and distinct, given the ambiguity and double-talk common to these occasions. The messages refer primarily to the domestic affairs, health and finance of the narrator herself, or occasionally of her female relatives. Only time will tell whether there is anything in it: several narrators say they are still waiting for the husbands, money or success they were promised! The air of objectivity is enhanced by this slight element of suspense, which narrators exploit by telling the story in strict chronological order without asides or digressions, and by structuring it according to a neatly matched before-and-after pattern. These are all rather good stories technically, but the cumulative effect is of detachment, the narrators perhaps taking most pleasure in simply 'telling-the-tale'.

Another small, but significant, point is that the cast of stories is all-female. The narrator, of course, is a woman, so is the fortuneteller, and the prophecies almost always relate either to the narrator herself or to female relatives, and are dominated by the female concerns of home and family.

Stella's story on page 124 is typical of accounts of visits to fortunetellers. She sets the date simply as 'once', refers throughout to the

fortuneteller as 'she', and is equally vague about other aspects of the
scene. For example, she simply speaks of her companion as 'the friend
I'd been with' instead of making her come alive for her audience or
naming her, and she makes no attempt to specify the interval between
the prediction and her subsequent engagement, as the teller of an ESP
story would have done. Only the fortuneteller's message is reported and
we are told nothing about how she arrived at her prediction. Again,
though we do (unusually for this type of story) get a little information
about how Stella felt about it all, this is confined to the introduction of
the story and there is no subjective comment to form a digression in the
main body of the account, which moves briskly on in lively and fairly
impersonal dialogue.

Norah's story which follows on page 125 – one of only three on the
subject of astrology – is equally distanced, vague and impersonal: it
seeks only to entertain for a moment. Whereas Stella's story is about
children and marriage, Norah's is about finance; between them they
therefore cover the topics which occur most frequently as predictions
about the future.

Occasionally, fortunetellers have more success – as in the following
two accounts both of which feature predictions about legs, which,
strangely enough, seem to be a preoccupation among the women I
interviewed. We have already met the first two speakers earlier in this
chapter. Sarah is the mother of Sylvia (who told the story on page 135–6),
who believes her to be psychic (see page 131). Dorothy is the lady
whose horoscope reminded her only of her shortcomings (page 125). It
is noticeable how both storytellers distance themselves, in one way or
another, from the events they relate:

Sarah's story

'Mind you! I went to a spiritualist's once. I *went* with the lady
next door, who lived next door to me. And my daughter that's
died, she was about ten *then*. And I went really for a *giggle* really.

'But she said . . . I went into this room and she said, "*Why* is
my leg hurting so terribly? It's my left leg." She said, "You're
going to *have* somebody *near* to you that's going to have *trouble*
with her left leg." Of course, I laughed it off!

'But, it would be a couple of days after . . . Yes, because it
was on the Saturday . . . And Laura went to the Sunday School
party. You know it was near Christmas time. And a *boy* put his
leg out like that and tripped her *up*. WELL, she had her *leg*
broken in *two* places. My DAUGHTER, you know.

'So *that* made me think. I thought, "WELL, how CAN you *feel* those things?"'

Dorothy's story

'When I was seventeen, I went to a person called ... Elsie Sylvia. She had an office at St Thomas's ... St Thomas's as it *used* to be, not as it is *now*.

'And I was having a love affair with a boy who was *shorter* than myself and I hated it, and yet I was KEEN on him, you see. And she said two things, and I've never forgotten them. She said, "That's just Nature's way of levelling things up! If all the short married the *short*, and all the tall married the *tall*, what a funny WORLD it would *be*!" you see.

'That passed on, and *then*, before I came out, she said, "Watch your legs!" I said, "I've got *wonderful* legs. Although I *say* it – LOVELY legs!"

'But, BLOW ME DOWN! – it's come to *pass* – the *leg* part, anyhow!

[G.B.: 'They've given you trouble since?']

'Well, since I had this *heart attack*. It's left my legs *disturbed*, and all sorts of funny, funny FEET and things.

'I've always remembered those two things.'

Overall, then, we find two very different types of experience told in very different ways. In stories about ESP, the women are careful to date the events clearly and to specify both the places and people involved: they try by all means to make the story both real and convincing. They tell of insights that came to them unbidden, as they went about their ordinary lives. In most cases these insights are purely subjective – a mood, a feeling, a sudden knowledge; in the few cases where something more objective is seen or heard, it is only the narrator who perceives the omen and who can interpret its significance. The women to whom these things happen are regarded as being more than usually sensitive, or, at least, in a more than usually sensitive mood or condition. Their intuitions are invariably other-person-centred: their concern is never with their own fate. In most cases, the other person whose distress or need they are intuitively responding to is a male member of their immediate family. All accounts of experiences of ESP are thus highly subjective and show the narrators as caring, intuitive, sensitive, loving, responsive to the needs of their family and menfolk.

In contrast, in telling stories about fortunetelling ventures, the women are much more careless and happy-go-lucky, taking little heed, it seems, whether they will be believed or not. They are vague about details, being content to say that the event happened 'once' or 'a long time ago', and not specifying very precisely who were the characters involved or where the events took place. These stories tell of visits to clairvoyants' offices, and are fairly objective accounts of the predictions made there. Rather than telling their listener how they *felt* about the visit, they concentrate on repeating the message they were given and saying whether it has (yet) come true; there is very little ego-involvement. They construct these stories dramatically, keeping to chronological order and endeavouring to present an entertaining account of their visit. The predictions almost invariably concern their own, not another person's, fate and keep to a range of topics conventionally considered to be narrowly feminine preoccupations.

When we list the main characteristics of the two sorts of events and the corresponding stories like this, it becomes plain why the women value one sort of encounter with the future and scorn the other. We can see that ESP experiences, as they see them, are geared towards the concerns of a person other than the self: they are intuitions, and they explain already-occurring strange states of mind satisfactorily, indeed flatteringly. On the other hand, one goes to a fortuneteller out of concern for one's own fate not another person's; it is a deliberately chosen action; it involves acquired skills rather than intuition; and, whereas the concept of ESP *explains* odd states of mind and/or perceptions, the practice of fortunetelling deliberately *introduces* an element of irrationality and strangeness into otherwise orderly lives. If we remember that the women are far more likely to accept a supernatural belief if it is other-person-centred, if it is geared to intuition, and if it helps to make the world seem safe and orderly, then everything falls into place. Plainly, the women are making moral judgements, accepting elements of the traditional folklore which fit in with their values and rejecting those that run contrary to them. At heart, this morality has much to do with a woman's conventional role and persona. Belief in ESP sanctions and enshrines the value of intuition, caring, interpersonal relationships and unassertiveness. The practices of fortunetelling, on the other hand, allow women to try independently to find out and perhaps control their future: it looks very much like improper inquisitiveness, self-seeking and vanity to be so concerned to master one's fate.

This morality comes into play even more forcefully when it is the women *themselves* who read the cups or the cards. This is the ultimate taboo. Six of the stories I collected about experiences of forewarning featured 'psychic' women telling fortunes for themselves or their friends. It is plain that this is considered to be an almost sinful exploitation of God-given powers, for in every case the results are dreadful. In one story, Clara has her hand read by a friend and within a year her favourite nephew dies a painful death; in Geraldine's case the result is a distressing domestic upheaval; and in Berenice's case an unfortunate marriage. Here the girl for whom Berenice is doing the predictions takes it all too literally for Berenice's taste and goes out determined to hunt down the ideal mate she was promised; when she decides she has found him, Berenice is appalled and deeply regrets the disservice she has done to the young man! In a fourth story, Alma reads the cups for her mother's friend and sees no future for her; and in the final pair, Rose tells first how she played with a Ouija board and ended up in hospital and then reads the cards for her husband's relatives and almost immediately afterwards their great-nephew contracts polio and dies in their house. In each case, then, 'psychic' women are seen to abuse their powers by 'delving' into the unknown: they are punished for their audacity by seeing far more than they bargained for. As Rose says, 'To me, it's a gift, and you don't abuse it.'

The tenor of the experiences and the morality in the stories can best be seen by looking at examples from Rose's and Alma's conversation, for both women not only tell a racy story but also are quite convinced that they really do have special powers which may be harnessed to good or ill. The cautionary tales they tell about the use and abuse of those powers are therefore well worth listening to:

Alma's story

'NOW, I'll tell you ONE thing! When I was younger I used to look into *teacups*.

'NOW, mother had a friend who was TERRIBLY superstitious, and whatever I *said*, she took for gospel. Things DID happen that way, but a lot of it didn't. But I know, the *last* time she asked me, she said, "Oh, you MUST read my CUP!"

'And I looked at it and I said, "Oh!" I said. "There's nothing *there!*"

'"Oh!" she said. "There MUST BE!"

'I said, "NO, there ISN'T!" I said. "Honestly," I said, "there's
nothing there AT ALL!" And I *couldn't* see a . . .

'WELL, she was very, very *offended* about this. And I said,
"No, there isn't."

'And when I came home, mother . . . "Oh!" she said. "Why
didn't you TELL her something?"

'I said, "LOOK, Mother! There was no *future* for her. None at
ALL!"

'She said, "There *must* have been!"

'I said, "There WASN'T."

'I said, "I couldn't see a THING in that cup," I said, "and I
got a QUEER FEELING when I picked it up," I said. "There
WASN'T ANYTHING THERE!"

'DO YOU KNOW! That next week, we were out, and we met a
friend, and she said, "OOH! Did you know about so-and-so . . ."
She'd been taken *ill*. She'd had a STROKE. And she only *lasted*
three days. The *next* thing we knew, my mother was going to
her FUNERAL. Well now, that was the *last time* that I
EVER . . .'

Rose's story (1)

'But I *don't believe in* delving, no.

'WE DELVED a few years ago. You know this damn silly
game that you play with a *glass*? – the Ouija board? *That* business,
and all the rest of it?

'And every time, this damn thing . . . This was *June*, was it?
. . . And this damn thing kept *saying*, "Rose is going . . . Rose is
going into *hospital*. Rose is going to have an *operation*." WELL,
there was no operation in my *mind*, was there the Devil!

'And three weeks after, Rose WAS in hospital and Rose *was*
having an operation.

'So, I decided that it was time we finished with that!'

[G.B.: 'So you didn't do it again?']

'NO NEVER! The TIMES people have said to me, "Tell my
fortune!" NO WAY!! You WON'T get me to tell fortunes. If
I can *see* it, I'll *see* it, but . . .'

Rose's story (2)

[Rose: 'What do you want me to tell you?'
     G.B.: 'Tell me how you think you're psychic.']

'Because I know what's going to happen. I've got a pretty good idea, yeah. *How* do I know? Inside THERE. And the fact also I've been able to tell fortunes by cards, and I was able to read cups, reading tea-leaves, and this was oh, forty, fifty years ago. I was young. I was in my teens then, you see, and I frightened myself to death. So I said, "NO WAY!" So I left the tea-leaf business alone.

'When I was married, and we'd been married Lord knows how long – the War interrupted, so of course we never had any children till 1947. Now, in that summer of '47, I used to tell all fortunes by *cards*.'

[G.B.: 'What's this? Tarot cards?']

'No, no. *Playing cards*. Each card has a meaning and all the cards together spell out a *message*.

'ANYWAY! I was about six or seven months pregnant and we *go* down to see my husband's aunt, and she was a great believer in the *cards*. And they have one son. NOW, he was very good in business. He was quite a top notch in Rolls-Royce.

'ANYWAY! We got down there on the Saturday afternoon and there was Auntie Edie, Uncle Bernard, who are my husband's aunt and uncle, myself (complete with *lump*, of course!) and my husband. And Cousin Charlie met us at Chesney station – with Rolls-Royce, of course, naturally! – and took us to *his* house.

'SO, we had a *terrific* THUNDERSTORM in the afternoon, so, to pass the time away, Charlie and his wife said, "Let's tell our FORTUNES, Rose!" So I said, "Oh, OK, then," never thinking anything about it.

'And they got the cards out and we started, you know. And ALL I could tell her was that ALL I could *see* and all I could *smell* – ALL I COULD SMELL – was FLOWERS and all I could *see* was a coffin SITTING there in the HALL on a BIER.

'Now, it was a *beautiful* house, with a great big square hall, you see. There's a *lounge* at the front, and there's a *dining*-room and there's a *morning*-room, and there's this, that and the *other*, you see.

'Went to bed at night. *Everybody laughed*! They thought, "Oh, she's *pregnant*," you see. So we went to bed at night, like, and I kept crying and my husband said to me, "What the HELL's the matter with *you*?" He says, "I can't *understand* you!"

'I said, "I want to go *home*! All I can see . . . I can ALL smell FLOWERS and all I can see is a *coffin* and it's on a *bier* in that hall!"'

'He said, "Oh, don't be SILLY, Rose!! *You'll* be all right. Get off to *sleep*!"

'NO SLEEP FOR ME!!

'We went home on the Sunday and Auntie Edie said to me going home on the train, "What was the *matter* with you yesterday, Rose?"

'So I *told* her, so I said, "There's a COFFIN. There's a FUNERAL in that house, you know."

'She says, "IS there?"

'I says, "Yes." I says, "I don't know who it *is*, but it's *definitely* in that house!"

'SO ANYWAY, I think it would be July 19th. NOW, in the *August* of 47, the great-nephew, he was fourteen years old, their only son – their only child, everything planned and a brilliant scholar – he came over to see his Auntie Edie and contracted polio, and in three weeks he was *dead*. Yes. AND HIS COFFIN STOOD ON A BIER IN THE HALL.

'It SO affected me, I said, "Never *again* will I tell a *fortune*!" FRIGHTENED me to DEATH! I said, "NO!"'

It seems clear from these accounts that most women believe that foreknowledge of future events *is* possible. They undoubtedly think that some people are given special gifts, and that even quite ordinary people may sometimes, somehow, get glimpses of the future if the initiating event affects them deeply enough. The mechanism by which this happens is a sensitivity to others that, so to speak, gets rubbed raw when disaster looms. The greater the attachment of one person to another, the more likely they are to be sensitive to events (future as well as present) that affect that person; the greater a person's general sensitivity to all living things, the more likely they are to be 'psychic'. The essential characteristic of the seer in either case is, then, that she is *reacting* to events already ordained, and she is doing this by means of a God-given sensibility that is created and consolidated by love of other people. This being the mechanism of the precognitive process, it must be a sinful distortion to use it to achieve selfish or trivial ends, to pry into the future or to attempt to thwart the will of God by preventing or avoiding one's predestined fate. A sharp line is therefore drawn between unsought (and therefore unexploitable) *experiences* of foreknowledge and *practices* designed to harness (and thereby run the risk of perverting) these powerful abilities. How far the women are likely to accept the various types of foreknowledge depends, then, to a large extent on whether the tradition is in accord with their sense of fitness and propriety. Supernatural experience that is not deliberately sought out is considered both safe and good because it is an extension of ordinary loving intuition. On the other hand, any attempt to deliberately seek knowledge of the future is dangerously audacious. It is bad enough when a woman visits a fortuneteller (though here the result may only be the dashing of her hopes), but it is distinctly wrong for a woman to take it upon herself to 'delve' into the unknown, to exploit her talent for worldly ends, and to seek for knowledge unbecoming to her station.[17] To break this taboo is to court retribution. This is the moral of the personal experience stories the women tell.

If it is powerfully stated in their narratives, we shall find it even more strongly evident when we look at what I think of as their 'dialogue of fear'.

THE DIALOGUE OF FEAR

Though belief in 'premonitions' is very widespread among the women I interviewed, there are, of course, a minority who discount the possibility that these things really happen. There are a few more who think it unlikely that people can be forewarned about trivial incidents through 'telepathy', and more still who think it unlikely that a death in the family would be presaged by 'omens'. When it comes to matters of fortunetelling and astrology, the position is reversed. The believers are in retreat and the sceptics are in the majority. In the answers to questions on these topics, therefore, we have the best insight into the psychology of disbelief. Judging by this evidence, the strongest motivation behind rejection and scepticism is fear.

It is significant that outright rejection of the possibility of being forewarned about future events is most frequently accompanied by an expression of the deterministic philosophy we discussed earlier in chapter 2. According to this view of life, God (or some unspecified operation) has set the world in motion and nothing can turn it from its course. The future is already ordained and advances on the individual like the infamous 'irresistible force'; people, however, are by no means 'immoveable objects'. Like trees in a gale, they have to bend and submit or be broken. As we saw before, women often adopt this philosophy as a defence mechanism against the vagaries of chance and fate. As a coping strategy, it operates in the paradoxical way that George Matheson's gloomy hymn describes:

> Make me a captive, Lord,
>   And then I shall be free;
> Force me to render up my sword,
>   And I shall conqueror be.
>   I sink in life's alarms
>   When by myself I stand;
> Imprison me within Thine arms,
>   And strong shall be my hand.
>
> My heart is weak and poor
>   Until it master find;
> It has no spring of action sure –
>   It varies with the wind.
>   It cannot freely move
>   Till Thou hast wrought its chain;
> Enslave it with Thy matchless love,
>   And deathless it shall reign.
>
> My will is not my own
>   Till Thou hast made it Thine;
> If it would reach a monarch's throne
>   It must its crown resign;
>   It only stands unbent,
>   Amid the clashing strife,
> When on Thy bosom it has leant
>   And found in Thee its life.

So, in submitting to their fate, the women say that 'you are given the strength' to endure it.

For women who have sought refuge in this cheerless stoicism, belief in the possibility of foreknowledge would be a breach in their defence against the world. So time and time again they reiterate the formulae of their faith:

'You see, I'm a practising Christian and that makes me believe that "What is to be, will *be*."'

'I just take everything as it comes. I always think, "Well, there's nothing I can *do* about it. What's going to come's going to *come*."'

'I'm sort of down to earth. I take things as they come.'

'I believe that what will be, *is*. If anything's going to happen, it *does*, whether you want it to or not.'

'I think life's what it *is*. It just *happens*.'

'I think that what happens, *happens*.'

'I do think you get the strength *given* to you, if you just have faith.'

In other, more personal, statements it is the anxiety, rather than the faith, that is uppermost. Here the defensive taboo against too much, or too premature, knowledge is quite evident:

'No. I don't want to *know*. In fact, if I *knew* that I was going to fall FLOP like that and break my hip – WELL!'

'Because one or two of my friends have had things told to them that have come true, and I don't want to *know*. So I don't go in for things like that. You'd never get *me* in one of those places!'

'No. What's going to happen, I'd rather let it *be* and *let* it happen. I don't *believe* in fortunetelling.'

'No. I'm *afraid* of those things.'

'I've often thought about it, but chickened out at the last minute. Not been *brave* enough to go in and find out what they were going to *tell* me.'

'No. I take things day by day, and I think if I went and had my hand read and she told me anything *wrong* was going to happen, it would mither me to death until that time was *there*.'

'I'm a day-to-day person, and if it comes, it *comes*. But I mean, if somebody says to me they *thought* something was going to happen, I would be so *worried*, so *ill*. I'm better not *knowing*.'

In these answers, the possibility of breaching the deterministic defence is acutely apprehended. The women cling fiercely to their ignorance and set up a taboo against knowledge. So they will rather reproachfully say that they 'don't *go in* for' fortunetelling and horoscopes, or they 'don't *believe* in it', in the sense of not *approving* of it, or they 'don't want to *know* about it'. Obviously, this attitude owes a lot to the Eden myth, but underneath the piety there might also be a bit of superstition – as if knowledge itself had malicious power to harm.

If, then, the women do actually read their horoscopes in the evening papers, or perhaps occasionally visit a fortuneteller, then they have to be careful how they admit to these peccadilloes. The most common tactic is to say that they do it 'for fun'. Twenty-six women responded to questions about horoscopes in this way; others say they do it 'for a giggle', 'out of habit', 'for devilment', or say 'I read it but I don't believe it.' By refusing to take things seriously, they provide themselves with a defence against both other people's criticism and the predictions themselves, thus depriving the future of its power to harm. This defensive attitude even creeps into answers framed as cautious justifications or qualified belief. Mary, for example, very typically says 'It depends whether the person reading it is going to tell you what they see or what they think it's best for you to know', seeming to imply that the latter might be the safer course of action.

Above all, this nervous, defensive dialogue is grounded as much in sexual roles and status as in religious or philosophical principle. The retreat from, or taboo against, knowledge can be seen as founded to a very large extent on an insistence on the maintenance of traditional virtues. The women obviously have immense respect for conventional female roles, and also a great measure of that diffidence born out of women's dependent social position. It is not very fanciful to suppose that, denied intellectual influence and socialized early into ignorance, the women should reject beliefs and practices that seem to offer power through knowledge. Their life-experiences – especially the disorientating one of bereavement – have also helped to establish stoicism and passivity as the proper virtues. The 'what will be, will be' maxim has served well to steer them through traumas and tragedies and to enable them to carry on. It is not likely that they would be willing to abandon such useful psychological armour for concepts which offer such doubtful benefits.

The sad side-effect of this psychological defence and the enshrinement of conventional female virtues is a retreat from positive action. If one copes with fate by being passive under its onslaughts and by raising passivity to the status of principle, then action, independence and responsibility become faults. Thus it is that dependence is sanctified as a virtue, and lack of curiosity is extolled as a becoming unwillingness to 'delve' into forbidden matters. Faced with any popular belief that purports to give control or knowledge, many women prefer ignorance.

It is very tempting to see this as an expression of a 'victim mentality'. Formulations of the stoic–passive philosophy, culminating, as they do, in maxims such as Evelyn's 'My father used to say that from the moment you're born to the moment you die, your life's mapped out for you, he says, there's NOTHING you can do to change it', strongly recall the conclusion of Margaret Atwood's fine feminist novel, *Surfacing*. When the nameless heroine surfaces from her healing madness, she re-emerges with a new resolution: 'This above all, to refuse to be a victim . . . I have to recant, give up the old belief that I am powerless and because of it nothing I can do will ever hurt anyone.'[18] That the women do feel powerless is evidenced by their ascription of their independent successes since widowhood to figures of power and authority – the dead husband or the lost mother – expressed in the constantly recurring phrase, 'I couldn't have done it on my own. There must have been help given'; in their ascription of observations and intuitions to heaven-sent 'premonitions'; and in their interpretation of any attempt independently to ascertain (and thereby control?) the future as either futile or wrong. It is easy to see these feelings as those of women who seek refuge in the role of victim – powerless and therefore absolved from both responsibility and blame.

The taboo against delving and the unwillingness to believe in fortunetelling and astrology, therefore, seem to be grounded in four complementary impulses: religious principle; philosophical bias; social values; and psychological defence. For these women, religious principle leads to the shunning of sought foreknowledge because it re-enacts the sin of Adam, who wilfully set out to acquire knowledge so dangerous that only God could handle it. Similarly, to seek deliberately to know the future breaches the deterministic philosophy which is many women's main defence against the cruelties of life and death. Thirdly, knowledge and power are considered unbecoming in a woman; and fourthly, action, which the possession of power and knowledge entails, is both frightening and foreign to their way of life.

Together, these impulses enshrine intuitive and unsought experiences of forewarning as feminine and valuable, but lead the women, often fiercely, to reject any deliberate attempt to catch and hold the future. Well might they say with Alexander Pope:

> Heaven from all creatures hides the book of Fate,
> All but the page prescribed, their present state:
> From brutes what men, from men what spirits know:
> Or who could suffer being here below?
> The lamb thy riot dooms to bleed today,
> Had he thy reason, would he skip and play?
> Pleased to the last, he crops the flowery food,
> And licks the hand just raised to shed his blood.
> Oh blindness to the future! kindly given,
> That each may fill the circle mark'd by Heaven:
> Who sees with equal eye, as God of all,

A hero perish, or a sparrow fall,
Atoms or systems into ruin hurl'd,
And now a bubble burst, and now a world.
    Hope humbly then; with trembling pinions soar;
    Wait the great teacher, Death; and God adore.[19]

NOTES

1   John Beaumont (1705), *An Historical . . . Treatise of Spirits.*

2   Taillepied (Summers edn), p. 87.

3   Lavater (1929 edn), p. 77.

4   Lavater (1929 edn), pp. 77–9.

5   Aubrey (1696), p. 35.

6   Aubrey (1696), pp. 37–8.

7   Kirk (1933 edn), pp. 78–9.

8   Baxter (1840 edn), p. 88.

9   Baxter (1840 edn), pp. 91–6.

10   Abercrombie (1841 edn), p. 296.

11   Glanvil (1676), p. 3.

12   Dr Henry More in a letter to Joseph Glanvil. Quoted in Glanvil (1681), p. 16.

13   Gomme (1890), p. 53.

14   Burne (1914), pp. 124–5.

15   Burne (1883), p. 276.

16   Quoted in Brand (1913 edn), pp. 665–7.

17   Cf. the following reflections by Henry Bourne in 1725: 'It becomes us not to prescribe Means to God, by which we may judge of our future Success, but to depend on his Power and Wisdom, his Care and Providence. The Observation of Omens . . . They are the Inventions of the Devil, to draw Men from a due trust in God, and make them his own Vassals. For by such Observations as these, they are the Slaves of Superstition and Sin, and have all the While no true Dependence upon God, no Trust in his Providence.' Bourne (1977 edn), pp. 74–5.

18   Atwood (1979), p. 191.

19   Alexander Pope, *Essay on Man*, III, 77–92.

6 The Ghost in Retrospect

History – a distillation of rumour.[1]

THOMAS CARLYLE

Ghost traditions have always had a role to play in explaining the oddities of human experience and in giving meaning, shape and form to concepts of the cosmos. The same beliefs, as well as bringing order and comfort to the lives of ordinary people, have from time to time been taken up and used by philosophers and divines to serve particular religious purposes, and by secular rulers to sanction custom and law, to enforce historical precedent, and to ensure the continuation of the social status quo. At the same time, of course, these tales of the unexpected have retained their power to thrill the imagination and have been at all times one of the most consistently popular types of narrative. I want to conclude, therefore, by looking briefly at some aspects of ghost traditions in a historical context, beginning at the Middle Ages and working forward to the present day.

There are several points which need stressing before I begin. The first is that in all ages, except the present, access to supernatural folklore is gained only through the writings of educated men: we cannot plug in directly to the voices of the people themselves. A history of ghost traditions is therefore necessarily not so much a history of folklore as a history of the educated élite's reactions to that folklore. We see the traditions through the eyes of men who had a variety of axes to grind; who were anxious either to exploit or to discourage popular beliefs in order to advance particular political, philiophical, religious or cultural causes. In other words, we meet traditions through the writings of people who were neither disingenuous nor disinterested informants, and it is impossible to be absolutely certain how far what they tell us is reliable. There is, necessarily, not only a lot of guess-work, but also some confusion and contradiction in any picture we may attempt to draw. There must, of course, always have been a vigorous belief in ghosts among the people at large, but we do not have direct access to it. In the sections below, therefore, I have tended to concentrate on the attitudes of educated people towards the supernatural, showing how it was viewed, used (and abused), and to show how the various stages of what we might call 'the life-cycle of ghosts' in educated thought have affected the way we think of ghosts today.

The next point I want to make is that the emphasis here will be on popular beliefs about spectres and apparitions, not about E S P and other related experiences. There are two main reasons for this. First of all, the historical aspects of the concepts of luck, magic, astrology and fore-knowledge have been very extensively described in Keith Thomas's modern classic *Religion and the Decline of Magic*; in such a short space as I have here, I could not in any way cover the subject in such detail, nor could I rival Thomas's scholarship. When it comes to the matter of ghosts, however, Thomas is very much briefer. So, here, there is a gap which genuinely needs to be plugged.

Secondly, the available literature on the supernatural is itself strongly biased towards discussion of ghosts and stories about the activities of spectres, apparitions and poltergeists. It is from religious writing that most information about supernatural traditions from the Middle Ages to the turn of the sixteenth/seventeenth centuries can be drawn; from medical and antiquarian texts that we learn most about the development of those traditions from the early eighteenth to the mid-nineteenth centuries; and in popular books and compilations of regional folklore that we have the most plentiful and vivid data from then on. Throughout all this literature, both sacred and secular, there is a similar concentration on ghosts. Though there are, of course, many stories and much dis-cussion about luck, fate and chance, they are fewer and more peripheral than stories about spectres and apparitions. This is because ghost tra-ditions supply not only the most dramatic, but also the most convincing, examples to use in an argument – whether the topic is the existence of purgatory or witchcraft, regret for the prisons of the mind created by mass superstition, or the displaying of country custom and belief. So, as far as ghosts are concerned, there is a wealth of relevant information on which we can draw to paint a picture of supernatural traditions in each succeeding age.

In order to marshal this mass of information into any sort of reason-able order and present an uncluttered picture of each development as it occurs, I have thought it best to keep the main discussion as free as possible from narrative, for most previous work on the subject has quickly got bogged down in storytelling and the thread of the argument has soon been lost. However, as there are very many good stories which not only have the power to thrill, but also serve to illustrate trends in the history of our concept of ghosts, I have included at least one of these as an appendix to each section by way of relief from an argument which at times, necessarily, becomes complex.

Lastly, this brief history comes with a disclaimer. I am not a historian but a folklorist. Though the ideas about developments in supernatural traditions are my own and are derived as far as possible from going back to the available literature in each age, ideas about the historical contexts in which those traditions flourished are necessarily drawn from the work of others.[2] My understanding is therefore at times a good deal less than I could wish for. Where there is not much literature available for consultation, in the form of contemporary treatises of ghosts or anti-quarian writings about popular traditions, there is what we might well call an 'unavoidable superficiality count' in my treatment of that period. The section on the medieval background, in particular, should be regarded as no more than the briefest run-in to the subject. The eigh-teenth century presents similar problems, for by then, as we shall see, educated opinion was so firmly set against the supernatural that even antiquarians paid scant attention to the popular ghost beliefs of the day and relied in the main on collating material from texts of the previous century.

I feel on safer ground for the seventeenth century, for there is a multiplicity of vernacular writing on the supernatural, which I have been able to consult; and, of course, when we come to the nineteenth century, by then 'Folklore' had been invented, there is a wealth of material, and I am dealing with the history of my own discipline.

The end-result is an overall unevenness of treatment, which I regret, but, given the constraints of trying to cover a vast subject in a short chapter, cannot easily remedy. Readers who want to know more are urged to consult the bibliography and the texts referred to in the notes at the end of the chapter.

DEVILS, MIRACLES AND PURGATORY:
THE MEDIEVAL BACKGROUND

In the history of conventional religion in Europe (Christianity as repre-sented by the official Churches), the ties between orthodox doctrine and the subterranean theology[3] of supernatural belief have been closer than is always recognized. In the first place, early Christianity had to take account not only of the dominant Graeco–Roman culture (rich in supernatural myth and legend), but also of its mother-religion. In particular, it took over key concepts from Judaism – doctrines of an afterlife and ideas about angels and demons.

Though, as Norman Cohn points out in his history of witchcraft, *Europe's Inner Demons*, the earliest biblical records do not recognize a power of evil separate from God, a crucial change is visible when the first Book of Chronicles came to be written. Here, in I *Chronicles* 21:1, it says that: 'Satan stood up against Israel and provoked David to number Israel.' It is in this account of David's taking a census of the tribes that, it seems, the word 'Satan' is first employed as a proper noun, and temptation seen as coming from an outside force opposed to God.

During the following centuries, Judaism elaborated a complex and comprehensive philosophy of demons, as a glance at the *Apocrypha*, compiled between the year 200 BC and the end of the first century AD, shows. Here we have many and various accounts of evil spirits working to thwart the divine plan, and it is this concept of the opposition of two kingdoms that Christianity was to take over and adapt to its own uses.

By the time of the New Testament, the world was imagined as divided into two embattled camps: on the one side, there was the power of good as represented by God, Jesus, the disciples and the faithful; on the other, there was Satan and his hosts of minor devils, whose role was to oppose the new religion. Throughout the history of the early Christian Church, Satan and his minions continued to be imagined much in the same way as they were portrayed in the New Testament and later part of the Old Testament. However, the early Church was optimistic about the outcome of the eternal struggle, believing that Satan would soon fall before the forces of good. In fact many Christians of this period believed that the return of Jesus was imminent, and that the Day of Judgement and the Millennium which would succeed it were not far away.

As time passed and these events did not come about, the question arose of what happened meanwhile to the waiting souls of the dead, and speculations about the existence of an afterlife took on new immediacy. As yet, however, ideas about what sorts of pleasures and pains this afterlife would bring, or where and what it consisted of, remained fluid and flexible (St Augustine, for example, still saw the souls of the dead as reposing in the bosom of Abraham as the Jewish religion had taught). But whatever or wherever the afterlife was, no one thought that it afforded chances of communication between the dead and the living.

Though the dead could be helped by the prayers of the living, all the contact was one-way, and no response could be expected from the otherworld. The only exception to this rule was made for the souls of martyrs and saints, who were thought capable on occasion of healing sickness or giving protection on a journey. It seems as though early Christianity deliberately chose to cut down on the number of spectral visitations in order to emphasize its separateness from the Mediterranean religions it saw itself as in competition with.

The spiritual atmosphere began to change, however, with the fall of the Roman Empire, when the main rival for converts ceased to be classical paganism, and Christianity found itself having to combat Celtic and Germanic religions. Then, missionaries abandoned their former reserve, and turned more and more to the miraculous supernatural in order to attract converts who were used to a colourful and dramatic faith. Tales of miraculous visitations, cures and conversions therefore began to proliferate, supplemented by a growing body of saints' legends and sacred wonder-tales. At the same time, the old demonology became increasingly assimilated into Christianity, so the number of supernatural entities and effects rapidly increased. In addition, the first stirrings of the doctrine of purgatory allowed there to be a *place* from which souls of the dead could operate in the world. So it was that the idea that contact was possible between this sphere and the world of the dead gradually became assimilated more and more into mainstream religious thought.

After about AD 1100, further developments took place in mapping out the supernatural in its religious aspects. Three interrelated changes in Christian doctrine undoubtedly helped to increase belief in ghosts. In the first place, the concept of purgatory as a resting place for souls, where they could be purified and made fit for heaven, was developed, refined, formalized and then established as an essential part of Church doctrine. Simultaneously, there was a change in the public face of Christianity, away from portraying Jesus as a hero victorious over death, sin and other religions, towards depicting him, as we do now, as the suffering crucified Lord. Thirdly, there was a parallel development in ideas about the Day of Judgement: whereas previously it had been thought of as a single event with a fixed date sometime in the (reasonably near) future, it began to be conceived of as a personal judgement at each individual death. Together these things, exacerbated no doubt by fear of the Black Death, which was decimating the population, meant that there was a rapid upsurge in anxiety about death. It is in this atmosphere that the earlier idea that the souls of martyrs and saints might communicate with the living if there was special need became extended, giving rise to a proliferation of reports about spirits of all types appearing to the living.

One of the few remaining guides we have to the ghost traditions of these troubled times are the 'exempla' – sermon manuals – which were written for the use of the clergy. Though we must be careful not to regard these stories as 'folklore', nor to place too great a reliance on them as indicating what supernatural beliefs would probably have been in the Middle Ages, we can at least regard them as useful indications of some of the sorts of things people might have found credible. We may assume that the clergy would not have deviated too far from the tenor of popular beliefs for fear of overreaching themselves and being received with incredulity. It must also be said that such stories, heard from the pulpit, told as true and coming with all the authority of the Church, would in turn have helped to shape public opinion and to mould the traditions of the day.

In these exempla we find two classes of apparition. Firstly, there are ghosts in the classical mould (hardly surprising when we consider the bias towards Graeco–Roman culture in the priestly education of the time), who mainly returned to demand proper burial. Secondly, there is a more utilitarian type of ghost, geared to educative purposes and designed to inculcate various aspects of Church doctrine. These come back to stress the importance of confession, absolution and the Last Rites; they are prone to insisting on the necessity of baptism for new-borns, to avoid the horrors of Limbo; they reassure their descendants of the value of giving alms and saying Masses to aid their progress in the next world; and they frequently insist on the correctness and wisdom of the Church's teaching on various doctrinal matters.

The exempla also indicate (and Pope Gregory the Great's *Dialogues*, still popular after 500 years or more, back them up on this) that spirits can be sometimes seen not only in this world but in the otherworld, too, through the dreams and visions of holy men. There are numerous accounts of hermits and ascetics being afforded visions of the death of prominent men, seeing them received with joy into heaven or, in torment of mind and body, condemned to the fires of hell. Elsewhere there are stories (still familiar in their general outlines today) of how, while the body of a sick man lies at death's door, his soul journeys to the gates of the otherworld, sees its joys or terrors, then is sent back to rejoin the body, which is restored to health and vigour, for either the sick man's time is not yet up after all or the angels have called the wrong Stephen or the wrong Simon. All these visions encourage the hearer to envisage heaven and hell in physical terms, as places with real, fixed locations, and to see the dead as continuing to inhabit their physical bodies. These ghosts are therefore not only distinctly material, but also recognizable people (which, incidentally, is one aspect of ghost belief which changed as the traditions became secularized in later ages).

What perhaps needs to be stressed in all this, however, is that the term 'ghost' is rather a misnomer for these visions and apparitions. In those days the word simply meant 'spirit' (as it does when we speak of 'the Father, Son and Holy Ghost') and it was as yet entirely free of the tricky, unpleasant connotations it has acquired since. The 'ghosts' that appear in medieval exempla and other clerical writing are just spirits of the dead – of saints, holy martyrs and restless sinners alike – all 'an integral part of an immense and ordered spiritual world'[4] and aligned, like the natural world, to the supreme purposes of God, the creator.

By the end of the medieval period, this complex world was envisaged by philosophers, divines and educated laymen alike as a series of links in one Great Chain of Being. All creatures, both natural and supernatural – fairies, elves, witches, devils, saints and martyrs, as well as man and beast, God and his angels – were thought to be linked hierarchically in a single, indivisible system. It was an intelligible and unified structure in which ghosts had their fixed place, just as *maleficium* (ill-wishing), fore-telling and magic had. Popular supernatural belief and magical practices were the baseline of a pyramid which extended upwards to the super-natural hierarchy of religion. Ghosts had a particularly important role in religion as well as folklore. They were essential intermediaries between the sacred and mundane levels of this pyramid – the vehicle of miracles and magic, the propagandist of divine laws, evidence against witches and, in the last resort, proof of the existence of God himself.

*   *   *

The story of the ghost which appeared to the philosopher, Athenodorus, is probably the most famous of all those in the old classical mould where the ghost requires burial. This account comes from the scholarly Capuchin friar, Fr Noel Taillepied, who says that it is contained in a letter from Pliny to Licinius Sura. Taillepied's *A Treatise of Ghosts* was compiled a year before his death in 1589, and contains not only a good deal of contemporary folklore, but also old tales and legends such as this one. This translation, the first into English, is by Montague Summers, and was published in the 1930s:

There was formerly at Athens a large and handsome house, which none the less had acquired the reputation of being badly haunted. Folk told how at the dead of night horrid noises were heard, the clanking of chains which grew louder and louder until there suddenly appeared the hideous phantom of an old man, who seemed the very picture of abject filth and misery. His beard was long and matted, his white hairs dishevelled and unkempt. His thin legs were loaded with a weight of galling fetters, that he dragged wearily along with a painful moaning; his wrists were shackled by long cruel links, whilst ever and anon he raised his arms and shook his gyves amain in a kind of impotent fury. Some few mocking sceptics who once were bold enough to watch all night in the house had been well-nigh scared from their senses at a sight of the apparition; and, what was worse, disease and even death itself proved to be the fate of those who after dusk had ventured within those accursed walls. The place was shunned. A placard 'To Let' was posted, but year succeeded year and the house fell almost to ruin and decay. It so happened that the philosopher Athenodorus, whilst on a visit to Athens, passed by the deserted overgrown garden, and seeing the bill, inquired the rent of the house, which was just such as he was seeking. Being not a little surprised at the low figure asked he put more questions, and then there came out the whole story. None the less he signed the lease, and ordered that one room should be furnished with a bed, chairs and a table. At night he took his writing tablet, style, books and a good lamp, and set himself as was his wont, to study in the quiet house. He had determined to concentrate upon some difficult problem, lest if he sat idle and expectant his imagination should play tricks, and he might see what in reality was not there. He was soon absorbed in philosophical calculations, but presently the noise of a rattling chain, at first distant and then growing nearer, broke on his ear. However, Athenodorus being particularly occupied with his notes, was too intent to interrupt his writing, until as the clanking became more and more continuous he looked up, and there before him stood the phantom exactly as it had been described. The ghastly figure seemed to beckon with its finger, but the philosopher signed with his hand that he was busy, and again bent to his writing. The chains were shaken angrily and with persistence, upon which Athenodorus quietly arose from his seat, and taking the lamp, motioned the spectre to lead before. With low groans the figure passed heavily through the spacious corridors and empty rooms until they came out into the garden, when it led the philosopher to a distant shrubbery, and with a deep sigh mingled with the night. Athenodorus, having marked the spot with stones and a broken bough, returned to the house where he slept soundly until morning. He then repaired to the nearest magistrates, related what he had seen, and advised that the spot where the ghost disappeared should be investigated. This was done and in digging they found, a few feet below the surface, a human skeleton, carious, enchained and fettered in gyves of a pattern many centuries old, now rusty and eroded, so that they fell asunder in flakes of desquamating verdigris. The mouldering bones were collected with reverent care and given a decent and seemly burial. The house was purged and cleansed with ritual lustrations, and never afterwards was it troubled by spectres and ill-luck.

The second story again comes from Taillepied, and is typically medieval. Here the ghost comes back to enforce, not one but three, religious messages. The story is plainly aimed as much at the clergy as at laymen: Taillepied's closing comment is as instructive as the story itself.

Melchior Flavin, a Franciscan Father, in his *De l'état des âmes après le trépas, comment elles vivent étant separées du Corps* records that Pope Innocent IV, during his residence in France, founded the nun's Charterhouse of Villeneuve ... owing to a vision seen by a holy Anchoret to whom there appeared a number of the departed ... Since this circumstance is very well known I will not enlarge upon it but rather here relate another incident which happened in France in the year 1238. At that time the Bishop of Paris was that holy and reverend prelate, William of Auvergne, whose writings are so generally esteemed and admired. There was held at the Dominican convent in Rue St Jacques a solemn conclave at which was present, amongst other learned doctors, Cardinal Hugues St Cher. The point under discussion was pluralism, and the members of the conclave were altogether of the opinion that no priest could with a clear conscience hold more than one benefice, if any second living was worth a sum exceeding fifteen livres parisis. The only dissentient from this was Maître Philippe, Chancellor of the University. A little after Maître Philippe fell ill, and being on his death-bed the good Bishop visited him, endeavouring to persuade him to relinquish the benefices he held. This, however, the sick man refused to do, for he presumptuously maintained to the last that he could assuredly be saved even if he were a pluralist. After his decease the Bishop was praying one night in the Cathedral of Nôtre Dame and the sound of Matins sweetly chanted in the choir still echoed in his ears when he beheld a dark shadowy figure, scarcely to be discerned in the dim flicker of the candles burning before distant shrines. The good prelate crossed himself and adjured this spectre in the name of God, if he were of God, to speak. 'Alas,' moaned the shade most piteously, 'I am not of God, for I am eternally separated from the God Who was my Maker.' 'Who art thou then?' asked the Bishop. 'I am that unhappy wretch, Philippe, sometime Chancellor of this University, and I am lost chiefly on account of three things. The first, because I was a pluralist. The second because I gave no penny of the rich incomes from my livings in charity to the poor as was my bounden duty, but I hoarded the gold. The third, because I led a wanton and evil life.' From this sad history it is evident that even lost souls can appear to men to warn them of their piteous estate, in order that the living may haply flee the wrath to come.

THE POLITICAL GHOST: 1550–1700

The role that ghosts played in the maintenance of a cosmic hierarchy is clear once you look at the decades following the Reformation. Ghosts became a central issue in theological battles about crucial religious matters. They were used as ammunition in fierce doctrinal arguments, firstly about the existence of purgatory, then about the existence of witchcraft, and finally about the existence of any sort of supernatural operation whatever.

Anyone setting out to study the literature on ghost belief is immediately struck by the volume of texts, both in Latin and the vernacular, which the period 1550–1700 threw up.[5] The sudden interest was neither fortuitous nor disinterested: ghosts were essential weapons in very serious and bitter wars. The first of these was fundamental to the growth and success of Protestantism in Europe.

The distinction between magic and religion in the medieval Church had been 'an impossibly fine one', according to Keith Thomas,[6] the Church acting as 'a repository of supernatural power which could be dispensed to the faithful to help them in their daily problems'.[7] In contrast, Protestantism, which had been steadily growing since the time of the Lollards, presented itself as a deliberate attempt to divorce religion from popular magic and superstition. Already in the fifteenth century, hagiography and pilgrimages were on the decline and there was a growing unease about the uses to which the rites of the Church were popularly put: by Tudor times there was a vigorous foundation of popular Protestantism. The Reformation in England, of course, initiated far-reaching attacks on the rituals of consecration and exorcism, on the Mass and other ceremonies, on the priesthood, on the fabric of the Church, on its rites, and on all magical elements of religious doctrine.

One major doctrinal debate of this nature concerned the existence of purgatory: the doctrine which had served its turn for four hundred years or more was under attack, Protestants arguing that, after the death of the body, the souls of the dead went straight to heaven or straight to hell according to their deserts, and that no subsequent action on the part of survivors could help them thwart their destiny. Men were saved by the faith they had shown during their life: no amount of prayers, alms, Masses or indulgences could therefore save them after their death. Odd though it might seem in these days, the existence or non-existence of ghosts was absolutely crucial in this important religious controversy. Crudely put, if ghosts existed, then so must purgatory, but if ghosts did not exist, then there was no evidence that purgatory did either. If, as the new Protestantism taught, the souls of the dead went straight to heaven or straight to hell, then there could be no such thing as ghosts, for the blessed would not want to leave heaven and the damned would not be allowed to leave hell. That empiricism, tradition and the Bible all joined to testify that souls of the dead had been, and were still, known to visit the mundane world proved – so the Catholic divines argued – that there was indeed a third realm in between the extremes of heaven and hell. As the reformer Ludowig Lavater pointed out, it was 'on those apparitions of spirits, as on a sure foundation, their purgatory [was] chiefly builded'.

The Catholics' neat and apparently conclusive argument put Protestant divines into an awkward position. Argument demanded that they should now reject the notion of ghosts and apparitions in entirety – to defeat the Catholic argument it was necessary to discredit all known examples of ghostly visitations – yet this could not simply be done. Not only was popular oral tradition in favour of the ghost, but also there were cases of ghostly apparitions in the Bible, most notably the appearance of the ghost of Samuel to King Saul under the mediumship of the Witch of Endor. All this evidence *had* to be either rejected or reinterpreted. For logical reasons it was not easy to reject it. As a member of the hierarchy of supernatural entities mentioned in the Bible and by the Christian Fathers, the ghost was vouched for on the highest authority. If the Bible and the Fathers could not be taken as authoritative on this matter, they could not be relied on in others. There was no logical place at which to put scepticism aside, and the whole edifice of religion was therefore threatened.

The answer to this dilemma was first to discredit as much of the evidence as possible, and then to redefine the remainder. In the writings of Ludowig Lavater we find the epitome of this approach. In discussing 'The Rhetoric of Tradition and Taboo' earlier, we saw how his *Of Ghostes and Spirites Walking by Nyghte* (translated into English in 1572) was designed to prove that ghosts were either the mistakes of silly, sick or unduly sensitive people, or the result of deliberate deceit, or some entirely natural thing misunderstood, or, alternatively (where none of these explanations applied), 'a good or evill Angell, or some other forewarning sent by God'. What they were not, and could not be, he argued, was 'the souls of dead men as some have thought'. A redefinitional process such as this was quite simple, intellectually satisfying, and could not be refuted on empirical grounds. If, the reformers reasoned, the ghost could not be a departed soul, and yet if it obviously existed, then it *had to be* another type of supernatural creature masquerading as the spirit of a dead man. There were two possibilities: it could be an angel sent from God to warn or comfort; or it could be a devil sent by Satan to alarm, deceive or entrap the unwary. The second of these possibilities was the more likely, because if God was Truth then he would not lightly deceive anybody, and moreover there was a precedent for thinking that the Devil could and did disguise himself, for early saints' legends frequently told of devils assuming shapes other than their own.[8] The standard Catholic position, therefore, was that ghosts existed and everybody knew that they did; and the standard Protestant position was that this just could not be so. Most people, they argued, were mistaken when they thought they saw a spirit, but Satan might disguise his devils in the shape of a spirit in order to wreak havoc with the lives and souls of poor mortals, and just occasionally God might send an angel on a special mission.

A direct reflection of the new thinking can be seen in one of the most familiar literary ghosts of this time – that is, the ghost of Hamlet's father. When confronted with this apparition, Hamlet's reaction is a combination of terror and attraction:

> Angels and ministers of grace defend us! –
> Be thou a spirit of health or goblin damned,
> Bring with thee airs from Heaven or blasts from Hell
> Be thy intents wicked or charitable . . .

Hamlet's choices are that the spectre is a 'spirit of health' from heaven or a 'goblin damned' from hell: initially he sees no third choice. It is not *his* suggestion that what he is seeing is the spirit of his dead father, but that of the ghost itself. Modern interpretations that see the tragedy of the play as stemming from Hamlet's vacillation and cowardice in not quickly revenging his father as the ghost demands may be way off-course. Though the ghost *says* it is the spirit of the dead king:

> Doom'd for a certain term to walk the night
> And, for the day, confin'd to waste in fires
> Till the foul crimes done in my days of nature
> Are burnt and purg'd away,

who knows whether it is telling the truth either about being in purgatory or about the manner of the old king's death? Certainly the destruction which the ghost's intervention lets loose on Hamlet, his family and the nation does not give one confidence in its altruism. Maybe Hamlet would have done well to be more circumspect, like the lady from Boulogne-sur-Mer in one of Fr Taillepied's tales, who resisted the attempts of her stepmother's spirit to speak to her, because 'she was convinced it was a lying demon trying to get in touch with her and entrap her'. At one time the desperate ghost even threw the baby into the fire 'in order to compel her to ask what it sought', yet the lady stayed mum for months on end before she finally gave way, spoke to the spirit, and thus allowed it to give its message.[9] By these standards, Hamlet's capitulation is precipitate and trusting in the extreme.

In similar vein, in Christopher Marlowe's *Doctor Faustus*, when the devil Mephistopheles appears to Faustus, he not only insists that he came of his own accord rather than because he was called up by Faustus, but also that, despite appearances to the contrary, he is in hell even as he speaks with Faustus in his study. When Faustus asks: 'How comes it then that thou art out of Hell?', Mephistopheles replies: 'Why this is Hell, nor am I out of it', and goes on to explain that he carries his own hell of regret and deprivation around with him wherever he goes. What is not possible, he stresses, is that, having lost heaven, he can be anywhere else but hell.

That the redefinition of the ghost held together for several generations can be seen in the fact that in 1718 Francis Hutchinson, vicar of St James's, Bury St Edmunds, and later to be Bishop of Down and Connor, was still putting forward the classic Protestant argument in his sermons, stressing that many night terrors were based on 'Heathenish Stories that the Holy Scriptures never Taught', that spectres were 'imaginary creatures of [our] own making', and that anyway: 'As we worship not Good Angels, so neither let us be in over great Dread or Terror for fear of bad ones.'[10]

Similarly, clergyman and antiquarian, Henry Bourne, when discussing 'whether evil spirits wander about in the Time of Night' in his *Antiquitates Vulgares* of 1725, explains that, though tradition testifies to the existence of spirits, 'What . . . could these have ordinarily been, but the Appearances of some of those Angels of Light, or Darkness? For I am far from thinking that either the Ghosts of the Damn'd or the Happy . . . returns here any more.'[11]

A similar notion can be seen in the popular work of Daniel Defoe, who, as late as 1729, under the alias 'Andrew Moreton', subtitled his *Secrets of the Invisible World Disclos'd*, 'an Universal History of Apparitions . . . Whether Angelicall, Diabolicall, or the Souls of the Departed'. It seems from this that, though the notion that ghosts might be the spirits of dead men had crept back, even in the eighteenth century apparitions were thought to be principally either angels or devils in disguise.

The Protestant reclassification of ghosts into messengers of a higher power, usually the servants of Satan, was never an easy matter. It undermined the belief in a unified creation, which had kept the world whole for several centuries, and it again fractured the realm of the supernatural into two opposed camps – evil against good. It also left people unable to interpret their experiences. Their life and salvation depended on guessing correctly whether the ghostly visitations to which they were accustomed were from angels or demons, but there was no easy way of telling them apart. Furthermore, the transformation was never really convincing nor ever fully completed. In the early days a formal belief in ghosts was a shibboleth that distinguished Catholic from Protestant; however, because the matter remained the subject of controversy, because the Protestant divines were attempting to re-structure ancient folklore at a stroke and because, as we shall see pres-ently, in time the ghost became a useful weapon in the armoury of Protestants, too, in the long run no settled patterns of belief emerged. There were Protestant philosophers and divines who believed in ghosts as spirits of the dead and there were Catholic scholars who utilized the notion that ghosts were or could be devils in disguise. Keith Thomas notes, for example, that, as late as the seventeenth century, belief in ghosts was to be found among almost all religious groups and at virtually every social level. Though in the early years of the Reforma-tion the matter of ghosts had been considered finally and conclusively settled, over the decades the old beliefs gradually regained their lost ground.

Indeed, by the later years of the sixteenth century, ghosts were posi-tively welcomed back in some Protestant circles, for a new enemy appeared, more threatening than the old faith – 'Sadducism',[12] that is, scepticism about the entire supernatural structure, God and all, and a stout reliance on the individual's ability to understand the world on his own terms and in his own way. This new attitude – so threatening to pious folk – was summed up in the reasoning of men like Thomas Hobbes and the 'mechanical philosophers' of the new scientific age:

We are not to renounce our Senses, and Experience [wrote Hobbes in *Leviathan*]: nor (that which is the undoubted Word of God) our natural Reason. For they are the talents which he hath put into our hands to negotiate, till the coming again of our blessed Saviour; and therefore not to be folded up in the Napkin of an Implicit Faith, but employed in the purchase of Justice, Peace, and true Religion.[13]

Such independent-mindedness and reliance on the individual's powers of judgement were entirely in tune with the spirit of the age, though historians point out that there had already been a consistent tradition of scepticism and religious free-thinking for many decades.[14] In 1573 it had been reported that a group of fenland sectaries had denied the existence of hell; in 1578 a Norfolk ploughwright had been burned for expressing the opinion that the New Testament was merely 'a story of men'; in 1589 Bishop Cooper had complained that 'the most part of men' held the clergy in 'loathsome contempt'; and in 1600 the Bishop of Exeter had confessed that in his diocese it was common for people to argue about whether God really existed or not. The middle decades of the seventeenth century had perhaps merely brought a lot of latent scepticism into the open. The Socinian sect now denied the divinity of Jesus and the Ranters repudiated the immortality of the soul; the 'Digger' Gerrard Winstanley alleged that heaven was 'a fancy your false teachers put into your heads to please you while they pick your purses', reproached the theologians of the universities Oxford and Cambridge because 'You doe not know that but as your fathers have told you; which may as well be false as true, if you have not better ground than tradition', and asserted (in an argument worthy of that later radical, William Blake) that God is 'the spirit and power that dwells in every man and woman'.[15]

Meanwhile the 'mechanical philosophy' was busy redefining the world and all that was in it. René Descartes spoke for all mechanical philosophers when he categorically stated that 'there exists nothing in the whole of nature which cannot be explained in terms of purely corporeal causes'.[16] This world of matter was an intricate and clever machine, no more; a machine which God had created and set in motion and then delivered into the hands of men. It followed that occult phenomena were either illusory or had a 'natural' (i.e. mechanical) explanation. Though it has been argued that the philosophy gained such rapid acceptance among educated Europeans because it was able to meet the challenges of both atheism and magic,[17] simultaneously upholding the social order and offering up the world to the control of men, there were yet many people who saw its denial of supernatural power as the ultimate threat to Christianity. Among the pious, it was convincing demonstration that a new age of atheism was coming upon them.

It was in the context of this feeling that a new use was found for spectres and apparitions. The utility of ghosts, as always, was that they were part of a widespread and well-established folklore, attested by both written and oral traditions and by the personal-experience accounts of honest, sincere and reliable people. If any supernatural entity existed, then surely ghosts did: if the supernatural existed, then the mechanical philosophy was undermined and the threat to Christianity beaten off.

As it happened, there were also other supernatural creatures for which there was (or appeared at the time to be) ample evidence – witches – and they, too, were pulled into the argument. In England there had been a severe persecution of witches under Elizabeth I and a second peak occurred under the Commonwealth. Though the confessions of the 'witches' were extracted under torture or the threat of torture, this did not invalidate the mass of evidence in the eyes of Church, State or ordinary people: any resistance to the torture was only seen as further proof that the accused were buoyed up by supernatural help from the Devil.

The evidence for the existence of both ghosts and witchcraft was thus extremely strong, being based on a combination of received tradition and validating testimony. In the battle against Sadducism, therefore, both were called upon to play their part by giving plain proof of the existence of a supernatural world. Dr Henry More, theologian and man of letters, summed up the position well in a letter to his friend Joseph Glanvil in 1681:

I look upon it as a special piece of Providence that there are ever and anon such fresh examples of Apparitions and Witchcraft as may rub up and awaken their benumbed and lethargic Mindes into a suspicion at least, if not an assurance that there are other intelligent Beings beside those that are clad in heavy Earth or Clay: In this, I say, methinks the Divine Providence does plainly outwit the Powers of the Dark Kingdom, in permitting wicked men and women and vagrant spirits of that Kingdom to make Leagues and Covenants one with another, the Confessions of Witches against their own Lives being so palpable an Evidence, (besides the miraculous feats they play) that there are bad Spirits, which will necessarily open a Door to the belief that there are good ones, and lastly that there is a God.' [18]

How long this argument was to seem both powerful and valid to con-servative minds is evidenced by the fact that, as late as 1768, John Wesley could write:

It is true likewise that the English in general, and indeed most of the men of learning in Europe, have given up all accounts of witches and apparitions, as mere old wives' fables. I am sorry for it; and I willingly take this opportunity of entering my solemn protest against this violent compliment which so many that believe in the Bible pay to those who do not believe [. . .] They well know (whether Christians know it or not), that the giving up of witchcraft is, in effect, giving up the Bible. [19]

In the late seventeenth century, pious men of letters therefore set about the task of collecting evidence of witchcraft and apparitions in a last-ditch battle to stave off what they saw as the growing atheism and materialism of the age. Among these, the most prolific were Henry More and Joseph Glanvil, along with Richard Bovet and George Sinclair, and the results of their efforts were three enormously influential compilations of stories of the supernatural: Glanvil's *Sadducismus Triumphatus* of 1681, Bovet's *Pandaemonium* of 1684, and Sinclair's *Satan's Invisible World Discovered* of 1685. These books constitute a reservoir of literary stories, personal experiences, folk legends and tales, rumours, news and gossip – stories of witches, poltergeists, apparitions, miraculous cures, demons, omens, warnings and deathbed experiences – polished up for public consumption and almost cynically designed as propaganda for a great cause. Though these should not be considered as collections of folklore (they were polemics), they do nevertheless have considerable interest for folklorists. Not only do they show how traditional ideas were utilized in theological politics, but also they indicate how a hundred years or more of using folklore in this manner affected the nature and content of the traditions themselves.

There is one obvious and discernible change – and that is, that though used in religious arguments, the ghosts themselves were credited most often with secular motives (where they had motives at all). In the Middle Ages, ghost traditions had been harnessed to the teaching of the Church and used to illustrate crucial doctrines such as the existence of purgatory and to validate central rites such as baptism, confession and burial. With the arrival of Protestantism, ghosts had been banished; in England the Church of England neither sanctioned them nor had any use for them – officially. Though ghosts, despite the ban, continued to exist, at a stroke they were deprived of all their religiously motivated behaviour. They could obviously no longer ask for alms and Masses, nor for prayers to speed their progress through purgatory, and they could not validate the Church's teaching in any respect because their very existence ran counter to official policy. Their only value in religious arguments was their mere existence – evidence of the immortality of souls and a supernatural sphere of operation. For this purpose, any sort of ghost would do.

In late-seventeenth-century educated literature, therefore, ghosts were often not necessarily credited with any real aims or motives at all, and where they were shown as purposeful, their purposes (for obvious reasons) were social rather than sacred. In Glanvil's stories, for instance, ghosts are seen most often as poltergeists or wraiths, or as geared to mundane affairs such as righting wrongs, gossiping about future conduct and achieving miraculous cures, or threatening or assaulting the living. In only three of his thirty-four 'Relations' are the ghost's words or motives sacred rather than secular. Bovet and Sinclair – less sober, better storytellers – have a much higher incidence of apparently motiveless apparitions (mainly incredible in the extreme). These include a personal experience story in which Bovet gives an account of seeing five 'very fine and lovely women', draped in white veils, process to his bedside in single file, and an equally preposterous tale of a manservant who was 'stripped of all his clothes after he was in bed' by apparitions of 'very beautiful young Women, whose presence lightened up the place, as if it had been day, though there was no candle near it'.[20]

Not to be outdone, Sinclair provides stories about 'an apparition to King James the fourth and his courtiers'; an 'apothecaries Servant that returned to the Shop after he had been dead'; 'a great Doctor of Divinity, that raise out of the Bier and spoke to all that were present'; and 'an apparition at Gladsmuir', a truly remarkable story of a murderer who will not die even though executed several times.[21]

The other result of the ghost being used as ammunition in theological argument was that ghost types became harshly polarized into good and evil manifestations. Firstly, the redefinition of ghosts in early Protestant doctrine stressed that, if not illusions, they must be either 'good or evil angels'. Secondly, the yoking together of witchcraft and apparitions in the battle against materialism nicely confused the boundaries between the two. Poltergeists, for example, which had earlier been implicitly grouped with ghosts and not always and necessarily thought to be malevolent,[22] by the mid-seventeenth century became examples of witchcraft and have never since lost the element of malice afore-thought. Thirdly, in radical Protestant thought the whole world was conceived of in starkly polarized terms. Richard Baxter, in his famous compilation of supernatural experiences *The Certainty of the World of Spirits Fully Evinced* (1691), for instance, called nearly every one of his collected examples either the work of the Devil or the providence of God.

What, then, may we conclude about the nature and content of ghost beliefs in the sixteenth and seventeenth centuries? From the mid-sixteenth century onwards, we see the truth of an established folklore being debated first by the proponents and adversaries of purgatory, then by the proponents and adversaries of witchhunting, and then by the proponents and adversaries of the new scepticism. By reading between the lines, we can get a good picture not only of how contemporary traditions were used as political weapons in these debates, but also of what these traditions probably were and how they were affected by contemporary debate.

From the various sources, 'political' writers like Glanvil as well as the antiquarians of the period, quite an elaborate picture builds up. It seems that for most of the sixteenth and seventeenth centuries, people believed in two overall classes of supernatural happenings. Firstly, there were non-human phenomena such as astral spirits, poltergeists, household familiars, ghosts in animal or fiery form, 'knockers' in mines and various other sorts of things that made unaccountable noises as warnings or advertisements of their presence. In addition, there were apparitions of (usually recognizable) people. Some of these were fetches and *doppelgängers*, and others were wraiths of the sick, the dying and the newly dead. Another large group of apparitions were human in shape but essentially alarming in nature. These were thought to be seen at night round the bed of the sleeper. Alternatively, they might haunt specific people or locations, usually betwixt-and-between places, where they would be seen by any unfortunate isolated or benighted person.

The most common type of apparition, however, was the ghost of some recognizable dead person, who returned for some specific purpose. There was a wide range of possible motives for such a visit. Ghosts might come back to issue warnings and prophecies; to reveal secrets such as murders, treasure or the hiding-place of wills and other lost documents; and to pay debts or otherwise rectify wrongs committed in life. They were also given to preventing injustices, revenging crimes, confessing to sins and seeking to clear their names. Sometimes they might return just out of affection for the past, to talk with their survivors, or to catch up on family gossip. Occasionally, they obstructed travellers, assaulted sceptics or knocked pedestrians over in the street; very occasionally in Protestant Britain, they asked for burial or prayers.

We can also see how that folklore was picked over, elaborated, polished up and used for specific purposes in theological politics. The result these processes had on the lore itself was to secularize supernatural traditions (and the behaviour of the visiting ghosts) and to polarize ghost-types into wholly good or wholly alarming manifestations of supernatural power.

There had always been, and continued to be throughout the sixteenth and seventeenth centuries, an undercurrent of fear of the dead, which expressed itself in stories about a variety of frightening or meaningless supernatural occurrences. Though there was a wide divergence of opinion about what benevolent apparitions might do, there was no dispute about what malevolent ones were capable of. Commentators differed, sometimes quite strongly, about what the functions of good ghosts were and how they might manifest themselves, some suggesting that, robed all in white and accompanied by music and sweet perfumes, they came to converse on spiritual matters and rock the baby's cradle, others suggesting that, haggard and dishevelled, they rose from the ground accompanied by mastiff dogs and demanded that the sword with which they had committed murder should be laid to rest beside their guilty corpses. Other ghosts guarded treasure, manifested themselves as disembodied hands, or led the percipient into the woods at midnight in order to reveal the hiding-place of lost documents: they were endlessly inventive in matters of appearance, purpose and destiny.

Yet, in all the texts from 1550 onwards, writers were in substantial agreement when it came to the matter of bad or neutral spirits. All agreed that bad spirits could exhibit themselves as malicious poltergeists, create domestic disturbances, injure the living (a favoured method was by burning or freezing the hand they grasped), pull bedclothes off sleepers or even get into bed with them.

They were equally in accord in declaring the existence of a wide variety of fairly neutral and more or less aimless ghosts – wraiths of the dying or newly dead and spirits who flittered about, closed doors mysteriously or were heard softly sighing, spitting and coughing on the stairs and in the corridors. The core of folklore on which all were agreed, then, was a group of traditions about meaningless or malevolent apparitions. In the supernatural folklore of the period, benevolence fluctuated, malevolence remained constant.

Fear and terror had been there all along, but it intensified with the Reformation. Before that, the Church provided rites of exorcism which allowed people to deal with the evil supernatural on its own terms, fighting evil magic with good. Protestantism had, of course, banned exorcism when it banned ghosts yet, ironically, by redefining ghosts in terms of devils it also increased the amount of evil abroad in the world. Though its aim was to free people from fear and superstition, and there must have been many who were indeed freed, yet there were many more who were plunged into even greater terror and anxiety. This should not be overstressed, but it was surely a contributory factor in the increased number of reports about manifestations of the evil supernatural – it is not surprising that by the end of the eighteenth and throughout the nineteenth centuries there should be an upsurge in stories about the laying of ghosts by bell, book and candle or by tricking them into bottles and throwing them in the Red Sea.

Again, in earlier days, when the Church had harnessed ghost belief to religious instruction, the Church's sanction of tradition had done much to civilize the supernatural and assuage fear, by providing as many good and caring apparitions as there were aimless and malevolent ones. When the Church withdrew its support and the number of ghosts with moral missions declined, the number of purposeless or evil ones expanded to fill the gap. The supernatural world thus began not only to be secular and polarized, but also to lose its sense of purpose.

* * *

No selection of supernatural narratives for the seventeenth century would be complete without Richard Baxter's famous, if repellent, tale of the manifestation which appeared to Mrs Bowen of Llanellin, Glamorgan, or his equally well-known story of the wraith of Mary Goffe. The two accounts provide diametrically opposed views of the supernatural. In the story of Mrs Bowen of Llanellin, the supernatural is shown in ugly light. The manifestation, though of a living not a dead man, is not only disgusting and terrifying, but also is plainly interpreted as the work of the Devil, as the references to darkness, noise, wind and the smell of sulphur testify. Baxter gives two separate accounts of this occurrence, which he has received from correspondents. The first is from Colonel Rogers, the Governor of Hereford, the second from Mr Maur. Bedwell (received via Mr Samuel Jones of Coedrehan).

Baxter's story of the wraith of Mary Goffe is also well-researched, his informant having taken evidence from the nurse and the minister attending the dying woman, from both her mother and father, and from two neighbours. In contrast to the story of Mrs Bowen, it is one of the most touching of the supernatural stories handed down to us from the seventeenth century.

The extracts are taken from Richard Baxter's *The Certainty of the World of Spirits Fully Evinced* (pages 9–16 and 49–52), first published in 1691:

Version 1

In the beginning of the late war, a gentleman of that county, being oppressed by the King's party, took arms under the Earl of Essex, and by his valour obtained a good repute in the army, so that in a short time he got the command of a lieutenant-colonel. But as soon as the heat of the war was abated, his ease and preferment led him to a careless and sensual life, insomuch that the godly commanders judged him unfit to continue in England, and thereupon sent him to Ireland, where he grew so vain and notional, that he was cashiered the army; and being then at liberty to sin without restraint, he became an absolute Atheist, denying Heaven or hell, God or devil (acknowledging only a power, as the ancient heathens did fate), accounting temporal pleasures all his expected heaven; so that at last he became hateful, and hating all civil society, and his nearest relations.

About December last, he being in Ireland, and his wife (a godly gentlewoman, of a good family, and concluded, by all the godly people that knew her, to be one of the most sincere and upright Christians in those parts, as being for many years under great afflictions, and always bearing them with Christian-like patience) living in this house in Glamorgan, was very much troubled one night with a great noise, much like the sound of a whirlwind, and a violent beating of the doors or walls, as if the whole house were falling to pieces: and being in her chamber, with most of her family, after praying to the Lord (accounting it sinful incredulity to yield to fear), she went to bed; and suddenly after, there appeared unto her something like her husband, and asked her whether he should come to bed. She, sitting up, and praying to the Lord, told him he was not her husband, and that he should not. He urged more earnestly: – 'What! not the husband of thy bosom? What! not the husband of thy bosom?' Yet had no power to hurt her. And she, together with some godly people, spent that night in prayer, being very often interrupted by this apparition.

The next night, Mr Miles (a godly minister), with four other godly men, came to watch and pray in the house for that night, and so continued in prayer, and other duties of religion, without any interruption or noise at all that night. But the night following, the gentlewoman, with several other godly women, being in the house, the noise of whirlwind began again, with more violence than formerly, and the apparition walked in the chamber, having an insufferable stench, like that of a putrified carcass, filling the room with a thick smoak, smelling like sulpur, darkening the light of the fire and candle, but not quite extinguishing it; sometimes going down the stairs, and coming up again with a fearful noise, disturbing them at their prayers, one while with the sound of words which they could not discern, other while striking them so that the next morning their faces were black with smoak, and their bodies swollen with bruises.

Thereupon they left the house, lest they should tempt the Lord by their over-bold staying in such danger, and sent this Atheist the sad news of this apparition; who coming to England about May last, expressed more love and respect to his wife than formerly; yet telling her, that he could not believe her relation of what she had seen, as having not a power to believe any thing but what himself saw; and yet would not hitherto go to his house to make trial, but probably will e'er long, for that he is naturally of an exceeding rash and desperate spirit.

August, 1656

Version 2

As to Col. Bowen's house, I can give you some brief particulars, which you may credit, as coming from such who were not so foolish as to be deluded, nor so dishonest as to report an untruth. What I shall write, if need were, would be made good both by ear and eye-witnesses. The gentleman, Col. Bowen, whose house is called Llanellin, in Gowersland, formerly was famous for profession of religion, but this day is the saddest man in his principles I know living. To me, in particular, he has denyed the being of the Spirit of the Lord: his argument thus – Either 'tis something or nothing; if something, show me, tell me what it is, &, and I believe he gives as little credit to other spirits as the Sadducees. At his house, aforementioned, he being then in Ireland, making provision for removing thither, these things happened. About December last, his wife being in bed, a gracious, understanding woman, and one whom little things will not affright; one in the likeness of her husband, and just in his posture, presented himself to her bed-side, proffering to come to bed to her, which she refusing, he gave this answer, 'What! Refuse the husband of thy bosom'; and after some time, she alledging Christ was her husband, it disappeared. Strange miserable howlings and cries were heard about the house, his tread, his posture, sighing, humming, were frequently heard in the parlour; in the day-time often the shadow of one walking would appear on the wall. One night was very remarkable, and had not the Lord stood by the poor gentlewoman and her two maids, that night they had been undone; as she was going to bed, she perceived by the impression on the bed, as if somebody had been lying there, and, opening the bed, she smelt the smell of a carcass somewhile dead; and being in bed (for the gentlewoman was somewhat courageous), upon the tester, which was of cloth, she perceived something rolling from side to side, and by and by, being forc'd out of her bed, she had not time to dress herself, such cries and other things almost amazing her, but she (hardly any clothes being on), with her two maids, got upon her knees by the bedside to seek the Lord; but, extreamly assaulted, oftentimes she would, by somewhat which felt like a large dog under her knees, be lifted a foot or more high from the ground. Some were heard to talk on the other side of the bed, which one of the maids harkening to, she had a blow upon the back. Divers assaults would be made by fits; it would come with a cold breath of wind, the candles burn blew, and almost out; horrible screekings, yellings and roarings, within and without the house, sad smells of brimstone and powder, and this continued from some nine at night to some three the next morning, so that the poor gentlewoman and her servants were in a sad case the next morning, smelling of brimstone and powder, and, as I remember, black with it, but the Lord was good, Fires have been seen upon the house and in the fields; his voice hath been heard luring his hawks, a game he delights in, as also the bills of the hawks. These are the chief things which I dare recommend upon credit, and I could wish, that they who question the existency of spirits had been but one night at Llanellin, to receive satisfaction to their objections [. . .]

Swansy
16 October, 1656

Mary, the wife of John Goffe, of Rochester, being afflicted with a long illness, removed to her father's house at West Mulling, which is about nine miles distant from her own: there she died, June the 4th, this present year, 1691.

The day before her departure, she grew very impatiently desirous to see her two children, whom she had left at home, to the care of a nurse. She prayed her husband to hire a horse, for she must go home, and die with the children. When they persuaded her to the contrary, telling her she was not fit to be taken out of her bed, nor able to sit on horseback; she entreated them, however, to try; 'If I cannot sit,' said she, 'I will lie all along upon the horse, for I must go and see my poor babes.'

A minister, who lives in the town, was with her at ten a clock that night, to whom she express'd good hopes in the mercies of God, and a willingness to die; 'But,' said she, 'it is my misery that I cannot see my children.'

Between one and two-a-clock in the morning she fell into a trance. One Widow Turner, who watched with her that night, says, that her eyes were open and fixed, and her jaw fallen; she put her hand upon her mouth and nostrils, but could perceive no breath, she thought her to be in a fit, and doubted whether she were alive or dead.

The next day, this dying woman told her mother, that she had been at home with her children. 'That is impossible,' said the mother, 'for you have been here in bed all the while.' 'Yes,' replied the other, 'but I was with them last night, when I was asleep.'

The nurse at Rochester, Widow Alexander by name, affirms, and says she will take her oath on't before a magistrate, and receive the sacrament upon it, that a little before two-a-clock that morning, she saw the likeness of the said Mary Goffe come out of the next chamber (where the elder child lay in a bed by itself, the door being left open), and stood by her bed-side for about a quarter of an hour; the younger child was there lying by her; her eyes moved, and her mouth went, but she said nothing. The nurse moreover says, that she was perfectly awake, it was then day-light, being one of the longest days in the year. She sate up in her bed, and looked steadfastly upon the apparition; in that time she heard the bridge-clock strike two, and a while after said, 'In the name of the Father, Son, and Holy Ghost, what art thou?' Thereupon the appearance removed, and went away; she slipp'd on her cloaths and followed, but what became on't she cannot tell. Then, and not before, she began to be grievously affrighted, and went out of doors, and walked upon the wharf (the house is just by the river side) for some hours, only going in now and then to look to the children. At five-a-clock she went to a neighbour's house, and knocked at the door, but they would not rise; at six she went again, then they arose and let her in. She related to them all that had pass'd; they would persuade her she was mistaken, or dreamt, but she confidently affirmed, 'If ever I saw her in all my life, I saw her this night.'

One of those to whom she made the relation (Mary, the wife of John Sweet) had a messenger come from Mulling that forenoon, to let her know her neighbour Goffe was dying, and desired to speak with her; she went over the same day, and found her just departing. The mother, amongst other discourse, related to her how much her daughter had long'd to see the children, and said she had seen them. This brought to Mrs Sweet's mind what the nurse had told her that morning, for, till then, she had not thought to mention it, but disguised it rather, as the woman's disturbed imagination.

The substance of this I had related to me by John Carpenter, the father of the deceased, next day after her burial, July the second. I fully discoursed the matter with the nurse, and two neighbours, to whose house she went that morning.

Two days after, I had it from the mother, the minister that was with her in the evening, and the woman who sat up with her that last night; they all agree in the same story, and every one helps to strengthen the others testimony.

They appear to be sober, intelligent persons, far enough from designing to impose a cheat upon the world, or to manage a lye, and what temptation they should lye under for so doing I cannot conceive.

In contrast, the antiquarian, John Aubrey, tells possibly the shortest ghost story on record in his *Miscellanies* of 1696. It is here reproduced in its entirety, and features a ghost with absolutely no purpose at all and a collector who in no way attempts to give it one (though, nevertheless, it neatly shows not only the way that ghosts were commonly assumed at the time to be either good or evil spirits, but also the correct manner of addressing them):

Anno 1670, not far from Cyrencester, was an Apparition. Being demanded, whether a good spirit or a bad? returned no answer, but disappeared with a curious Perfume and a most melodious Twang.

In the same book, Aubrey also has (pages 61–5) a series of stories all obviously in lively circulation between 1640 and 1696, when the book was compiled, which show apparitions in a variety of contemporary shapes – as wraiths of the dying and as purposeful ghosts, insisting on justice for their children or trying to persuade them to mend their evil ways, desiring alterations to social situations prevailing in the mundane world. The contrast with the religious purposes shown in Fr Taillepied's stories is very plain:

ANNO 1647, the Lord MOHUN's Son and Heir (a gallant Gentleman, Valiant, and a great Master of Fencing and Horsemanship) had a Quarrel with Prince GRIFFIN; there was a Challenge, and they were to Fight on Horse-back in Chelsey-fields in the Morning – Mr MOHUN went accordingly to meet him; but about EBERY-FARM he was met by some who quarrell'd with him and Pistol'd him; it was believed, by the Order of Prince GRIFFIN; for he was sure, that Mr MOHUN being so much the better Horseman & would have Killed him, had they Fought. In JAMES-STREET in COVENT-GARDEN did then Lodge a Gentlewoman a Handsome Woman but Common, who was Mr MOHUN's Sweet-heart. Mr MOHUN was Murthered about Ten a clock in the Morning; and at that very time, his Mistress being in Bed, saw Mr MOHUN come to her Bed-side, drew the Curtain, looked upon her and went away: She called after him but no answer: She knock'd for her Maid, ask'd her for Mr MOHUN; she said, she did not see him, and had the Key of her Chamber door in her Pocket. This account my Friend aforesaid, had from the Gentlewomans own Mouth, and her Maids.

A parallel Story to this, is, that Mr BROWN (Brother-in-law to the Lord CONNINGSBY) discovered his being Murthered to several. His Phantome appear'd to his Sister and her Maid in FLEET-STREET about the time he was Killed in HEREFORDSHIRE, which was about a Year since, 1693.

Sir WALTER LONG of DRAYCOT (Grandfather of Sir JAMES LONG) had two Wives; the first a Daughter of Sir — PACKINGTON in WORCESTER-SHIRE; by whom he had a Son: His second Wife was a daughter of Sir JOHN THINNE of LONGLEAT; by whom he had several Sons and Daughters. The second Wife did use much Artifice to render the Son by the first Wife (who had not much Promethean Fire) Odious to his Father; she would get her Acquaintance to make him Drunk; and then expose him in that Condition to his Father; in fine she never left off her attempts, till she had got Sir WALTER to disinherit him. She laid the Scene for the doing this, at BATH at the Assizes, where was her Brother Sir EGRIMOND THINNE an Eminent Serjeant at Law, who drew the Writing; and his Clerk was to sit up all Night to Engross it; as he was Writing, he perceived a shadow on the Parchment, from the Candle: he look'd up, and there appear'd a Hand, which immediately vanish'd; he was startled at it, but thought it might be only his Fancy, being sleepy; so he writ on; by and by a fine White-hand interposed between the Writing and the Candle (he could discern it was a Womans Hand) but vanish'd as before; I have forgot [whether] it appeared a Third time. But with that, the Clerk threw down his Pen, and would Engross no more, but goes and tells his Master of it, and absolutely refused to do it. But it was done by somebody, and Sir WALTER LONG was prevailed with to Seal and Sign it. He lived not long after; and his Body did not go quiet to the Grave, it being arrested at the Church-porch by the Trustees of the first Lady. The Heir's Relations took his part, and Commenc'd a Suit against Sir WALTER (the second son) and compell'd him to accept of a Moiety of the Estate; so the Eldest Son kept South-Wranchester, and Sir WALTER, the Second Son, Dracot Cernes &. This was about the middle of the Reign of King JAMES the First.

I must not forget an Apparition in my Country, which appear'd several times to Doctor TURBERVILE's Sister, at SALISBURY; which is much talk'd of. One Marry'd a second Wife, and contrary to the Agreement and Settlement at the first Wife's Marriage, did wrong the Children by the first Venter. The Settlement was hid behind a Wainscot in the Chamber where the Doctor's Sister did lie: And the Apparition of the first Wife did discover it to her. By which means Right was done to the first Wife's Children. The Apparition told her that she Wandred in the Air, and was now going to God. Dr TURBERVILE (Oculist) did affirm this to be true . . .

One Mr TOWES who had been School-fellow with Sir GEORGE VILLERS, the father of the first Duke of BUCKINGHAM, (and was his Friend and Neighbour) as he lay in his Bed awake, (and it was Day-light,) came into his Chamber the Phantome of his dear Friend Sir GEORGE VILLERS: Said Mr TOWES to him, Why, you are Dead, what makes you here? said the Knight, I am Dead, but cannot rest in peace for the Wickedness and Abomination of my Son GEORGE at Court. I do appear to you, to tell him of it, and to advise and dehort him from his Evil ways. Said Mr TOWES, the Duke will say, that I am Mad, or Doat. Said Sir GEORGE, Go to him from me, and tell him by such a Token (some Mole) that he had in some secret place, which none but himself knew of. Accordingly, Mr TOWES went to the Duke, who laugh'd at his Message. At his return home, the Phantome appeared again; and told him, that the Duke would be Stab'd (he drew out a Dagger) a quarter of a Year after: And you shall outlive him half a Year; and the warning that you shall have of your death will be, That your Nose will fall a-bleeding: All of which accordingly fell out so. This account I have had (in the main) from two, or three; but Sir WILLIAM DUGDALE affirms what I have here taken from him to be true, and that the Apparition told him of several things to come, which proved true, e.g. of a Prisoner in the Tower, that should be honourably delivered. This Mr TOWES had so often the Ghost of his old Friend appear to him, that it was not at all terrible to him. He was Surveyor of the Works at WINDSOR (by the favour of the Duke): being then sitting in the Hall, he cried out, The Duke of BUCKINGHAM is stabb'd: He was stabb'd at that very moment.

This relation Sir WILLIAM DUGDALE had from Mr PINE (Neighbour to Mr TOWES without BISHOPSGATE) and they were both great lovers of Musick, and sworn Brothers . . .

THE DECLINE OF THE PURPOSEFUL GHOST: 1700–1840

'I have said it before, and I say it again', wrote Pierre Bayle[23] towards the end of the seventeenth century, 'it is the purest delusion to suppose that because an idea has been handed down from time immemorial to succeeding generations, it may not be entirely false.' The development of modern science and the mechanical philosophy which accompanied it revolutionized educated men's ideas about the world and threw out the traditional concepts of several centuries. By the middle of the seventeenth century, the Royal Society was already congratulating itself for this achievement. In his history of the Society (1667), Thomas Sprat explained that:

as for the TERRORS and MISAPPREHENSIONS which commonly confound weaker minds, and make men's hearts to fail and boggle at Trifles; there is so little hope of having them removed by speculation alone, that it is evident they

were first produc'd by the most CONTEMPLATIVE men among the AN-
CIENTS; and chiefly prevail'd of late years, when that way of LEARNING
flourish'd.

But now everyone could rejoice that:

from the time in which the REAL PHILOSOPHY has appear'd, there is scarce
any whisper concerning such HORRORS: Every man is unshaken at those
Tales, at which his ANCESTORS trembled: the cours of things goes quietly
along, in its own true channel of NATURAL CAUSES and EFFECTS. For this
we are beholden to EXPERIMENTS; which though they have not yet completed
the discovery of the true world, yet they have already vanquish'd those wild
inhabitants of the false worlds, that us'd to astonish the minds of men. A
Blessing for which we ought to be thankful, if we remember, that it is one of
the greatest Curses that God pronounces on the wicked, THAT THEY SHALL
FEAR WHERE NO FEAR IS.[24]

Certainly, the last of the Witchcraft Acts was dismantled in 1736 and by
the same date clergymen and philosophers had ceased to take an interest
in ghosts and apparitions. In the face of the eighteenth century's
overpowering confidence that nature was subdued and irrational fears
abolished, it is not surprising that belief in the supernatural should go
underground. At least in public, educated men began to repudiate tradition, feeling that belief in ghosts was somehow vulgar and disreputable. So, the process begun in the early years of the Reformation
was finally consummated a century and a half later.

The changed world-view brought about by experimental science
and Cartesian philosophy created a universe which could run without
outside help from supernatural sources. A 'cosmology in which God
is effectively relegated to a spectator's seat while the Devil drops from
view'[25] had no place for apparitions at all. The ghost was doubly
stranded. Forsaken by the clergy and abandoned by the educated laity,
the ghost that appeared in the literature became increasingly purposeless because there was no authoritative voice with a vested interest
in *giving* it purpose. Already the polarization of the supernatural had
isolated and foregrounded 'bad' ghosts, secularization had deprived
'good' ghosts of their spiritual functions, and doctrinal changes had
further eroded the idea that there might be rhyme and reason in supernatural visitations (for once man is saved by faith and deeds avail him
nothing, there is no reason why ghosts should be restless because of
good deeds left undone). Finally, when science and rationalism created
a world in man's image and there was no longer a place for magic
and mystery, when State as well as Church repudiated the super-

natural, then there simply became less and less for ghosts to *do* – except hang round aimlessly and cause mischief, like adolescents on a street corner.

In earlier centuries the world had been thought of as a semi-magical place, and strange creatures such as ghosts had had their due rank and function: when the world became a machine, there was no room left for them, no possible role for them to play, no place for them to return from, no reason for them to bother people. They *could* only be illusory, private experiences or meaningless, inharmonious intrusions. They literally had no *raison d'être*.

For the folklorist or historian of ideas, the eighteenth century creates particular difficulties, for, despite this official scepticism, at a private and personal level many people continued to believe in ghosts, omens and divination. Throughout the century, there was a wealth of popular occult literature: the works of seventeenth-century collectors such as Glanvil, Bovet and Sinclair were still (according to Francis Hutchinson) to be seen in tradesmen's shops and farmers' houses and exerting a considerable influence on the minds of young people;[26] and antiquarians were amassing significant amounts of information about popular concepts of the supernatural, mainly culled from village custom and country belief. Nor was such belief confined to the 'vulgar', uneducated, or rural people. There remained a significant number of educated people who still, in the privacy of their own hearts, clung to the old ideas (Keith Thomas notes, for example, that belief in ghosts was 'a reality in the eighteenth century for many educated men, however much the rationalists laughed at them').[27]

But there are two grave difficulties about using contemporary material to reconstruct or interpret the folklore of the age. The first is that we have no way of knowing what the folklore *meant* to the people who transmitted it. Antiquarians, for example, recorded their information either 'blank' without comment, or with a commentary full of reproofs and sneers that established their intellectual respectability in the face of their material. The second problem is that, whereas this information is thus all description, the information we get from the previous century is all interpretation, so there is apparently a huge difference between the ghosts of one century and the ghosts of the next. There seems to be an enormous shift in supernatural folklore. But we cannot be certain how far that shift is real and how far it was the product of the very different attitudes which educated commentators brought to their accounts of ghost traditions. Judging by much popular literature and antiquarian writing, meaningless and malevolent manifestations by the early eighteenth century had almost completely crowded out the purposeful supernatural.

This is plain if we look at probably the best account of early eighteenth-century ghost traditions – Henry Bourne's *Antiquitates Vulgares* of 1725. It is worth looking at Bourne's descriptions of local beliefs in some detail and noting the perspective from which he himself regards them. As curate of All Saints' Church, Newcastle-upon-Tyne, he explicitly says that his intentions are to give 'An Account of several of [the common people's] Opinions and Ceremonies with Proper Reflections upon each of them; shewing which may be retain'd, and which ought to be laid aside.' In his preface he explains that many of the customs and beliefs he will describe, though once general in the land, would now 'have little or no being, if not observed among the Vulgar', but it is not his intention either to condone old superstitions or to suppress innocent customs. His aim is to 'make known their End and Design' in order to sift the wheat from the chaff, to clear folklore of superstition and regulate it for the advantage of its adherents. Thus chapter 6, for example, is headed: 'Of the Time of Cock-crow: Whether evil Spirits wander about in the Time of Night; and whether they fly away at the Time of Cock-crow. Reflections upon this encouraging us to have Faith and Trust in God.'

The main interest for us today, however, is not the comforting reflections, but the descriptions of the traditions themselves. We read, for example, that:

It is a received Tradition among the Vulgar, That at the Time of Cock-crowing, the Midnight Spirits forsake these lower Regions, and go to their proper Places. They wander, say they, about the World, from the dead Hour of Night, when all Things are buried in Sleep and darkness, till the Time of Cock-crowing, and then they depart. Hence it is, that in Country-Places, where the Way of Life requires more early Labour, they always go chearfully to Work at that Time; whereas if they are called abroad sooner, they are apt to imagine every Thing they see or hear, to be a wandring Ghost.[28]

Likewise chapter 7, which deals with fear of churchyards and promises that since the arrival of Protestantism there is nothing to fear in them, tells us that:

The most ignorant People are afraid of going through a CHURCH-YARD at Night-time. If they are obliged upon some hasty and urgent Affair, they fear and tremble, till they are beyond its Bounds, but they generally avoid it, and go further about [. . .] The reason of this Fear is, a Notion they have imbib'd, that in CHURCH-YARDS there is a frequent walking of Spirits at the DEAD-TIME of Night.[29]

Elsewhere he tells of whole families spending winter evenings telling ghost stories (often of their own personal experiences), and adds that this practice greatly adds to the fear-level of the community. Shepherds are especially prone to telling these stories, he says, and there are few of them who cannot recount meeting fairies, or apparitions in the shape of cows, dogs and horses, or the Devil himself with his cloven foot.

At other times, he says, country storytellers tell tales of haunted houses. Almost every village is said to have one and there are lively rumours about how it came to be haunted (whether by murder, sudden death or accident) and what tricks the restless spirit gets up to. 'Another Tradition they hold, and which is often talk'd of', he claims, 'is, that there are particular Places alotted to Spirits to walk in' and that such places are dangerous at night: 'Nay, they'll further tell you, that some Spirits have lamented the Hardness of their Condition, in being obliged to walk in cold and uncomfortable Places, and have therefore desir'd the Person who was so hardy as to speak to them, to gift them with a warmer walk, by some well grown HEDGE or in some SHADY VALE, where they might be shelter'd from the rain and Wind.'[30]

There is no doubt that Bourne is here describing at first hand the folklore of ghosts and hauntings to be found in towns and villages in the early eighteenth century. His comment that this is all 'Legendary Stories of Nurses and Old Women'[31] is a slur which folklorists are very familiar with: it is usually a sure guide to the existence of a genuine folklore! Bourne's frequent use of the word 'formerly' should not be taken literally either: folklore is one of those things that commentators invariably see as a thing of the past even while they describe its present forms. Again, Bourne's ascription of the traditions to 'Vulgar' (i.e. uneducated and/or working) people living in the country is also a first-class guide to the existence of folklore, though again we should not take this literally: it has always been the custom for commentators on folklore to see it as confined to classes and regions to which they themselves do not belong.

Throughout his very full descriptions it is clear, then, that Bourne is entirely *au fait* with local traditions and, perhaps in the deepest recesses of his heart, more than a little sympathetic to them. As a later commentator on the passage has it: 'I cannot help thinking, that the NURSE prevails over the PRIEST in it. The good man ... had played the Conjuror so far as to RAISE us Spirits, but does not seem to have had so much of the SCHOLAR in him as to have been able to LAY them.'[32]

But how different Bourne's picture of supernatural traditions is from that of Glanvil, Bovet, Sinclair and other writers of the previous century! Though it seems that people believe as much as ever in a supernatural world, it appears to be a *different* supernatural world that they believe in.

The countryside is now haunted by a variety of terrors. Chief among these are the ghosts of the restless dead who 'walk' in set places – the room where they died, old houses, dark lanes and churchyards. Night and loneliness are to be feared as their walking time and cock-crow will send them back to their graves. As well as these recognizably human ghosts, the benighted traveller may be unfortunate enough to encounter fairies, goblins, demons, ghosts in animal shapes, fiery ghosts and ghosts of headless horsemen. Though these spectres may complain about having to walk in chilly and uncomfortable places, they never explain why they have to 'walk' in the first place, nor has the poor person whom they ac-cost any means of halting their perambulations. As far as the commen-tators at least are concerned, gone are the days when ghosts were part of the real world or had their proper place in a purposeful natural/supernatural system: they are no longer real, they have no purpose, and are part of no system. They are random effects.

Later in the century, antiquarians were still painting a very similar picture of a world haunted by meaningless and terrible (though ridicu-lous and incredible) apparitions. In 1787, Francis Grose published *A Provincial Glossary* to which he appended *A Collection of Local Proverbs and Popular Superstitions*. In the introductory chapter, Grose gives the acid-tongued but entertaining description of the tales which 'antiquated maiden aunts and cousins' told to children and which 'embittered the lives of a great many persons of all ages' quoted earlier in chapter 3. He is in accord not only with Bourne but also with all earlier and later writers of this period in his fierce opposition to these traditions. To recapitulate, this is the folklore he describes:

The room in which the head of a family had died was for a long time un-tenanted, particularly if they had died without a will, or were supposed to have entertained any particular religious opinion. But if any discontented maiden, or love-crossed bachelor, happened to dispatch themselves in their garters, the room where the deed was perpetrated became for ever after uninhabitable, and not infrequently nailed up. If a drunken farmer, returning from market, fell from Old Dobbin, and broke his neck . . . that spot was ever after haunted and impassable. In short, there was scarcely a bye-lane or cross-way but had its ghost, who appeared in the shape of a headless cow or horse, or clothed all in white glared with its saucer eyes over some gate or stile. Ghosts of superior rank, as befitted their station, rode in coaches drawn by six headless horses, and driven by headless coachmen and postillions. Almost every ancient manor house was haunted by one or other of its former masters or mistresses . . . and as for the churchyards, the number of ghosts that walked there, according to the village computation, almost equalled the living parishioners.[33]

If we are to believe the antiquarians, therefore, towards the end of the eighteenth century, as at the beginning, the folklore of ghosts was still dominated by aimless and nameless terrors of various sorts, fear of which even the most strenuous efforts of clergymen and educators had been unable to remove. Hauntings were still purposeless, unless the terror they inspired was purpose enough; apparitions were still of indeterminate shape and fearful aspect; and the populace was still powerless to remove them from their midst.

Now, strangely enough, Grose also devotes a section of his next chapter to ghosts and apparitions, but this description is very different – it is an account which appears to refer to a wider context than country villages and, moreover, relies on the old concept of a purposeful supernatural world, as a selection of quotations shows:

A ghost is supposed to be the spirit of a person deceased who is either under command to return for some special errand such as the discovery of a murder, or to procure restitution in land or money unjustly held from an orphan or widow, or having committed some injustice while living, cannot rest until that is redressed. Sometimes, the occasion of spirits revisiting this world is to inform their heirs in what secret place or private drawer in an old trunk they have hidden the title deeds of the estate, or buried their money or plate. Some ghosts of murdered persons whose bodies have been secretly buried cannot be at ease until their bones have been taken up and deposited in consecrated ground.

The coming of a spirit is announced, some time before its appearance, by a variety of loud and dreadful noises . . . At length the door flies open, and the spectre stalks up to the bed's foot, and opening the curtains, looks steadfastly at the person in bed by whom it is seen . . . It is here necessary to observe, that it has universally been found by experience, as well as affirmed by diverse apparitions themselves, that a Ghost has not the power to speak until it has first been spoken to; so that, notwithstanding the urgency of the business on which it might come, everything must stand still till the person visited can find sufficient courage to speak to it, which sometimes does not take place for many years.

Ghosts have undoubtedly forms and customs peculiar to themselves.[34]

In this sour and funny passage, ghosts not only return for all the familiar old reasons from treasure to murder, but they also actually still try to communicate with the world of the living and influence its affairs.

In the contrast between these two passages, we see the dilemma of the eighteenth century. Take away all sense of reason and purpose from ghosts by outlawing them and sneering at them, and they necessarily become both intrusive and incredible, reduced to haunting lanes and bye-ways in unlikely forms. But when, *nevertheless*, there yet remains a vigorous undercurrent of belief in ghosts, and when many people, educated as well as 'vulgar', go on seeing apparitions, *then explanations are called for*. Contemporary philosophy provides no explanations whatsoever, so writers fall back on those of previous generations. This poses a very difficult problem for the historian or folklorist interested in reconstructing the traditions of the eighteenth century. By refusing to take contemporary popular traditions seriously and making no effort to analyse or understand the reports of haunted houses and churchyards which they collected, antiquarians of the period deprived themselves (and consequently us, too) of any knowledge of the rationale behind popular supernatural belief. We, like them, simply do not know whether there was any rhyme or reason for ghosts of 'headless cows and horses', or for spectres' lamentations about the cold and draughty walking places allotted to them. We do not know why such ghosts were thought to come back, why they came back in that form or place, or what they were supposed to be doing there – if anything. It *looks*, of course, as if the supernatural world has become almost entirely purposeless, for believers as well as sceptics. But we cannot be certain.

Instead of trying to make sense of the supernatural beliefs they observed around them, when they needed to provide a sensible rationale for ghosts, antiquarians turned to the traditions of the seventeenth century and found suitable explanations in the thinking of previous generations. It does not, for example, take a Sherlock Holmes to notice the similarity of Grose's second account to the picture of ghosts painted in Baxter's and Aubrey's stories or to observe that, from beginning to end, it is liberally sprinkled with references to Joseph Glanvil's *Sadducismus Triumphatus*. The passage both begins and ends with references to this work and five of Glanvil's twenty 'Relations' about ghosts and poltergeists are quoted. In fact, if you read Glanvil's stories first and then turn to Grose, one begins to sound very like a witty paraphrase of the other, and it looks very much as if Grose lifted the whole of his second passage straight out of *Sadducismus Triumphatus* or some other earlier text.

In general, when educated eighteenth-century writers did not present supernatural occurrences as obviously meaningless – delusions or 'legendary stories of nurses and old women', and therefore in no need of explanation, understanding or analysis – like Grose they picked over the concepts of the seventeenth century to find a suitable explanatory framework for their descriptions. Ironically, this picking-over of older traditions, like the ignoring of the rationale behind the contemporary ones, also creates a strong impression of a supernatural world grown fragmentary and increasingly purposeless. One reason for this is that each writer chose different bits of the older tradition to provide the rationale he needed. Thus Grose, in picking over Glanvil, omitted all references to ghosts who guard treasure or return to give warnings, discover murder or revenge crimes, yet apparitions with just these purposes were at that very time being spoken about in the *Gentleman's Magazine* and other reputable and influential journals. So older traditions of purposeful ghosts may have been kept alive (or half-alive) in educated thought, but only in a fragmented form.

Again, despite the fracturing and the lack of consensus, nevertheless there was, over the period as a whole, a steady trend in writers' choices among the older traditions, which also showed itself in a decline in concepts of purpose. After the Reformation, writers had gradually ceased to attribute religious functions to ghosts: after the scientific revolution, they also gradually ceased to attribute moral functions to them. When picking over older literature to find an explanatory framework that suited their purposes, they tended more and more to discard accounts of ghosts who rectified wrongs committed in life, or confessed to sins, or desired to prevent injustices. They preferred, instead, to make use of picturesque tales of apparitions that guarded treasure or revealed murder or other fell secrets – no doubt because these did not threaten their world-view or hold them up to the ridicule of their peers. Most significantly, in eighteenth- and early nineteenth-century writings, ghosts became much more silent and passive than they had been earlier. If they had a purpose, it was seldom stated outright. They observed a Trappist code of conduct. It was the *percipient*'s task to interpret their appearance, and the ghosts themselves did little or nothing to aid that interpretation. Ghosts might 'appear' but they very seldom either 'did' or 'said' anything at all.

The literary traditions which the eighteenth century passed on to the nineteenth century therefore show – with what justice we cannot be certain – a supernatural world grown increasingly meaningless and purposeless. Gone for ever, it seems, were the old ghosts who, amidst thunder and lightning, stalked up to sleeping people and loudly demanded their services in some mission of mercy, or who, surrounded by sweet music and ethereal light, spoke of the joys of heaven and salvation. Now, who could know why a ghost might appear? Or in what shape? Or whether it had any reason for its visit at all?

If, in contrast, ordinary people transmitted a folklore which, despite appearances to the contrary – appearances which educated men created out of their own unwillingness to try to understand that folklore in its own terms – *was* purposeful and *was* part of a meaningful concept of the Cosmos, we shall never know. In the end, the supernatural folklore of the eighteenth century remains something of an enigma to us, for those who might have explained it declined to do so. Rationalism was all the rage, the supernatural 'obviously' illusory, or a meaningless and motiveless intrusion into the 'real' world of matter, and the ghost a mere shadow of its old self – like life itself, according to Macbeth:

> . . . but a walking shadow, a poor player
> That struts and frets his hour upon the stage
> And then is heard no more: . . . a tale
> Told by an idiot, full of sound and fury
> Signifying nothing.

*   *   *

The Cock Lane poltergeist excited public attention for a full five years during the mid 1700s. Here, the case is discussed with all the trappings of eighteenth-century rationalism by the poet, novelist and dramatist, Oliver Goldsmith. The knockings and scratchings at the house in Cock Lane were attributed to the ghost of the common-law wife of one Mr K— , who was thought by many (including the lady's family) to have poisoned her in order to come by her small inheritance. Goldsmith's presentation of what he sees as the facts, his sneering language and dismissive logic, are just as interesting as the story itself and entirely representative of the official attitude of his age.

While we must admire the passion with which he defends a defenceless man and upholds the principles of natural justice, we must note that the account contains a lot of special pleading and logical sleight-of-hand. All those who believe in the ghost are 'credulous', low-class, 'ignorant publicans', and so on; all those who disbelieve it, of the highest rank and probity. Then again, the ghost is accused of being silent and purposeless, yet it was the thinking of rationalists like Goldsmith himself which had caused this state of affairs: suddenly the eighteenth-century materialist is judging a ghost by the standards of seventeenth-century mystics. No wonder he finds it lacking!

The following account is a series of extracts from Goldsmith's pamphlet, *The Mystery Revealed*:

It is somewhat remarkable, that the Reformation which in other countries banished superstition, in England seemed to encourage the credulity of the vulgar. At a time when Bacon was employed in restoring true philosophy, King James was endeavouring to strengthen our prejudices, both by his authority and writings. Scot, Glanville, and Coleman, wrote and preached with the same design; and our judges, particularly Sir Matthew Hales, gave some horrid proofs of their credulity.[35]

Since that time, arguments of this kind have been pretty much rejected by all but the lowest class. The vulgar have indeed, upon several occasions, called for justice upon supposed criminals, and when denied, have often exercised it themselves: their accusations, however, in general fell upon the poor, the ignorant, the old, or the friendless, upon persons who were unable to resist, or who, because they knew no guilt, were incapable of making an immediate defence.

But of all accusations of this nature, few seem so extraordinary, as that which has lately engrossed the attention of the public, and which is still carrying on at an house in Cock Lane near Smithfield. The continuance of the noises, the numbers who have heard them, the perseverance of the girl, and the atrociousness of the murder she pretends to detect, are circumstances that were never perhaps so favourably united for the carrying on of an imposture before. The credulous are prejudiced by the child's apparent benevolence: her age and ignorance wipe off the imputation of her being able to deceive, and one or two more, who pretend actually to have seen the apparition, are ready to strengthen her evidence.

Upon these grounds, a man, otherwise of a fair character, as will shortly appear, is rendered odious to society, shunned by such as immediately take imputation for guilt, and made unhappy in his family, without having even in law a power of redress. Few characters more deserve compassion, than one, that is thus branded with crimes without an accuser, attacked, in a manner, at once, calculated to excite curiosity, and spread defamation, and all without a power of legal vindication.

[Here Goldsmith gives a full account of Mr K—'s history, his relationship with his lady, his exemplary behaviour during her illness (smallpox complicated by advanced pregnancy) and grief at her death.]

A person who behaved in so fair and open manner, might surely have no reason to expect reproach . . . he might rest in security, that no accusation or calumny . . . could affect him . . . but he was attacked from a quarter, that no person in his senses could in the least have imagined, in a manner, that but to mention, would have excited the laughter of thousands . . ., all of a sudden, he was surprised with the horrid imputation of being a murderer, of having murdered the person he had held most dear upon earth, of having murdered her by poison: and who is his accuser? Why, a ghost! The reader laughs: yet, ridiculous as the witness is, groundless as the accusation, it has served to make one man compleatly unhappy [. . .]

The story of the ghost is in brief, as follows: for some time a knocking and scratching has been heard in the night at Mr P—s's, where Mr K—formerly lodged, to the great terror of the family; and several methods were tried, to

discover the imposture, but without success. This knocking and scratching was
generally heard in a little room, in which Mr P—s's two children lay; the eldest
of which was a girl about twelve or thirteen years old. The purport of this
knocking was not thoroughly conceived, till the eldest child pretended to see
the actual ghost of the deceased lady . . . When she had seen the ghost, a weak,
ignorant publican also, who lived in the neighbourhood, asserted that he had
seen it too; and Mr P—s himself, (the gentleman whom Mr K— had disobliged
by suing for money) he also saw the ghost at the same time: the girl saw it
without hands, in a shrowd; the other two saw it with hands, all luminous and
shining. There was one unlucky circumstance however in the apparition: though
it appeared to several persons, and could knock, scratch, and flutter, yet its
coming would have been to no manner of purpose, had it not been kindly
assisted by the persons thus haunted. It was impossible for a ghost that could
not speak, to make any discovery; the people therefore, to whom it appeared,
kindly undertook to make the discovery themselves; and the ghost, by knocking, gave its assent to their methods of wording the accusation; thus there was
nothing illegal on any side, Mr K—'s character was blackened, without an
accuser; the persons haunted only asked questions, no doubt, merely from
curiosity, without any assertion that could be reprehended; and answers by
knocking could by no means be looked upon as a legal cause of impeachment.
Thousands, who believed nothing of the matter came, in order, if possible, to
detect its falsehood, or satisfy curiosity; and the words poison and murder
being frequently joined with the name of the supposed offender, that name
became every where public, joined to an accusation which, whether believed or
not in itself, is to a sensible mind sufficient misery: to become every where
remarkable by imputed guilt, is certainly a state of uneasiness, that only falls
short of a consciousness of real villainy.

When therefore the spirit taught the assistants, or rather the assistants had
taught the spirit (for that could not speak) that Mr K— was the murderer, the
road lay then open, and every night the farce was carried on, to the amusement
of several, who attended with all the good-humour, which spending one night
with novelty inspires; they jested with the ghost, soothed it, flattered it, while
none was truly unhappy, but him whose character was thus rendered odious,
and trifled with, merely to amuse idle curiosity.

To have a proper idea of this scene, as it is now carried on, the reader
is to conceive a very small room with a bed in the middle, the girl at the
usual hour of going to bed, is undressed and put in with proper solemnity;
the spectators are next introduced, who sit looking at each other,
suppressing laughter, and wait in silent expectation for the opening of the
scene. As the ghost is a good deal offended at incredulity, the persons present
are to conceal theirs, if they have any, as by this concealment they can only
hope to gratify their curiosity. For, if they shew either before, or when the
knocking is begun, a too prying, inquisitive, or ludicrous turn of thinking,
the ghost continues usually silent . . . The spectators therefore have nothing

for it, but to sit quiet and credulous, otherwise they must hear no ghost, which is no small disappointment to persons, who have come for no other purpose.

The girl who knows, by some secret, when the ghost is to appear, sometimes apprizes the assistants of its intended visitation. It first begins to scratch, and then to answer questions, giving two knocks for a negative, and one for an affirmative. By this means it tells whether a watch, when held up, be white, blue, yellow, or black; how many clergymen are in the room, though in this sometimes mistaken; it evidently distinguishes white men from negroes, with several other marks of sagacity; however, it is sometimes mistaken in questions of a private nature, when it deigns to answer them: for instance; the ghost . . . called her father John instead of Thomas, a mistake indeed a little extra-ordinary in a ghost; but perhaps she was willing to verify the old proverb, that it is a wise child that knows its own father. However, though sometimes right, and sometimes wrong, she pretty invariably persists in one story, namely, that she was poisoned, in a cup of purl, by red arsenic, a poison unheard of before, by Mr. K— in her last illness; and that she heartily wishes him hanged.

It is no easy matter to remark upon an evidence of this nature; but it may not be unnecessary to observe, that the ghost, though fond of company, is particularly modest upon these occasions, an enemy to the light of a candle, and almost always most silent before those, from whose rank and understanding she could most reasonably expect redress. When a committee of gentlemen of eminence for their rank, learning, and good sense, were assembled to give the ghost a fair hearing, then, one might have thought, would have been the time to knock loudest, and to exert every effort; then was the time to bring the guilty to justice, and to give every possible method of information; but in what manner she behaved upon this test of her reality, will better appear from the committee's own words, than mine.

[Here Goldsmith transcribes the overwhelmingly negative report of the investigating committee, which concludes, 'It is therefore the opinion of the whole of the assembly, that the child has some art of making or counterfeiting particular noises, and that there is no agency of higher cause.' Goldsmith then goes on in his own voice . . .]

The ghost knows perfectly well before whom to exhibit. She could as we see venture well enough to fright the ladies, or perhaps some men, about as courageous as ladies, and as discerning; but when the committee had come up, and gathered round the bed, it was no time then to attempt at deception, the ghost was angry, and very judiciously kept her hunters at bay [. . .]

The question in this case, therefore, is not, whether the ghost be true or false, but who are the contrivers, or what can be the motives for this vile deception? To attempt to assign the motives of any action, is not so easy a task as many imagine. A thousand events have risen from caprice, pride or mere idleness, which an undiscerning spectator might have attributed to reason, resentment, and close laid design. It would not therefore become me, who have now been endeavouring to vindicate innocence, to lay the blame upon any individual on earth, tho' never so rationally to be suspected; All I shall say is, that, as the reader may remember, Mr K — has many who owe him an ill will. His landlord at one house, whom he arrested for money lent him, had cause of resentment; his landlord in Cock Lane, the father of the child, whom he was obliged to sue from similar motives, was, it is to be supposed, willing enough to retaliate the supposed injury. But above all [his lady's] relations, who had filed a bill in chancery against him, just two months before this infernal agent appeared to strengthen their plea. [. . .]

I have now as briefly, and indeed as tenderly as I could, stated the whole of this most surprising transaction, and the reader by this time sees how far Mr K — is culpable. He sees him living affectionately with a woman as his wife, whom the laws of nature allow him to love, but the strictness of the canon law forbade him to marry. He sees every possible method taken to preserve this woman's reputation and life, and the most reputable persons produced, as witnesses of her end. He sees men of the highest rank, both for birth, character, and learning, joined to acknowledge the whole of the pretended ghost, as an imposition upon the public; and lastly, he sees those who pretend to bear witness to the accusation, persons of a mixed reputation, of gross ignorance, great cruelty, and what is more, armed with resentment against him [. . .]

But still it seems something extraordinary, how this imposition could be for so long carried on without a discovery. However . . . [it] was the observation of Erasmus, that whenever people flock to see a miracle, they are generally sure of seeing a miracle; they bring an heated imagination, and an eager curiosity to the scene of the action, give themselves up blindly to deception, and each is better pleased with having it to say, that he had seen something very strange, than that he was made the dupe of his own credulity.

THE RISE OF THE ROMANTIC GHOST:
1840–1920

It is characteristic of that fashion in attitudes we call 'the spirit of the age' to swing like a pendulum from one extreme to another. So the world-view which had conquered the seventeenth century and dominated the eighteenth, in time produced its own antithesis out of its own excess. The logical culmination of the mechanical philosophy was the appropriation of nature for mankind's use, the growth of technologies which could harness the energy of nature and people alike, and the downgrading of the individual to the status of a cog in the cosmic and commercial machine. From the mid-eighteenth century onwards, the industrial revolution and the conformist mass society were on their way – developments which, not unnaturally, disturbed many thinking people. Out of this disquiet, the romantic movement was born. As David Wright says in a luminous essay, the romantic movement was:

a birth of a new kind of sensibility which had to do with the new kind of environment that man was in the process of creating for himself. If the individual was on the way to being regimented, then poets and artists, with as it were intuitive prescience, began to seek to balance the scale by giving the greatest value to individual consciousness.[36]

One of the romantic movement's most famous evangelists, the poet Wordsworth, expressed this well in his Preface to the second edition of *The Lyrical Ballads* (1800), an essay which became a touchstone for the movement:

a multitude of causes, unknown to former times, are now acting with a combined force to blunt the discriminating powers of the mind . . . The most effective of these causes are the great national events which are daily taking place, and the increasing accumulation of men in cities, where the uniformity of their occupations produces a craving for extraordinary incident, which the rapid communication of intelligence hourly gratifies. To this tendency of life and manners the literature and theatrical exhibitions of the country have conformed themselves [. . .] Reflecting upon the general evil, I should be oppressed with . . . melancholy, had I not a deep impression of certain inherent and indestructible qualities of the human mind [. . .] and did I not further add to this impression a belief, that the time is approaching when the evil will be systematically opposed, by men of great powers.[37]

Along with the often passionately felt need to emancipate the individual from the grasp of mass popular culture and pre-digested thought, there went an equally ardent desire to emancipate nature from the grasp of the industrialists – to assert the value of people and the natural world against those who would see both as merely convenient resources for the amassing of wealth. Wright notes that: 'This may be why another Romantic trait was a nostalgic looking back at the past, as if there to seek the reassurance of a ruder, but simpler, less complicated way of life than that which the present offered or the future promised. Not only was it a looking back at a less-civilized bygone age but also an attempt at its imaginative recreation.'[38] By the mid-eighteenth century, England was already being transformed to an industrialized capitalist nation: by 1780 the leading spirits of the romantic movement were trying to halt, subvert, or at least provide an antidote to, this process.

After about 1820, however, the initial fiery reforming passion burnt out: industrialization and urbanization were established and the French Revolution, which many had seen as a struggle for the rights of the individual, was betrayed. Whereas the first wave of the romantics had a radical political zeal, which kept them at the periphery of society and a sense of vision which led them fiercely to defy public taste, the second wave of romantics became assimilated (in a sense 'synthesized') into the establishment. Wright, for example in a wonderful selection of adjectives too good not to quote, speaks of the 'self-consciousness', 'vaporous intellectual rhetoric', 'treacle', 'macabre sensationalism', 'gothic glooms' and 'spiritual vulgarity' of the later poets.

All this is relevant to any discussion of 'The Rise of the Romantic Ghost'. We must remember that any history of the supernatural concepts of the past is necessarily (though unfortunately) primarily the history of educated people's reactions to traditional ideas, and that those reactions are conditioned by the prevailing philosophy. We see ghosts through the cultural spectacles of each succeeding age, or, to change the metaphor, we see them wearing the 'ideal corsets' which each intellectual fashion dictates. By 1840 these 'ideal corsets' were being provided by antiquarians and collectors of peasant bygones (and after 1878 by the Folklore Society) whose attitudes and ideas were permeated through and through by the spirit of romanticism.

What is fascinating about the folklore of the nineteenth century ('folklore' in the sense of the study of tradition, not the tradition itself) is how directly it reflects the values, virtues and vices of the movement which gave it birth. It is as if all the stages of the romantic movement from the late eighteenth to the mid-nineteenth centuries are somehow distilled in the folkloristic work of 1840 to 1920.

At its best, it was motivated by a genuine zeal to rescue old values and old culture and return to the verities of rural life and simple values; it found much of its impetus in a real respect for and interest in the individual mind and heart and a campaigning enthusiasm to reform a debased public taste fed on the pap of a popular culture seen as inferior, inadequate and depraved. At its worst, it turned so to speak 'gothic' and, with the tastelessness of the fag end of the romantic tradition, regurgitated its *own* sort of pap, a mixture of the patronizingly and self-consciously 'quaint', the macabre and the ghoulish, the lip-licking sensationalist and the just plain stupid.

The Folklore Society and its work of course suffered from one grave temporal disadvantage. The organized study of popular beliefs, customs, tales and songs did not get underway until the middle of the nineteenth century. By then Victoria was on the throne and England was the leading industrial country in the world. Romanticism as a radical movement was already out, and 'romance' was in. Even the best of the work of the early folklorists is therefore often marred by the sentimental, sententious, self-conscious and histrionic spirit of the later romantics, and none of it has the radical political zeal which characterized the early movement, and, fortunately for its adherents, kept them social outsiders. The early folklorists were all *insiders* – clergymen, men of letters, publishers, journalists, gentlefolk – middle-class Victorians with time and/or money to devote to their hobby: frankly 'bourgeois'. Necessarily, they looked at the rural life and country customs they studied with the preconceptions of their time and class.

As an object-lesson in the attitudes and methods of nineteenth-century fieldworkers, it is worth looking at song-collecting. The work of men like Cecil Sharp and other leading figures in the folksong world is very well-documented because their notebooks and manuscripts remain to us. By analogy, then, we can reconstruct the attitudes of legend-collectors (whose methods are less well-documented) and explain the forms in which supernatural beliefs and stories come down to us.

There were two main periods of song-collecting – the first around 1840 with the 'Percy Society', which defined its task as the publication of ancient ballads, songs, plays, verse and popular literature; the second about thirty years later, possibly as a response to the publication in 1866 of Carl Engel's *Introduction to the Study of National Music*. The mainspring of the first period was an interest in the past; that of the second period more difficult to define, but certainly clogged with sentimentality and a cloying desire for moral reform, the songs being almost invariably described as 'wholesome', 'simple and artless', 'a refining influence', and so on. Something of the flavour of the enterprise is reflected in Sir Hubert Parry's inaugural address to the Folk Song Society in 1899. 'Folk music is among the purest products of the human mind . . . We are beginning to realize . . . how much joy there lies in the simple beauty of primitive thought and the emotions which are common to all men alike, even the sophisticated.'[39] Likewise the *Handbook of Suggestions for the Consideration of Teachers* (1905) states that: 'National or folk songs . . . are the expression in the idiom of the people of their joys and sorrows, their unaffected patriotism, their zest for sport and the simple pleasures of a country life.'[40] Unfortunately, the more the collectors collected, the more they found that the songs 'the people' sang were no such thing at all. They were often not the 'simple art' of the 'folk' (in the sense the collectors defined the terms), but the products of broadside balladeers,

Georgian songsters and Victorian music halls – in the collectors' eyes 'the dross of centuries'.[41] The majority of what they found therefore was discarded as not 'folk song', though it had been sung by just those people they regarded as 'the folk' – a neat illustration of how, when two arbitrary definitions encounter each other, the result is a circular trap of begged questions. Moreover, though, as musicians, they approved the tunes of the songs that did get through their definitional net, as *gentlemen* they could not approve the *words*. These were 'corrupt' as prudish Victorians saw it, neither 'wholesome' nor a 'refining influence'. They were, in fact, often lewd, crude and rude, full of dialect words, 'incorrect' grammar, lines that would neither scan nor rhyme, and – worse still! – shockingly frank about sex (the Revd Sabine Baring-Gould, for example, noted that on occasion 'the coarseness of the original words obliged me to re-write the song').

Almost identical attitudes and processes are observable in the collections of regional folklore and legends, which are our chief source of information about ghost traditions from 1840 onwards. There are the same preconceptions about what the nature and content of folk traditions are, the same selectivity, the same zeal to rescue (and, if necessary, imaginatively re-create) the remnants of a lost *Merrie England*, the same nostalgia for the past, the same lack of realism about rural life. Above all, there is the same lack of scruple about 'improving' traditions, re-writing, polishing, refining, altering – in short, making them over in the collector's own image. Naturally, such wholesale criticism cannot be applied to every nineteenth-century collector of regional folklore (there are very honourable exceptions), but, nevertheless, as a crude generalization, it sums up their attitudes and methods.

Influenced by romanticism, historicism and nationalism, folklorists went in active search of quaint country customs, 'superstitions' and what Robert Hunt with unconscious irony called 'wild tales'. Naturally, they found what they were looking for. And it is out of this jumble of bits and pieces of more or less unreliable information that we are left to construct our history of ghostlore in the nineteenth and early twentieth centuries.

What makes the task even more difficult is that, by the mid-nineteenth century, the battle for the supernatural had long ago been lost. The religious, philosophical, scientific and medical establishments for decades had united to assert that there could be no possible vestige of truth in the pre-Enlightenment world-view, and that anybody who still believed in the supernatural was either a charlatan, a crackpot, or a victim of the most ignorant superstition. Folklorists very naturally brought these attitudes to their collections of supernatural lore and legends. As there was no possibility that the beliefs of their informants could be in the slightest 'true', there was no onus on the collector to take them seriously or record them accurately.

In addition, there was a strong incentive to select beliefs expressed in story-form, rather than as plain assertion or reasoned argument. Though legends no doubt make more entertaining reading than sober discussions, there are drawbacks in relying too heavily on such material. Most obviously, there are many other reasons for telling a legend than simply to express belief. I may tell a legend, say about a boggart, for any one of the following reasons (among others): because I like telling stories, because I want to entertain my visitor and persuade him/her to stay a little longer, because my grandmother used to tell the story, or because boggarts hold no fear for me so I prefer to talk about them rather than the things that do actually frighten me. In addition to these drawbacks that pertain to any day and age, there were obstacles peculiar to the nineteenth century, which hampered the early collectors. First, and most obviously, there were no tape-recorders: collectors therefore could only note down the broad outlines of any legend they were told. There was no way of recording the details of the description or the style of the telling: that was provided by the collectors when they prepared the manuscript for publication. The published legend then was, in a very real sense, the collector's not the informant's. It was the collector's world-view and attitudes that infused it.

The end-result of all these influences was, for want of a ready-made term, a 'literary-fying' of ghosts. The supernatural world as it appeared in most early collections of regional folklore was a sort of story-book version of the traditions discussed by Bourne in 1725 and decried by Grose in 1787. The *essence* was still the same, but the *spirit* was entirely different. Ghosts were still either malicious and mischievous, or passive and purposeless, and almost invariably silent. Their image (or imagery), too, remained the same. They were still portrayed as denizens of churchyards, crossroads, bye-lanes, old houses, ruined castles; lovers of night, haters of day; averse to priests, fond of children; prone to assuming the shapes of animals or to donning shrouds or luminous clouds; haunters of stairs, lingerers at doors, peerers through windows, hoverers by beds. Yet somehow all the fight had been taken out of them. They had been exorcised by laughter and disinfected by a strong dose of the picturesque. Poltergeists were replaced by prankish bargeists or boggarts; headless cows and horses had user-friendly names or turned out to be pigs, donkeys or washing hanging on a line; the haunted manors were now the walking places of 'ladies' of various hues but no great threat; and the really obstreperous ghosts were invariably 'laid' by a whole cricket-team of holy men at prayer.

For the most part, no great care was taken to make any sort of *sense* of these stories. They were simply 'stories' (i.e. untrue tales) and not *expected* to make sense: they were curiosities rather than realities. There was no attempt to put them in context, either: we do not know when or why or how or to whom the legends were told. Often an account of the supernatural folklore of a region was no more than a list of entities supposed to inhabit/haunt the area. Harland and Wilkinson's *Lancashire Legends* of 1867 is typical, in this respect no better, no worse than most. We are told that there were supposed to be 'boggarts' at Boggart Hole Clough, Greenside Farm cottage, Clegg Hall, Clock House, Thackergate and Clayton Hall; that locals were scared of the 'Nutman', 'Grindylow', 'Jenny Green Teeth', 'Peg o' Lantern', black dogs and corpse-candles; that the ghost of one George Marsh haunted Smithills Hall, that the path from Fairfield to Ashton Hill Lane was haunted by a shadowy 'lady' who glided in front of pedestrians then disappeared into the mist, and that at Ince Hall there was a ghost with a deep interest in a forged will; that at Greenside Farm there had been a murder in the shippon so nowadays the cows would not stay tethered in their stalls and that Clayton Hall boasted a 'Bloody Chamber' with an ineradicable blood-stain. One would think that such a wealth of information would need a bookful of explanation. Harland and Wilkinson reveal all in five pages. Such accounts do not tell us what ghost traditions meant to the informants: they only tell us what they meant to the collectors – which was *precisely nothing*.

There was, however, the occasional collector (to whom we should be eternally grateful) who was broadminded enough to attempt to understand local traditions in their own terms, and took them seriously enough to get them into some sort of order. Thanks to such collectors, we can begin to make sense of the mishmash of information in the work of all the others. The boggarts, black dogs, bloody chambers and exorcisms fall into place and we can begin to pick out the outlines of nineteenth-century ghostlore.

Charlotte Burne was just such a collector. She devotes two chapters of her *Shropshire Folklore* (1883) to the supernatural. The second of these seems very dated now, presenting an 'explanation' of supernatural traditions based on the theory of cultural evolution so popular in her day and asserting that: 'It is indeed an axiom of Folk-Lore that the demons and evil beings of folk-tales are the Gods of earlier myths, fallen from their high estate, but neither forgotten nor supposed to be mere crea-tures of the imagination.'[42] In the earlier chapter, however, she gives us the result of her on-the-spot observations, telling us that Shropshire people used four types of expression when speaking of ghosts. They might say that there was 'summat to be sid' [seen], or a 'frittening', or that somebody 'came again', or – worst of all – 'came again very badly'.

'Summat to be sid' consisted of animal ghosts, or human revenants in animal form, and various non-human phenomena. These might be colts or bulls, headless pigs, black dogs with red eyes, or simply what in the dialect was called the 'know' of a dog. 'Frittenings' were hauntings by headless ghosts or shapeshifters, indelible bloodstains and supernatural curses – on the whole, nameless and apparently purposeless terrors, or the supernatural record of a hideous crime. Examples she gives are 'John Viam's Curse', the ineradicable bloodstains at Plaish Hall, Card-ington, and 'Clatterin' Glat' – an unmendable hole in a hedge (in Shropshire dialect a 'glat' is a hole and 'to glat' is to mend a hole). Local legend asserted that a murderer had dragged his victim through a hedge, tearing a great gap in it. Though he mended the hole to conceal his crime, it had mysteriously opened up again by the morning. Since then the hedge had never allowed itself to be successfully repaired.

Revenants who 'came again' were either unpopular or wicked people, suicides, night-riders, or people who had left unfinished business or were so fond of their lifetime pursuits that they couldn't bear to leave them. Revenants who 'came again very badly' were ghosts of a par-ticularly horrific or persistent nature (these eventually had to be 'laid' to get rid of them).

These four categories, based on the terms local people actually used to describe hauntings, bring order and system to supernatural belief – or, more properly, allow us to recognize that there *was* order and system in supernatural beliefs. In Shropshire traditions, as represented by Burne, there is a clear hierarchy of hauntings from the purposeless to the purposeful, and from the merely 'scary' to the truly terrifying and awe-ful.

In the main, this is pretty much the same picture of the supernatural as we find in eighteenth-century antiquarian writing. On the one hand, we find an array of wild and weird purposeless apparitions, confined to certain locations, usually dark or lonely places with unpleasant associa-tions or a history of eccentricity and sorrow, and 'liminal' places and times, that is, betwixt-and-between, neither/nor regions – doorways that are neither 'inside' nor 'outside', staircases that are neither 'upstairs' nor 'down', graveyards where former friends lie 'there' but 'not there', twilight between dark and day, midnight between today and tomorrow. On the other hand, we read of ghosts in human shape – some of wicked people, purposeless, deliberately frightening, out of control; some purposeful and therefore less horrifying.

It is quite likely that a similar classification of hauntings underlay the folklore collected from other regions, and that from the higgledy-piggledy jumble of legends and legend-summaries in the compilations of many other nineteenth-century folklorists a similar belief-system could be disinterred. Certainly, the majority of regional collections from about 1860 to 1890 feature a very similar *range* of ghosts, though naturally the individual detail varies. Overall, then, work like Burne's is very valuable in illuminating the structure of belief that informed the legends collected in the nineteenth century.

Even Burne, though, has the bias of her age and time. Though much, or most, of her material appears to have been taken from oral sources and reproduced in a form as close as possible to the original, yet, even so, much *is* rewritten in a literary style. The 'literary-fying' and its effects are plain in the story which follows – worth quoting in full:

A very weird story of an encounter with an animal ghost arose of late years within my own knowledge. On the 21st of January, 1879, a labouring man was employed to take a cart of luggage from Ranton in Staffordshire to Woodcote, beyond Newport, in Shropshire, for the use of a party of visitors who were going from one house to the other. He was late in coming back; his horse was tired and could only crawl along at a foot's pace, so that it was ten o'clock at night when he arrived at the place where the highroad crosses the Birmingham and Liverpool Canal. Just before he reached the canal bridge, a strange black creature with great white eyes sprang out of the plantation by the road-side and alighted on his horse's back. He tried to push it off with his whip, but to his horror the whip went THROUGH the Thing, and he dropped it to the ground in his fright. The poor tired horse broke into a canter, and rushed onwards at full speed with the ghost still clinging to its back. How the creature at length vanished the man hardly knew. He told his tale in the village of Woodseaves, a mile further on, and so effectually frightened the hearers that one man actually stayed with his friends there all night, rather than cross the terrible bridge which lay between him and his home. The ghost-seer reached home at length, still in a state of excessive terror (but, as his master assured me, perfectly sober), and it was some days before he was able to leave his bed, so much was he prostrated by his fright. The whip was searched for next day, and found just at the place where he said he had dropped it.

Now comes the curious part of the story. The adventure, as was natural, was much talked of in his neighbourhood, and of course with all sorts of variations. Some days later the man's master (Mr B— of L—d) was surprised by a visit from a policeman, who came to request him to give information of his having been stopped and robbed on the Big Bridge on the night of the 21st January! Mr B—, much amused, denied having been robbed, either on the canal bridge or anywhere else, and told the policeman the story just related. 'Oh, was that all, sir?' said the disappointed policeman. 'Oh, I know what *that* was. That was the Man-Monkey, sir, as *does* come again at that bridge ever since the man was drowned in the Cut!' [43]

This story would plainly not have been originally told like this at all. Apart from obvious give-aways like the length and construction of the sentences, the choice of vocabulary and the dissociative humorous asides, the story has been provided with a verbal punchline (a rare thing in natural memorate) which *explains* the occurrence. A literary story always has to have the ends tied up, to arrive at a dénouement, to be resolved: personal experience stories of supernatural events rarely are so neatly and finally rounded off.

The need for literary stories to 'end properly' has a direct effect on re-written supernatural memorate and legend. To look right on paper, they too have to have neat resolutions. The onus is on the collector/re-writer to provide a convincing ending in terms of a tidy or dramatic explanation of the events. Over time, therefore, one curious result of the 'literary-fying' of oral legends of the supernatural was the reinstatement of the purposeful ghost, and the institutionalization of the connection between apparitions and unnatural deaths or wicked lives.

From the time of the Reformation onwards, ghosts had lost one *raison d'être* after another. First, they had lost their religious function, then they lost many of their moral functions, too. Then, during the eighteenth century, writers had picked over the various social functions left to ghosts, utilizing picturesque behaviours and discarding many of the more utilitarian ones. By the 1860s, there was only a narrow range of functions left for ghosts to perform: they could return for love of the life they had left, to guard treasure, complete unfinished business, or issue warnings. At least, these are the purposes attributed to them in the regional folklore collections of the period. This did not leave much in the way of variety if explanatory frameworks and neat endings were called for. This may be why, from the final decades of the nineteenth century onwards, a type of ghost began to appear which, though not entirely novel, had not made much of an impact in the traditions of previous centuries. These were the helpful ghosts of strangers. They were often associated with a particular location and often assisted travellers or brought them to the assistance of others. None of the ingredients of these legends considered separately was new, but the combination of the ingredients had not often come together in this particular way before.

Helpful ghosts had been known, of course, since the Middle Ages, but they almost invariably had appeared to people who had known them in life. Indeed most or all purposeful ghosts of any sort had haunted *people* not *locations*. The ghost of an unknown person appearing on a mission of mercy in a particular place and at a time of particular danger was a real rarity. It is possible that such legends had been transmitted in former times but had been ignored by writers because there was more exciting material to hand; or maybe that the continual arrangement and rearrangement of motifs, which constitutes the flux of oral tradition, simply by chance brought these elements together for the first time in the mid-nineteenth century; or maybe the proliferation of bad and meaningless supernatural manifestations created a need for more good ones (a sort of 'supply and demand' mechanism). But, however that may be, certainly these ghosts were *useful* to nineteenth-century compilers of legends, and in time such accounts became more numerous as subsequent workers went over and over the same ground, borrowing from each other to create ever larger compilations.

One interesting corollary of the rise of the stranger-ghost is that, for the first time in tradition, a person might not recognize that the ghost *was* a ghost, and might mistake it for a living person. This opened up a large new vista to the imagination, and from about 1900 there was a proliferation of ghosts of the 'phantom hitchhiker' (see pages 64–5) and 'ghostly guardian' varieties.

The second result of the 'literary-fying' of the supernatural – the formalizing of the connection between ghosts and unnatural deaths or wicked lives – had been rather longer in the making. It is so set now in our mental habits that it seems strange to reflect that this apparently necessary connection did not exist in medieval thought nor in the writings of the sixteenth century. Though apparitions *might* be of people who had lived or died violently, they might just as easily be of people who had led blameless lives and died quietly in their own beds. Indeed, apparitions were not even necessarily of *dead* men at all: they might just as easily be wraiths of the living.

By the end of the seventeenth century, subtle changes were, however, beginning. The average compilation of supernatural stories would be given half-and-half to tales of apparitions on the one hand, and to accounts of poltergeists and witchcraft on the other. Though many of the apparitions were still of living people, many more were of people who appeared at the moment of their death (as in Aubrey's story of Mr Mohun) or had been dead some time. Eight out of every ten of these sorts of apparitions were still, however, of blameless people who had died natural deaths. Only a minority were the ghosts of murdered men, and there is something peculiar and significant about most of these. Two famous, and typical, seventeenth-century ghosts of this variety were Anne Walker (or Waters) and Mr Bower. The ghost of Anne Walker appeared to tell neighbours who it was had murdered her, and a trial was based (and the culprit convicted) on her evidence; the ghost of Mr Bower appeared in prison to a highwayman who then told his interrogators that the ghost had informed him that his cell-mates were the murderers (they were duly executed for the crime). All very convenient. It is hard to avoid thinking that in one case the appearance of the ghost was a way of pointing the finger of suspicion without identifying the real accuser (as, for instance, Goldsmith argues so forcefully in his exploration of the Cock Lane case), and that, in the other, it was a device for shifting suspicion or neatly clearing up two crimes for the price of one. There is, of course, a long tradition of supernatural accusations of this kind.

This brings us to the case of 'spectral evidence'. There was in seventeenth-century thought, as we saw earlier, a close connection between ghosts and witches. In practice, this often manifested itself through the belief that witches could not only cause poltergeist-effects, but could also go visiting their victims in the form of spectres. So if Goody Blake, who thought that Goody Smith was bewitching her, could testify that she had seen the spectre of Goody Smith standing in her doorway smirking, then that was sufficient evidence to get a conviction for witchcraft. As Francis Hutchinson passionately argued in an essay which put the final nail in the coffin of witchcraft as an indictable offence:

in other cases, when wicked or mistaken people charge us with crimes of which we are not guilty, we clear ourselves by showing that at that time we were at home, or in some other place, about our honest business. But in prosecutions for witchcraft, that most natural and just defence is a mere jest; for if any wicked person affirms, or any crackbrained girl imagines ... that she sees any old woman ... pursuing her in her visions, the defenders of ... witchcraft ... hang the accused parties for things that they were [supposed to be] doing when they were, perhaps, asleep upon their beds, or saying their prayers, or, perhaps, in the accuser's own possession, with double irons upon them.[44]

The appearance of a spectre was thus regarded, for many decades, as incontrovertible evidence of witchcraft. In this way, a strong connection was forged between apparitions and people who led wicked lives. So, seventeenth-century traditions not only encouraged a strengthening of the connection between death and apparitions, but also the building of a close link between evil and spectres.

It was in the eighteenth century that the idea of *unnatural* deaths being the cause of hauntings began to get established. Certainly, in the antiquarian writing of this period, the violence formerly attributed to the behaviour of ghosts gets transferred to their past life. As ghosts become, as it were, *more* sedate, the manner of their death becomes *less* sedate. Besides, there was a strong psychological incentive among writers on the supernatural to link ghosts with unnatural death. For those writers who did not simply dismiss them as 'superstition' or (grudgingly) accept them as 'tradition', a *causal* framework was often a welcome alternative to the *explanatory* framework provided by older traditions. Where writers were unwilling to hazard a guess about the *purpose* of a ghost's return (or to venture to suggest that they had a purpose at all), they often fell back on the idea that there might at least be a *cause* for their restlessness. The obvious cause was that they had died before their time; the obvious reasons for dying before one's time are suicide, murder or mistreatment.

By the nineteenth century, the relationship between apparitions and wicked lives or violent deaths is just assumed. It is the *logic* that underpins all accounts of purposeless manifestations in human form. Purposeless animal ghosts need no explanation or are incapable of being given one: purpose*ful* lifelike ghosts provide their own explanations. The real trouble comes with apparitions that look like humans but seem to have no role to play in the human world. If their actions *after* death have no logic, it follows that any rationale must be found in events *before* their death. The havoc they wreak after their death therefore gets explained by the havoc of their life or dying. Either they are assumed to have had a malice so intense that it cannot die, or they are assumed to have had a death so cruel that the death itself cannot die and goes on being re-enacted somehow. The after-death hauntings are mirror-images of the pre-death emotions. So wicked men 'come again very badly' in deliberately horrific forms and with malicious persistence, and will not be quiet until they are 'laid' by all the resources which wisdom and intelligence can muster; and the victim-ghosts endlessly try to enlist the support of the living to avenge their misery.

The making of folklore into literature, which took place during the last half of the nineteenth century, has had important effects on present-day thinking about the supernatural. On the one hand, a crucial element of the stereotype of ghosts, which had earlier seemed to be dying out, was re-established in tradition; on the other hand, elements which had before been growing only slowly suddenly fused. So, we find two old ideas given new life and force. The belief that ghosts have *reasons* for their visits was revived in such a way as to lead to the emergence of a new variety of apparition, the ghost of a helpful stranger; and the belief that ghosts have *causes* for their restlessness also solidified and fastened itself, so to speak, on the notions of unnatural death and evil lives. These are ideas, as we have seen, that are fundamental to the supernatural folklore of ordinary people today and which give their beliefs their rationale.

There was another consequence of the 'literary-fying' of the supernatural, which has had repercussions just as wide. Once tidied up, rounded off and romanticized, ghost stories became 'fixed' in print. Whereas a story in oral tradition gets adapted by each successive person who tells it, a written story is quoted more or less verbatim. So the more a written story is repeated, the more it stays the same, and the result is the growth of an 'official' or 'writers'' version of supernatural folklore.

This process and its consequences are very apparent in the work of folklorists after about 1880 or 1890. Whereas earlier workers had for the most part compiled their own legend-collections, those who followed seemed content to borrow from any old source they could lay their hands on. Scissors and glue in hand, they took to their armchairs and snipped bits from seventeenth-century texts, mid-nineteenth-century regional folklore collections, contemporary ghost gazetteers and guide-books to haunted inns, then pasted them at random into one big volume. As Derbyshire folklorist S. O. Addy remarked in 1907:

Although in these days the word Folk-lore has become part of the common speech, and the subject is in some degree familiar to everybody, little original research is done. Even the Folk-lore Society, instead of collecting fresh material – and there is plenty to be had – has been printing under the name of County Folk-lore, a farrago of material from local histories and guide-books, of which not one item in twenty is worth repeating.[45]

'Worth repeating' or not, such items *got* repeated, not just once, but time and time again. Thanks to this continual borrowing, there grew up a received body of tales, which by 1920 was accepted as 'the' folklore of ghosts.

There are three elements in this official folklore. First, we find stories from seventeenth-century texts, chosen for their weirdness or pathos, or because they feature famous people. Most collections contain a selection of the following stories. For strangeness, the story of Anne Walker is very popular, as is another accusatory ghost who gave evidence of her own murder, Mary Barwick. For weirdness of another variety, writers like to include Joseph Glanvil's account of 'The Ghost of Major Sydenham' (see pages 62–4) and another of his quite preposterous tales, 'The Daemon [or 'Drummer'] of Tedworth' (see page 84). Pathos is provided by Richard Baxter's story of the wraith of Mary Goffe who visited her far-distant children as she lay dying and John Aubrey's account of how, while the poet John Donne was abroad, he saw an apparition of his wife weeping and carrying a dead baby in her arms (she had just given birth to a stillborn child). Other phantoms of the famous are the 'fetch' of Lady Diana Rich, a story again taken from Aubrey, and his account of the ghost of the first Duke of Buckingham's father, who came back to try to curb his son's wild excesses.[46]

The second element of this official legendry comes from journals and year-books from the 1780s onwards. Again, most of these feature a cast of famous people or have considerable novelty value. Of the latter, the most often quoted is Robert Chambers's account of 'The Golden Knight of Bryn yr Ellyllon' (see chapter 1) and the story of 'The Mannington Ghost' in which a studious man, burning the midnight oil in the library of Mannington Hall, is kept company all night by the quiet ghost of a distinguished-looking old scholar.[47]

The final element is composed of borrowings from the collections of regional folklore made in the 1860s and 1870s. This provides endless accounts of 'cauld lads', brown, white and grey 'ladies', boggarts of all kinds, black dogs and white deer, rustling ghosts, exorcisms, and the re-enactments of famous battles preferably from the Civil War.

The reliance of writers – popularizers and folklorists alike – on this bookish approach has had far-reaching consequences. Lack of research, and reliance on previously published legend-collections, meant that for years nobody got round to seeking up-to-date information or querying received ideas. Anything that deviated from the official version could be simply dismissed as 'not folklore'. Students, scholars and general readers alike were therefore gulled into thinking that the subject was well-researched and supernatural traditions were thoroughly understood, though one sometimes suspects all that many nineteenth-century re-searchers really knew about was their own group folklore.

The consequences of all this are felt even today. This rich official tradition nowadays provides a constant material-bank for writers and film-makers, and perpetuates a concept of the supernatural which, being based on tales from the folklore of the past not the present, seems outdated and irrelevant, and is therefore almost universally rejected. Yet in the privacy of their own hearts and minds many people cherish beliefs about divine providence and the relationship between life and death that are in the truest and simplest sense of the word 'super-natural'. Official tradition cannot really hope to mediate the unofficial beliefs, for there is little in common between them. For that, to some degree, folklorists have to blame their predecessors.

*   *   *

The four illustrations below are taken from Charlotte Burne's *Shropshire Folklore*, Charles Hardwick's *Traditions, Superstitions and Folklore* (*chiefly Lancashire and the North of England*) and Ella Leather's *The Folklore of Herefordshire*. Each is typical in its own way of the legends to be found in nineteenth-century compilations. The first is a well-told and typical story about a ghost who 'comes again very badly' in the shape of an animal (a 'Roaring Bull'). It tells why the ghost was so evil and how it was eventually exorcised despite its strength by twelve parsons, and 'laid', as all the worst ghosts are, in the Red Sea. Typical folktale motifs in the story are the fact that the ghost comes as noise and wind (a 'rush'), the ancient association between witchcraft and wind being evident here; the fact that the wisest parson is also blind; that the day is saved at the last moment by the twelfth and oldest man; the crack in the church wall; and the association between horses, water, candles and ghosts. The story comes from Charlotte Burne's *Shropshire Folklore*, which was compiled from the collection of an earlier fieldworker, Georgina Jackson, and published in 1883. As usual, the collector's opening and closing comments are almost as interesting as the text itself. Charlotte Burne, unlike many, does set the story in at least its geographical context, but her closing remarks are plainly designed to poke gentle fun at her informant and hence his belief in the Roaring Bull:

Let us now cross the county, from north-east to south-west. 'The Roarin' Bull o' Bagbury', although he has been 'laid' for generations, is still talked of about Bishop's Castle and all along the Shropshire side of the Border. Hyssington, the scene of his conquest by the assembled parsons, is a parish partly in Shropshire and partly in Montgomeryshire, which here runs up into Shropshire in a peninsular form. 'There's a prill [brook] o' waiter as divides the sheeres', said William Hughes. This, if I understand aright, is the very streamlet crossed by Bagbury Bridge, where the bull asked to be laid, so altogether the story may be said to belong to both counties. It was thus taken down in 1881 from the narration of an old farmer named Hayward.

'There was a very bad man lived at Bagbury Farm, and when he died it was said that he had never done but two good things in his life, and the one was to give a waistcoat to a poor old man, and the other was to give a piece of bread and cheese to a poor boy, and when this man died he made a sort of confession of this. But when he was dead his ghost would not rest, and he would get in the [farm] buildings in the shape of a bull, and roar till the boards and the shutters and the tiles would fly off the building, and it was impossible for any one to live near him. He never come till about nine or ten at night, but he got so rude at last that he would come about seven or eight at night, and he was so troublesome that they sent for twelve parsons to lay him. And the parsons came, and they got him under, but they could not lay him; but they got him, in the shape of a bull all the time, up into Hyssington Church. And when they got him into the church, they all had candles, and one blind old parson, who knowed him, and knowed what a rush he would make, he carried his candle in his top boot. And he made a great rush, and all the candles went out, all but the blind parson's, and he said, "You light your candles by mine." And while they were in the church, before they laid him, the bull made such a burst that he cracked the wall of the church from top to bottom, and the crack was left on purpose for people to see. I've seen it hundreds of times.

'Well, they got the bull down at last, into a snuff-box, and he asked them to lay him under Bagbury Bridge, and that every mare that passed over should lose her foal, and every woman her child; but they would not do this, and they laid him in the Red Sea for a thousand years.

'I remember the old clerk at Hyssington. He was an old man then, sixty years ago, and he told me he could remember the old blind parson well.'

But long after the ghost had been laid in the Red *Say*, 'folk were always frightened to go over Bagbury Bridge', said John Thomas. 'I've bin over it myself many a time with horses, and I always got off the horse and made him go quietly, and went pit-pat, ever so softly, like this, for fear of *him* hearing me and coming out.' And the old man got up and stumped about the cottage in his heavy boots, making a very unsuccessful attempt to show how gently he could walk.

The second story also comes from *Shropshire Folklore* and features a 'Madam', a common name for a female ghost of an upper-class variety. Again similar folktale and witchcraft motifs can be seen in this story (note especially how a black cat somehow gets involved and how, as in the story of 'The Roaring Bull of Bagbury', there is physical evidence of the ghost's existence – here a turned boulder, there a crack in the church wall). Like the previous story, this ends with an exorcism. Here, how-ever, the ghost returns because it had a miserable death rather than a wicked life. The author's dissociative remarks are once more rather blatant; she obviously does not care to link herself too closely to the stories she relates:

A far more appalling 'Madam' is Madam Pigott, the ancient terror of Chetwynd and Edgmond. Village tradition (utterly unsupported by genealogical evidence) declares that long ago, no one can tell when, some one or other of the many Madam Pigotts who have in turn reigned in the family mansion at Chetwynd, was an unloved and neglected wife. When her baby was born, so the story goes, her husband showed no anxiety for her safety, provided his child lived, and on being told of her extreme danger only replied that 'one should lop the root to save the branch'. Neither mother nor child survived, but after her husband had thus cruelly willed her death, Madam Pigott's spirit could find no rest. Night after night, exactly at twelve o'clock, she issued from a trap-door in the roof of Chetwynd (old) Rectory, and wandered through the park and the lanes in the direction of Edgmond, turning over, as she passed it, a large boulder-stone by the roadside between Edgmond and Newport. Her favourite haunt was a steep, dark, high-banked lane, properly called Cheney Hill, but nearly as well-known by the name of Madam Pigott's Hill. Near the top of it was a curiously-twisted tree-root, called Madam Pigott's Armchair. On this, or else on the old stone wall of Chetwynd Park just above it, Madam Pigott used to sit, 'on a moonshiny night', combing her baby's hair; and if some belated rider passed by (especially if he were on any errand concerning a woman in the same circumstances as herself), she and her black cat would spring up behind him and cling fast, notwithstanding all his efforts, till she came to a 'running water', then she could go no farther.

At last she became so troublesome that twelve of the neighbouring clergy were summoned to lay her, by incessantly reading psalms till they made her obedient to their power. Mr Foy, curate of Edgmond, has the credit of having been the one to succeed in this, for he continued to 'read' after all the others were exhausted. Yet at least ten or twelve years after his death, some fresh alarm of Madam Pigott arose, and a party went in haste to beg a neighbouring rector to come and lay the ghost! And to this day, Chetwynd Hall – which some say was the starting-point of this ghostly ramble – has the reputation of being haunted, and many a strong young groom or ploughboy still shrinks from facing 'Madam Pigott's Hill' after dark.

This wild and gruesome myth is familiar to the poor folk for miles around Chetwynd.

The third story is probably the best-known of all stories about boggarts. It is quoted here from Charles Hardwick's significantly entitled *Traditions, Superstitions and Folklore (chiefly Lancashire and the North of England), their affinity to others in widely distributed localities, their Eastern Origin and Mythical Significance*, published in Manchester in 1872. Here there is far more comment, both overt and implied, than in Charlotte

Burne's stories, as well as a good many sneers at other writers. The affinity between boggarts and poltergeists is quite apparent, though the boggart is made into an entirely unserious and ultimately comic character. The text speaks for itself:

I may just remark, *en passant*, that the word 'traditions', as applied to nearly the whole of these stories, is a sad misnomer. The tales might perhaps with propriety, be termed *nouvelletes*, or little novels; but when put forth as 'traditions', in the true acceptation of the term, they are worse than useless, for they are calculated equally to mislead both the antiquary and the collector of 'folk lore'. Croker makes the scene of his story what was once a retired and densely wooded dell, or deep valley, in the township of Blackley, near Manchester, called to this day, 'Boggart Ho' Clough'. This boggart sadly pestered a worthy farmer, named George Cheetham, by 'scaring his maids, worrying his men, and frightening the poor children out of their senses, so that, at last, not even a mouse durst shew himself indoors at the farm, as he valued his whiskers, after the clock had struck twelve'. This same boggart, however, had some jolly genial qualities. His voice, when joined with household laughter, on merry tales being told and practical jokes indulged in, around the hearth at Christmastide, is described as 'small and shrill', and easily 'heard above the rest, like a baby's penny trumpet'. He began to regard himself at last as a 'privileged inmate' and conducted himself in the most extraordinary manner, snatching the children's bread and butter out of their hands, and interfering with their porridge, milk and other food. His 'invisible hand' knocked the furniture about in the most approved modern style of goblin or spiritual manifestation. Yet, this mischievous propensity did not prevent him from occasionally performing some kindly acts, such as churning the cream and scouring the pans and kettles! Truly, he was a 'tricksty sprite'. Croker refers to one circumstance which he regards as 'remarkable', and which will remind modern readers very distinctly of a 'spiritual' exhibition which recently attracted much public attention. He says – 'the stairs ascended from the kitchen; a partition of boards covered the ends of the steps, and formed a closet beneath the staircase. From one of the boards of this partition a large round knot was accidently displaced, and one day the youngest of the children, while playing with the shoe-horn, stuck it into this knot-hole. Whether or not the aperture had been formed by the boggart as a peep-hole to watch the motions of the family, I cannot pretend to say. Some thought it was, for it was called the boggart's peep-hole; but others said that they had remembered it before the shrill laugh of the boggart was heard in the house. However this may have been, it is certain that the horn was ejected with surprising precision at the head of whoever put it there; and either in mirth or in anger the horn was darted forth with great velocity, and struck the poor child over the ear.' To say the least of it, it is rather remarkable that the mere substitution of the words *structure* or *cabinet* for *closet*, and *trumpet* for *horn*, to say nothing of the peculiar quality of the boggart's voice, should make the whole so eloquently suggestive of the doings of a certain 'Mr Ferguson' and his friends the Davenport Brothers, and other 'spiritual manifestations' recently so much in vogue. All this supernatural mountebanking was, it appears, taken in good part by Mr Cheetham's family, and when the children or neighbours wished for a little excitement they easily found it in 'laking', that is, playing, with this eccentric and pugnacious disembodied spirit.

But Mr Boggart eventually returned to his old avocations, and midnight noises again disturbed the repose of the inmates of the haunted house. Pewter pots and earthen dishes were dashed to the floor, and yet, in the morning they were found perfectly uninjured, and in their usual places. To such a pitch at last did matters reach, that George Cheetham and his family were observed one day by neighbour John Marshall sullenly following a cart that contained their household goods and chattels. What transpired is best told in Mr Croker's own words:

'Well, Georgy, and soa you're leaving th'owd house at last,' said Marshall.

'Heigh, Johnny, my lad, I'm in a manner forced to it, thou sees,' replied the other, 'for that wearyfu' boggart torments us soa, we can neither rest neet nor day for't. It seems loike to have a malice agains t'young uns, an' it ommost kills my poor dame at thoughts on't, and soa, thou sees we're forced to flit like.'

He had got thus far in his complaint when, behold, a shrill voice, from a deep upright churn, the topmost utensil on the cart, called out, 'Ay, ay, neighbour, we're flitting, you see.'

'Od rot thee,' exclaimed George, 'If I'd known thou'd been flitting too, I wadn't ha' stirred a peg. Nay, nay, it's no use, Mally,' turning to his wife, 'we may as weel turn back again t'ould hoose as be tormented in another that's not so convenient.'

The final story comes from Ella Leather's *The Folklore of Herefordshire* compiled in 1912. She calls it 'The Guide of the Black Mountain', and it is a very typical legend about the helpful ghost of a stranger. The way it is told is in keeping with all legends of this type, beginning with an assertion of belief based on personal experience, containing an account of an entirely silent ghost, and ending with a neat dénouement that proves the supernatural nature of the disappearing stranger.

A few years ago a man was driving a lady from Longtown to Llanveyno, and she, being a stranger, questioned him concerning the 'Apparition of our Lady' at Llanthony. He replied that he did not believe in it at all; there were indeed spirits to be seen on the mountain, but they were different. He had seen, and he knew. Once he went to see friends at Llanthony, and was returning directly over the mountain to Longtown, when a fog came on suddenly and he lost his way. He was standing, quite at a loss, when a man came towards him, wearing a large broad-rimmed hat and a cloak. He did not speak but beckoned, and the man followed him, until he found himself in the right path. Turning round, he thanked his unknown friend, but received no reply; he vanished quickly in the fog. This seemed strange, but he thought no more till, on visiting his friends at Llanthony later, they asked if he reached home in safety that evening, as they had been anxious.

When the stranger in the broad-rimmed hat was described they looked at each other in surprise. 'What!' they said, 'tell us exactly what his face was like.' He described the stranger more minutely. 'It was T— H—, for sure,' they cried, 'he knew the mountain well, and HE HAS BEEN DEAD THESE TWO YEARS.'

NOTES

1   Thomas Carlyle, *History of the French Revolution*, 1, vii.
2   For the early sections of this chapter, I am much indebted to Keith Thomas (1971), as also to the following works: Norman Cohn, *Europe's Inner Demons* (1976); R. C. Finucane, *Appearances of the Dead* (1982); Brian Easlea, *Witchhunting, Magic and the New Philosophy: An Introduction to the Debates of the Scientific Revolution 1450–1750* (1980); Richard Bowyer, 'The Role of the Ghost Story in Mediaeval Christianity' (1981); W. M. S. Russell, 'Greek and Roman Ghosts' (1981); J. R. Porter, 'Ghosts in the Old Testament and the Ancient Near East' (1981); and to the work of Alan MacFarlane, Alan Kors and Edward Peters, Christopher Hill, Rossell Hope Robbins, George Lyman Kittredge, R. H. Tawney, Mary Douglas and H. C. Lea (for details see the bibliography).
3   This very apt term was coined by a sociologist of religion, David Martin. See Martin (1967), p. 74.
4   Bowyer (1981), p. 177.
5   Unfortunately, in such a short space as this allows, quotations and reference to this vast array of literature are necessarily extremely selective. Those interested in following up the subject further might begin by looking up some of the texts omitted from this discussion – in particular works by Scot, Bekker, Le Loyer, Beaumont and Kirk (for details see the bibliography).
6   Thomas (1971), p. 30.
7   Thomas (1971), p. 32.
8   Lea (1957), p. 65.
9   Taillepied (Summers edn), p. 101.
10 Hutchinson (1720 edn), pp. 332–3.
11 Bourne (1977 edn), p. 40.
12 'For the Sadducees say that there is no resurrection, neither angel, nor spirit.' Luke, 23:8.
13 Hobbes (1957 edn), p. 199.
14 The following examples are drawn from Keith Thomas, Christopher Hill and Brian Easlea.
15 See Sabine, ed. (1941); Hill, ed. (1973); Brailsford (1983) and Easlea (1980).
16 In *Principles of Philosophy*. Quoted Easlea (1980), p. 111.
17 Principally by Easlea (1980).
18 Glanvil (1681), p. 16.
19 *The Wesley Journal*, 25 May, 1768. Quoted in Hole (1957), pp. 32–3.
20 Bovet (1951 edn), pp. 122 and 133.

21 Sinclair (1969 edn), pp. 102–8, 156–8; 187–90 and 190–2.

22 See, for example, Robert Kirk's description of poltergeists: 'The Invisible Wights which haunt houses seem rather to be some of our Subterranean Inhabitants [i.e. members of the 'Secret Commonwealth' of elves, fauns and fairies that his title refers to] than Evil Spirits or Devils, because tho they throw great stons, pieces of Earth, and wood at the Inhabitants, they hurt them not at all, as if they acted not maliciously like Devils, but in Sport like Buffoons and drols.' Kirk (1976 edn), p. 85.

23 Pierre Bayle, *Pensées diverses sur la Cométe*. Quoted by Easlea (1980), p. 217.

24 Thomas Sprat, 'The History of the Royal Society of London'. Quoted by Easlea (1980), p. 212.

25 Easlea (1980), p. 217.

26 Hutchinson (1720).

27 Thomas (1971), p. 591.

28 Bourne (1977 edn), pp. 37–8.

29 Bourne (1977 edn), pp. 59–60.

30 Bourne (1977 edn), pp. 84–5.

31 Bourne (1977 edn), p. 41.

32 Brand (1810 edn), p. 78.

33 Grose (1790 edn), pp. 2–3.

34 Grose (1790 edn), pp. 5–11.

35 King James I was author of a treatise on demonology and a firm believer in witchcraft. The 'Glanville' referred to is Joseph Glanvil, author of *Sadducismus Triumphatus* (1681); 'Coleman', presumably, is the turncoat cleric Edward Coleman, conspirator in the 'Popish Plot', arraigned and executed for high treason in 1678; 'Sir Matthew Hales' is the judge, Sir Matthew Hale, who greatly encouraged witchhunting and presided over a very controversial witchcraft trial at Bury St Edmunds in 1662. The slur against Reginald Scot, one of the bravest opponents of witchcraft as an indictable offence, is entirely unjustified.

36 David Wright, in his 'Introduction' to *The Penguin Book of English Romantic Verse* (1973), p. xiv. Another very readable introduction to the spirit of the romantic movement may be found in John Summerson's discussion of the architecture of the period in *Spirit of the Age* (1975), pp. 129–50.

37 William Wordsworth, 'Preface' to the 2nd edition of *The Lyrical Ballads*, p. 13.

38 Wright (1973), p. xvii.

39 Quoted in Dean Smith (1954), p. 11.

40 Quoted in Reeves (1958), p. 5.

41 Quoted in Reeves (1958), p. 22.

42 Burne (1883), p. 131.

43 Burne (1883), pp. 106–7.

44 Quoted in Robbins (1981), p. 254.

45 S. O. Addy, 'Derbyshire Folk-lore', in Cox (1907), p. 346.

46 For an account of 'The Ghost of Anne Walker' see Webster (1667), pp. 295–6; for 'Mary Barwick' see Aubrey (1696) and Hole (1940), p. 28; for 'The Daemon of Tedworth' see Glanvil (1681), pp. 71–94; for 'The Wraith of Mary Goffe' see Baxter (1840 edn), pp. 96–100; for 'The Wraith of John Donne's Wife' see Aubrey (1696), p. 60; for 'The Fetch of Lady Diana Rich' see Aubrey (1696), p. 76; and for the Buckingham ghost see Aubrey (1696), pp. 64–5.

47 Hare (1896), vol. 6, p. 304.

Afterword

Since 1920, British folklorists have, with only a few exceptions, opted out of the study of supernatural folklore and the collection of supernatural narratives. It is primarily therefore through the *popular* stereotype that ghost beliefs are most clearly seen today. Because it *is* a mass stereotype, it necessarily reflects the values of the age: that age is, of course, one in which the supernatural is seen as dangerous superstition if actually believed, though just harmless fun and thrills if not believed. According to this stereotype, what supernatural concepts cannot be is valuable, useful, or worthy of serious consideration.

The end-result is a trivializing of the supernatural by the mechanisms of commerce. The supernatural has been taken over by TV, films and ghost-hunters in such a big way that shows and books can almost provide a classification system for popular notions about ghosts. So we find, for example, that ghosts may be allowed to exist on what we might call the 'Scoobie-Doo' level, where they are either tameable or friendly, or turn out to be frauds and fakes; that they are also allowed existence on the 'Haunted Inns of England' level, where they are regarded as tourist attractions, a speciality of the house, synthetic (and profitable) thrills; or they may appear in 'Hammer House of Horror' mode, where they are allowed to be threatening, but only to those deliberately seeking to be (safely and temporarily) threatened. In other words, as forms of entertainment. So the supernatural has been officially demoted to the nursery world of grown-ups and children alike, where it is frankly so synthetic a concept that it can serve no useful purpose at all.

Yet people continue to have experiences which demand explanations – explanations which nature and science as we define the terms today cannot provide – and they continue to need more than merely material things. There is in many people a yearning for something magical and mystical, which not only gives glamour to a humdrum world, but may also be a sort of baseline of a religious impulse, a thirst for the holy in the everyday. The experiences can only be explained, and the impulses satisfied, by belief in a sphere of life that is above the 'natural'.

Neither our formal culture, our modern world-view, nor our popular traditions (now hi-jacked to provide little thrills for big kids) can supply us with an organized 'official' belief-system through which these needs can be met. People turn, therefore, to *un*official channels – to informal opinion expressed through the medium of a network of face-to-face conversations. They, as it were, 're-invent' tradition all over again and make old ideas live once again – valid, vital and useful – through the folklore they offer each other in their personal experience stories, discussions and exchanges of ideas.

At this informal level, there continues to be a very widespread belief in the supernatural, which has kept some traditions alive almost unchanged, despite the onslaughts of secularism, rationalism and materialism, and which has led to others being adapted to modern conditions. People still continue to believe in poltergeists, and in fetches, wraiths and warning ghosts, more or less as they did in the sixteenth and seventeenth centuries. There is also a heartfelt popular tradition that the souls of the family dead – continuing to exist somehow, somewhere, some way – can exert an influence over the lives of the living and be communicated with if necessary.

One of the particular interests of the present study has been in establishing that, in a typical community today, the experience of seeing a ghost, or at least the phrase 'seeing a ghost' is restricted in use (and therefore no longer usable for serious studies of supernatural belief). As the women I interviewed see it, 'ghosts' are features of haunted houses, essentially phenomena limited to special classes of place, such as houses where suicides or murders have been committed or where former residents have suffered intense unhappiness. The crimes and sorrows leave their mark on the building in the form of 'waves' of 'energy', which manifest themselves as mysterious noises, self-opening doors, flying objects, the switching on and off of lights without human agency, or spirits which interfere with living residents. These are in essence very similar to the characteristics of haunted houses in the popular stereotype today, and in much of the folklore of previous centuries as well, though less exotic, marvellous and baroque than, say, the seventeenth century could boast.

At the other end of the spectrum from 'ghosts' and haunted houses, women today have an informal belief in a variety of friendly apparitions of dead members of the family, personal to the percipient rather than peculiar to any location. These supernatural 'witnesses' of earthly life are expressions of an unchanging need for an effective, organized and unified Cosmos where both the dead and the living, both the divine and the mundane, can exist side-by-side in mutual harmony. They are, in a very real sense, direct descendants of the old purposeful ghosts, though domesticated, made simpler and more personal.

Supernatural concepts, just as in the past, take their impetus from, and are shaped by, a comprehensive world-view. The sphere of operation of the medieval revenant was a world of religious and moral obligation, rites and observances: that of the present-day 'witness' is an orderly, caring, domestic sphere, reflecting an orderly, caring creation supervised by a personal God. So the women's views about the status of the spirits of the dead are fitted into a wider belief-system. Belief in esoteric psychic powers is widespread, expressing itself through the concepts of pre-monitions, omens, second-sight and telepathy. Together, these concepts have two vital psychological functions. Firstly, they are strenuous attempts to bring rhyme and reason to a chaotic world. Secondly, they give the highest sanction to traditional female values and are thus the strongest justification for the lives the women have led and the duties which they have given their lives to performing. Beliefs in revenants, premonitions, and so on, are thus one aspect of a unified, consistent religious or moral philosophy – as they always have been. Far from being 'irrational', they are the results of a rationalizing impulse, and far from being 'superstitious', they are the results of hours of careful thought and corporate discussion, the consequence of an ongoing dialogue between the adherents of two opposed world-views – the supernaturalist and the rationalist – and two psychological impulses – cultural tradition and social taboo.

Commentators who have claimed that supernatural belief is 'obviously' much diminished in modern Britain have, I would suggest, been deceived by the official world-view into not recognizing the existence of an entirely different unofficial one. When we know where to look and how to ask, it is very easy to find plenty of evidence for the existence of a very substantial supernatural belief-tradition today.

If this book has succeeded in demonstrating that supernatural belief is still alive and well and living in the hearts of ordinary people, I am well content – though, as T. C. Lethbridge once pointed out, 'it may not be a great achievement to prove something exists when all the world knows that it does'. That, however, is inevitably, and by definition, the fate of the folklorist.

Appendix

Some Linguistic Clues to Belief and Disbelief

Degree of Belief	*Linguistic Clues*
Convinced Belief	'I firmly believe' 'I do believe in *that*!' 'Yes. Oh, yes!' 'Without question' 'I've proof of *that*' prompt or precipitate reply prompt initiation of narrative
Some Belief	'Not *really*, but . . .' 'Possibly there's something *in* that' 'I think there *could be*' 'I don't say I *believe* it, but . . .' falling–rising intonation
Unsure/Uncommitted	'I don't know' 'I don't take much notice of that kind of thing' 'I get a bit mixed up about that' unstressed intonation hesitation unaccompanied by embarrassment
Some Scepticism	'I don't think so, *really*' (compare 'Not *really*, but . . .' When expressing scepticism the pause occurs *before* 'really'. Absence of qualifying 'but')
Convinced Disbelief	'No' 'I don't believe in *that*!' 'I just don't *see*!' laughter grimaces headshakes embarrassment absence of stress on words expressing belief/ understanding/knowledge (compare stress patterns in 'Some Belief' category)

Select Bibliography

Abercrombie, John, M. D., 1841. *An Enquiry Concerning the Intellectual Powers and the Investigation of Truth*, eleventh edn, London, John Murray. First published in 1830 (Edinburgh, Waugh and Innes.)

Abrahams, Roger D., 1977. 'Toward an Enactment-Centred Theory of Folklore', in William Bascom, ed., *Frontiers of Folklore*, A A A S Symposium, 5, Boulder, Colorado, Westview Press, pp. 79–120.

Addy, Sidney Oldall, 1907. 'Derbyshire Folk-lore', in the Revd Charles J. Cox, ed., *Memorials of Old Derbyshire*, London/Derby, Bemrose and Sons, pp. 346–70.

Atwood, Margaret, 1979. *Surfacing*, London, Virago.

Aubrey, John, 1696. *Miscellanies*, London, Edward Castle.

Ballard, Linda-May, 1981. 'Before Death and Beyond: Death and Ghost Traditions with Particular Reference to Ulster', in: Hilda R. Ellis Davidson and W. M. S. Russell, eds., *The Folklore of Ghosts*, The Folklore Society, Mistletoe Series, London, D. S. Brewer, pp. 13–43.

Barrett, Sir William Fletcher, 1926. *Death-bed Visions*, London, Methuen.

Bascom, William, 1965. 'Four Functions of Folklore', in Alan Dundes, ed., *The Study of Folklore*, Englewood Cliffs, New Jersey, Prentice Hall, pp. 279–98.

—, ed., 1977. *Frontiers of Folklore*, A A A S Symposium, 5, Boulder, Colorado, Westview Press.

Bauman, Richard, 1977. *Verbal Art as Performance*, Prospect Heights, Illinois, Waveland Press.

Baxter, Richard, 1840. *The Certainty of the World of Spirits Fully Evinced*, London, H. Howell. First published in 1691.

Beardsley, R. H. and Rosalie Hankey, 1942. 'The Vanishing Hitchhiker', *California Folklore Quarterly*, 1, pp. 303–35.

Beaumont, John, 1705. *An Historical, Physiological and Theological Treatise of Spirits, Apparitions, Witchcraft and Other Magical Practices*, London, D. Browne.

Bekker, Balthasar, 1695. *The World Bewitched*, London, R. Baldwin. First published in 1691.

Ben Amos, Dan, 1971. 'Towards a Definition of Folklore in Context', *Journal of American Folklore*, 84, pp. 3–15.

Bennett, Sir Ernest, 1939. *Apparitions and Haunted Houses*, London, Faber and Faber.

Bennett, Gillian, 1986. 'Heavenly Protection and Family Unity: The Concept of the Revenant among Elderly Urban Women', *Folklore*, 97: i, pp. 3–14.

Bennett, Gillian, Paul Smith and J. D. A. Widdowson, eds., 1987. *Perspectives on Contemporary Legend II*, Sheffield, CECTAL, Sheffield Academic Press.

Blacker, Carmen, 1981. 'The Angry Ghost in Japan', in Hilda R. Ellis Davidson and W. M. S. Russell, eds., *The Folklore of Ghosts*, The Folklore Society, Mistletoe Series, London, D. S. Brewer, pp. 95–105.

Blauner, Robert, 1966. 'Death and Social Structure', *Psychiatry*, 29, pp. 378–94.

Boas, Franz, 1896. 'The Growth of Indian Mythologies', *Journal of American Folklore*, 9, 32, pp. 1–11.

—, 1910. *Kwakiutl Tales*, New York/Leiden, New York: Columbia University Press, Leiden: E. J. Brill.

—, 1911. *The Mind of Primitive Man: A Course of Lectures Delivered Before the Lowell Institute, Boston, Mass., and the National University of Mexico, 1910–1911*, New York, Macmillan.

—, 1915. 'Mythology and Folk-tales of the North American Indians', in *Anthropology in Northern America*, New York, G. E. Stechert, pp. 306–49.

—, 1932. *Bella Bella Tales*, Memoirs of the American Folklore Society, 25, New York, G. E. Stechert.

Bourne, Henry, 1977. *Antiquitates Vulgares: or the Antiquities of the Common People*, New York, Arno Press. First published in 1725.

Bovet, Richard, 1951. *Pandaemonium: or the Devil's Cloister*, Aldington, Kent, Hand and Flower Press. First published in 1684.

Bowlby, John, 1961. 'Processes of Mourning', *The International Journal of Psychoanalysis*, 42:4–5, pp. 317–40.

—, 1969–80. *Attachment and Loss*, International Psychoanalytic Library, 79, London, Hogarth Press.

Bowyer, Richard A., 1981. 'The Role of the Ghost Story in Mediaeval Christianity', in Hilda R. Ellis Davidson and W. M. S. Russell, eds., *The Folklore of Ghosts*, The Folklore Society, Mistletoe Series, London, D. S. Brewer, pp. 177–92.

Brailsford, H. N., 1983. *The Levellers and the English Revolution*, edited by Christopher Hill, Nottingham, Spokesman.

Brand, John, 1810. *Observations on Popular Antiquities: including the whole of Mr Bourne's 'Antiquitates Vulgares', with Addenda to every chapter of that work: As also an Appendix, containing such Articles as have been Omitted by that Author*, second edition, London, W. Baynes. First published 1777. Reprinted in 1913 as *Observations on Popular Antiquities, chiefly illustrating the origin of our vulgar customs, ceremonies and superstitions, with the additions of Sir Henry Ellis*, London, Chatto and Windus.

Bray, Anna, 1844. *Legends, Superstitions and Sketches of Devonshire on the Borders of the Tamar and Tavy*, London, J. Murray.

Briggs, Katharine, M., 1962. *Pale Hecate's Team*, London, Routledge and Kegan Paul.

—, 1977. *British Folktales and Legends: A Sampler*, London, Paladin.

—, 1977. *A Dictionary of Fairies*, Harmondsworth, Penguin.

Brown, Theo, 1979. *The Fate of the Dead: A Study in Folk Eschatology in the West Country after the Reformation*, The Folklore Society, Mistletoe Series, London, D. S. Brewer.

Browne, Ray B., 1975. *A Night with the Hants and other Alabama Folk Experiences*, Bowling Green, Ohio, University Press.

Burne, Charlotte Sophia, 1883. *Shropshire Folklore: A Sheaf of Gleanings from the notebooks of Georgina Jackson*, London, Trench Trübner.

—, 1914. *The Handbook of Folklore*, Publications of the Folklore Society, 73, London, Sidgwick and Jackson.

Butler, Jon, 1983. 'The Dark Ages of American Occultism, 1760–1848', in Howard Kerr and Charles L. Crow, eds., *The Occult in America: New Historical Perspectives*, Urbana/Chicago, University of Illinois Press, pp. 58–78.

Calmet, Augustin, 1850. *The Phantom World*, edited and translated by the Revd Henry Christmas, London, Richard Bentley. First published in 1746.

Chambers, Robert, 1869. *The Book of Days: A Miscellany of Popular Antiquities in Connection with the Calendar*, London/Edinburgh, W. R. Chambers.

Clodd, Edward, 1895a. 'Presidential Address', *Folk-Lore*, VI, pp. 54–81.

—, 1895b. 'A Reply to the Foregoing "Protest"', *Folk-Lore*, VI, pp. 248–58.

—, 1896. 'Presidential Address', *Folk-Lore*, VII, pp. 35–60.

Cohn, Norman, 1976. *Europe's Inner Demons*, St Albans, Paladin.

Cox, The Revd Charles J., 1907. *Memorials of Old Derbyshire*, London/Derby, Bemrose and Sons.

Crowe, Catherine, 1852. *The Night Side of Nature: or Ghosts and Ghostseers*, 2 vols., London, Routledge, third edition. First published in 1848.

Daillon, Jacques de, 1723. *Daimonologia: or a treatise of Spirits wherein several places of Scripture are expounded, against the vulgar errors concerning witchcraft, apparitions etc.*, London, no publisher accredited.

Danielson, Larry, 1979. 'Toward the Analysis of Vernacular Texts: The Supernatural Narrative in Oral and Popular Print Sources', *Journal of the Folklore Institute*, 16:3, pp. 130–54.

—1983. 'Paranormal Memorates in the American Vernacular', in Howard Kerr and Charles L. Crow, eds., *The Occult in America: New Historical Perspectives*, Urbana/Chicago, University of Illinois Press, pp. 196–217.

Davidson, Hilda R. Ellis and W. M. S. Russell, eds., 1981. *The Folklore of Ghosts*, The Folklore Society, Mistletoe Series, London, D. S. Brewer.

Day, J. Wentworth, 1954. *Here are Ghosts and Witches*, London, Batsford.

Dean Smith, Margaret, 1954. *A Guide to English Folk Song Collections 1822–1952*, Liverpool, University Press, in association with the English Folk Dance and Song Society.

Defoe, Daniel, 1706. *A True Relation of the Apparition of one Mrs Veal, the next day after her death: to one Mrs Bargrave at Canterbury. The 8th of Sept., 1705*, London, B. Bagg.

—, 1822. *The Political History of the Devil, ancient and modern*, Durham, G. Walker. First published in 1726.

—, *alias* Andrew Moreton, 1729. *The Secrets of the Invisible World Disclos'd*, London, J. Clarke, A. Millar, C. Rivington and J. Green.

Dégh, Linda, Henry Glassie and Felix J. Oinas, eds., 1976. *Folklore Today: A Festschrift for Richard M. Dorson*, Bloomington/London, Indiana University Press.

Dingwall, Eric J., Kathleen M. Goldney and Trevor H. Hall, 1956. 'The Haunting of Borley Rectory: A Critical Survey of the Evidence', *Proceedings of the Society for Psychical Research*, V:51: part 186.

Dingwall, Eric J. and Trevor H. Hall, 1958. *Four Modern Ghosts*, London, Gerald Duckworth.

Dorson, Richard M., 1964. *Buying the Wind: Regional Folklore in the United States*, Chicago/London, University of Chicago Press.

—, 1968. *The British Folklorists: A History*, London, Routledge and Kegan Paul.

—, ed., 1968. *Peasant Custom and Savage Myth*, 2 vols., London, Routledge and Kegan Paul.

—, ed., 1972. *Folklore and Folklife*, Chicago/London, University of Chicago Press.

Douglas, Mary, ed., 1970. *Witchcraft: Accusations and Confessions*, London/New York, Tavistock Publications.

Dundes, Alan, 1964a. *The Morphology of the North American Indian Folktale*, Helsinki, Folklore Fellows Communication, 195.

—, 1964b. 'Texture, Text and Context', *Southern Folklore Quarterly*, 28, pp. 251–65.

—, 1975. *Analytical Essays in Folklore*, The Hague, Mouton.

—, ed., 1965. *The Study of Folklore*, Englewood Cliffs, New Jersey, Prentice Hall.

Dyer, T. F. Thiselton, 1898. *The Ghost World*, London, Ward and Downey.

Easlea, Brian, 1980. *Witchhunting, Magic and the New Philosophy: An Introduction to the Debates of the Scientific Revolution 1450–1750*, Brighton, Harvester.

Ellis, Bill, 1987. 'Why are Verbatim Texts Necessary?' in Gillian Bennett, Paul Smith and J. D. A. Widdowson, eds., *Perspectives on Contemporary Legend II:* Sheffield, CECTAL, Sheffield Academic Press, pp. 31–60.

Evans, George Ewart, 1970. *Where Beards Wag All: The Relevance of Oral Tradition*, London, Faber and Faber.

—, 1976. *From Mouths of Men*, London, Faber and Faber.

Fine, Elizabeth, 1984. *The Folklore Text: From Performance to Print*, Bloomington/London, Indiana University Press.

Finucane, R. C., 1982. *Appearances of the Dead: A Cultural History of Ghosts*, London, Junction Books.

Frazer, Sir James George, 1934. *The Fear of the Dead in Primitive Religion*, 2 vols., London, Macmillan.

—, 1963. *The Golden Bough: A Study in Magic and Religion*, abridged edn, London, Macmillan. First published in 1922.

Freud, Sigmund, 1913. *The Interpretation of Dreams*, authorized translation of third edn, edited by A. A. Brill, London, G. Allen.

Fromm, Erich, 1951. *The Forgotten Language: An Introduction to the Understanding of Dreams, Fairy Tales and Myths*, English translation New York, Rinehart. First published in 1934.

Gauld, Alan and A. D. Cornell, 1979. *Poltergeists*, London, Routledge and Kegan Paul.

Georges, Robert, 1969. 'Towards an Understanding of Storytelling Events', *Journal of American Folklore*, 82, pp. 313–28.

Giraud, Louis S., 1927. *True Ghost Stories Told by Readers of the 'Daily News'*, London, Fleetgate Publications (Daily News Book Dept).

Glanvil, Joseph, 1676. *Essays on Several Important Subjects in Philosophy and Religion*, London, J. D.

—, 1681. *Sadducismus Triumphatus*, London, Thomas Newcomb.

Glick, Ira O., Robert S. Weiss and Colin Murray Parkes, 1974. *The First Year of Bereavement*, New York/London, John Wiley and Sons.

Goldsmith, Oliver (attributed), 1742. *The Mystery Revealed*, London, W. Bristow in St Paul's Churchyard and C. Etherington, York.

Gomme, George Lawrence, 1885. *English Traditions and Foreign Customs: A Classified Collection of the Chief Contents of the Gentleman's Magazine from 1731–1868*, London, Elliott Stock.

—, 1890. *The Handbook of Folklore*, London, Nichols and Sons, for the Folklore Society.

Gorer, Geoffrey, 1955. *Exploring English Character*, London, Cresset Press.

—, 1965. *Death, Grief and Mourning in Contemporary Britain*, London, Cresset Press.

Green, Celia and Charles McCreery, 1975. *Apparitions*, London, Hamish Hamilton.

Grimm, Jakob and Wilhelm, 1884. *Grimm's Household Tales with the Authors' Notes*, translated and edited by Margaret Hunt, with an introduction by Andrew Lang, 2 vols., London, Henry G. Bohn. First published in 1812.

Grose, Francis, 1790. *A Provincial Glossary with a Collection of Local Proverbs and Popular Superstitions*, London, S. Hooper, second edition. First published in 1787.

Gumperz, J. J. and Dell Hymes, 1972. *Directions in Sociolinguistics: The Ethnography of Communication*, New York, Holt, Rinehart and Winston.

Gurney, E., F. W. H. Myers and F. Podmore, 1886. *Phantasms of the Living*, London, Society for Psychical Research.

Halpert, Herbert and J. D. A. Widdowson, 1984. 'Folk-narrative Performance and Tape Transcription: Theory *vs* Practice', in Reimund Kvideland and Torunn Selberg, eds., *Papers: The 8th Congress of the International Society for Folk Narrative Research, Bergen, 12–17 June 1984*, Bergen, pp. 225–32.

Hand, Wayland D., 1971. *American Folk Legend*, Berkeley/Los Angeles/London, University of California Press.

—, 1976a. *American Folk Medicine*, Berkeley/Los Angeles/ London, University of California Press.

—, 1976b. 'Folk Belief and Superstition: A Crucial Field of Folklore Long Neglected', in Linda Dégh, Henry Glassie and Felix J. Oinas, eds., *Folklore Today: A Festschrift for Richard M. Dorson*, Bloomington/London, Indiana University Press, pp. 209–19.

—, Anna, Casetta and Sondra B. Thiederman, eds., 1981. *Popular Beliefs and Superstitions: A Compendium of American Folklore Compiled by Newbell Niles Puckett*, Boston, Massachusetts, G. K. Hall.

Hare, Augustus J. C., 1986. *The Story of My Life*, 6 vols., London, George Allen.

Hardwick, Charles, 1872. *Traditions, Superstitions and Folklore (Chiefly Lancashire and the North of England)*, Manchester, A. Ireland.

Harland, John and T. T. Wilkinson, 1867. *Lancashire Legends*, London, F. Warne.

Henderson, William, 1973. *Folklore of the Northern Counties*, Wakefield, E. P. Publishing. First published in 1866.

Hill, Christopher, ed., 1973. *Winstanley: The Law of Freedom and Other Writings*, Harmondsworth, Penguin.

Hobbes, Thomas, 1957. *Leviathan*, Everyman's Library, London, Dent. First published in 1651.

Hole, Christina, 1940. *Haunted England*, London, Batsford.

—, 1957. *A Mirror of Witchcraft*, London, Chatto and Windus.

Hone, William, 1832. *The Year Book*, London, Thomas Tegg.

Honko, Lauri, 1962. *Geisterglaube in Ingermanland*, Helsinki, Folklore Fellows Communication, 185.

Hufford, David J., 1976. 'A New Approach to the Old Hag', in Wayland D. Hand, ed., *American Folk Medicine*, Berkeley/Los Angeles/London, University of California Press, pp. 73–85.

—, 1982a. *The Terror that Comes in the Night: An Experience-centred Study of Supernatural Assault Traditions*, Philadelphia, University of Pennsylvania Press.

—, 1982b. 'Traditions of Disbelief', *New York Folklore*, 8:3–4, pp. 47–55.

Hunt, Robert, 1865. *Popular Romances of the West of England: or The Drolls, Traditions and Superstitions of Old Cornwall*, Series 1 and 2, London, John Camden Hotten.

Hutchinson, Francis, 1720. *An Historical Essay Concerning Witchcraft with observations tending to confute the vulgar errors about that point*, London, R. Knaplock and D. Midwinter, second edition. First published in 1718.

Ingram, John H., 1884. *The Haunted Homes and Family Traditions of Great Britain*, Series 1 and 2, London, W. H. Allen.

Jahoda, Gustav, 1969. *The Psychology of Superstition*, London, Allen Lane.

Jones Ernest, 1931. *On the Nightmare*, International Psychoanalytical Library, 20, London, Hogarth Press.

Jones, L. C., 1944. 'The Ghosts of New York: An Analytical Study', *Journal of American Folklore*, 57, pp. 237–54.

—, 1959. *Things that Go Bump in the Night*, New York, Hill and Wang.

Jung, Carl Gustav, 1964. *Collected Works*, Volume 8, London, Routledge and Kegan Paul.

Kastenbaum, Robert J., 1981. *Death, Society and Human Experience*, St Louis/ Toronto/London, V. C. Moseby.

Kerr, Howard and Charles L. Crow, eds., 1983. *The Occult in America: New Historical Perspectives*, Urbana/Chicago, University of Illinois Press.

Kirk, Robert, 1976. *The Secret Commonwealth and A Short Treatise of Charms and Spells*, edited by Stewart Sanderson, The Folklore Society, Mistletoe Series, London, D. S. Brewer. Written in ?1691. Also edited by Andrew Lang and reprinted at Stirling by Eneas MacKay, 1933.

Kittredge, George Lyman, 1929. *Witchcraft in Old and New England*, New York, Russell and Russell.

Kors, Alan C. and Edward Peters, 1973. *Witchcraft in Europe 1100–1700: A Documentary History*, London, Dent.

Krohn, Kaarle, 1926. *Die folkloristische Arbeitsmethode*, Cambridge, Massachusetts, Harvard University Press.

Kvideland, Reimund and Torunn Selberg, eds., 1984. *Papers: The 8th Congress for the International Society for Folk Narrative Research, Bergen 12–17 June 1984*, Bergen.

Lang, Andrew, 1873. 'Mythology and Fairy Tales', *Fortnightly Review*, 19 (May), pp. 618–31.

—, 1885. 'Comparative Study of Ghost Stories', *The Nineteenth Century*, 17 (April), pp. 623–32.

—, 1887. *Myth, Ritual and Religion*, London, Longman's, Green and Co.

—, 1893. 'Comparative Psychical Research', *The Contemporary Review*, 64 (Sept.), pp. 372–87.

—, 1894a. *Cock Lane and Common-Sense*, London, Longman's, Green and Co. See also new edition published in 1896, London, Longman's, Green and Co.

—, 1894b. 'Ghosts Up To Date', *Blackwoods*, 155 (Jan.), pp. 47–58.

—, 1894c. 'Ghosts Before the Law', *Blackwoods*, 155 (Feb.), pp. 210–22.

—, 1895a. 'Ghost Stories and Beast Stories', *The Nineteenth Century*, 37 (Feb.), pp. 258–70.

—, 1895b. 'Protest of a Psycho-folklorist', *Folk-Lore*, VI, pp. 236–48.

—, 1895c. 'The Wesley Ghost', *The Contemporary Review*, 68 (Aug.), pp. 288–98.

—, 1897a. *Dreams and Ghosts*, London, Longman's.

—, 1897b. 'Ghosts and Right Reason', *The Cornhill Magazine*, 75 (May), pp. 629–41.

Lavater, Ludowig/Lewes, 1929. *Of Ghostes and Spirites Walking by Nyghte*, Oxford, reprinted for the Shakespearean Association at the University Press. First published in English in 1572.

Lea, H. C., 1957. *Materials Towards a History of Witchcraft*, arranged and edited by Arthur C. Howland, New York/London, Thomas Yoseloff.

Leather, Ella M., 1912. *The Folklore of Herefordshire*, Hereford/London, Hereford: Jakeman and Carver, London: Sidgwick and Jackson.

Lee, Frederick George, D. D., 1875. *The Other World, or Glimpses of the Supernatural*, London, Henry S. King.

—, 1885. *Glimpses in the Twilight*, Edinburgh/London, Blackwood.

Legman, Gershon, 1964. *The Horn Book: Studies in Erotic Folklore and Bibliography*, London, Cape.

—, 1968. *The Rationale of the Dirty Joke*, New York, Grove Press.

Le Loyer, Pierre, 1605. *A Treatise of Spectres or Strange Sights*, London, Z. Jones. First published in 1856.

Lethbridge, T. C., 1961. *Ghost and Ghoul*, London, Routledge and Kegan Paul.

Levitt, Eugene, 1952. 'Superstitions Twenty-five Years Ago and Today', *American Journal of Psychology*, 65, pp. 443–9.

Lewes, Mary L., 1911. *Stranger than Fiction*, London, William Rider and Son.

Lindemann, Erich, 1944. 'Symptomatology and Management of Acute Grief', *American Journal of Psychiatry*, 101, pp. 141–8.

MacFarlane, Alan, 1970. 'Witchcraft in Tudor and Stuart Essex', in Mary Douglas, ed., *Witchcraft: Accusations and Confessions*, London, Tavistock Publications, pp. 81–102.

Malinowski, Bronislaw, 1966. *Coral Gardens and Their Magic*, London, Allen and Unwin.

—, 1982. 'Myth in Primitive Psychology', in *Magic, Science and Religion and Other Essays*, London, Condor. First published in 1926.

Marris, Peter, 1958. *Widows and their Families*, London, Routledge and Kegan Paul.

—, 1974. *Loss and Change*, London, Routledge and Kegan Paul.

Martin, David, 1967. *A Sociology of Religion*, London, SCM Press.

Mather, Cotton, 1862. *Wonders of the Invisible World*, Library of Old Authors, London, John Russell Smith. First published in 1692.

Mather, Increase, 1684. *An Essay for the Recording of Illustrious Providences. Wherein an account is given of many remarkable events which have happened in this last age, especially in New England*, Boston, G. Calmet.

Montell, William, 1975. *Ghosts Along the Cumberland: Deathlore in the Kentucky Foothills*, Knoxville, University of Kentucky Press.

— and Barbara Allen, 1982. 'A Biographical Approach to the Study of Memorates', *International Folklore Review*, 2, pp. 85–104.

Müller, Max, 1871–6. *Chips from a German Workshop*, 4 vols. New York, Scribner, Armstrong and Co.

New Larousse Encyclopedia of Mythology, The, with introduction by Robert Graves, 1959. London/New York/Sydney/Toronto, Hamlyn.

Nixon, H. K., 1925. 'Popular Answers to Some Psychological Questions', *American Journal of Psychology*, 36, pp. 418–23.

Olrik, Axel, 1965. 'Epic Laws of Folk Narrative', in Alan Dundes, ed., *The Study of Folklore*, Englewood Cliffs, New Jersey, Prentice Hall, pp. 129–41.

Opie, Peter and Iona, 1959. *The Lore and Language of Schoolchildren*, Oxford, Clarendon Press.

Owen, Robert Dale, 1861. *Footfalls on the Boundary of Another World*, London/New York, Trench Trübner.

Parkes, Colin Murray, 1982. *Bereavement: Studies of Grief in Adult Life*, London, Tavistock Publications.

—, and Joan Stevenson Hinde, eds., 1982. *The Place of Attachment in Human Behaviour*, London/New York, Tavistock Publications.

Perrault, Charles, 1922. *The Fairy Tales of Charles Perrault*, illustrated by Harry Clarke, with an introduction by Thomas Bodkin, London, Harrap.

Porter, J. R., 1981. 'Ghosts in the Old Testament and the Ancient Near East', in Hilda R. Ellis Davidson and W. M. S. Russell, eds., *The Folklore of Ghosts*, The Folklore Society, Mistletoe Series, London, D. S. Brewer, pp. 215–38.

Propp, Vladimir, 1968. *The Morphology of the Folktale*, translated by Laurence Scott, second and revised edition with a preface by Louis A. Wagner, new introduction by Alan Dundes, Austin/London, University of Texas Press. First published in English in 1958. First published 1928.

(Lord) Raglan, 1965. 'The Hero of Tradition', in Alan Dundes, ed., *The Study of Folklore*, Englewood Cliffs, New Jersey, Prentice Hall, pp. 142–57.

Ralya, Lynn L., 1945. 'Some Surprising Beliefs concerning Human Nature among Premedical Psychology Students', *British Journal of Educational Psychology*, Volume 15, pp. 70–5.

Rees, W. Dewi, 1971. 'The Hallucinations of Widowhood', *British Medical Journal*, 4 (Oct.–Dec.), pp. 37–41.

Reeves, James, ed., 1958. *The Idiom of the People: English Traditional Verse from the Manuscripts of Cecil J. Sharp*, London, Heinemann.

Robbins, Rossell Hope, 1981. *The Encyclopedia of Demonology and Witchcraft*, New York, Bonanza Books. First published in 1959.

Roby, J., 1900. *Traditions of Lancashire*, sixth edn, Manchester/London, John Heywood.

Rockwell, Joan, 1981. 'The Ghosts of Evart Tang Kristensen', in Hilda R. Ellis Davidson and W. M. S. Russell, eds., *The Folklore of Ghosts*, The Folklore Society, Mistletoe Series, London, D. S. Brewer, pp. 43–72.

Russell, W. M. S., 1981. 'Greek and Roman Ghosts', in Hilda R. Ellis Davidson and W. M. S. Russell, eds., *The Folklore of Ghosts*, The Folklore Society, Mistletoe Series, London, D. S. Brewer, pp. 193–214.

Sabine, G. H., ed., 1941. *The Works of Gerrard Winstanley*, Cornell, Wisconsin, University Press.

Schulz, Richard, 1978. *The Psychology of Death, Dying and Bereavement*, Reading, Pennsylvania., Addison-Wesley.

Scot, Reginald, 1651. *The Discoverie of Witchcraft*, London, R. C. First published in 1584.

Sidgewick Henry, Alice Johnson, W. H. Myers, Frank Podmore and Eleanor Mildred Sidgwick, 1894. 'Report of the Census of Hallucinations', *Proceedings of the Society for Psychical Research*, 10, pp. 25–442.

Sidney, Sir Philip, 1959. 'An Apology for Poetry', in H. A. Needham, ed., *Sidney: An Apology for Poetry and Shelley: A Defence of Poetry*, London, Ginn and Company.

Sinclair, George, 1969. *Satan's Invisible World Discovered*, Gainsville, Florida, Scholars' Facsimiles and Reprints. First published in 1685.

Strömbäck, Dag, ed., 1971. *Leading Folklorists of the North*, Oslo/Bergen/Tromsø, Universitetsforlaget.

Summerson, John, 1975. 'Landscape with Buildings', in *Spirit of the Age*, London, BBC.

Taillepied, Fr Noel, n.d. *A Treatise of Ghosts*, translated and edited by Montague Summers, London, Fortune Press/Charles Skilton. First published in Paris, 1588.

Tawney, R. H., 1964. *Religion and the Rise of Capitalism*, Harmondsworth, Penguin. First published in 1926.

Thomas, Keith, 1971. *Religion and the Decline of Magic*, Letchworth, Weidenfeld and Nicolson.

Thompson, Stith, 1955. *The Motif Index of Folk Literature: A Classification of Narrative Elements in Folk-Tales, Ballads, Myths, Fables, Medieval Romances, Exempla, Fabliaux, Jest Books, and Local Legends*, revised edition, Copenhagen, Rosenkilde and Bagger.

Towler, Robert, 1974. *Homo Religiosus: Sociological Problems in the Study of Religion*, London, Constable.

—, *et al.*, 1981–4. 'Conventional Religion and Common Religion in Great Britain', *Leeds Religious Research*, The University of Leeds, Department of Sociology.

Tylor, Edward B., 1873. *Primitive Culture: Researches into the Development of Mythology, Philosophy, Religion, Language, Art and Custom*, 2 vols., second edition, London, John Murray.

Vansina, Jan, 1965. *Oral Tradition: A Study in Historical Method*, London, Routledge and Kegan Paul.

Warburton, F. W., 1956. 'Beliefs Concerning Human Nature Among Students in a University Department of Education', *British Journal of Educational Psychology*, pp. 156–62.

Ward, Donald, 1977. '"The Little Man Who Wasn't There": Encounters with the Supranormal', *Fabula*, 18, pp. 212–25.

Webster, John, 1667. *The Displaying of Supposed Witchcraft*, London, J. M.

Weiss, Robert S., 1982. 'Attachment in Adult Life', in Colin Murray Parkes and Joan Stevenson Hinde, eds., *The Place of Attachment in Human Behaviour*, London/New York, Tavistock Publications, pp. 171–84.

Wilson, William A., 1975. 'The Vanishing Hitchhiker Among the Mormons', *Indiana Folklore*, 8, pp. 80–97.

—, 1982. 'On Being Human: The Folklore of Mormon Missionaries', *New York Folklore*, 8:3–4, pp. 5–27.

Wordsworth, William and Samuel Taylor Coleridge, 1952. *The Lyrical Ballads*, London, Methuen. First published 1798.

Wright, A. R., 1927. 'The Folklore of the Past and Present', Presidential Address to the Folklore Society, *Folk-Lore*, 38, pp. 13–39.

Wright, David, ed., 1973. *The Penguin Book of English Romantic Verse*, Harmondsworth, Penguin.

FOR THE BEST IN PAPERBACKS, LOOK FOR THE

In every corner of the world, on every subject under the sun, Penguin represents quality and variety – the very best in publishing today.

For complete information about books available from Penguin – including Pelicans, Puffins, Peregrines and Penguin Classics – and how to order them, write to us at the appropriate address below. Please note that for copyright reasons the selection of books varies from country to country.

In the United Kingdom: For a complete list of books available from Penguin in the U.K., please write to *Dept E.P., Penguin Books Ltd, Harmondsworth, Middlesex, UB7 0DA*

In the United States: For a complete list of books available from Penguin in the U.S., please write to *Dept BA, Penguin, 299 Murray Hill Parkway, East Rutherford, New Jersey 07073*

In Canada: For a complete list of books available from Penguin in Canada, please write to *Penguin Books Canada Ltd, 2801 John Street, Markham, Ontario L3R 1B4*

In Australia: For a complete list of books available from Penguin in Australia, please write to the *Marketing Department, Penguin Books Australia Ltd, P.O. Box 257, Ringwood, Victoria 3134*

In New Zealand: For a complete list of books available from Penguin in New Zealand, please write to the *Marketing Department, Penguin Books (NZ) Ltd, Private Bag, Takapuna, Auckland 9*

In India: For a complete list of books available from Penguin, please write to *Penguin Overseas Ltd, 706 Eros Apartments, 56 Nehru Place, New Delhi, 110019*

In Holland: For a complete list of books available from Penguin in Holland, please write to *Penguin Books Nederland B.V., Postbus 195, NL–1380AD Weesp, Netherlands*

In Germany: For a complete list of books available from Penguin, please write to *Penguin Books Ltd, Friedrichstrasse 10 – 12, D–6000 Frankfurt Main 1, Federal Republic of Germany*

In Spain: For a complete list of books available from Penguin in Spain, please write to *Longman Penguin España, Calle San Nicolas 15, E–28013 Madrid, Spain*

FOR THE BEST IN PAPERBACKS, LOOK FOR THE 🐧

A CHOICE OF PENGUINS AND PELICANS

The Literature of the United States Marcus Cunliffe

The fourth edition of a masterly one-volume survey, described by D. W. Brogan in the *Guardian* as 'a very good book indeed'.

The Sceptical Feminist Janet Radcliffe Richards

A rigorously argued but sympathetic consideration of feminist claims. 'A triumph' – *Sunday Times*

The Enlightenment Norman Hampson

A classic survey of the age of Diderot and Voltaire, Goethe and Hume, which forms part of the Pelican History of European Thought.

Defoe to the Victorians David Skilton

A 'Learned and stimulating' (*The Times Educational Supplement*) survey of two centuries of the English novel.

Reformation to Industrial Revolution Christopher Hill

This 'formidable little book' (Peter Laslett in the *Guardian*) by one of our leading historians is Volume 2 of the Pelican Economic History of Britain.

The New Pelican Guide to English Literature Boris Ford (ed.)
Volume 8: The Present

This book brings a major series up to date with important essays on Ted Hughes and Nadine Gordimer, Philip Larkin and V. S. Naipaul, and all the other leading writers of today.

Adieux Simone de Beauvoir

This 'farewell to Sartre' by his life-long companion is a 'true labour of love' (the *Listener*) and 'an extraordinary achievement' (*New Statesman*).

British Society 1914–45 John Stevenson

A major contribution to the Pelican Social History of Britain, which 'will undoubtedly be the standard work for students of modern Britain for many years to come' – *The Times Educational Supplement*

The Pelican History of Greek Literature Peter Levi

A remarkable survey covering all the major writers from Homer to Plutarch, with brilliant translations by the author, one of the leading poets of today.

Art and Literature Sigmund Freud

Volume 14 of the Pelican Freud Library contains Freud's major essays on Leonardo, Michelangelo and Dostoevsky, plus shorter pieces on Shakespeare, the nature of creativity and much more.

A History of the Crusades Sir Steven Runciman

This three-volume history of the events which transferred world power to Western Europe – and founded Modern History – has been universally acclaimed as a masterpiece.

A Night to Remember Walter Lord

The classic account of the sinking of the *Titanic*. 'A stunning book, incomparably the best on its subject and one of the most exciting books of this or any year' – *The New York Times*

FOR THE BEST IN PAPERBACKS, LOOK FOR THE 🐧

A CHOICE OF PENGUINS AND PELICANS

The Apartheid Handbook   Roger Omond

This book provides the essential hard information about how apartheid actually works from day to day and fills in the details behind the headlines.

The World Turned Upside Down   Christopher Hill

This classic study of radical ideas during the English Revolution 'will stand as a notable monument to . . . one of the finest historians of the present age' – *The Times Literary Supplement*

Islam in the World   Malise Ruthven

'His exposition of "the Qurenic world view" is the most convincing, and the most appealing, that I have read' – Edward Mortimer in *The Times*

The Knight, the Lady and the Priest   Georges Duby

'A very fine book' (Philippe Aries) that traces back to its medieval origin one of our most important institutions, modern marriage.

A Social History of England   New Edition   Asa Briggs

'A treasure house of scholarly knowledge . . . beautifully written and full of the author's love of his country, its people and its landscape' – John Keegan in the *Sunday Times*, Books of the Year

The Second World War   A. J. P. Taylor

A brilliant and detailed illustrated history, enlivened by all Professor Taylor's customary iconoclasm and wit.